Beltane

A Spellworkers' Chronicles Novel

Alys West

Typesetting and Design Fabrian Books – fabrianbooks.com.

For Janey,
because without your support and encouragement
this book
would never have been finished.

Prologue

The gate slammed. He spun to face the woman stalking across the lawn towards him.

"What the hell do you think you're doing?" Maeve shouted. She was tall, with short blonde hair and sharp features. In the dim light of the full moon, she looked younger than he'd expected.

"Taking her away from you."

"Who are you? Her pitiful excuse of a boyfriend?"

He edged backwards towards the gate. "It doesn't matter who I am." Scanning the garden, he searched for something he could use to create a distraction. "But I know who you are, Maeve Blackwell, and don't think for one minute you're going to get away with this."

She was only a few short steps away from him now. Her lips bent into a cruel parody of a smile. "Oh, I think I will."

Drawing on awen, the earth's energy, he felt it pulse through the ground into his feet. Without his staff it was only a puny trickle but it would have to do. He shaped it in his mind, raised his hand and released an eddy of wind. It picked up the dried autumn leaves scattered over the garden. He pushed his hand out and they swirled into Maeve's face.

He sprinted towards the gate. As his fingers reached to touch the handle, he was grabbed from behind. He looked over his shoulder, saw nothing.

What the hell? The invisible force tightened and flung

him backwards. For several terrible seconds he was airborne then his back smacked into something solid. His head whipped back, his skull connected, his teeth rattled. Pain spun nauseatingly through him as his vision blurred.

Branches towered above his head. A mocking laugh floated across the garden. Blinking, he tried to focus, to fight the barrier that held him. "My dear boy, you can stop struggling. I'm not going to let *you* escape as well."

As she drew closer, he struggled harder. He'd massively underestimated her power, thought she was one of the Glastonbury crazies, messing with forces they didn't understand. Seeing her cold, blue eyes he knew he would pay for that mistake with his life.

"That little trick of yours was very revealing." She pressed a hand against his chest. "What are you?" Even through the force field he felt her drawing energy from him. Fighting desperately, his feet scrabbled against the trunk, his fingers digging into the bark. Her eyes widened. "A druid. Now that is a delightful surprise!"

"Screw you!" he spat.

Her hand whipped out and slapped him across the face. "Quiet." She paced away across the lawn. Desperately, he tried to draw awen from the tree. His heart pounded and he could barely focus. A tiny amount seeped into his fingers. *It wasn't enough.* He fought to quell the panic, tried again. The flow strengthened. If he had enough time he could use it to break the force field. If not, he would die here.

When she turned, he saw the glint of sharp steel in her hand. She pointed the athame at his heart. "You really are the answer to all my prayers. But as you've dropped in so unexpectedly I'm going to have to keep you safe until I'm ready."

"Ready for what?" But he had a terrible feeling that he already knew the answer.

"Never you mind. Now I suggest you keep still. The

more you struggle the more it will hurt." She raised the athame and pressed it against his neck. He flinched away and she pressed harder until the blade pierced the skin. "And the more I'll enjoy it."

Raising her hands, she spoke words he didn't understand. The force field lifted slightly and, for a second, hope surged through him. He dragged more awen into his body, tried to focus it against the invisible bonds that held him.

Something gripped his ankle. He looked down. Roots snaked out of the ground, twisting around his legs. He struggled and a branch whipped down fastening around his neck. His hands were suddenly free. He grabbed at the branch, his fingers scrabbling to get a hold. It tightened, threatened to choke him. Trying to prise it away, another branch twined around his hands, yanking them backwards.

He fought with everything he had left. He swore and struggled but the tree was stronger. His torso sank into the trunk. Bark crept over his body and up his neck. He screamed, an agonising howl of pain. As the wood covered his face the last thing he heard was Maeve laughing.

Chapter 1

Zoe Rose dumped her bags at her feet. On the blue gate in front of her was a sign that read *Anam Cara Healing Retreat* in purple script. Angels with outstretched wings surrounded the lettering. She pressed the button on the intercom and looked up. To her right, partially hidden behind a row of houses was Glastonbury Tor. On her left beyond the main road the ground sloped sharply down to the Somerset Levels.

The intercom crackled and a voice with a strong Australian accent said, "Hello?"

"Hi I'm Zoe Rose. I rang up a few days ago to book a room."

"Sure, I remember. I'll open the gate."

A loud buzzing came from the intercom. Zoe quickly hefted her rucksack onto her back, picked up her portfolio and pushed open the gate. The scent of spring flowers immediately surrounded her. Zoe smiled. Her friend Anna had promised that Anam Cara was a haven and she wasn't wrong. The garden was beautiful. A narrow stream flowed past her feet to cascade into a wide pool filled with water lilies. Ivy clung to the high walls and climbing roses trailed over a trellis that arced over the centre of the path. A magnolia tree bloomed in the centre of a flower bed filled with tulips.

Exhaling deeply, Zoe felt tension ease from her shoulders. This was why she'd come. Earlier in the week she'd been ready to abandon her dream of being a full time illustrator and hand back the commission to illustrate the children's book on the legends of King Arthur. It was Anna who'd calmed her down and talked her into coming to Glastonbury. It wasn't just the idea of working in the place that was believed to be Avalon that had convinced her but Anna's description of the healer, Maeve. Her friend had stayed at Anam Cara a couple of times in the past year and found her amazingly wise, intuitive and nurturing. Zoe was looking forward to meeting the woman whom her usually cynical friend raved about.

Following the path past a single storey building, Zoe headed towards the cream pebbledash house. As she stepped through the trellis, the ground floor of the house became visible. Outside the French windows was a stone table with a circular top of grey granite.

Stomach clenching, Zoe froze.

At the centre of the table was a vase filled with leaves and twigs around which clustered feathers and crystals. Four fat purple candles with blackened wicks stood at the edge like points on a compass.

A shiver crept up her spine as memories of blood, terror and despair flooded through her. She blinked. Took a step back and looked again. She'd seen this table before. Not the stuff cluttering the top of it; that she didn't remember. But the table was locked in her memory and she didn't know why.

She glanced back towards the gate. She didn't want to stay here anymore. As she was about to move a loud voice said, "Zoe! How lovely to meet a friend of Anna's."

A tall, thin woman walked down the path from the house. She had short blonde hair highlighting remarkable cheekbones in a face that could be anywhere between forty five and sixty. She wore elegant clothes of glacial blue and ash grey that flowed around her narrow figure. A silver pendant with a large white stone hung around her neck.

The woman stretched out her hands. “Welcome to Anam Cara.”

Zoe stepped towards her and found herself being hugged as if they were old friends. The hug lasted a second or two longer than felt comfortable and when the woman released her Zoe hastily pulled away. Her gaze rose to the woman’s face. Her eyes were a washed out blue with bloodshot rims. Watery and unfocused, they seemed at least twenty years too old for her face.

Zoe swallowed hard. Who was this woman? Whoever she was she knew instinctively that she didn’t like her. “It’s nice to be here,” she said. “I’m looking forward to meeting Maeve. Anna’s told me so much about her.”

“My dear child.” The woman laughed. “I’m Maeve!”

Zoe’s face stiffened as she tried to stop her smile slipping. “Oh! Sorry. I didn’t realise.” This woman was nothing like Anna’s description. She’d been expecting an earth mother dressed in tie-dyed clothes, probably with hennaed hair and wearing a lot of crystals.

“Helena will help you with your bags.” Maeve gestured to the plump girl in her mid-twenties who stood by her shoulder.

“There’s no need,” Zoe said. “I can manage.”

“I’m sure you can, dear. But you’re here to relax, remember. Helena will take them up to your room.” At Maeve’s words, Helena came forward and Zoe reluctantly relinquished her luggage.

“What brings you to Glastonbury, dear?” Maeve said, heading back to the house.

“I’m an artist. I’m illustrating a children’s book on the legend of King Arthur. I’m... well, I’m hoping to be inspired by Glastonbury. You know, the Isle of Avalon and all that.” She tried to sound confident as if she did this kind of work all the time. She wasn’t going to tell Maeve this was her first commission for a decent sized publisher that was actually paying her market rates.

"And have you been here before?"

"I came to the festival a few years ago."

Maeve gestured dismissively. "That's not the same thing at all. The festival is an abomination on our doorstep. Causes nothing but disruption. The locals can't abide it."

Unable to think of a tactful response Zoe kept her mouth shut. Opening the door to a large half-glass porch, Maeve added, "You must show me some of your work, my dear. It's a blessing to have creative people in the house. They bring such positive energy with them."

Behind the healer's back, Zoe screwed up her nose. She was pretty certain her energy was anything but positive. In the hall, Maeve lingered for a moment before a large mirror. After running her fingers through her blonde hair, she strode up the wooden stairs. Zoe trailed behind. On the right, at the top of the stairs, a pine door stood open.

"This is my stellar room," Maeve said. "All of the rooms have a theme. It challenges perceptions which is vital when you're working on the plane of the spirit."

The room had white walls and a midnight blue ceiling decorated with silver stars. The bedside lamp and mirror were shaped like stars. The bed linen and curtains were blue with yet more stars – gold this time. A print of Vincent Van Gogh's 'Starry Night' hung above a double bed.

Unable to repress a grin at the decor, Zoe walked over to the window. At least she had a view of the garden and the Tor. She glanced down. And she couldn't see the weird stone table from here.

Turning to Maeve, standing in the doorway, she said, "Thanks. It's... special."

Maeve's mouth pressed into a thin line, her eyes narrowed. "You'll have karmic wave healing during your stay."

The words were a command, spoken so emphatically that Zoe felt compelled to say 'yes, of course.' Opening her mouth to say the words, she thought *what...?* Glancing up, she met Maeve's cold, glassy eyes. Goosebumps prickled the back of Zoe's neck. Quickly looking away, she said, "What's karmic healing?"

"Karmic wave, dear. It's a wonderfully deep and holistic healing that works emotionally, spiritually and physically. All my guests have it while they're here."

"Oh, yes. I remember now. Anna said she'd had it." Her friend had experienced a strong reaction and been under the weather for a day or two afterwards. Zoe couldn't afford to lose that kind of time. She had a deadline.

"Which day do you want your healing?"

"I'm not sure I can fit it in. I'm here to work."

"It will help you with your work. You do look a little tense, dear, and I'm sure that isn't helping you be creative."

Zoe crossed her arms. Maeve couldn't be more right but she wouldn't give her the satisfaction of knowing it. "I really don't think I've got time."

"Don't decide now, dear," Maeve said, her watery blue gaze fixed on Zoe. "See how you feel in a day or two when you're more relaxed and in tune with being here."

"Sure if you like. But I don't think I'll change my mind."

"We'll see." Maeve smiled a little smugly. Striding across the landing she turned a corner and disappeared down a shadowy passage.

Zoe closed the door with a little more force than necessary, headed back to the window and looked up. The grey tower was a reminder of the mediaeval abbey that had once flourished on the Tor. The turf terraces winding around its lower slopes seemed like a path climbing to the summit. Being this close to the Tor, the myths of fairies, dragons and druids that seemed absurd in London suddenly weren't so unbelievable.

Her gaze dropped to the garden. So far it was the only good thing about Anam Cara. Maeve was nothing like she'd expected and the stone table was weird beyond belief. Chewing on her bottom lip she tried to figure out why it seemed so familiar. She'd not been to Glastonbury before, not stepped foot inside Anam Cara before today. So why had the table made her feel so inexplicably terrified?

Dropping onto the bed, she stared up at the stars on the ceiling. Why had she let Anna talk her into this? She couldn't even find somewhere else to stay. Maeve had insisted that she pay for four nights in advance and that had cleared out her bank account. She'd had to borrow the money for the coach fare from Anna.

She tugged her hair out of its ponytail. She'd have to try to make the best of it. At least Glastonbury was as wonderfully alternative as she'd expected. On the walk from the town centre she'd passed a shop selling witchcraft supplies, been handed a flyer for a goddess workshop, and seen a man with long grey hair and a beard clad in sky blue robes.

Grabbing her bag, she pulled out her mobile. Tapping her finger on the screen she dithered over what to say. Not wanting to tell Anna she'd taken an almost instant dislike to the healer whom her friend found so inspirational she eventually settled on "*Just arrived. Glastonbury fab. Anam Cara not exactly what I expected. Ring soon x*". Then she sent short – journey fine, arrived safely - messages to her mum and her sister, Mia.

When she couldn't find any other reason to linger in her room she headed for the kitchen in search of a cup of tea. It was a relief to find that, among the extensive selection of herbal teas, Maeve had Tetley's.

Holding a mug she wandered out into the garden. Two wooden recliners with white cushions stood on the lawn in the afternoon sunshine. Zoe pushed off her pumps and stretched her legs out. Her head fell back as she enjoyed the warmth of the sun on her skin. It was late April but it felt more like June.

Something soft brushed against Zoe's hand. She opened her eyes to see a large white cat rubbing its body against the chair. "Hey, puss." Zoe clicked her fingers. The cat looked nonchalantly at her and then strolled across the lawn curling up elegantly in a patch of sunshine. The itch to draw was suddenly intense. Hoping the cat wouldn't move, she ran upstairs and grabbed her sketchpad and pencil case.

Back in the garden the cat remained in the same spot. After studying him for a few minutes she started to sketch. It felt good. She'd missed this effortless flow during the recent weeks of artist's block. The cat moved and yawned. She tore off that page and started again, sketching his face, unearthly pink eyes and short, sharp teeth.

The breeze freshened. A gust eddied around the garden, rustling her pad and lifting the first sketch. It drifted across the garden but, with her focus locked on the cat, Zoe barely noticed. She tore off page after page as she sought to capture the essence of the animal.

When the cat eventually strolled away, Zoe sketched a last few lines and looked up. The light had changed and suddenly she felt chilly. Pulling her thin cardigan around her, she walked across the grass to retrieve the page that had blown away. It lay on the ground in the dim shade of a large tree. She bent, picked it up. Straightening, she gasped.

There was the face of a man in the trunk.

It looked spookily real. Nothing like the usual images of the Green Man carved in stone or wood. It seemed totally organic as if the tree had sprouted a face. She reached up to trace its contours with her fingers. The face was handsome with a wide forehead, straight nose, strong cheekbones and a square chin. The unseeing gaze of the deep set eyes was fixed on the house. The mouth was twisted into a grimace as if the face was in pain. Zoe ran her fingers over the untidy, wavy curls of his hair. They made him seem so lifelike, as if he would speak at any moment.

"Are you the spirit of this place?" she whispered. It should have seemed weird to be talking to a wooden face but actually it didn't. Something about the Green Man felt familiar. "I bet you could tell me about Maeve. What is her problem? I mean I just don't get it. Anna said she was wonderful but I *really* don't like her."

Zoe giggled as she realised that the most words she'd spoken since arriving at Anam Cara were to a tree. Was this the hippy, Glastonbury effect working on her already? Because oddly enough, it didn't seem weird at all.

She reached up and touched his bark covered cheek. "I think you are a tree spirit," she whispered. "And maybe I'm being ridiculous but who cares? I need all the help I can get. If you do wishes or anything like that then please help me. I need to be inspired and I mean, *really* inspired. These King Arthur pictures have to be as good as anything I've ever done because this is my big chance. Please, please don't let me blow it."

She stared at his blank eyes. A long moment passed. She was sharply aware of the rough texture of the bark beneath her fingers, the smell of damp earth, the birds singing in the branches above her head. "Thanks for listening," she breathed.

Inhaling deeply, she leaned her back against the trunk. If she was really honest she'd been tense for weeks. She wasn't enjoying life as an aspiring artist any more. She'd expected that by now, five years after graduation, life would be easier. Yet she was still working two other jobs just to pay the rent. Being constantly on the brink of bankruptcy was no joke. It was fine when she'd first left Goldsmiths because her friends were penniless too but now they were all, Anna included, busy climbing career ladders and their salaries made her income look like pocket money. Her friends were no longer happy with 'all you can eat buffets' and restricted view seats at the theatre. They had the money to enjoy a different lifestyle and Zoe, still determinedly chasing her dream, felt left behind.

When this commission had unexpectedly come her way she'd believed it was her big chance. Until everything she drew was unoriginal, uninspired or the sick ghost of someone else's work. She spent hours at her drawing table with nothing to show for it except eyes red from crying and mountains of discarded paper, fit only for recycling. If she couldn't break through the block while she was here she had no hope of delivering the commission and her dream was dead. She'd have no choice but to get a proper job.

"Zoe! What are you doing?" Maeve called, her voice high and sharp.

Startled, Zoe looked round. The healer stood by the recliners, hands on hips, her face creased into lines of controlled rage. Reluctantly Zoe pushed away from the trunk and walked towards the healer.

"What were you doing by that tree?" Maeve's foot tapped impatiently.

"One of my drawings blew away. I went to pick it up." She glanced back at the wooden face; saw that his empty eyes watched her.

"Oh!" Maeve's hands slipped from her hips. "Have you been working on your book?"

Holding up the sketch, Zoe said, "Actually I've been drawing your cat."

Maeve bent to look at the sketches scattered on the recliner. "And are these Persia as well?"

"Yes. I got a bit carried away but he's a joy to draw." Zoe gathered up the sketches and handed them to Maeve. "So elegant. I love the way he moves."

"She," Maeve said as she leafed through the sketches. "These are very good. Very good indeed. This one in particular is remarkable." Maeve held out the picture of the cat yawning. "You've captured the spirit of Persia. Most people just see the smooth coat of the domestic cat but you've caught the killer within."

"I'm glad you like it." Seeing the pleasure on Maeve's face, Zoe said impulsively, "You can keep it if you like."

"How kind. Thank you, my dear." Maeve's smile warmed her watery eyes.

Perhaps they'd just got off on the wrong foot, Zoe thought smiling back. Maybe in time she could come to like Maeve as much as Anna did. "I was just wondering, the face in the tree over there, is it a Green Man?"

"Yes but it's a modern interpretation." Turning her back on the face, Maeve couldn't have made it any clearer that she didn't want to talk about it.

Irritated by the healer's response, Zoe folded her arms and continued. "I was just admiring him. He's most unusual. I love that he's got hair rather than the usual leaves around his head. Makes him look so realistic."

"It's really not that interesting." Maeve spoke slowly, emphasising each word. Her eyes narrowed, staring directly at Zoe as if trying to imprint a message in her brain. Again Zoe felt the strange compulsion to agree and was about to say 'yes, you're right' when she remembered that the Green Man intrigued her.

"Actually I'd like to draw him." She gestured towards the tree. "The light's wrong now but maybe tomorrow if it's a nice day."

Maeve blinked and then her face tightened. "I thought you said you were working on a book on King Arthur. A Green Man won't help you with that."

"I've got some freedom with the inner covers and I think he would work well there. You could say the Green Man is one of our remaining links to the world of myth and folklore," Zoe said improvising quickly. She had no definite plans for the inner covers but this could work. It was as good an idea as any she'd had so far. She wasn't pushing this just to annoy Maeve. Although that was rapidly becoming an unexpected bonus.

The healer's eyes narrowed. "We're about to start the evening meditation and, as it's such a lovely day, we're going to meditate around the Earth Mother's Altar. *You'll join us*." She spoke the final words with calm emphasis. Again Zoe felt the strange compulsion to agree. She blinked and looked away from Maeve's glassy blue eyes.

"It'll be good for you," the healer said. "You must open your mind to release your creativity."

"Where's the Earth Mother's Altar?" As the words left Zoe's mouth she had an uncomfortable feeling she already knew the answer.

Maeve pointed to the stone table. "It's over there, dear. You saw it as you came in."

Zoe shook her head. "Then no. Thanks. I'm going to walk into Glastonbury and get something to eat."

"Tomorrow then!" Maeve said, as she walked away. It sounded like a command.

Goosebumps again prickling the back of her neck, Zoe watched Maeve cross to the granite table. What was it about the damned thing that freaked her out so much? She ran back into the house and grabbed her bag and jacket. She wanted to be out of here before the meditation started. She didn't want to witness what went on around Maeve's altar.

***

Dropping three cushions on the ground around the table, Maeve took a box of matches from her trouser pocket and lit each of the candles. There would be only Tanya and Helena for the meditation. It was hardly worth doing at all.

She'd such hope of the new girl. When she'd hugged her she'd caught a flicker of silver in her aura. Silver was always enticing as it indicated awakening of the cosmic mind. She'd expected an opportunity for further investigation during the meditation.

Until the girl turned out to be impervious to her powers of persuasion. Her strength must be waning faster than she'd realised if a slip of a girl could withstand her so easily. Zoe looked waif-like and delicate with her flowing brown hair and big, doe eyes but she was infuriatingly resistant.

That this girl – the only one for years that she couldn't influence - had noticed the face and, even worse, was clearly fascinated by it, made for an unwelcome complication. She could only hope that the girl's interest would be transient. If not, Zoe would have to be watched.

Settling cross legged on the cushion, Maeve reminded herself that she only had to maintain her careful facade for five more days until Beltane. After that, if all went to plan - and after six months of meticulous research and preparation there was no reason to think it would not – she'd be strong enough to no longer need what her guests unwittingly gave.

Chapter 2

By half past eight Zoe was desperate for a distraction, any distraction. She'd eaten the sandwiches, salad and fruit she'd bought from the Co-op in the town. Then deciding to do some work she'd looked again at the manuscript of the six tales of King Arthur until the familiar panic swamped her. It was bad enough at home feeling like her one talent had abandoned her but at least she had friends, two other jobs and her housemates to take her mind off it. Anam Cara wasn't the comforting haven she'd craved. Here she felt exposed, every emotion, every thought amplified.

Figuring there must be a television in the place somewhere she headed downstairs. As she stepped into the kitchen an Australian voice said, "Hey, Zoe! How you doing?" Helena and another woman sat around the dining table.

"I'm fine, thanks," Zoe said.

"Do you want to join us?" Helena gestured to the bottle of red wine and the glasses on the dining table. She wore black clothes that did nothing for her, clinging to her plump body and draining all colour from her complexion.

"Yeah, that'd be great! Thanks." Zoe started to pull out a chair and then realising it gave an uninterrupted view of Maeve's altar, walked around the table and sat next to the other woman.

"I'm Tanya," she said, pouring wine into the glass that Helena pushed towards Zoe. She appeared to be in her early thirties, gently rounded with ample chest and hips.

She looked very polished in an aubergine jersey dress with impeccable make-up, manicured nails and perfect hair.

"Nice to meet you." Zoe picked up her glass and gestured towards her companions. "Cheers!"

"I'm just reading Tanya's angel cards," Helena said, tucking strands of frizzy brown hair behind her ears.

"What are angel cards?" Zoe said. A pack of oversized cards lay on the table. In front of Tanya, two cards had been turned over. A third lay face down.

"They're messages from our guardian angels. Tanya asked about her future and these two cards show her past and her present. The next one -" Helena pointed at the third card "- is about her future."

"I came here because my relationship ended," Tanya said. "I'd been with Nick nearly a year and I really thought it was going somewhere, you know. Then he said we'd grown apart and he couldn't see his future with me. But he was lying. I found out last week that he's sleeping with Danielle from the accounts department." Tanya's eyes filled with tears that she tried to blink away.

"I'm sorry to hear that," Zoe said softly. She could empathise. She'd felt that kind of pain after she'd ended it with Gareth. The lies had made it worse, made it cut deeper.

Tanya turned the final card over and read the words printed on it. "It's always darkest before the dawn. Don't give up before the miracle occurs." An angel in front of a sunrise illustrated the meaning.

Tanya looked at it uncertainly for a long moment. "Is this telling me to keep hoping that things will get better?"

"If the meaning's unclear to you at the moment then you need to meditate on it. In time it'll come clear," Helena said.

"Alright." Tanya still looking confused. "And if I'm still unsure I'll ask Maeve about it on Monday when I have my healing."

"She'll help you interpret what it means," Helena said. Shuffling the cards, she turned to Zoe, "Shall I do yours?"

Zoe held her hands up. "I don't really believe in angels. Won't that get in the way?"

"You might not believe in angels but they believe in you," Helena said, with the same calm, superior smile that Maeve had.

Zoe hesitated. She didn't want to be rude but something in Helena's words made her uncomfortable. "Maybe later, okay?"

"What brings you to Glastonbury?" Tanya said.

"I'm an artist." Zoe grimaced. "Well, I'm trying to be. This could be my big chance but I seem to be screwing it up." Pushing her hair away from her face, she told them about the King Arthur project and, unlike with Maeve, she found it easy to share her worries about the commission. They both assured her that Maeve fostered such a wonderful, nurturing environment she'd have no problem being creative at Anam Cara.

"That's what my friend Anna said when she talked me into coming here. But I'm just not feeling it," Zoe said.

"It took me a while to settle in. When I first arrived I thought I'd made a dreadful mistake. It seemed so *hippy*." Tanya pronounced the word with derision. "But when I got to know Maeve and we really talked I knew I'd come to the right place."

"So being here is helping you get over Nick?" Zoe said.

"I feel like a different person and I've only been here three days. I was so angry and hurt. This isn't how my life is supposed to be." Tanya's voice rose as a tear crept down her cheek. "Maeve is helping me to let go of that negativity and to value myself again. She's amazing. I've never met anyone like her."

"Meeting Maeve changed my life," Helena said. "I

was going nowhere before I met her. I'd come to Europe doing the backpacking thing and all I'd seen were beaches and bars. I landed up here by accident. I didn't realise it at the time but now I reckon it was meant to be."

"It's a shame you missed the meditation this afternoon," Tanya said. "We had a great session. Really powerful."

"I'm not that into meditating," Zoe said.

"You know I'd never meditated before I came here but I'm going to keep it up when I go home. I felt amazingly calm after the session today. It's almost like being on drugs. That is -" Tanya added hastily "- I'm guessing that's what drugs are like. I've not actually taken any."

"I've done plenty of pot and I'm telling you meditating's better. You don't get the down," Helena said.

"Honestly Helena, you make me feel like I've never lived!" Tanya laughed. "My only vice is a glass of wine at the end of a day."

From then on the conversation flowed effortlessly. Tanya talked more about Nick and the breakup of their relationship. Helena admitted she'd been drifting. When she spoke about Maeve she sounded almost reverential. She planned to go home to Melbourne in the autumn and, because she wanted to be a healer too, had enrolled on a reflexology course.

Walking upstairs with Tanya sometime around eleven, still chatting away, Zoe thought that maybe coming to Anam Cara hadn't been such a big mistake after all.

***

She woke feeling exhausted. It'd been a night of nightmares, the worst she'd had since the autumn. Twice she'd woken and had to draw the dreams before she could go back to sleep. Hauling herself out of bed, she walked across the wooden floor to open the curtains. It was another bright sunny day.

Turning from the window, Zoe's shoulders tensed as she picked up her sketchpad. Since October her fear of the dreams had intensified. On a deep breath, she flipped the pad open to see what she'd drawn. Eyes widening, her hand rose to her throat.

The drawing showed a man standing in a garden. *This garden. The one outside her window!*

She sank into the chair. Sucking in a deep breath, she studied the rough sketch. It was dark and raining heavily. A light above the gate illuminated the garden showing the broken wreck of one of the trees by the boundary wall. The stub of the trunk still stood, cleft down the middle and hollowed out. Branches, twigs and leaves littered the garden.

The man stood on the lawn, staring at the house. Poised to run, a look of terror and confusion in his face. He was tall with a broad chest, long, strong legs and bare feet. Dirt streaked his face; his square chin was dark with stubble. He had a gash above one eyebrow. Blood dripped from cuts on his hands. A rip in his trousers revealed a gash on his thigh. A deep cut on his chest stained his t-shirt.

Zoe closed her eyes and then looked again. But the picture remained the same. She shoved her hand through her hair. What the hell was wrong with her subconscious?

Turning the page she saw the same man limping in bare feet along a dark road. A single lamppost lit the night as rain sheeted down. His mouth was a thin line. Rain streaked the dirt on his face. Blood smeared his forehead. He held his injured hands cradled to his chest.

She recognised the sign for the Chalice Well on the road into Glastonbury. She shuddered. She'd walked past there yesterday evening.

There had to be a sensible explanation. She refused to

contemplate anything else. This was *so* not the time to think about the dreams she'd had of Mia with a baby before her sister announced her pregnancy. Or, prior to her Mum announcing she planned to move, the restless nights when she'd woken to find drawings of strangers in her childhood home.

It was nothing like those things. They were flukes. She'd discussed them with Anna and they'd decided her subconscious picked up on signals from her family and reflected them in her dreams. These drawings must be a reaction to her uncertainty about staying here, her dislike of Maeve and the stress she was under with this commission. Totally understandable in the circumstances. Absolutely nothing to worry about.

But even if that was true – and the freaked out part of her brain was far from convinced – these pictures left her with two unanswerable questions. *Who was this guy? And what was he doing in her dreams?*

***

Maeve woke feeling her age. Every bone in her body ached. Her vision was blurred and her breath rattled in her chest. Eventually she found strength to throw back the bedclothes, reached for the stick she kept by the bed for days like this and heaved herself up. Then slowly, painfully, she crossed the room and drew the heavy velvet curtains. The soft pile was sandpaper against her skin. The rattle of the curtain rings on the wooden pole sounded as loud as clogs on cobbles. Light flooded the room. She winced and turned away.

Bent almost double, she made for the table. She flicked the switch on the kettle and picked up a jug. Above the table were two rows of silver canisters. Placing the stick where she could easily reach it, Maeve leaned on the table and took down three of the canisters. Today she needed fennel, to reduce the sensitivity which increased as her strength lessened; rosemary for the muscle pains and sage for her mental exhaustion. She spooned a teaspoon of each into a jug, added two spoons of powdered bone and poured on boiling water.

She bent to open the small fridge beneath the table and took out a small vial containing a ruby red liquid. Shaking it, she realised it was almost empty. She'd been rationing herself for the past month but she had barely enough to last to Beltane. She stirred the contents of the jug, poured them into a mug and added a couple of drops from the vial.

A little later, fortified by her infusion, Maeve walked unaided to the window. It was another warm day. The unseasonable weather would benefit the garden. She surveyed it, picking out jobs that needed to be done. Helena could weed the flower beds, plant out the gladioli and acidantheras and....

Was Zoe standing under the tree? She peered closer. The girl held a sketchpad. Damn her! Why was she so fascinated with it? Maeve wanted to rush down there, rip the pad from the meddling child's hands and tear the drawing into tiny pieces. But she couldn't leave her rooms until she'd put her face on.

In front of the mirror above the fireplace, Maeve placed her hands on her face and murmured the familiar words. She peered myopically at her reflection. She looked exactly the same. Repeating the words, she spoke slower and more loudly. This time her reflection changed a little but not nearly enough.

Dropping into a chair she ran her hands through her short blonde hair. It would be a mistake to waste the little power she had left on vanity. She'd have to stay in her rooms and rest. Tomorrow she'd get a boost of energy to see her through to Beltane. Only five more days, she reminded herself. Then she'd be strong enough to dispense with the masquerade.

Moving to the window again, she looked down. Zoe had finished her drawing. With the pad tucked under her arm she leant against the tree. Maeve froze. If the blasted girl looked above her head then she would have to act, regardless of the effect her appearance would have on her guests. Peering more closely, she forced her weak eyes to focus. How strange. It looked like the girl was talking to herself.

Only when Zoe returned indoors did Maeve move to the door and call for Helena. The girl's unfortunate fascination with the tree had to be addressed. The instructions might be considered peculiar but Helena was so wonderfully pliant Maeve knew that she wouldn't question them.

***

Zoe spent the day at Glastonbury Abbey. Legendary burial place of Arthur and Guinevere, it was the obvious place to start. She knew that was probably a myth, that the remains found by the monks in the twelfth century were almost undoubtedly a fraud. But she decided to disregard that. Like the mediaeval pilgrims who had flocked here she hoped to find King Arthur at the abbey.

She spent an hour or so wandering around the site imagining the butter coloured stones as they must have been before the monastery's dissolution. Eventually she sat on the warm grass by the site of Arthur's reputed tomb, took out her sketchpad and let her mind wander, thinking about him as a man not a legend. When she drew it felt effortless as if she'd never been blocked. After several versions, she nodded. The man on the paper looked like a soldier and a statesman, calm in a crisis and measured in his judgments, capable of inspiring his warriors and leading his country.

After her sandwich lunch, she walked back to the grave to see if Guinevere would appear in the same way as Arthur. She closed her eyes and tried to think of Camelot's queen. Instead the Green Man came to mind. She took out the sketch she'd drawn earlier. On a fresh sheet of paper she redrew the face, changing his grimace to a half smile. She gave him a strong muscular body, added armour and a sword. "Are you Lancelot du Lac?" she whispered. Answering her own question, Zoe said quietly, "I think you might be."

By the time she left she felt more positive than she'd done in weeks. Walking up the hill to Anam Cara made her hot and a little sweaty and when she opened the gate she wanted only a long, cold, glass of water.

Helena knelt by a flower bed. "Hey, Zoe. Did you find King Arthur?" she said, dusting earth from her hands.

"You know, I think I did. I've been to the abbey. It's a fabulous place, very atmospheric. I feel like I've made some real progress." Zoe's hands moved rapidly as she spoke, underlining her excitement.

"That's great." Helena smiled. "Look, if you've not got anything planned for this evening then Tanya and I are going to the New Moon Cafe for a bite to eat and a few drinks. If you'd like to join us?"

"Sound's good. Count me in."

"Alright then. We thought we'd go after the meditation. Say about seven? Maeve's resting. But Penny and Tony arrived earlier and Penny's going to guide the meditation. As it's another nice day we'll do it around the altar. Take advantage of what you Brits call sunshine."

"I think I'll skip it, thanks. I'll see you later." Zoe headed towards the house. She glanced across at the Green Man and changed her mind. She'd asked for his help yesterday and today she'd made more progress than she had in weeks. Just in case it was down to him, she wanted to thank him.

"What you doing?" Helena called. Zoe glanced back. Helena walked briskly across the lawn, the trowel she carried pointing at Zoe's chest.

"I... nothing." Zoe shrugged, before turning and heading towards the house.

***

Surprisingly the New Moon Cafe was the place to be in Glastonbury on a Sunday evening. A local singer/songwriter would be playing later and, if the number of teenage girls piling into the place were anything to go by, then he was going to be cute.

With the meal they shared a bottle of white wine and then another. The audience of teenage girls cheered and wolf whistled when the singer came on. After a few covers of songs about unrequited love, Tanya stood. "This is the last thing I need," she said, "I'm going to get another drink." She was gone a while and returned with a third bottle of wine and a blonde haired, well-built man whom she introduced as Dave. Zoe had barely said hi before Tanya launched into a story that involved a lot of giggling and touching his arm.

"Good to see Tanya enjoying herself," Zoe said quietly to Helena.

"I suppose," Helena replied. "But it could be too soon. Her angel cards said she needed to take time to figure out what she really wants."

"Well, I admire her ability to bounce back. After I split up with my ex it was about six months before I looked at another guy."

"Break ups are tough. It's important to take time to heal."

"Yeah but I think I'm past it now. It ended really badly. I found out that he was playing internet poker, like, all the time. He'd been borrowing money off me for a while and that caused me a problem, because I don't earn much and I couldn't afford to keep subbing him. When I found out about the poker, I tried to talk to him about it but he said it was nothing to do with me and anyway it wasn't a problem, he had it under control."

"I'm guessing that was a big fat lie."

"And you'd be right. A couple of weeks later he asked me to lend him money, more than I could possibly afford. I told him I couldn't and he said okay, he understood. But when he'd gone I found he'd taken all the money in my purse. When I confronted him about it, he lied. That was it, I ended it."

"Sounds like you're better off without him."

"Yeah. I can see that now but I still feel like an idiot for believing in him." Zoe smiled wryly. "Okay, that's enough about me. What about you? Anyone special in your life?"

"Nah, I'm sworn off men at the moment. I talked about it with Maeve and we decided it was for the best until I sorted my head out. Look, why don't you talk to Maeve about your breakup?" Helena leaned forward, her face getting rather too close to Zoe's.

"Oh, I don't think so," Zoe murmured, shifting away.

"Maeve's a great listener. She'd be able to help you put it in perspective and forgive yourself for trusting this guy."

"Honestly, I'm fine. There's no need."

"Sure, you're fine. But are you great?" Helena said, getting closer again. "Cos if you want to be great then you should talk to Maeve about it. Maybe it's blocking your creativity and that's why you're struggling with this project."

"Look, Helena, I really don't feel comfortable talking to Maeve about stuff like this." Zoe's hand rose to form a barrier between them.

"I know it's difficult to open up to people at the

beginning. But once you get over that then you'll realise that she's amazing. She's the wisest person you'll ever meet."

"I'm really pleased Maeve's helped you, Helena. Honestly, I am. It's just not the right thing for me, okay?" Zoe stood up. "I'm going to the ladies."

There was, of course, a queue for the toilet. While she waited Zoe indulged in figuring out how she'd draw Helena – it was kind of cathartic when people annoyed her - and decided she'd be a ventriloquist's dummy perched on Maeve's knee.

As she walked back into the cafe the singer introduced REM's *Everybody Hurts*. Winding through the crowd to her seat, she started singing along. Then she giggled. She must be drunk!

While she'd been away, Tanya and Dave had got even closer. Dave's arm now rested on the back of Tanya's chair and she leaned in with her hand on his knee. Helena had disappeared. However her jacket still hung on the back of her chair so it was too much to hope that she'd run home to Maeve.

Sinking into her chair, Zoe listened to a Nick Drake cover and stifled a yawn. The bad night's sleep had caught up with her. She didn't want to be a lightweight and duck out early but she was shattered. She tried to quell her yawning but it was no good. She wanted nothing as much as her bed.

Leaning over, she said to Tanya. "I'm sorry but I'm going to have to call it a night. I'm shattered."

"You poor thing. Will you be alright walking back on your own?"

Zoe nodded. There was no way she'd tear Tanya away from Dave's company. "I'll be fine. Where's Helena?"

Tanya gestured to the back of the café. "I think she went outside for a cigarette."

"Tell her I said 'bye' will you?" Zoe said, stifling

another yawn.

Outside she found her knees were rather too relaxed. She couldn't be that drunk, could she? She shrugged. It felt kind of humid. Or was that just the wine? No point putting her jacket on. The air felt nicely cool on her bare arms.

As she walked she started singing *Everyone Hurts,* humming the tune when she couldn't remember the words. The lyrics made her think of the man from her pictures. Where was he going through the rainy night? And what had made him so unhappy? *Honestly, Zo get a grip. He's only a picture.*

The walk was *so* much further on the way back. Why did Maeve have to build Anam Cara at the top of a stupid hill anyway? Thunder rattled across the sky, making her jump. She looked up in time to see lightning flash across the sky. Just what she needed to get caught in a thunder storm. Thank Christ, she was nearly there. As the road curved round she saw the absurdly high wall of Anam Cara. Maeve took the privacy of her guests so seriously anyone would think she ran an exclusive rehab clinic.

She bungled the security code twice before she got it right. When the gate finally opened, the light above it shone over parts of the garden while others were deep in shadows. Thunder rumbled again, a crack of lightning following it. It sounded nearer this time.

It wasn't raining yet and she wanted to talk to the Green Man. To avoid the altar, she cut across the lawn to the tree. In the darkness under the canopy of leaves, she rested her hand on the trunk. "I've come to say thanks. I know I've had a few drinks but I don't want you to think I don't mean this. I don't go round chatting up all the trees, you know. I'm not that kind of girl!" Zoe laughed. Then startled by how loud it sounded, clapped her hand over her mouth. She dropped her voice to a whisper. "Oops, don't want to wake Maeve. I wanted to tell you that I found King Arthur and Lancelot today. I'm making progress and it feels good, like maybe I can do this after all. And I wanted to say thank you."

Lightning flashed momentarily illuminating his frozen face with cold light. "I know it's stupid but I feel like you're really listening," Zoe whispered. The shadows hid the trunk again and she reached up to find his face. Her hand swept across the rough bark, searching for his features. Her fingertips brushed against something soft. She whipped her hand back, stifling a shriek.

Peering upwards, she wished she'd got a torch. Then she remembered she'd got a phone. Reaching into her bag, she pulled out her mobile and touched the screen. The thin stream of bright light shone through the camera lens. Stretching up, she waved the phone at the trunk and, as lightning lit up the night again, she glimpsed a scrap of something against the bark. Angling the beam to shine on it, she stood on her tiptoes and reached up. A little above the Green Man's face and to the left, closer to the wall, was that it?

Her body pressed against the trunk. As thunder echoed, she realised that this was an insane place to be. She should give up and go inside before she got struck by lightning. But her fingers closed around soft cloth. It was attached to the tree. Trying to turn it towards the light, she wobbled back on her heels. Her fingers didn't get the message to let go.

Something tumbled to the ground. "Shit!" Zoe bent to pick it up. By the light of her phone she could see that it was barely bigger than her hand, roughly made, like a miniature scarecrow. Its head was a ball covered in beige cloth with a face scrawled on. The arms and legs were untidy sausages with frayed, raggedy edges. Wool had been knotted around its neck like a noose.

The really odd thing – weirder even than it being attached to the tree – was that a strip of bark encased the torso, arms and legs of the doll, bound there with black wool.

Thunder reverberated across the sky again. Zoe shivered. The doll looked like something from a horror film and she'd seen enough of those to know this was a portent. Moments after the character found it they'd be slaughtered by the psycho-killer.

Hearing a thud she spun round. The gate slammed back on its hinges. "Zoe! What are you doing?" Helena shouted.

Thank God, it's Helena, not an axe murderer! Then she remembered she held the doll. "You startled me! Are you on your own? Tanya was waiting for you," Zoe babbled, shoving the doll into her bag and heading towards the house.

"Tanya's with Dave. I came after you." Helena strode up the path towards Zoe. Thunder sounded, louder again.

"Really, there was no need. I was fine walking back on my own." Zoe reached the path and turned to Helena. The Australian stopped a foot away, her arms folded across her chest.

"I'm not worried about that. What I want to know is what you were doing -" Helena pointed "- by that tree?"

Zoe hesitated. There really wasn't a sensible explanation for standing under a tree during a thunder storm. But why was Helena so uptight about it? She clearly wasn't worried that Zoe was about to get electrocuted.

She opened her mouth to lie. Then lightning flashed again, almost instantaneously followed by thunder and the first fat drops of rain landed on her bare arms. In unison she and Helena glanced up at the sky. Rain streamed down, soaking into Zoe's hair and thin top, trickling down her face. She sprinted for the house, threw open the porch door and stumbled inside, Helena a step behind her. Rain blurred the windows and hammered on the roof.

Brushing water from her face, Zoe walked into the hall and started up the stairs. Helena called after her, "You haven't told me what you were doing by that tree."

Zoe hesitated before she replied. "Why does it matter what I was doing?"

"It's not a good place to be. Maeve said…"

Zoe's hands flew up. "Oh, if *Maeve* said!"

"What's that supposed to mean?"

"I'm just pretty tired of hearing you repeat what Maeve says all the time!" Without waiting for a reply she stomped up the remaining stairs. Closing her bedroom door, she leaned against it for a minute. Snatching her towel from the radiator, she dried her arms, her hair. Anam Cara just kept on getting weirder. Had she really just been warned off from standing by a tree?

Her smile faded when she remembered the doll. She took it from her bag, rested it on her palm and studied it. The scrawled face glowered at her and she shivered. Not surprising that you're scowling, she thought, with your arms and legs all tied up like that. Digging around in her bag, she found her pencil case and took out her scissors.

Carefully snipping through the black wool that bound the doll, she unwrapped the bark and gently straightened its arms and legs. She dropped the scraps of wool and the bark in the waste paper basket. The doll lay limp on the quilt. It should have been only a crudely made child's plaything yet there was still something about it that reminded Zoe of her nightmares. No way could she sleep tonight with it scowling at her.

Walking across the room, she opened the top drawer of the chest, dropped the doll inside and slammed it shut.

Chapter 3

A thunderous crack jerked Zoe from sleep. A loud creaking which sounded ominously close was followed by a sharp rattling against the windows. Half asleep, she rolled onto her back. A second later, a scream tore through the house.

She flung herself out of bed and opened her door. Tanya appeared in the doorway opposite, still fully dressed. “Did you hear that?” she said.

“You could hardly miss it. Do you think everyone’s okay?”

“I don’t know.” Tanya moved to stand close to Zoe. “Maybe it’s something to do with what happened in...” She broke off as a loud thud resounded through the ceiling.

“It’s coming from upstairs.” Zoe walked across the landing and switched on the light. “Whose room’s that?”

“Maeve’s I think but I’ve never been up there.”

Several loud crashes reverberated through the house making the ceiling shake. A hairline crack appeared spewing a thin trail of plaster dust. The door across the landing opened. A middle aged man with grey hair and a neat beard stepped into the light in navy blue pyjamas, fumbling with his glasses. “Are you alright?” he said, blinking at them through his lenses.

“Oh, Tony!” Tanya walked towards him, one hand outstretched. “Do *you* know what’s going on?”

Tony frowned. “Can’t say I do. We were asleep until the explosion in the garden woke us. And then we heard the scream and Penny asked me to find out if anyone needed any help."

Footsteps echoed along the dark corridor that ran behind the bathroom. Helena stepped into the landing. She wore sleep shorts and a baggy grey t-shirt and carried an electric kettle. "Sorry about the disturbance. Everything's fine. You can go back to bed."

A babble of enquiries burst from Tony and Tanya. Waiting until there was a pause, Zoe said, "Helena, what the hell's going on?"

"Everything's fine," Helena repeated. "Maeve asked me to apologise for disturbing you. Persia brought a mouse in. Gave Maeve quite a fright, I can tell you. She's sorry about the noise. That was me trying to catch it. It's a tricky little beggar but I've got it cornered now." Helena glanced at each of them as she spoke, her gaze darting quickly away.

Zoe waited until Tanya and Tony said goodnight and returned to their rooms. "What's really going on?" she said, her voice low. "Because if you're asking me to believe that Maeve got spooked by a mouse I'm just not buying it."

"I don't care whether you *buy it* or not." Holding the kettle in front of her chest, Helena glared at Zoe. "That's what happened."

Turning away, Zoe muttered, "Whatever." She closed her door and turned the key in the lock. A headache was building behind her left temple. Picking up the glass of water from the bedside cabinet she tried to think. None of this added up. Maeve wasn't the screaming type and definitely not about something as trivial as a mouse. She could probably stun it with a single steely glance. Plus there was no way a mouse would make that amount of noise.

And that was only what had been going on inside the house. She walked over to the window and pulled the curtains open. Then she gasped.

The garden was a wreck. But much, much worse than that, it was a 3D replica of her drawing. A tree had been destroyed leaving only a shattered stub. Peering through the rain, her eyes opened wider when she realised it was the Green Man's tree.

It must have been struck by lightning. *Dear God! What if it had happened earlier?* Zoe shuddered. What had she been thinking to stand under it in a thunder storm? She needed her head read.

And maybe she did, she thought, snatching her drawing pad from the bedside table and flipping it open. Frantically she looked between the picture and the garden. The only difference was that the man was missing from the scene outside her window.

If she could dream and draw the carnage in the garden before it happened then there was no reason to think the man was simply a figment of her imagination. But where had he come from? And where had he gone?

She traced her fingers across the drawing pad, lingering on the wounds on the man's face, the gashes on his leg and chest, his cut hands. The rattling against her window must have been splinters from the exploding tree. If he'd been in the garden when the tree exploded then he was lucky to have suffered nothing worse.

Flipping to the next page in her pad, she looked at him on the road to Glastonbury; rain pouring down exactly as it did outside her window. This could be happening right now. And somehow, impossibly, she'd drawn it yesterday.

She shuddered, feeling suddenly sick. What the hell was happening to her? This was entirely different to the dreams she'd had about her family. There was no way she could have known the Green Man's tree would blow up in the middle of the night.

That could mean only one thing. She'd dreamt and drawn the future. Sinking to the floor by the bed she curled up, wrapping her arms around her bent knees.

Was there some way to stop these dreams? A switch in her head she could flip so it didn't happen again? What good could come of seeing things before they happened? She'd end up as one of those women who rang the police to report a murder that had not yet been committed. Someone who others thought of as mad or delusional or both.

Climbing into bed, she curled into a tight ball willing herself not to dream again.

***

Finn McCloud had slept soundly. Six months ago he would have said he'd slept like a log. Now he'd never use that phrase again.

He levered himself from the lower bunk he'd inhabited for the latter part of the night and made his way to the bathroom. The communal facilities in the hostel could not be described as luxurious but no shower had ever felt so good. His stiff muscles eased a little under the hot water. He inspected the wounds on his body, decided it was too risky to heal them here.

Leaving the cubicle he caught sight of himself in the mirror above the row of wash basins. His eyes widened at the face staring back at him. Deep gashes on his forehead and his hands, bruises blackening on his sunlight starved skin, dark circles under his eyes. No wonder the night porter had needed some cold hard cash before he'd agree to let him in.

Being in no way fastidious Finn was surprised, when he returned to the dorm, to find how much he didn't want to put back on the torn, blood stained clothes he'd arrived in. As they were all he had, he pulled them on. Reluctantly, because it was one of his least favourite activities, he added shopping to his mental list of things that couldn't be avoided today.

Stepping out of the hostel into a grey overcast day, he smelt rain in the squally wind. His first stop was the chemist where he bought plasters and other essentials. Returning to the hostel, he patched up his wounds, shaved and yanked a comb through his hair.

He had a tenner left. That should buy him breakfast. The cafe opposite the abbey provided him with a full English which he wolfed down like a man facing starvation. Sitting at the back of the room, facing away from the door, he read the paper while he drank his coffee. It was depressing how few things had changed in his absence. The world's trouble spots were still troublesome. The same group of charlatans were still bungling running the country. The economy hadn't improved and, Finn knew from experience, that had the knock-on effect of keeping environmental issues low on the government's list of priorities.

Which meant that a new job would be harder to come by. Add to that the fact that he'd gone AWOL from his last one. With good reason. Unfortunately not the kind of reason he could explain to a prospective employer. All in all it would make his search for employment interesting to say the least. But that was a problem for another day. He had – with only four days until Beltane - to deal with what was going down in Glastonbury before he could start to think about putting his life back together.

He walked the length of the cafe to the counter to pay his bill. A guy with dreads, a baggy shirt and drooping trousers ambled from the kitchen and started fumbling with the till. Finn dropped his ten pound note on the counter and turned away, his eyes idly raking over a notice board on the opposite wall. Brightly coloured flyers and leaflets for alternative therapies, self-help workshops and tarot card readings covered it. No wonder Cat felt at home here. His sister was a sucker for all this crap.

The words *Anam Cara Healing Retreat* caught his eye. Striding over he snatched the flyer from the wall. There was a picture of a garden together with promises of sanctuary, healing and transformation. He ripped the paper into two before his fist tightened crushing the pieces into a tight ball.

"What do you think you're doing, man?" the dreadlocked guy called, shambling from behind the counter.

Finn dropped the screwed up paper onto a dirty plate. "Leaving," he said.

Chapter 4

Zoe woke to a hangover. The headache had become a dull throb filling the left side of her cranium but she didn't feel sick. One the other hand, she didn't exactly feel ready for breakfast either. She yawned hugely. She'd not had nearly enough sleep. She'd heard the clock in the hall chime three before she'd slept and then, in the cold light of dawn, she'd been yanked awake by another dream.

Gingerly she stood up. She only felt slightly worse when she was upright. Crossing the room, she tentatively opened the curtains. In the morning light the full devastation to the garden was apparent. The trunk of the Green Man's tree had been cleft in two. Debris was everywhere. Branches and leaves scattered over the garden, crushing plants and filling up the pond.

Taking her pad from the chest of drawers, Zoe flipped it open at her drawing of the garden and compared it again with the reality outside her window. The drawing remained the same. The realisation in the middle of the night that she could draw the future hadn't been another dream.

But what about the dream that had come with the dawn? With shaking fingers she turned the page. "Not again," she whispered. Suddenly she did feel sick. Her eyes flicked upwards. There was no doubt.

In the drawing the man stood in front of the tower on the Tor. It was night, the moon partly hidden by a cloud. He wore dark clothes - a fleece, walking trousers, boots, a beanie hat - and held binoculars. A small pack rested against the wall of the tower. His gaze was fixed in the distance. His jaw was tense, his eyes narrow.

She looked up again. Traced with her artist's eyes the shape of the Tor, the angle of the tower. It's as if he's looking down here. As if he's watching me.

Who the bloody hell are you? And why do I keep drawing you?

Abruptly she spun away, hauled her rucksack from the floor to the chair and started tossing clothes into it. Then, hairbrush in hand, she stopped. She was finally making progress with King Arthur. If she went home and the block returned then she'd hate herself. It wasn't like she didn't have these strange dreams at home. For nearly a week before Halloween last year she'd had a nightmare every night.

She put her hairbrush back on the chest of drawers and rummaged in her bag for some painkillers. She needed coffee and time to think before she made a decision.

Half an hour later she wandered into the kitchen to find Tony sat at the table next to a middle aged woman. That must be Penny, Zoe thought, taking in her long steel grey hair. She wore shapeless clothes in earthy shades and no makeup. Tanya, looking slightly paler than usual in blue loungewear, stared out the French windows. Helena was in the kitchen, cutting up a grapefruit. She wore a grey t-shirt which matched the colour of her face.

"Good day," Helena said.

"I'm not so sure." Zoe's hand massaged her temple. "You look about the way I feel."

"I had a real bad night. Woke up feeling like I'd never been to sleep." Helena attempted to stifle a yawn. "How are you?"

"Just a headache." She took a seat at the table, poured coffee into a mug and considered whether toast was a good or bad idea. The others were talking about the thunder storm and the devastation in the garden.

"Can lightning destroy a tree so completely?" Zoe said.

"I've never seen anything as extreme, but it's possible," Tony said. "When the lightning strikes the electric current is carried by the water in the sapwood. That's the wood immediately below that bark. The current heats the water and when it boils the pressure of the steam makes the tree explode."

"Why do you ask, dear?" Maeve's distinctive voice came from behind Zoe. She whipped her head round wincing as her headache objected. Maeve stood in the kitchen, elegant in grey linen trousers and an ice blue cardigan.

"I was just wondering," Zoe mumbled.

The healer walked over and took the empty chair at the head of the table. Helena stood behind her. "I do apologise for the disturbance last night. Naughty Persia brought a mouse home. I'm afraid I'm rather frightened of mice. Helena was very brave. She caught it and disposed of it. But it was total mayhem for a little while as she and Persia both tried to catch the mouse at the same time." Maeve finished with a light laugh.

The explanation sounded like a work of not particularly good fiction. Zoe blinked in surprise when the other guests nodded and smiled before asking Maeve how she felt this morning.

"I'm fine. I'm simply sorry that I disturbed you all last night," Maeve said. While the healer's attention was on the other guests, Zoe looked directly at her. She intended to glance quickly away but found herself staring. Maeve looked older, visibly aged from when she'd seen her last, less than forty-eight hours before. A myriad of lines scored her face. Her skin sagged into pouches under her eyes and made jowls along her jaw line. Beneath her makeup her watery eyes were puffy and bloodshot.

"As long as you're alright now, that's all that matters," Penny said. "But Maeve, your garden! I nearly cried when I saw what had happened. All your hard work gone to waste. And just before Beltane too."

"It's very sad but nature renews. I never forget that." Maeve smiled. Turning to Tanya, she said, "My dear, I'd like to move our appointment to eleven."

"Oh yes, that's fine. I am feeling a little fragile this morning. Entirely self-inflicted I'm afraid. I'm sure the healing will help." Tanya rubbed her fingers over her forehead as she spoke.

"Excellent. I'll see you at eleven in the treatment rooms." Maeve stood up and moved through to the kitchen. Helena followed. "Is that my breakfast? Helena, what did I say about grapefruit juice?"

Helena mumbled something which Zoe didn't catch. "No, I'll get it!" Maeve snapped. Opening the fridge she fired instructions at her employee about organising the clean-up of the garden.

Tanya turned to Zoe. "Your room overlooks the garden, doesn't it?" When she nodded in response the other woman added, "Did you look out the window after the tree blew up?"

"I did when I went back to my room after we'd all been out on my landing. Why do you ask?" Deciding to risk a slice of toast Zoe buttered it as she spoke.

"I was wondering if you saw anyone in the garden."

Zoe looked at her in surprise. Had Tanya seen the man from her picture?

"What did you say?" Holding a carton of juice, Maeve walked swiftly over and stood next to Tanya's chair, staring down at her. Helena followed, hovering uncertainly behind her employer.

"It's probably nothing." Tanya already appeared less certain. "I'd not been back long and I was getting ready for bed when I heard the tree explode. I looked out of the window and I thought I saw someone moving about outside."

"Are you sure, dear? It was very dark. And none of us were outside, were we?" Maeve looked around the table. In turn Penny, Tony and Helena shook their heads. When Maeve turned to her, Zoe channelled her inner teenager and shrugged insolently.

"You see, we were all tucked up in our beds. There couldn't have been anyone in the garden." Maeve's tone was calmly reasonable as if she spoke to a misbehaving child.

"I must have got it wrong. To be honest, I'd had a fair bit to drink last night so I could easily have imagined it," Tanya said with a little laugh.

Maeve smiled condescendingly. "That's right dear. Well, I really must get on." She walked briskly through the kitchen, dumping the carton on the worktop as she passed. "Helena, I asked you to bring my breakfast to the office." Zoe watched for a reaction from the Australian, a look or a gesture to indicate she felt put upon by her employer. But Helena simply poured juice into a glass and then carried the tray out of the door.

Frowning, Zoe looked around the table at her fellow guests. Tony was topping up his and Penny's coffee cups from a cafetiere. Tanya was half way down a bowl of muesli. They all appeared oblivious to Maeve's rudeness. Just as they'd apparently accepted her explanation about the disturbance in the night.

Penny smiled at Tanya. "What kind of healing are you having?"

"Karmic wave therapy. Maeve says it's amazing and heals on lots of different levels. You know, emotionally and spiritually as well as physically," Tanya said.

"I had it last time I was here," Penny said. "It is a deep form of healing but for me, at least, that came at a price. I had the worst healing crisis I've ever experienced."

"What's a healing crisis?" Tanya's forehead creased with lines.

"It means that you feel worse before you feel better. It's to do with the way in which your body eliminates toxins after healing. I do massage and reflexology and I tell my clients that they might feel a bit lethargic or have a headache the day after the healing. If it went on any longer than that I don't think any of them would come back." Penny smiled. "You'll need to be extra careful as you were drinking last night. To be honest, I'm surprised Maeve didn't reschedule your appointment. I'd have thought she'd want to wait until this afternoon, at least, to give you time to rehydrate."

"Maeve told me I might feel tired the day after but said it was part of the healing process and nothing to worry about," Tanya said.

"Penny was under the weather for a week after she had karmic wave healing when we were here last year." Tony's arm rose to rest on the back of his wife's chair. "I've told her that I don't think she should have it again. It may have done her good in the end but I don't think it was worth feeling that bad to get there."

"Yes, I know." Penny gave her husband a fond but slightly exasperated look. "But I think I had a bit of an extreme reaction. I was run down at the time so that might be why. And it was Beltane so that could have made it more intense."

"What's Beltane?" Zoe asked.

"Beltane's the first of May and it's one of the most sacred times of the year," Penny said. "It marks the start of spring and is a fertility rite. Maeve usually has a ceremony to celebrate. It's a wonderfully positive evening with drumming, chanting and dancing. Very transformational. We all bring an item to signify what we want to change in our lives in the coming season and throw that into the ceremonial fire."

“That sounds very...erm...interesting,” Zoe said.

“Beltane’s a really important time of the year for pagans,” Penny said. “It was the ancient Celts’ festival of fire to welcome the spring. Druids kindled fires on the tops of hills which were believed to have fertility and healing powers. We’ve been coming to Maeve’s Beltane ceremonies for the past five years. It’s such a shame she’s not celebrating it this year. We’re getting together with a group of other pagans in Avebury on Thursday but it won’t be the same.”

Surprised by Penny’s casual admittance that she and Tony were practising pagans, Zoe couldn’t stop her overactive imagination from painting a picture of witches dancing naked around a ritual fire.

Tanya pushed her chair from the table and stood up. “I guess I’d better go and get ready for my healing.”

Penny gave her a reassuring smile. “Don’t let my experiences of karmic wave put you off. Just make sure you drink lots of water before and after the healing.”

“Oh, okay,” Tanya said and then she grinned. “But I’ve got a date this evening. What’s he going to think if I only drink water?”

Zoe looked up. “With Dave?”

“Yes.” Tanya’s face was bright with excitement. “Because I’m leaving tomorrow, he’s skipping cricket training so he can take me out tonight.”

“That’s great. Where are you going?” Zoe said.

“Somewhere he knows in Wells. He’s picking me up at seven.”

Zoe smiled. “I hope you have a great time.”

There was silence for a few moments after Tanya left then Penny said, “What are you doing today?”

“I’m going to look for the Lady of the Lake,” Zoe replied which, of course, led to explaining her reasons for coming to Glastonbury. Soon Penny and Tony were suggesting sites connected to Arthurian legend that she should draw. While she made mental notes of the places they mentioned she wondered if subconsciously she'd already decided to stay.

"There's a walk along the River Brue that gives a good view of the Tor," Penny said, leaning towards Zoe. "When you see the view over the Levels it's easy to imagine Glastonbury as the Isle of Avalon. We're walking into town this morning. We could show you where the walk starts if you like?"

"That would be really helpful. If you're sure I'm not putting you out?" Zoe said.

"Not at all." Tony glanced at his watch. "Can you be ready in about ten minutes?"

"No problem. I'll meet you in the garden if that's alright?"

She drained her coffee cup and headed through the kitchen. In the hall she caught sight of the broken husk of the Green Man's tree and, after a quick glance over her shoulder, hurried into the garden. The carpet of green leaves was slippery beneath her feet. Twigs snapped as she trod on them. A blustery wind swirled debris around her ankles.

The Green Man's tree had been cleft down the middle into two shattered halves joined only by the root system. Resting her hand on the bark, she craned forward to peer through the V formed by the bisected trunk. The wood in the centre of each half had been roughly hollowed out. It looked bizarrely like someone had started to make a canoe from the trunk without bothering to fell the tree first.

Zoe stepped back to look at the Green Man's face. She wanted a final moment with him before the chainsaws moved in. He'd been her lucky charm. If she decided to stay then she would miss his handsome face.

It wasn't there. In its place was an oval that had been ripped in two as the trunk had split. She reached up to touch the half of the oval closest to her. The bark felt strangely soft beneath her fingers. It was as if the Green Man had been erased by the storm. But that was impossible. Of all the things lightning could do, removing a carving wasn't one of them. The fear and uneasiness she'd felt since arriving here, that had magnified when she found the doll last night, formed into a churning ball of nausea in the pit of her stomach.

She waited, hoping for the same sense of reassurance that she'd felt when she talked to the Green Man. Instead the queasiness intensified. Goosebumps broke out on the back of her neck. Abruptly and absurdly she wanted to cry. Turning her back on the broken ruin of the tree she hurried into the house.

Back in her room the sketches of the mystery man lay where she'd left them on her unmade bed. It was obvious from the conversation at breakfast that she couldn't leave them there. She slipped them into her portfolio and then, prompted by the obscure sense of fear that the Green Man's missing face had produced, she looked around for somewhere to hide it. Under the bed was the only possibility and she slid it as far as she could reach.

Hurriedly she shoved her pencil case, sketchpad and umbrella in her bag. After glancing at the overcast skies she screwed up her cagoule and pushed that in too. She really hoped she wasn't going to have to wear it. It was the world's least flattering garment. Grabbing the bulging bag, she ran down the stairs, through the porch and into the garden. Then she stopped.

Maeve stood by the Green Man's tree talking to two men. A chainsaw rested on the grass by the feet of the taller man. He was a good-looking guy, broad shouldered with chin length brown hair. A skinny lad in his late teens leaned on a rake, obviously bored. "I want the wood cut into logs that I can use for a fire," Maeve said.

Zoe stepped back into the open door of the porch – out

of Maeve's line of sight – and checked her watch. What was keeping Penny and Tony? They'd said ten minutes and it was nearer fifteen.

"There's one more thing, Dylan," Maeve said. "I want you to find something for me. Something that was on the tree but that has gone missing since the explosion."

Zoe peered around the door frame. "It's a small doll, about so high." Maeve's fingers moved a couple of inches apart. "Made of wood and cloth and wrapped in bark."

Shit! The doll! How had she forgotten about it? For a second, she stared at the figures on the lawn as if they were actors in a play.

"In all of this, you want us to find a doll?" Dylan said, his voice incredulous.

"Yes, it's of great sentimental value. There'll be a bonus for you and Kyle." Zoe heard Maeve say as she turned and ran through the porch.

She stopped abruptly when she saw Penny and Tony coming down the stairs in a clatter of walking boots. "Sorry, we're a bit late. Are you ready to go?" Tony said.

"Erm, I just forgot something. I'll only be a minute," Zoe said. "I'll catch you up."

"Are you alright?" Penny said. "You look a bit pale."

"Yes. Fine," Zoe called as she sprinted up the stairs.

She slammed the door shut behind her and strode to the chest of drawers. Yanking open the top drawer she pulled the doll out. She'd expected it would have lost its power overnight. That the bright light of day would be a reality check to her silly, drunken fears.

Only it wasn't. The doll's roughly scrawled face leered at her. Its miniature arms and legs hung limply, twisted from imprisonment in the bark binding. Even at ten thirty on a grey, Monday morning and nursing a hangover, it was still the freakiest thing she'd ever seen in real life. She had to get it out of here before Maeve found out she'd taken it. And worse, hacked it apart with her scissors. She stuffed the doll into the depths of her bag and ran for the door.

***

Maeve walked slowly across the lawn, pausing to pluck the heads from broken flowers. Earlier, not long after dawn had unobtrusively crept across the sunless sky, she'd inspected the damage. It was cruelly, mercilessly extensive. Her spring flowers obliterated, the pond leaking and choked with foliage, shrubs and rose bushes crushed. Years of hard work wiped out in a single moment. In the gentle early morning light she sat by the pond and let grief wash over her. Other women would have cried. Maeve hadn't wept in decades. She didn't now.

Fury had tempered the grief. Her loss was far greater than the devastation that surrounded her. But she wouldn't mourn until it was certain that what had been lost could not be recovered.

Returning to her office she threw her sunglasses on the desk. It took a massive effort of will to stay upright. Every step sent jolts of agony through her body. Sunlight felt like needles in her eyeballs. The exhaustion from yesterday had been compounded by a night without rest and the brutal backlash that had overwhelmed her when the spell on the tree had recoiled.

At the moment of explosion, pain had ripped a scream from her throat, buckled her legs and almost rendered her senseless. Struggling to retain consciousness, she'd fought against her growing awareness of the tree's destruction. Crawling over to the window and hauling herself up, she'd been desperate for her sense of disaster to be dispelled.

It hadn't been. The garden was destroyed. The Beltane sacrifice was lost. For a while after that she'd been beyond control. In the cool light of day she somewhat regretted that. It had resulted in unnecessary questions from her guests. When the exquisite release of destruction had waned, she'd become aware that she was dangerously weakened. She'd dragged herself, using stick and wall as support, to Helena's room. The girl slept soundly which had made it easy to take what she needed. She'd been careful to limit herself. She needed Helena to be able to do her work and there would be a further boost in the morning.

Hearing the roar of the chainsaw Maeve's hand moved to rest on the black leather cover of her grimoire. She had to find out what had caused the catastrophe. Only then could she formulate a plan to regain what she'd lost.

The defences that she'd placed on the boundaries of her property remained intact. An inspection of the tree had revealed that lightning was a convenient explanation but not the actual cause. She'd taken the precaution of adding a few scorch marks to the trunk to add veracity.

Her hours of deliberation since first light had proved inconclusive. She needed the poppet. Dylan and Kyle had to find it. With the poppet in her hands she could identify the force that had destroyed the tree.

After glancing at the clock she left the office, walked through the house to the French windows and along the path to the garden wing. More slowly than usual she prepared the treatment room. Lighting candles, putting the anodyne New Age music on the CD player, plumping the pillows on the couch.

She heard a tentative tap on the door. Opening it, she welcomed Tanya. The girl stood hesitantly in the doorway, fidgeting with the zip on her hooded top. Pressing her lips together, Maeve explained what would happen during the healing. When Tanya was settled on the couch with a soft fleece blanket over her, Maeve asked her to close her eyes. Repeating the same mantras again and again, she emphasised the most important word. "*Relax*, you're safe here. *Relax* and engage with the healing energy."

As Tanya's breathing slowed, Maeve placed her hands a centimetre above her guest's forehead and concentrated on Tanya's aura. A dirty brown overlaid her energy field showing that, despite all the time she'd spent listening to the girl whinge about her broken relationship, Tanya continued to hold on to negative emotions. Maeve's hands moved up and down stirring the air above Tanya's body. As the negativity was removed, Tanya's aura glowed in swirls of bright orange and emerald green.

Maeve smiled. That was exactly what she needed.

Chapter 5

Leaving the cafe Finn headed for the bank hoping that his tramp-like appearance wouldn't count against him. The girl behind the counter was pretty but not too bright. It took him twenty minutes to convince her that although his debit card had expired he was the same Finn McCloud named on his account and it was not contrary to bank procedures to give him access to his money.

Back on the High Street he spotted a bus heading for Street and jumped on it. He knew from his visit in October that it was impossible to buy anything practical in Glastonbury. The shopping village in Street had a couple of decent outdoor shops and he quickly purchased a complete change of clothes, spares to keep him going for at least a week, new boots and a small rucksack. In a cubicle in the toilets he stripped off his clothes. He placed his hands over the gash on his chest and closed his eyes. When he looked down the cut had shrunk to a thin pink line. He did the same with the wound on his thigh until sweat poured down his face. Too much, too soon, he realised. His other injuries would have to wait. After putting on his new clothes, he shoved his old kit in the bin and packed his old boots and the spares in his rucksack.

He decided to walk back to Glastonbury. It was only a couple of miles. He needed the earth beneath his feet. To feel, however weakly, the connection to its energy.

Ignoring the busy main road, he took a route that cut across the Somerset Levels. He soon realised that his mind was much keener on this walk than his body. His legs were stiff. After ten minutes his back started to ache.

He slowed his pace, his stride shortened by the tightness in his muscles.

When he reached the river he followed it and saw the Tor in front of him. An uncomfortable reminder of the mistakes he'd made. Blind, stupid mistakes that could easily have been fatal. It was only the knowledge that Cat had escaped that made him any less furious with himself.

He would have to ring both his sister and his Mum when he got back to Glastonbury. He was being a prat to have put it off this long. But he wasn't ready to deal with their reactions. At least there was no pressure to contact his father. Six months without contact would barely be noticed.

On the path ahead of him was a figure. Drawing closer he was surprised to see a young woman sitting on the ground. As he got nearer he saw that she stared at the Tor for long moments before bending her head to a book resting on her bent knees. He realised that she was drawing. She was so intent that he didn't want to disturb her even by walking past. He was in no hurry. It was no big deal to wait a while.

Finn had been lucky enough to see otters frolicking off the Outer Hebrides, elephants bathing in Botswana and humpback whales in the icy waters of Alaska. This woman was as fascinating to watch as the best of them. Her left hand moved swiftly over the paper, then stopped and hovered, while she studied the view in front of her. The wind teased at her long brown hair, plucking tendrils from her ponytail and blowing them around her face. The coat she sat on flapped in the breeze. She was oblivious to these distractions.

Drizzle started to fall. The woman held out her palm and looked up at the overcast skies. Standing, she picked her coat from the ground. The wind caught the waterproof making it billow and as she fought to hold it her sketchpad fell from her hand. Three sheets of white paper blew in tumbling arcs towards the river. Finn focused his mind and reached out to stop them.

***

Zoe tried to grab the pages but she was much too slow. She dropped her coat and ran, knowing as she did that it was hopeless. The sketches were a dozen steps ahead of her heading inexorably towards the river.

But then the pages stopped. Miraculously, as if they'd hit an invisible wall, they fell on the very edge of the river bank. She dashed to catch them before another gust caught them. She'd not be that lucky twice.

A tall man, in black fleece and jeans with a rucksack on his back, strode towards them. He reached the pictures before she did, bent to pick them up. As he straightened she thought *I know you from somewhere*.

"Have you lost something?" The man smiled as he held the sketches out to her. A quick, ready smile.

"Thanks. I thought there was no way they weren't going in the river. Thanks for grabbing them."

"No problem. Seems like the Lady of the Lake is just trying to get back to the water." The man's smile widened into a grin.

"You recognised her?"

"Sure. How many other women lurk in lakes brandishing swords?"

"Sorry. That must have sounded like a really silly question." Heat crept over her cheeks. "It's just that I'm illustrating a children's book about King Arthur. And, to be honest, it's not been going very well. So it's great that you recognised the Lady of the Lake straight away. Makes me think I'm doing something right after all."

"I'm no expert on art or King Arthur but they look good to me," the man said.

Zoe pushed damp hair from her eyes and stole a glance at him. He was looking past her, his gaze fixed on the path as if he was about to walk away. The silence was on the edge of becoming uncomfortable when he said, "I'm Finn, by the way."

"Hi. I'm Zoe." She smiled up at him. *Boy, was he tall!* He looked to be in his early thirties. The dark circles under his eyes and his pallid skin made him look exhausted. He had a bruise on one cheekbone and a plaster above his left eye.

Her coat, lifted by the wind, suddenly turned clumsy cartwheels across the path. "Oh my God!" Zoe said, trying ineffectually to grab it. Finn ran forward on long, strong legs and caught it. Seeing him grimace, she found herself wondering if his injuries weren't only on his face.

"Thanks again." Zoe laughed to cover her embarrassment. "I want you to know that I don't usually have this many problems with my possessions."

"Don't worry about it. Do you want to put this on?" Finn held the cagoule out for her.

It was a delightfully gentlemanly gesture. Only problem was she really didn't want him to see her in it. But as the thin drizzling rain had become persistent she decided it would seem ridiculous to refuse. "Yes, thanks," she murmured. Aware of Finn's closeness, she slipped her arms into the sleeves.

"But you haven't got a coat. You're going to get soaked. You can borrow my umbrella if you like?" Zoe slid her pad - now safely enclosing her sketches - inside her bag and rummaged until she found a pink and purple umbrella.

"Thanks, but it's not my colour," Finn said. "You use it. I don't mind getting wet. I'm used to being outside in all weathers." Rain slid over his cheekbones and soaked into his hair until it looked almost black. She stared at him. Why did she feel like she'd seen his face somewhere before?

Opening her umbrella she tried to remember where.

The wind caught it and blew it inside out. Finn reached up, grabbed one side and pulled it the right way round. "Careful or you'll take off."

Zoe tried to close it but the umbrella resisted. Finn moved to stand between her and the wind. Immediately it collapsed. Zoe kept her head down as she stuffed it back in her bag. "Thanks," she muttered.

"No problem." His voice sounded different. She glanced up and saw he was trying not to laugh. "I'm glad *you're* enjoying this! I couldn't be more embarrassed."

"If you're going back to Glastonbury I'll walk with you. Just in case anything else you own decides to blow away."

"Thanks."

"No problem." Finn laughed. Zoe glared at him. He laughed harder. It was a deep, rich sound and annoyingly infectious. Her frown faltered and then she found she was laughing.

"This weather doesn't bother you at all?" As Zoe turned towards the town, the rain blew straight into her face. Reluctantly she pulled her hood up.

"It's not that big a deal. I'm outside a lot for my work."

"What do you do?"

"I'm a conservationist."

"Wow! That sounds...green," Zoe said and then bit her bottom lip. Could she come up with anything more inane?

"It's not always that straight forward. The green agenda is increasingly complex and always short of money. I try to take the jobs that are about protecting habitats, conserving species. Those are the ones that are really worthwhile."

"Are you working on anything interesting at the moment?"

"I've... been...abroad. Working." From beneath her hood Zoe peeked up at him. His face looked tense, closed off.

"Anywhere nice?"

"Erm...New Zealand."

"Ooh, that sounds exciting! What were you doing out there?"

"I was working on a project on...soil erosion."

"That sounds -" Zoe hesitated, trying to find a suitable word "- interesting."

"Actually it was. To me at least."

"But New Zealand! That's somewhere I'd love to go. It looks amazing." Finn didn't respond. He stared into the distance as if his thoughts were far away. The moment filled with silence until Zoe said, "Were you there for long?"

"I…six months."

"Wow! You're so lucky." She stole another glance at him. His forehead was creased, his shoulders hunched. She dropped her gaze to her feet wondering if it would be rude to ask more questions.

"But what about your job? Getting paid to draw King Arthur? Nice work if you can get it, I'd say!" Finn's voice was light and teasing. Zoe looked at him in surprise. He was grinning at her now. Whatever the shadow had been it had passed.

"Being an illustrator's harder than it looks. Or at least it is for me. And this is the first paid commission that I've had. I have to do other things so I don't end up starving in a garret." Zoe's hands moved as she spoke, decorating her words.

"Such as? No, let me guess." Finn stopped and reached towards her. His hand hovered an inch from her sleeve. Zoe saw that there were plasters on three of his fingers and across his palm. "Juggler?" She shook her head, trying not to laugh. "Okay then. I've got it. You're an umbrella tester."

"No!" She pushed his arm away, grinning up at him. "I teach adult education art classes but that's part-time and it's only for half the year so I have to work at the Clapham Picturehouse as well."

"Do you like teaching?" Finn started walking again and she had to hurry to keep up with his long stride.

"I love it. It's really rewarding to see the students improve and turn out work they're proud of. I'm hoping that this King Arthur project will lead to more illustrating work and then I'll be able to give up the cinema job." Zoe was surprised she'd said so much. It seemed that as long as she wasn't looking at Finn's face he was really easy to talk to.

"Sounds like a plan. I hope it works out for you."

"I'm feeling a bit more optimistic about it. I was really struggling with this project at home and then my best friend suggested that I came here. You know, because of the Isle of Avalon and Arthur's grave. And it's really helping. I'm actually making progress." Zoe paused to detour around a large puddle. "So that's why I'm in Glastonbury on a rainy day in April. What about you?"

"You could say I'm here for my job too." Deep furrows appeared on Finn's forehead. She'd definitely seen that look before. But where?

"Where's home?" Finn added.

"Lewisham, South London."

"But that's not where you're from originally?" It was barely a question.

"No, I'm from Scarborough. How did you know?"

"I did my MSc in Leeds. Your accent reminds me of the people that I met when I lived there."

"You can take the girl out of Yorkshire." Zoe quoted with a reluctant smile.

"There's nothing wrong with that. Scarborough's great. I went over a few times when I was in Leeds. Had probably the best fish and chips I've ever tasted."

"I'm glad you liked it. Lots of people think it's..." Zoe paused, trying to find a way to describe some of the less positive reactions to the town she loved.

"A bit overly candyflossed?"

Zoe laughed. "Yes, exactly that. I've been in London for eight years but I still miss it. Especially the sea. I go back when I can. My Mum moved to Whitby about a year ago but whenever I visit I make sure I spend a day in Scarborough."

"If you miss the sea you'd have liked Glastonbury before the Levels were drained. Back then all of this was covered in water." Finn gestured to the flat landscape around them. Zoe was disappointed to see that the outskirts of the town were rapidly getting closer.

"I like it now. I love how open minded and creative people are. It's such a nice change from London. I just wonder if they take it a bit too far sometimes."

"Crystals and auras not your thing?"

"I don't mind that. It's the pagan stuff that's a bit weird for me." Zoe wasn't sure why she was telling him this. Except she needed to talk about it and Finn was a good listener.

"What do you mean by pagan?" Finn's grey eyes were intent on her face.

Zoe hesitated. She'd sound paranoid if she told him about the creepy doll which she'd thrown into the River Brue (hopefully it had now sunk to the bottom, never to be seen again). Or insane if she talked about the Green Man's face disappearing. "Well, at the place where I'm staying they have this stone altar with candles on which I find really creepy. And I met this couple over breakfast who actually told me they're pagans and they usually come here for some big celebration on May Day. It just seems a bit much to me."

"I wouldn't worry about that. Most of what goes on at Beltane is harmless."

Zoe threw a doubtful glance at him. "*Most* of it is harmless?"

"A few people take it to extremes."

"What kind of extremes?" Zoe's imagination was working overtime again with images of blood and sacrifice.

"Drugs. Sex. Some people embrace the fertility rite a little too wholeheartedly."

They reached a stile and Finn stood back to let her go first. She put her foot on the flat wooden step. Finn stretched his hand out and she took it. To hell with being an independent woman. What mattered was getting over this stile without falling flat on her bum.

"You're very well informed about this whole Beltane thing," Zoe said, as they crossed a road that led into a modern housing estate.

"I have an interest in folklore. And my Mum's Irish. From Donegal. I spent a lot of time there when I was growing up. Beltane's still a good excuse for a party in parts of Ireland."

"I'm guessing you're named after one of your Irish ancestors?" Zoe grinned at him.

"Actually, Mum named me after a legendary Irish warrior, Fionn mac Cumhaill. Much to my father's disgust. But he'd agreed she could name their first son and, for all his faults, he does stick to his word. And as my surname's McCloud his Scottish heritage is obvious."

"Finn McCloud." Zoe rolled the name around her mouth. "Nice! I'm Zoe Rose."

"Pretty!" Finn smiled and she wasn't sure he was only talking about her name.

A warm glow started to grow inside her, protecting her from the rain and the chill spreading through her body from her wet clothes. There was a moment's silence and then she blurted out, "You don't sound very Scottish."

"That's because I've never lived in Scotland. We moved around a lot when I was younger. Father was a doctor in the army."

They turned along a tree-lined lane. The canopy of leaves provided some shelter and the rain eased to a light drizzle. In a few minutes they'd reach the main road where he'd go down the hill into town and she'd head back to Anam Cara to dry out. Before they got there she wanted to know if she would see him again. Because that would definitely make her decide to stay. He was the most interesting guy she'd met in ages. And it seemed that he liked her too. He'd not been adverse to a bit of flirting and he'd held her gaze for far longer than was necessary on more than one occasion.

"Are you in Glastonbury for long?" she said.

"I'm not sure."

Zoe took a deep breath and decided to go for it. "You see, I was wondering if we could meet up sometime. I'd like to buy you a drink as a thank you for all your help today. If you'd not been around I'd have lost my morning's work, my coat and my umbrella." She hoped she sounded casual. As if she wasn't really asking him on a date.

Finn gazed fixedly at the road ahead. "I'd like that but I'm not sure of my plans yet."

She hesitated and then said quickly, "What if we swap numbers and then if you decide to stay you can give me a ring?"

"I gave my mobile to my sister. Long story." There was a pause. She was about to tell him to forget it when Finn added, "But you could give me your number and I'll call you when I know what I'm doing."

He smiled fleetingly. Was he simply being polite? She wasn't sure but it was too late now. Tearing a piece of paper from her sketchpad, she scribbled her mobile number on it. "Here you go." His fingers brushed hers as he took the scrap of paper.

Silence stretched uneasily between them. Zoe could hear cars passing on the main road. Their steps slowed as they climbed the steep incline to the junction but in only a few minutes they would say goodbye.

Deciding to just keep talking, she said the first thing that came to mind, "As I really don't think I can get any wetter when I get back to Anam Cara I'm going to have a hot shower and..."

Finn grabbed her arm and pulled her to a stop. "Did you say Anam Cara?" He bent slightly to look her straight in the eye.

"Yes, that's where I'm staying. Why? Do you know it?"

"Yes." Finn took his hand from her arm but his gaze didn't leave her face. "How is Maeve?" he said slowly. "You must feel lucky to be staying there."

Zoe frowned. "Is she a friend of yours?"

"No."

"Oh, that's okay then. Because I can't stand her. But everyone else thinks she's great. My friend Anna – it was her idea that I came here – she raves about Maeve. And all the other guests think she's this wonderful healer. If I could afford it I'd leave tomorrow." It was such a relief to express her real feelings that it took Zoe a second to realise that Finn was staring at her, his mouth slightly open.

"You're serious? You don't like her?"

"I don't know why you're so surprised." Zoe folded her arms. "I can't be the only person who doesn't get on with her."

"You have no idea," Finn said quietly. Zoe was trying to figure out what he meant by that when he added, "Whatever you do, don't let her give you any healing."

"Why do you say that?"

"Maeve Blackwell is not a healer. She claims to be but she can no more heal than your umbrella can fly to the moon."

"On this morning's performance I think you're

underestimating the umbrella." Zoe's grin faded when she saw that he was serious. "Anyway there's no need to worry because I wasn't planning on having any healing. I'd rather walk bare foot across hot coals than let Maeve put her hands on me!"

She thought Finn would laugh but he didn't. As they fell into step again he muttered something which sounded like, "At least you'll be safe."

It was such an unlikely thing to say that Zoe thought she'd misheard. She was going to ask him to repeat it but then she saw his narrowed eyes and tense jaw. Hoping it was a safer subject, she said, "How do you know Maeve?"

There was a long moment before Finn replied, his voice hard edged, "Because of my sister. Catriona stayed at Anam Cara. I had to come to get her."

There's so much more to that than you're telling me, she thought. He really was a man of light and shade. Sometimes so relaxed and fun to be with and then it was like he clouded over. If she were drawing him she'd....

She lurched to an abrupt halt. How could she have been so blind? It'd been staring her in the face since she met him. *Literally in the face. His face.* And the plasters! Could there be any more clues? And she'd missed them all because she was too busy flirting with him.

Finn walked on a few steps. He turned, looked puzzled. "Where'd you go?" When she didn't respond he walked back. "What's wrong? You look like you've seen a ghost."

"I'm fine," Zoe mumbled through dry lips, forcing her feet to move.

"Are you sure? You look really pale." Finn sounded concerned which would have pleased her five minutes ago. Now it wasn't helping at all.

She was sure though. Finn was the man from her pictures. She'd dreamed him and drawn him. And then, unbelievably, failed to recognise him.

Suddenly she was painfully aware that she was walking down a quiet country lane with a man that she'd met less than an hour ago. A man who'd been in Anam Cara's garden in the middle of the night. He'd made it clear he was no friend of Maeve's. So what was he doing there?

Ugly words like trespass and burglary popped into her mind. Instantly, she pushed them away. But was that a mistake? After she'd got it so wrong with Gareth she wasn't sure.

"How long are you staying at Anam Cara?" Finn said.

"Until Wednesday," Zoe said absently. Questions were seething through her brain. Was she brave enough to ask them? The main road was only a few metres away. It was now or, quite possibly, never. "You said you picked your sister up from Anam Cara? Was that recently?"

"October last year. Why?"

"Have you been back since?"

There was a pause that stretched and stretched. Eventually Finn said, "That's an odd question."

"Is it? Forget it then." She hung back, giving herself time to think. He clearly wasn't about to open up and tell her why he'd been in Maeve's garden last night. But could she really expect that? He knew even less about her than she did about him.

The lane climbed steeply to the junction with the main road. "Is that the A39?" Finn said, turning up the collar of his fleece. When Zoe frowned, he added, "The road that Anam Cara's on?"

"Yes."

He reached in his rucksack and pulled out a black hat, tore a cardboard tag from it and put it on over his wet hair. The hat drew attention to the bones in his face. Finn briefly closed his eyes and Zoe couldn't help staring, tracing with her eyes the features that she'd drawn with her pencil. She had the strangest feeling that she'd seen his face somewhere more solid than a dream.

"I'll say goodbye here."

"If you're wanting to go back into town I'm pretty sure it's quicker if you go down the main road."

"Actually, I've come further out of my way than I'd realised. I'll head back -" Finn nodded in the direction they'd come "- this way."

"Sorry." Zoe's hands swept upwards emphasising her apology. "I should have asked you where you were going."

"And I should have realised. I don't know what's wrong with me. Usually my sense of direction's better than this." Finn glanced towards the main road. "I know it's a lot to ask as we've only just met but would you do me a favour?"

"What kind of favour?" If there was one thing she'd learned from her relationship with Gareth it was that a smart woman found out what the favour involved before making any promises.

"Will you not tell Maeve that we've met?"

"Why not?"

"I'd rather she didn't know I'm in Glastonbury."

"Because...?" Zoe scanned his face, trying to get some clue as to what was behind his request.

"Because I need to talk to Cat and… sort out some other things before Maeve and I meet again." Finn glanced away, his jaw tense.

There was so much more to it than that. But she wasn't going to refuse. She liked him. More than that she felt a connection to him. Okay, that might be because she'd dreamed about him before she met him. And she needed time to figure out whether she could trust that, trust him. Yet, pushing that aside, what he'd asked wasn't a big deal. It wasn't like she and Maeve sat down for cosy chats.

"Okay. As far as Maeve's concerned we never met."

"Thanks. I appreciate it." Finn stretched his right hand towards her. Zoe stared at it, suddenly awkward. Reflexively her hand rose, touched his. He covered it with his other hand, looked intently at her. She felt a strange tingling over her skin where they touched. She was embarrassed to feel a blush creeping over her cheeks.

"It's been good to meet you, Zoe Rose." Finn looked in her eyes and she knew he was trying to tell her goodbye. He wouldn't ring.

"You too. And thanks for your help...with everything."

"Take care." For a moment all she saw was Finn; his warm smile, his eyes, the feel of his hands wrapped around hers. Everything else – road, rain, confusion – faded.

Then a van rushed past them. The moment evaporated. Zoe pulled her hand away, uncertain whether he'd felt it too. "See you soon?" She couldn't help making it a question, hoping he'd agree and she could dismiss the sense of finality. Finn didn't speak. He looked down at her, his grey eyes lingering on hers. He hadn't said it but she could see it in his face. She said the word for him. "Goodbye then."

Raising her hand in an awkward wave, she turned away. Eyes on the wet tarmac she trudged up the incline. She'd gone six steps when she heard him call, "Don't forget what I said about the healing."

She looked back. He raised his hand before he walked away.

Chapter 6

Finn strode swiftly down the lane, turning repeatedly to look behind him. What had he been thinking? Had he been so distracted by a pretty face that he'd lost all sense of direction? It was insanity to be this close to Anam Cara in broad daylight. As soon as he'd realised he'd shielded himself but that could easily turn out to be too little, too late.

He was crap at this. He was completely and totally unprepared to take on Maeve. He'd proved that spectacularly in October. What the hell did he think he was doing taking another shot at her?

Pushing his aching legs to maintain their pace, he ran his hand over his wet face. He knew the answer to that. Running and hiding were the easy options. He knew he couldn't live with himself if he took them.

Not for the first time he wished The Order was still around. It'd been their sacred duty to deal with problems like this. But he was six years too late. He was on his own unless he could talk his friend, Winston, into helping.

Until he got his staff back he had to stay hidden, watch from the shadows and find out if Maeve was working alone or leading something bigger. His gut feeling was that she was a loner but he needed to be sure.

He should have asked Zoe more questions. It was better luck than he deserved that she wasn't one of Maeve's groupies. Once he'd found that out he'd had the perfect opportunity to pick her brain. And he'd been so surprised he'd wasted it.

Perhaps he should meet her for that drink. Just to find

out more about Maeve and Anam Cara. Finn smiled. Zoe had been fun to be with in a rainstorm that would have drowned a lot of people's good humour. Think what a good time they'd have in a decent pub with a few drinks, maybe a bite to eat. Especially if she wore something more flattering than that ugly cagoule.

Focus. He was in the middle of the most dangerous thing he'd ever done. This wasn't the time to start dating. And Zoe deserved better than that. She was a nice girl. She should be left alone to draw King Arthur and then go back to London to get on with the rest of her life.

He shouldn't have said he'd ring her. He'd only done it to erase the disappointment that had flitted across her expressive face. He'd tried, when they said goodbye, to let her know that he wouldn't call. As she turned away he thought, with more regret than he'd anticipated, that she got the message.

Turning onto the road that led back to the centre of Glastonbury he occupied his mind with practicalities. The location of the hostel on the main street meant he couldn't spend another night there. This was a small town and there'd be too many opportunities for him to be seen coming and going. He needed somewhere quiet and isolated, where no one would notice if he was out half the night. A place on the opposite side of town to Anam Cara.

Should he have warned Zoe to leave? He'd stopped himself because obviously he couldn't tell her the truth. She'd never believe that. But he could have lied. Said Maeve gave her guests food poisoning or cloned their credit cards. Instead all he'd done was warn her about the healing. Would that and her ability to see through Maeve be enough to keep her safe?

And why had she suddenly stopped and looked frightened? What was that all about? She'd been like an open book up until that point. Then immediately afterwards she'd asked when he'd last been at Anam

Cara. Had she seen him in the garden last night? He'd seen movement at one of the upstairs windows, instantly feared it was Maeve. If that had been Zoe then what else had she seen?

There was no point thinking about it. He'd decided not to see her again. That was the end of it. First priority was making sure he could defend himself. Which meant he had to see to his sister. If he was going to Melton he needed transport. He'd have to hire a car. Expensive but not impossible now that he was reunited with his bank account. And he needed food and a few beers. It was a bloody long time since he'd had a beer.

The residential streets turned into shops and cafes as he approached the centre of the town. He pulled his hat lower, hunched his shoulders and kept his head down. His eyes scanned the roads. Searching for one face among the pedestrians shielded by umbrellas or behind the windscreen of passing cars.

Hurrying through the door of the hostel, he asked the man behind the desk if there was a phone he could use. He couldn't put it off any longer.

He was directed to a shabby cubicle under the stairs. It was clearly built for midgets. Hunched over, his shoulders pressing against the low ceiling, it took him a few seconds to remember how to use a pay phone. He stuck two pound coins in the slot and dialled his sister's mobile.

Listening to it ring, he felt himself tense at the thought of Cat's reaction to hearing his voice. But the voice that answered was his mother's. "Mum?" he managed to croak before his throat closed up.

"Finn? Oh sweet Jesus, is that you?" Maggie McCloud's voice cracked as she spoke. He tried to reassure her but he couldn't find the words. A barrage of exclamations and questions erupted down the line swiftly followed by stifled sobs. Crammed into the tiny scruffy space, Finn felt totally bloody helpless as he listened to his mother cry.

At the end of the call, his face contorted with bleak fury. He'd stayed calm while speaking to Maggie, promised that he'd be at her house tomorrow or Wednesday at the latest. When he slammed the phone down his rage exploded. "The fucking evil bitch! I'm going to fucking kill her!" His fist whipped out, once and again, slamming against the thin plywood wall.

Then he slumped forward. His forehead rested on the cold metal of the payphone. He'd thought he'd saved Cat. Turned out he'd only done half the job. She still suffered, was still in pain.

After a long moment he fed in more coins and dialled again. When a deep Scottish voice answered, he said, "Winston? It's Finn."

"Bloody hell, Finn! Where've you been for all these months?"

"It's a long story. I ran into some trouble."

"In Glastonbury. I know. I came to look for you."

"You did?" Again Finn found himself lost for words. He'd not expected that.

"Aye, you rang me remember? The night you disappeared. When I rang back I got your Mum. She told me what'd been going on. How your sister had turned up but you'd gone missing. I spent a week down in Somerset trying to track you down."

"Thanks." Finn swallowed hard. He'd forgotten about the phone call. If only he'd waited...

"Come on then, where've you been hiding since Samhain?"

Finn winced. "Not hiding. Hidden. Look, I'm using the pay phone at the hostel and I don't know who might be listening so I'll keep it short. The trouble I ran into is still here. I need your help to tackle it."

"Count me in," Winston said.

Chapter 7

What is it with Glastonbury? Zoe slammed her feet down as she tramped up the hill to Anam Cara. Why was everything that had happened since she'd arrived freaky or scary? Or both?

And now Finn was part of that. He'd seemed to be just a normal guy when they'd met by the river. Well, not entirely normal because he was interesting and attractive and - God only knew - that didn't happen every day. But then it turned out that he's not just a guy, he's *the* guy. The one from the garden, the one from her drawing. The one that she'd dreamed about *three* times before she met him.

And that gave a whole new meaning to meeting the man of her dreams. A meaning she seriously didn't want to get into because she was so *not* together about this whole seeing the future thing. Not that it mattered anyway because she was almost one hundred per cent sure that she wouldn't see him again.

Turning the corner of Anam Cara's high wall, she reached the gate. Her eyes widened as she saw, hanging from a rusty nail above the gate, a bunch of foliage tied with brown ribbon.

On tiptoes she stretched up to get a better look. The wide shiny leaves she recognised as bay, and the dark green, prickly one was obviously holly. She couldn't identify the frond of long, thin leaves, evenly spaced along a central spine.

Why did Maeve keep hanging things from her property? This was like something from folklore. But

Maeve didn't seem the kind to go in for superstitious nonsense. There must be some reason for the bundle of leaves. And the damned doll. Because otherwise why was Maeve so desperate to find it? She'd said it was for sentimental reasons but Zoe had trouble imagining Maeve being sentimental about anything. Least of all a crude, ugly doll.

Had it been a mistake to throw it in the river? She could have brought it back, dropped it somewhere in the garden and kept her fingers crossed that Dylan or Kyle found it. It was too late for that now. She'd rather enjoyed its watery end. As the doll sank there'd been a sweet sense of release as if her late night terrors went down with it.

Zoe frowned as she realised that people behind this gate were probably still looking for the damned thing. If only she could come clean and tell them they weren't going to find it. But then she'd have to admit that she'd taken it. And she couldn't do that. She didn't want to face Maeve when she was angry. She was unnerving enough when she was pretending to be pleasant.

Punching in the security code, Zoe pushed opened the gate. Keeping her head down, she hurried along the path. The roar of a motor startled her and she looked up to see Dylan standing over the felled trunk of the Green Man's tree, a chainsaw snarling in his hands.

Zoe blinked and quickly looked away. *Get a grip,* she told herself. *The Green Man's gone. Stop reacting like Dylan's dismembering the corpse of an old friend.*

She detoured around Kyle who was wielding a dripping angler's net as he removed debris from the pond. Helena, wearing extremely unflattering blue overalls, raked leaves into piles on the lawn. She called hello and Zoe returned the greeting but didn't slow her pace.

Striding through the house and running up the stairs she couldn't stop herself from scanning nervously around. In the safety of her room, she kicked off her soggy trainers and stripped wet jeans from her chilled legs. Then she hauled her portfolio from under the bed and took three drawings from it. Dropping them on the bed she climbed under the covers.

She balanced the sketches of Finn on her bent knees. Staring at them, she searched for details that she'd missed before. She'd forgotten, in the shock of realising who he was, that he looked terrified in this picture. She traced a finger over his ripped, dirty clothes. "What were you doing, Finn?" she whispered. "You don't look like a thief or an axe murderer. So why were you here?"

Her mind ran back over the time she'd spent with him, seeking clues that she'd missed, words that could have a different meaning. Were his moments of withdrawal anything to do with Anam Cara? She tried to remember what had triggered his silence. It was hard to recall his exact words but she didn't think there was a pattern.

Unless - she reran the conversation in the lane just before they'd said goodbye - it was something to do with his sister. He'd said he met Maeve because of her, that Catriona had been staying at Anam Cara. But that - Zoe counted back on her fingers – was six months ago. What had brought him here on Sunday?

She wished now that she'd asked more directly. She could have pretended that she'd seen him in the garden from her window. Only she'd not thought of that at the time. She'd just wanted to avoid anything that could end up with her revealing that she'd dreamt about him. She could all too easily imagine the look of horror on his face if she'd said that. It would have been a sure fire way to guarantee never seeing him again.

Not that she was going to anyway. Despite the moment of connection when he'd taken her hand - which seemed to say more than all the words that they'd exchanged - she was sure he wouldn't ring.

Her stomach growled and she glanced at her watch,

surprised to find it was almost 3 o'clock. Deciding to have a quick shower and then raid the stash of food hidden in the bottom drawer of the bedside cabinet, she picked up her towel and headed for the bathroom.

Half an hour later - dressed in the warmest clothes she'd brought with her - she draped the wet towel over the radiator beneath the window. On the windowsill, between a polished piece of rose quartz and a star shaped candle was a clear glass jar filled with leaves.

Certain it hadn't been there earlier Zoe picked it up. The leaves were the same as those suspended above the gate and there was also something that rattled. She poked at the foliage. Something pricked her finger.

Instinctively, she stuck it in her mouth. Bringing the container up to eye level, she peered through the bottom and shook it gently. Hidden amongst the foliage were pins and needles. Zoe slammed the jar down and stepped away from it. What kind of person put a jar of needles in a guest's room? The thing should have a health warning.

Sinking down on the bed, Zoe closed her eyes. She'd had enough. She'd come here to draw. All she wanted was a nice B&B for a few days where she could concentrate on King Arthur. She did not want spooky bloody dolls, tables that triggered inexplicably brutal emotions or freaky psychic dreams.

Which brought her back to the decision that she'd been putting off since this morning. Except now she definitely didn't want to leave. Okay, so Finn might not ring but Glastonbury was a small town. Maybe she'd bump into him. And now she'd met him the dreams didn't seem so scary. It wouldn't be a stranger she was dreaming of. It'd be Finn.

But there was no way she could endure two more nights at Anam Cara. There must be a normal bed and breakfast somewhere in Glastonbury. There was a tourist information office on the main street; she could go there and plead with them to find her somewhere else. It was worth working extra shifts at the cinema for a month to get out of this mad house.

With the decision made Zoe pulled open the bottom drawer of the bedside cabinet to reveal half a packet of chocolate hobnobs and an apple. Not what you'd call a healthy, well balanced lunch but better than nothing. As she bit into the apple there was a knock on the door. About to shout 'come in' she spotted her sketches of Finn lying on the bed.

"Just a minute," she called. Sliding them into her portfolio, she kicked it under the bed and hurried to open the door. Tanya leant against the doorframe. Her face was ashen and creased with pain, her skin covered in a thin film of sweat.

"Oh my God! Are you alright?" Zoe asked.

"I don't feel well." Tanya's voice was low as if it hurt to talk. "Have you got any painkillers?"

"Sure. Come and sit down while I dig them out for you." Zoe held the door open. Tanya stepped forward and then swayed, bumping against the wall. Zoe placed her hand under her friend's elbow and gently guided her towards the bed.

"Bad head?" Zoe said, trying to keep the shock at Tanya's appearance out of her voice.

"Shocking." Tanya's whisper was followed by a dry, rasping cough.

"Has it just come on? You seemed okay at breakfast."

"I woke up with it about half an hour ago. I was really tired after the healing. Maeve said I should rest and I went straight to bed. I slept for over two hours but I'm still exhausted. I've drunk loads of water like Penny said. But it's not doing any good." Tanya's face crumpled. Her voice was thick with tears. "It's not just my head. My chest feels really tight like I can't catch my breath. And I feel sick."

"You poor thing." Zoe rummaged in her bag until she found the packet of painkillers and pressed them into Tanya's limp hand. Registering the heat emanating from Tanya's skin, she said, "You're really hot. Do you think you're coming down with something?"

"I don't know. I feel kind of shivery." Standing, Tanya coughed wheezily again.

"Can I get you anything else?" Zoe hovered by Tanya's shoulder waiting to catch her if she wobbled again.

"If it's no trouble, more water would be good. I can't believe how thirsty I am."

"No problem. You go and lie down and I'll bring it to you." Zoe waited while Tanya walked slowly, one hand pressed to her temple, across the landing.

Running down to the kitchen, Zoe wondered if this was the healing crisis that Penny had talked about at breakfast. As she flipped open cupboards looking for a glass, she remembered Finn's warning about Maeve's healing abilities. Could this be why he'd said Maeve wasn't a healer? Walking back up the stairs, the words that she'd thought she misheard popped into her mind. He couldn't really have said, "at least you'll be safe", could he?

Tanya's room was larger than hers, decorated in shades of purple, with windows on two sides. Her friend lay fully dressed under the patchwork quilt, her head turned into the crook of her raised arm.

"Here's the water." Zoe put the glass on the bedside cabinet. Tanya murmured her thanks. "Would you like me to draw the curtains?" Tanya nodded and Zoe walked to the window.

A jar of leaves stood on the windowsill just like in her room. Picking it up, she shook it and heard it rattle. More needles. As she pulled the curtains together she saw that there was an unobstructed view of the entire garden.

"You know you said there was someone in the garden last night." Zoe glanced over her shoulder at Tanya. "Was it a guy? Tall, kind of good looking, in his early thirties?"

"Maeve said there was no one there," Tanya said faintly.

"Yeah, I know. I was just wondering what you thought you saw." Zoe walked to the other window.

"I thought it was a man. But I was wrong. There was no one there." Tanya sounded close to tears and instantly Zoe felt bad about asking questions.

"Yes, of course. Sorry. Forget I asked, okay?" Zoe tweaked the curtains together until only the merest sliver of light slipped into the room. "Is there anything else you need or shall I leave you to rest?"

"Thanks. I'm going try to sleep it off. Got to be better for tonight."

"Well, shout if you need anything." Zoe gently closed the door, the sound of coughing following her out.

Back in her room she picked up the discarded apple. The exposed flesh had gone an unappetising shade of brown and she tossed it into the bin. What if Finn was right? What if Maeve had done something to make Tanya ill? Only why would she? What could she possibly gain from making her guests poorly?

She shook her head. She was being ridiculous, reading things into Finn's words that didn't belong there. Tanya had been drinking last night. She could have the hangover from hell. Or be coming down with flu. And alright, Penny had a bad reaction too but she'd said she was run down when she had the healing. Then what about Anna? She'd suffered after having healing with Maeve. Weren't three bad reactions more than a coincidence?

Grabbing her coat and the chocolate hobnobs, she locked her door and then hesitated. Should she tell Tanya that she was going out? She didn't want to disturb her if she were sleeping. Maybe she could ask Helena to check on her later.

Slipping her arms into her cagoule, Zoe took the stairs slowly, stopping in the hall to look through the porch. Dylan and Kyle were in the garden. Continuing into the kitchen, she saw Helena emptying the dishwasher.

"Hi Zoe, how you doing? Do you want a brew? Maeve always has a cup at this time and I'm making for the guys out there."

"No thanks, I'm going out. Can you do something for me?"

"Sure. What do you need?"

Looking at Helena's eager smile, Zoe realised that she might be able to answer some of her many questions. "How long have you worked here?"

"It's been five months now."

"So you weren't here in October?"

"No, I started in the middle of November."

"I don't suppose you know who worked here before you?" Zoe said, hoping it sounded like a casual enquiry.

"There wasn't anyone. Anam Cara had been closed for a while when I got here."

"Do you know for how long?" Zoe had assumed Catriona had been a guest but if Anam Cara had been closed then what was she doing here?

"Over a month, I think. There was a lot of work getting it ready for guests."

Realising she didn't know when in October Catriona had stayed, Zoe tried a different tack. "Did Maeve say why it was closed?"

"No. Why are you asking?" Helena crossed her arms and a frown creased her plump face.

"Just curious." Zoe shrugged slightly. "I actually wanted to talk to you about Tanya. She's not well. When I spoke to her a while ago I told her to shout if she needed anything but then I remembered I had to pop out. So I was wondering if you'd look in on her."

“Yeah, no problem. I’ll go up later to see if she needs anything.” Helena filled the kettle and put it on to boil.

“Thanks. I’m just a bit worried about her. She looked awful. But she thinks she’ll be well enough to meet Dave tonight so I suppose she can’t feel that bad.”

“She’ll be lucky.” Helena leaned against the counter. “It takes at least twenty four hours.”

“What does?”

“Oh, it’s nothing to worry about. Maeve says karmic wave therapy works on such a deep level that the body has to take time out to deal with it.”

“Are you telling me everyone has this kind of reaction after karmic wave therapy?”

“Not everyone reacts in the same way. But there’s nothing to worry about. Most people are better in a day or two.” Helena’s voice was calmly reassuring.

“But not everyone?” Zoe stepped forward. Was this why Finn had come to get his sister? Had Maeve given healing to Catriona and she’d been ill after it?

Helena glanced away. “No, some people take a bit longer to get over it.”

“Like how much longer?”

“I can’t say for certain because most of them have gone home by then.” Helena turned to take mugs and a china cup from the cupboard.

“But some people stayed, right? How long did it take them to get over it?”

“It’s only happened a couple of times. Maeve said that they must have caught a virus before the healing and that’s why it took them a while to -” Helena hesitated, her back still turned to Zoe “- bounce back.”

“Just how long until they *bounced back*?” Remembering the look on Finn’s face when he’d talked about his sister Zoe couldn’t hide her anger.

Helena turned, her arms crossed. “There’s no need to worry, you know. Tanya will be great in a day or two.

Everyone who has karmic wave therapy says it's transformational. Maeve's always getting emails and cards from people thanking her and saying how much she's helped them."

"So feeling really rubbish for a day or two is a known side effect of this type of healing?" Zoe said. When Helena looked blank, she added, "It happens with the other healers who do karmic wave therapy as well? All their patients get really sick for a day or two but then feel great afterwards?"

"I don't know."

"What do you mean you don't know? You must have asked."

"Maeve said..." Helena's voice was flat as if she were reciting a mantra.

"But what about the other healers doing karmic wave therapy?" Zoe repeated. When Helena looked at her blankly, she added, "Please tell me there *are* other healers doing it?"

"I don't know. Maeve says..."

"But she's been trained?" Zoe spoke more loudly to be heard over the noise of the kettle. "I mean, she has qualifications or certificates or something?"

"Maeve says that healing is instinctual. You know, a gift."

"A gift! Is it a gift to make people ill before you make them better? What kind of healing is that? Tanya didn't know it would make her feel this bad or she'd never have agreed to it. You know how much she's looking forward to this date with Dave. She wouldn't do anything that would risk her missing that." Voice rising above the clamour of the boiling kettle, Zoe's hands sliced through the air to emphasise her words.

The kettle clicked off. In the sudden silence, there were two quick footsteps. "Good afternoon girls," Maeve said.

Zoe swung round. *Please God, let Maeve not have heard what she'd just said.* Then she gasped. At breakfast the healer, had looked drained, exhausted and – not to put too fine a point on it - old. Now, in the bright afternoon light shining through the kitchen window, she looked rejuvenated. Her skin glowed with health, the deep lines had melted away and her eyes were bright. She looked ten, maybe even fifteen, years younger.

Zoe stared at the transformation. Maeve must have been without her makeup this morning and whatever brand of cosmetics she used they were doing an incredible job. She looked like she'd had a facelift in the six hours since breakfast.

"Zoe dear, you look startled. Is everything alright?" Maeve smiled.

"Sure. I'm...I'm fine."

"Zoe came to tell me that Tanya's not well," Helena said.

"And you're worried about her, dear? There's really no need. It's usual for people to feel a little under the weather after karmic wave therapy. It heals on such a deep level that the body needs time to recover." Her hand stretched towards Zoe's shoulder in a gesture that would have been comforting from anyone else. Instinctively, Zoe stepped beyond Maeve's reach. The healer's mouth tightened into a thin line.

"That's exactly what Helena said." Zoe forced her eyes away from Maeve's startlingly changed face.

Turning to her employee, Maeve said, "Have they found it?"

Zoe frowned. Were they talking about the doll? Her thoughts slid guiltily to the moment when she'd thrown into the river.

"No, sorry. Not yet," Helena said.

"Then they'll have to leave the clean-up and focus on the search. I want it found." Pivoting on her heel, Maeve strode towards the door. She stopped abruptly, looked Zoe up and down. "You were in the garden this morning. Maybe you saw what I'm looking for? A doll made of wood and cloth, about two inches tall."

"No." The word came out of her mouth too loudly. "No, I haven't, that is, I didn't see a doll. I just went to see the tree. That's all." Zoe's eyes were fixed on the polished wood floor. As the silence lengthened she felt compelled to meet Maeve's gaze.

"Alright, dear," Maeve said with a smile.

For a second Zoe felt relief. Then she realised the smile didn't warm the healer's cold eyes. She waited until Maeve entered the porch before hurrying over to Helena. Keeping her voice low, she said, "What's so special about this doll?"

"I don't know." Helena frowned. "But if it's more important than tidying up the garden then she must really want it back."

"Why do you say that?"

"Maeve adores her garden. It's her passion and her joy. If finding this doll's more important than getting the garden put to rights..." Helena shrugged before she picked up the tray and carried it out of the kitchen.

Then it'd been a huge mistake to chuck the doll in the river. If only she'd never taken the damned thing. If she'd had any idea last night of the stress it would cause she'd never have cut the doll from its stupid bark binding.

Before the thought was completed, she was sprinting across the hall and up the stairs. She fumbled with the key, turning it the wrong way before the door unlocked. Crossing the room, she snatched up the bin, scrabbling through its contents of uneaten apple, screwed up paper and used cotton wool balls until her fingers closed around the curl of bark. She stuffed it in her coat pocket. Pulling out the scraps of black wool, she shoved those in too.

Locking the door behind her, she raced down the

stairs. Then stopped abruptly.

Maeve stood in the doorway of the porch, watching Dylan and Kyle work. She would have to walk past her. After the questions in the kitchen she didn't think she could face it. Not with the wool and bark stuffed in her coat pocket.

She was heading back to the stairs when she remembered the French windows. They were too close to the stone table but that had to be a better option than hiding in her room. She hurried through the kitchen and hesitated, her hand on the door handle. Four black candles stood, equally spaced, around the rim of the table and a vase of foliage, like the one in her room, was at its centre.

Taking a deep breath, Zoe opened the door and stepped out. Immediately, the same intense feelings hit her. Her heart pounded, her breath caught in her throat. Cringing away from the table she pressed herself against the pebbledash wall.

An image flashed across her mind. A young woman lying on the table, moaning in agony as blood dripped from a gash on her arm.

She lurched away from the table and ran for the gate. Before she reached it, she had the unmistakable sense of being watched. Yanking the gate open, she glanced over her shoulder. Maeve hurried along the path towards her. "Zoe, dear! I just wanted to ask..."

Zoe whipped through the gate and kept running until it slammed behind her.

Chapter 8

Zoe's hasty exit confirmed Maeve's suspicion. Every instinct that she'd gained during her interminable years as a school mistress told her that the girl had lied. Admittedly the attempt had been clumsy and unconvincing. And far more revealing than Zoe realised.

Turning back to the house, Maeve passed Helena raking up leaves. "My office. Now!"

Sitting behind her desk, her hand settled on the worn black cover of a large book. There was a tentative knock on the door. "Come!" Maeve rapped out the word. Helena hovered in the doorway.

"Close the door," Maeve said. Eyes fixed on the floor, Helena complied.

"Look at me." When the girl's gaze met hers, Maeve said, "Why were you talking to Zoe about things which do not concern her? You know I will not stand for people gossiping behind my back."

"Oh, Maeve." Helena's eyes welled with tears. "I'm so very, very sorry. It was all a mistake. She started asking me all these questions and I didn't..."

"What kind of questions?" Maeve interrupted. "Tell me exactly what she asked."

Shuffling her feet as she struggled to answer Maeve's cross-examination Helena paraphrased her conversation with Zoe. When Maeve felt confident she'd extracted everything relevant from Helena's memory, she put her hand on the girl's wrist and said, "There will be no repeat of this afternoon's unfortunate behaviour. If Zoe asks any more questions, then leave the room immediately and come and find me." Helena responded with a stream of apologies and assurances that Maeve cut through saying, "Has Zoe gone out for long?"

"She told me she was going into town but she didn't say how long she'd be. Did you want her?"

"No. You can go."

Picking up her delicate china cup, Maeve's rejuvenated features settled into a scowl. The girl was more astute than she'd given her credit for. When she'd finished her tea, she took a bundle of keys from a locked drawer. Briskly she walked upstairs. The house was quiet. Tanya was the only other occupant and she was in no position to interfere. Maeve turned the key, stepped into the stellar room and closed the door.

Sometime later she emerged and locked the door. Her face was taut with fury, her eyes hard as glacial ice. Her fingers gripped a strand of black wool.

***

Zoe swore under her breath when she saw the closed door of the Tourist Information Office. It wasn't even 5 o'clock yet. And now she was stuck at Anam Cara for the night. That reminded her of the bark and scraps of wool in her pocket. She dumped them in a rubbish bin, wandered up the High Street and through the open doors of the Earth Cafe.

Ordering a latte, she sat in the window to do some people watching. She found the diversity of people in Glastonbury fascinating. Hippies and Crusties passed, followed by a woman dressed as a pixie and a group of slightly bemused looking tourists. But she knew that wasn't the only reason she'd chosen this seat. She hoped she'd see Finn.

Drinking her coffee she started to relax. Lying was seriously bad for her stress levels. Thank God, Maeve had seemed to buy it. If only she could be sure that the healer hadn't overheard her in the kitchen.

She really shouldn't have got so wound up with Helena. If Helena wanted to have blind, unquestioning faith in Maeve then that was her business. It was just irritating as hell to be around. And odd because Maeve wasn't even that nice to her. She treated her like a slightly dim servant. After putting up with that any normal person would be desperate to dish the dirt behind Maeve's back.

Zoe pulled her mobile from her bag. If Helena wouldn't answer her questions then she'd Google. She started with 'Karmic Wave Therapy'. It wasn't a huge surprise to find that the only exact match was Anam Cara's website. Reading the quote from Maeve about its amazingly beneficial effects for mind, body and spirit and the glowing reviews on the testimonials page, her brow furrowed. If other people had been as ill as Tanya then why hadn't they complained? Or did they, as the testimonials claimed, end up feeling so fabulously revitalised that they thought the healing crisis worth the end result?

Googling 'healing crisis' brought up an abundance of natural therapy sites. There was a divergence of opinion as to the causes of the crisis. However the general consensus was that the body expelled toxins during the healing that created symptoms like a bad hangover which often lasted between one and three days.

The sheer number of sites and variety of opinions made Zoe wonder if she could rely on any of them. They were written by people who claimed, like Maeve, to be healers. But exactly what qualifications or experience did they have? If anyone could set up as a healer and make whatever claims they liked then how did people know who was for real and who was a charlatan? And which was Maeve? It was so very tempting to believe she was a fraud but then wouldn't her guests experience nothing at all? Obviously something was going on. The question was what? Because she was sure Finn hadn't been at Anam Cara to complain about his sister having a headache for a couple of days.

Her stomach growled. Figuring that as she'd missed lunch she was entitled to a decent meal she ordered veggie lasagne. When she'd finished eating she had another coffee, took out her sketchpad and redrew the crumpled pictures of the Lady of the Lake that Finn had rescued this morning. As usual she became absorbed in her work, adding to and improving what she'd done earlier. When she looked up she was surprised to see it was half past seven. Wanting to put off returning to Anam Cara for as long as possible she considered ordering another drink. But the thought of walking back in the dark stopped her. After the day she'd had who knew what phantoms her mind would conjure from the twilight.

She dawdled on the way back, thinking about Finn, wondering what he was doing this evening. As she opened the gate her stomach clenched. Crossing the garden, she glanced at the stump of the Green Man's tree. She wanted to tell him about Finn and her suspicions about Maeve. She knew she'd have felt better afterwards. Somehow reassured.

She shook her head. Back in London she'd have considered that one small step from unhinged. But Glastonbury was making her reconsider her definition of crazy. After all, talking to trees was far less strange than drawing the future.

She headed straight for her room. Half way up the stairs she met Helena carrying a can of furniture polish and a duster. "Hi, how you doing?" Zoe said.

"Fine." Helena stared over Zoe's right shoulder.

"Please tell me you're not still working?"

"Maeve's gone out. I want to clean her office before she gets back."

"Oh, right." For some reason Zoe had the idea that Maeve never left Anam Cara, that she was a constant presence like a spider lurking in the centre of her web. "How's Tanya?"

"She's okay," Helena muttered, pushing past Zoe.

"Did she go to meet Dave?"

"Yes." Helena clumped heavily downstairs.

Maeve's office door was shut with more than necessary force. Zoe raised her eyebrows. Was the chill in the atmosphere because Helena hadn't forgiven her for what she'd said earlier? Zoe turned and headed downstairs. If Maeve wasn't around she wasn't going to hide in her room until bedtime.

Maeve clearly didn't encourage people to watch TV as the only set was in a small, cramped lounge behind the kitchen. Zoe slipped off her coat and sank into the sofa. She flipped through the channels and settled on a rom-com movie that she'd seen before. It was comfort viewing. But she couldn't engage with the plot. Her mind churned over everything that had happened since she went to bed last night. It seemed like far more than twenty four hours since she'd left the cafe and trailed drunkenly back here.

Her mobile rang. Hoping it was Finn, she frantically scrambled through her bag to find it and was sharply disappointed to see Anna's name on the screen. Yesterday she'd been waiting for her best friend to call. Today she couldn't handle talking to anyone else who unquestioningly adored Maeve. She let the phone ring.

A little later a loud buzzing sounded from the hall. Fearing it signalled Maeve's return, Zoe tensed. She heard Helena's voice but couldn't make out the words. A door banged. Voices were raised, Helena's and a man's with a Somerset accent. Tanya's name spoken again and again. Something about a doctor.

Zoe scurried to the kitchen door. Dave stood in the

hall, his arms around Tanya who slumped against him, her head resting on his chest. Helena bustled around them.

"What's wrong? What happened?" Zoe said, shocked to see that, despite her elegant red dress and fabulous heels, Tanya looked paler and sicker than she'd done this afternoon.

"She's not well," Dave said. "She should be in bed. Can you show me which is her room?"

"Sure." Zoe picked Tanya's red suede bag from the floor and headed up the stairs.

"Tanya, we need to get you up to bed. Can you walk?" Dave said to her, his voice soft. Feebly apologising for the inconvenience she was causing, Tanya allowed her arm to be placed over Dave's shoulders. Murmuring constant encouragement, Dave half carried her up the stairs.

Zoe steered them into Tanya's room, Helena trailing behind them saying, "If only Maeve was here. She'd know what to do." Zoe resisted the impulse to say, 'I think she's done more than enough,' as she slid Tanya's beautiful shoes from her feet and placed them under a chair.

Dave helped Tanya under the covers. "I'll ring you tomorrow. You're not to worry about this evening." He took her hand. "Just concentrate on getting better so we can rearrange."

Zoe abruptly felt *de trop* and left them to it. Hovering on the landing, she waited for an opportunity to speak to Dave. Helena hurried past and returned carrying a large bowl that she took into Tanya's room. When Dave emerged, Zoe said, "What happened?"

"I don't exactly know," Dave said as they slowly descended the stairs. "She looked a bit pale when I picked her up. I asked if she was alright and she said she was fine. After we'd had our starters she went to the bathroom. She was gone so long I was starting to think maybe she'd done a runner." Dave smiled weakly. "But she hadn't. She'd been throwing up in there and then passed out. When she came back to the table she looked bloody awful, white as a sheet, shaking like a leaf. I wanted to call an ambulance but she wouldn't let me. Said that I had to bring her back here." Dave halted in the porch and added quietly, "And then the bloody woman who works here refused to ring for a doctor."

"Helena?"

"Yeah, that's the one. Said she couldn't do anything 'til Maeve got back."

"You think Tanya needs to see the doctor now?" Zoe said, walking across the lawn. Twilight seeped into the shadowy corners of the garden.

"I know I'd feel better if I knew she'd seen a proper doctor. All this healing nonsense, that's what got her into this mess in the first place."

"Tanya told you about that?"

"She said she only started to feel bad after she'd had her session with Maeve. And it don't take a genius to put two and two together and make four, now does it?"

"No," Zoe said. "I've been wondering about that myself."

"She said you took care of her this afternoon. Will you keep an eye on her? Make that Helena ring for a doctor if she gets worse?"

"Yes, of course." They'd reached the gate. Zoe pulled it open. A large black car stood in front of it.

"Thanks." Frowning, Dave looked back at the house. "That makes me feel better about leaving her here."

Zoe stepped closer to him. "Why? What's wrong with here?"

"People talk about it. And the woman who owns it. I'd always thought it was complete rubbish but when I saw that -" Dave nodded at the bundle of leaves above the gate "- I wasn't so sure."

"What's that got to do with it?"

"Probably nothing. My Gran was always filling my head with superstitious nonsense." Dave walked around his car. "Seems like some of it must have stuck."

"Dave, please! What do people say about this place?"

With the driver's door open, he looked at her over the car's roof. "It's nothing to worry about, Zoe. It's only gossip and old wives tales."

"About what?" Zoe cried as the door slammed shut. The headlights swung in an arc as the car reversed into the road.

Zoe stared after it. What had Dave meant? What could Maeve be doing in Glastonbury - where alternative lifestyles were the norm - that stirred up gossip? And what had that got to do with the bundle of leaves above the gate? He could at least have told her what his Gran said. It was alright him dismissing his worries. He wasn't the one who had to spend another night here.

Goosebumps rose on the back of her neck. Feeling as if someone watched her, she instinctively looked around. She couldn't see anyone but the sensation persisted. She lifted her eyes to the Tor. She'd drawn Finn up there. Was he watching her now?

Chapter 9

In the shadow of the tower, Finn's grip tightened on his binoculars as he watched Zoe go back into Anam Cara. It was one thing knowing she was staying there. Something else to see that gate close behind her.

Watching her talk to the big guy had made him smile. Her body language was as revealing as if she had a thought bubble above her head. Her hands had whisked through the air in confusion and increasing agitation. When the bloke drove away she'd stared after him, arms folded across her chest, obviously pissed off.

Earlier the man had helped a woman into the house. That had brought back memories Finn didn't want to think about. If he needed another justification for what he planned then he had it. Maeve continued to steal from her guests.

A movement in his peripheral vision startled him. He looked up to see a bat circling overhead, dipping and swooping in its flight. He focused the binoculars on it. Identified it as a common pipistrelle. Turning back to Anam Cara, he waited.

Earlier he'd watched Maeve take her car from the garage at the rear of her house and head down the road into town. It'd be ironic, he'd thought, if she was searching for him as he watched Anam Cara.

The wind was picking up. Stepping into the lee of the tower he flipped the collar of his fleece up. It was a reflexive action. He was in no danger of getting cold. Awen spiralled upwards from the ground beneath his feet, warming his blood and soothing his aching muscles.

Much later, when night had settled like a cloak around the Tor, he saw a light go on in a first floor room, a slim figure drawing the curtains. He was surprised at the wave of fury that pulsed through him. How he wanted to storm down there, kick the gate in and get her out.

Like that went so well the first time.

Zoe's different, he told himself. She can see through Maeve. She's been warned.

The light went out. Finn stiffened and then forced himself to relax. Zoe had a window in her room. She could come and go as she wanted. It wasn't the same at all.

But it was too déjà-bloody-vu for words. Almost exactly six months later. Same hill, same house. Watching and waiting in the dark.

Four days in October but it had felt like forty. Four days since his Mum had rung with the news that his sister hadn't turned up for work for the second day in a row and her colleagues couldn't contact her. Four days since the police had been called. Countless hours at the police station. Question after intrusive question as the investigators picked over every detail of his sister's life. His mother edging closer to a breakdown with every day of silence. Four sleepless nights. Nothing to do but wait. And all the time, like poison festering in a wound, he knew he'd let Cat down.

With the benefit of hindsight he could see that when he stood here in October he'd not been thinking straight. Guilt had been like acid in his gut. He remembered the almost perfect circle of the moon casting a ghostly light over the Levels. Every time he'd looked at it his panic had sharpened. Because the next night the moon would be full. On Samhain.

For that reason he'd acted alone. Climbing the wall into Anam Cara, not waiting for Winston to return his call. He'd told himself that, even if his friend could get away, there was nothing he could do. Winston was in Glasgow. It'd be hours before he arrived. If he was right then Cat didn't have that long.

When he found her in that tiny, windowless room - terrified, barely able to stand – he knew he'd done the right thing. A feeling that was extremely short lived. Because he'd not planned how to get them out of there. And he'd catastrophically underestimated Maeve.

A car stopped outside Anam Cara and a figure got out. He saw blonde hair in the car's headlights. She put her car in the garage, walked to the gate and entered. She was alone.

Hands curled into fists, he waited and watched.

Chapter 10

Maeve locked the gate and turned towards the house. The glow of the street lights diluted the darkness, revealing the outlines of her garden. Slipping off her shoes, she strolled across the lawn and sat on the stone bench by the pond. The darkness obscured and softened but couldn't erase the damage. The garden had been her haven. She'd lost that today. Together with the key to her future.

Whatever happened in the next few days she had to leave. That had always been part of her plan. A necessary sacrifice to bring to fruition her new life. She'd made arrangements. The house would go on the market a week today. By then she'd expected to be far from here.

Maeve's hands tightened on the edge of the bench. If next week was not the fresh start she craved, if she were forced to continue the facade in a new location then leaving would be unbearable.

She knew she'd stayed too long. She should have left eight or ten years ago. Before tongues started to wag. She'd seen the signs many times. Always before it had provoked her to sell up and move on. This time she'd disregarded them, told herself that in this community, at this time, she could never be remarkable.

She no longer knew or cared if that were true. If people talked about her it hadn't affected trade. As long as guests came seeking healing she could survive.

She'd not realised how dissatisfied she'd become with mere survival until last autumn when prayers she'd never dared to formulate had been answered. To have the future she'd worked and planned for snatched away was intolerable. To lose her garden in the process was unendurable.

Maeve stared into the depths of her ruined pond. She would make them suffer. The price she would exact, the pain she'd leverage from them would be recompense for every broken leaf and tattered flower.

Because more than her plants had taken root in this garden. She'd broken her own rules and committed part of herself to this place. It had been a kind of homecoming. Back in England, close to her birthplace and the graves that marked her ancient grief. Creating the garden had been an act of worship to the powers that sustained her. Unexpectedly it had also brought her peace.

Hearing a rustle from the shrubbery, her head jerked round. Persia slunk onto the lawn, her body low to the ground, hunting prey in the shadows. Cats are fortunate, Maeve thought as she stood. They don't have to hide their true nature.

Back on the path, she slipped on her shoes and crossed to the garden wing. Entering, she rapped sharply on the door on the left and said, "Helena, I want to see you in my office. Now!"

After a few seconds she heard a muffled incoherent response. "Get up, get dressed and be there in five minutes," Maeve said. Back in the house, she left her office door ajar and sat behind her desk, tapping her foot as she waited.

Looking rather less than half awake, Helena appeared in the doorway. "Is something the matter? Is it about Tanya? Because I told her I couldn't call the doctor until you'd seen her. I hope that was alright. I didn't..."

"Quiet! Close the door and sit down."

Helena perched on the edge of the brown leather armchair. Opening her desk drawer, Maeve took out a single strand of black wool and held it up. "Do you know what this is?"

Helena shook her head.

"It's from the doll that's missing. The doll that I've been looking for since dawn. Do you know where I found this piece of wool?"

"No," Helena murmured, her eyes fixed on the floor.

Quashing the impulse to tell her to speak up, Maeve said, "I found it in Zoe's room. Can you tell me how it got there?"

"No." Helena's voice was even quieter.

Maeve leaned forward. "That, my dear Helena, is simply unacceptable. On Saturday the doll hung on the tree in the garden. I saw it myself. But, as you know, I was indisposed on Sunday. What did I ask you to do for me?"

"You asked me to watch Zoe when she was in the garden and keep her away from the tree." Helena looked up. "And I did! In the afternoon, she was heading towards the tree and I asked her what she was doing and she stopped and went in the house. Then in the evening..." Helena's hand rose to her mouth. "Oh!"

"Tell me!"

"I'd forgotten what with everything else. And it was only a few minutes. I didn't think..."

"Stop babbling!" Maeve walked across the room to stand over Helena. "Tell me, slowly and clearly, what happened on Sunday evening."

"We went into town to the New Moon Cafe, that is Zoe and Tanya and I went and, well, Tanya met Dave there. He's the bloke she went to meet this evening, the one who brought her back when she got sick. She chatted to him all night and I was talking to Zoe. Anyways, I went out the back and..." Helena's gaze dropped to the floor as her words sped up. "And while I was gone Zoe, kind of, left. When I found out that she'd gone, I headed back but she got here before me. And I asked her what she was doing but then it started to rain so she came in anyway and went to bed."

"I see." Maeve paced in front of Helena's chair. "Where was she when you arrived?"

"Standing under the tree that the lightning hit. I remember thinking didn't she know better than to stand there in a thunder storm."

"How long had she been in the garden before you got back?"

"I don't know." Helena shrugged. "Five minutes maybe?"

Maeve raised an eyebrow.

"Definitely no more than ten."

"And tell me, what were you doing 'out the back', as you so eloquently put it?"

Helen's face crumpled, tears filling her eyes. "I'm real sorry Maeve. It was only one. And I was away for five minutes. No more. I didn't even finish it."

Maeve's hand whipped down and struck the girl across the face. Her palm tingled with the impact. She permitted herself a swift smile.

Helena gasped. Tears slid down her pudgy face. She cradled her cheek. "I...I'm sorry. I didn't know she'd got the doll, I swear. I didn't know anything about the doll until this morning."

"But it's too late for sorry." Maeve returned to her chair. "I wondered when you came here if I could trust an addict but you were so pathetically keen to change that I gave you a chance. I was wrong. Your inability to resist a quick joint has done more damage than you can possibly imagine." Maeve stared at Helena as if she were an insect squashed under her foot. "I require your help until Friday. Then you will leave."

"Please, Maeve! Don't make me go. I'm real sorry." Helena sobbed, tears dripping from her cheeks. "I won't let you down again. I promise."

"Be quiet! You will leave on Friday. And you will not

mention this conversation to anyone, is that clear?" Maeve said emphasising each word.

Helena nodded. Cringing away, she backed towards the door. "Shall I go now? Or is there anything else you want?"

Maeve waved her hand in dismissal. When the door closed, she massaged her temples. Exhaustion threatened. The energy she'd taken this morning was waning. She must rest. But not until she'd confronted the source of her problems.

She walked upstairs. Removing her shoes, she unlocked the door. Stepping inside she stood for a moment waiting for her eyes to adjust, then approached the bed. Zoe slept, vulnerable as a child, one hand tucked under the pillow. Reaching out, Maeve encountered no barriers, no protections. Her hand rested on the girl's hair. She was defenceless. How unexpected.

The healer placed her other hand on Zoe's. Through the touch connection she focused on the girl's aura. Violet and lavender pulsed gently; dark blue and muddy grey swirled around. How satisfying, Maeve reflected, to see the colours of fear in the girl's aura. To know she felt it, even if she didn't show it. And the fear encroached on Zoe's creativity.

As Maeve watched silver darted like fireflies across the aura, briefly repelling the darker colours. When the sparks died, the cloudiness slowly leeched back. She waited, barely breathing, for more silver to manifest but it didn't come.

She pulled her hands away and walked to the window. Zoe's aura was vastly different to the steady golden glow of power she'd expected. The silver sparks were interesting. But in this intermittent form, they showed only weak and unfocused potential. There had been times when silver sparks would have been enough to tempt her. She desperately hoped those days were over.

Moving back to the bed Maeve studied the girl's face. She needed answers. Perhaps the unconscious mind would be receptive. Bending lower, she began to whisper in Zoe's ear.

Chapter 11

To escape from the nightmare Zoe forced her eyes open. She'd dreamed of a pitch-dark room. She knew she wasn't alone but she couldn't see anyone or anything. Only hear a low voice that whispered to her. Only feel cold, clammy hands clutching at her. Pawing her hair, her face, her arms. She'd tried to scream, found herself mute. Tried to fight but was caught in an iron grip. The voice laughed as she'd struggled and the sound followed her back to consciousness.

Pushing her hair away from her face she sat up, yawned, and blearily reached for her watch on the bedside cabinet. It took a moment to focus on it. The hands weren't in the position she expected. How could it be nearly half past nine? She'd set her alarm for eight. She never slept through it.

Throwing back the bedclothes, she stood. Exhaustion saturated her body but she kept moving. There was something she needed to do. She just couldn't remember what. Throwing on the first clothes she saw she hurried downstairs.

The kitchen was empty. A place was set at the head of the table. Zoe reached for orange juice, poured cereal into a bowl. Concentrating on eating and not looking through the French windows at the stone table outside, she wondered why she felt so damned tired after she'd had so much sleep. She heard footsteps. Offered a half formed prayer that it wasn't Maeve and felt instantly relieved when Helena said, "Good day."

Zoe opened her mouth to repeat the greeting. The

words died on her lips. A bruise blackened Helena's eye and cheek. "Are you okay? What happened?"

"I walked into a door."

"Oh my God! Does it hurt?"

"Not really," Helena said, her voice expressionless, as she stacked dirty mugs and plates on the kitchen counter.

"Sorry to be so late for breakfast. I slept through my alarm."

"Doesn't matter to me."

Surprised at the response, Zoe raised her eyes from her muesli. The Australian stared out of the kitchen window. Then as if she felt Zoe's gaze, she forced an unconvincing smile and said, "Do you want coffee?"

"Yes, thanks." A few minutes later, Helena put a cafetiere and brown toast in front of her. Zoe poured herself a cup, adding an extra teaspoon of sugar hoping it would kick-start her sluggish brain. As she sipped it, she suddenly remembered Tanya. She'd been really worried about her last night. How had that fallen out of her head this morning? "How's Tanya? I hope she's feeling better. Dave was really worried about her last night."

"I don't know."

"You mean you've not been to check on her?" When Helena shook her head, Zoe said, "Well, I'll go up in a minute." The flash of irritation brought last night back into sharper focus. She'd been pissed off with Helena when she wouldn't call the doctor and insisted on waiting for Maeve's return.

"Let me know if she wants anything." Helena brushed her hand over her damaged cheek and winced.

Seeing that, Zoe's anger evaporated. "Look, tell me to mind my own business if you want, but are you okay?"

"I'm fine." Helena's chin wobbled.

"If there's something you'd like to talk about then..." Zoe broke off when, tears streaming down her face, Helena met her gaze.

"I'm leaving that's all." Helena scrubbed her hand over her cheeks. "But I can't talk to *you* about it," she sobbed and then ran clumsily from the room.

Staring after her, Zoe shook her head. This place went from bizarre to bizarrer. Tanya had better be on the mend because promise or no promise she was getting out of here today.

When she'd finished her breakfast she walked slowly upstairs and gently knocked on Tanya's door. "Come in," she heard.

The room smelt of stale sweat and sickness. In the dim light of the closed curtains, Zoe saw lines of pain creasing Tanya's face. A sheen of sweat and the smudged remnants of last night's make-up clung to her pallid skin. Dark circles pooled under her eyes.

Zoe looked at the bowl of vomit. "Bad night?"

"Awful," Tanya said. "I can't even keep water down. My head's pounding and I'm absolutely freezing." Feeling as if she channelled her Mum, Zoe touched Tanya's forehead. She was burning up.

"I'll get rid of this. Then we need some fresh air in here." Nose wrinkling, Zoe carefully picked up the bowl.

Tanya turned her head on the pillow. "Please....don't....I..."

Someone has to and you can be sure it won't be Maeve, Zoe thought as she disposed of its contents in the bathroom. Returning to Tanya's bedside, she said, "You need to see a doctor."

"I thought I should see what Maeve says first. It's just that..." Tanya trailed off, biting her lower lip.

"What?"

"You did tell her I wasn't well, didn't you?"

"Yes, of course. I told her yesterday afternoon."

"Oh, that doesn't explain it then." Tanya looked intently at her hands as they pleated the bedclothes.

"I'm sorry you've lost me. Explain what?"

"It's just that I've not seen her since my healing session yesterday."

"I *can't* believe that she's not..." Seeing Tanya's forehead wrinkle, Zoe bit back her rant. "This is a lot more than a healing crisis," she said, trying to sound calm. "Maybe you've got some bug or a virus. Whatever it is you need to see a doctor."

When her friend nodded weakly, Zoe ran downstairs. How could Maeve be so unfeeling? Tanya was suffering and she'd just left her for Helena to take care of. And now Helena was having some kind of meltdown and didn't seem to care either.

Zoe wandered through the downstairs rooms calling Helena's name. There was no response. She stepped into the porch and scanned the garden. Dylan and Kyle were hard at work again. They told her that they'd seen Helena head out of the gate a few minutes before.

Zoe returned to the hall and stood for a moment trying to figure out what to do. She had to find a number for the nearest surgery. She ran back upstairs and grabbed her mobile. No signal. Not wanting to disturb Tanya to borrow her phone, she realised she'd have to do this the old fashioned way.

There wasn't a telephone directory in the lounge, kitchen or dining room. Finding herself in the hall, Zoe stared at Maeve's office door. That was the obvious place to keep directories.

With her hand an inch above the door handle, Zoe hesitated. She was pretty sure Maeve would have a fit if she found her in there. Then she gave a tiny shrug. If the healer didn't want people in there she should take better care of her guests. Looking around, she eased open the door. Stepping inside she left it slightly ajar, figuring that way she'd have some warning if someone came.

Half packed boxes cluttered the office floor. Framed watercolours and old photographs were stacked against the walls. Focusing on the shelves above the untidy desk, Zoe scanned the spines. There were a load of really old volumes with titles that had almost disappeared with age, glossy hardbacks on gardening and a selection of classic novels. On the second shelf she spotted the Yellow Pages and next to it the telephone directory.

Reaching up, she pulled the directory down and balanced it on a pile of papers. Flipping through it she found the number for the Glastonbury Surgery. She looked around for something to write with. A biro was lodged under a pile of books. Trying to extract it, she dislodged the top volume.

The sound of it hitting the wooden floor was impossibly loud. Zoe froze. Seconds passed unbelievably slowly. She released the breath she'd been holding and bent to pick up the book.

It had fallen open, its pages splayed either side of the spine. Lifting it she saw a folded sheet of paper and snatched it up with her free hand. The smell of ancient dust filled Zoe's nostrils. The pages were thick and marked with little brown smudges.

As she put the bookmark back, her eyes read the first sentence. '*The holder must renounce his staff by breaking it. The pieces must be burnt in the fire kindled in the centre of the circle.*' Beneath was a diagram. She scanned the circle of dots with crosses in its centre. Read its title. '*Fig. 148: configuration of the circle.*'

A thought flickered in her brain. As she tried to pin it down she heard a noise. Her head jerked round. Her eyes scanned her limited view of the hall. All she could see was a sliver of polished floorboards and cream walls. But if Maeve came in and found her holding this book...

Zoe thrust it on to the desk. She grabbed the telephone directory and held it in front of her chest like a shield. It was her reason for being here. But she knew Maeve wouldn't care. She would be totally and terrifyingly furious.

Painfully conscious of her heart pounding, she stared at the doorway. She heard the noise again. Her grip on the directory tightened.

A flash of white. Persia curled around the doorframe, stopping to rub her head against it. Zoe's hand rose to her throat. *Damned cat.*

She reopened the directory and, with trembling fingers, scribbled the number on her hand. Returning it to the shelf, she carefully lodged the biro under the pile of books and balanced the black volume on top. Printed on the spine in faded gold letters was the title, "*The Seventh Book.*" For a reason she couldn't identify, Zoe's stomach clenched.

At the door she listened. Heard the gurgle of the dishwasher and Persia's claws clicking on the floorboards. Peeking out she saw the hall was empty. She stepped out and, eyes darting, slid the door closed.

Heart still beating too fast, she rushed upstairs, tapped on Tanya's door and went in. "I've got the doctor's number. Do you want me to ring them for you?"

"No. I can do it. You've been really kind, Zoe. I don't know what I'd have done..."

"Have you got your phone?" Zoe said, as she scribbled down the number, her voice artificially high and bright. "Is there anything else you need?" After taking a thick blanket from the wardrobe and spreading it over the bed, she slid open a window and promised to pop back before she went out.

In her own room, she leaned against the door pressing her palm against her chest. What the hell had she been thinking? She had to get out of Anam Cara before she got herself into any more trouble.

After a quick shower, she put on her denim skirt with leggings and a purple t-shirt. Snatching her sketchpad from the bedside cabinet, she stuffed it in her bag and grabbed her velvet jacket.

When she returned Tanya seemed a little brighter. She'd spoken to the surgery and expected the doctor later that morning. Anxious to be gone Zoe hovered just inside the door, trying not to fidget, as Tanya fretted over how the doctor would get in and whether Helena would try to send him away. Offering to tell Helena to expect him, Zoe escaped. Again she couldn't find the Australian and, not knowing what else to do, she scribbled a note and left it in the kitchen, and then apologetically asked Dylan to open the gate when the doctor arrived.

Feeling she'd done everything she could she went straight to the Tourist Information. Which turned out to be a depressing waste of time. All of the available single rooms were seriously out of her price range. It turned out that Anam Cara was cheap.

Almost too cheap, Zoe thought as she left the Tourist Information, clutching a leaflet about the Abbey's upcoming mediaeval weekend. Close by was the hostel and she peered through the window. It didn't look like her kind of place.

If she still had a credit card then there'd be a way out of this mess. But the credit card had been chopped into little pieces after she'd indulged in one too many 'cheering up' shopping trips after the split with Gareth. She toyed with the idea of ringing her Mum and asking for a loan. Ruled it out as she'd worked hard to keep the full extent of her financial crisis from her family. She didn't want to waste all that effort and she could totally live without the lecture.

So it came to a choice. Stick it out at Anam Cara. See if the hostel could find her a bed. Or blow her budget on two nights in one of the nice B&Bs and have to go home before the weekend.

She didn't want to spend another minute at Anam Cara but it would be really stupid to go further into debt to escape it. What was the worst that could really happen? Maeve had accepted her lie about the doll. If she was challenged about going into the office she had a good excuse. If she stayed out of Maeve's way, kept a very low profile and only went back to sleep couldn't she survive another day or two?

Because she really wanted to be in Glastonbury. The creative vibe of the place was infectious. She felt more connected to her work than she'd done since graduation. If she could just focus and stop being distracted by the total bizarreness of Anam Cara she had a real chance of being ready for the meeting with the publishers. Which was a panic-inducing mere eight days away.

She glanced at the leaflet in her hand. The mediaeval weekend at the Abbey would be perfect King Arthur material. There'd even be re-enactors doing battle in full armour. She couldn't miss that.

And there was always the possibility she might bump into Finn.

Decision made she went into the hostel. As an almost beggar, she couldn't be choosy. However basic the accommodation might be, however many people were zipping rucksacks at five in the morning it had to be less stressful than Anam Cara. The desk clerk told her they were fully booked until Thursday. Without letting herself remember exactly how much she hated hostelling, she reserved a bed in the dorm for three nights from Thursday. On asking about cancellations, the clerk told her to ring tomorrow to see if any beds had come free. Zoe pulled out her pad to write down the number. Opening it she saw a drawing.

Of Finn.

She stared at it. The clerk recited the number. She heard the words but they made no sense. "Do you want this number or not?" the guy said.

"Yes. Sorry," Zoe replied, without looking up from

the picture. The man gave her the telephone number again, speaking slower this time as if he thought she wasn't all that bright. She scrawled it down and left.

There were metal chairs and tables outside the hostel. Sitting, Zoe took a deep breath and looked at the picture.

The drawing showed him standing on a hill that rose sharply behind him. The sun was a ball, partly hidden by wisps of cloud, sinking - or maybe rising – over his right shoulder. His heavily bandaged hand rested in a sling. Surgical padding protected his collar bone. A wide gash on his cheek bone was taped together. He looked utterly exhausted. The palm of his uninjured hand rested against the trunk of a small tree. Its branches were gone, only stumps remaining. Finn's head was bowed as if he prayed. Circular rows of streamers fluttering in the breeze obscured the lower part of the trunk.

Was this the Holy Thorn? She'd seen something similar in the books she'd read back in London. But that tree had its branches intact.

Shaking her head, she tried to remember when she'd drawn this. She'd felt dislocated all morning but this was major. How had she forgotten waking in the night to draw? She tried to recall what had happened after she went to bed last night. She'd taken ages to fall asleep. But then what?

Fragments of a dream - grabbing, clammy hands touching her face – resurfaced. She shuddered. Why the hell hadn't the nightmare forced her awake? Then it'd be safely trapped on the page. Not lurking in the depths of her subconscious making her feel, even in the bright light of day, obscurely frightened.

If only she could talk to him. She traced his face with her fingertip. How had he got even more banged up than yesterday? She closed her eyes. Tried to think back, to recover any trace of this dream. There was nothing. The dream of the dark room and the clutching hands blocked the earlier one.

A tall man with untidy, dark hair walked past her. For a moment she thought it was Finn then he turned and she saw his face. Her eyes dropped to the drawing. She had so much to tell him. About Tanya being ill and what she'd found out about karmic wave healing. To somehow find a way to explain about the doll which didn't make her sound completely insane. And ask the questions she'd not been brave enough to put to him yesterday. But what if she never saw him again? What if the dreams were just dreams and didn't mean anything?

But they meant one thing. Finn would be on this hill at sunset (or was it sunrise?) either tonight or some other evening. She didn't have to wait to bump into him. She could hang out on this hill casually waiting for him to turn up.

She knew it was a crazy plan but she didn't care. If this is what it took then she'd do it but first she needed to pin down exactly what she'd drawn. Clutching her sketchpad, she returned to the Tourist Information. After a barrage of garbled questions, she learned that she'd drawn a sunset and that tonight the sun would sink behind the horizon at around quarter past eight. Clasping a map of the town, helpfully marked with the location of the Holy Thorn on Wearyall Hill, she stepped into the street and looked at the sky. There were clouds gathering but the sun still shone.

The possibility of seeing Finn later made everything seem more bearable. Even two more nights at Anam Cara. She ducked into the bakers to buy a sandwich and a Diet Coke for lunch before heading up the High Street to the Chalice Well.

She couldn't help glancing repeatedly at the sky as she walked. The sun was her only guide as to whether she'd drawn Finn on the hill later today or some other evening. So far she'd drawn the future the night before it happened.

She was clinging to the hope that this would be the same. If it clouded over this evening there'd be little point going to the hill to look for Mr McCloud.

After paying the entry fee, Zoe wandered through the quiet gardens surrounding the Chalice Well hoping to find inspiration for the story of the grail quest. Peering into the well's depths she wondered if the story was true. Had Joseph of Arimathea brought the chalice from the Last Supper here? Did the spring water run red and have healing powers because he'd buried it in this spot? It seemed unlikely but she couldn't deny the sense of peace in the garden.

She found a seat built into the stone wall, closed her eyes and tried to conjure up the grail quest. It was harder than it should have been. Her mind kept creeping away to thoughts of Finn. Wondering what he was doing, what would bring him to the Holy Thorn. Eventually she focused enough to make some progress.

She left at about half past five relieved that she'd produced a few basic sketches of Sir Galahad and the grail story. She walked slowly back into the town, aware that she had over two hours to kill before sunset. Despite the nerves filling her stomach, she knew she should eat. She stopped at the Earth Café and ordered a bowl of chips. She ate them distractedly, her mind busy with planning what she'd say to Finn and staring out of the window watching the sky.

As the clock's hands eased towards half past seven she had to move. She spent five minutes in the ladies brushing her hair out of its ponytail and applying lip-gloss before paying her bill. Outside, she immediately looked up.

Big, white, candyfloss clouds were gliding across the sky partially obscuring the sun. A breeze had picked up. She told herself it could still be alright. The fat clouds might blow away. The sun could still set as she'd drawn it.

Fuelled by nerves and anticipation she hurried down the High Street. Seeing a display in a shop window she skidded to a halt. Two mannequins, one male, one female, stood by a fire unconvincingly fashioned from orange paper and fairy lights. The woman wore clinging white robes, had artificial flowers in her straight black hair and held a crystal wand. The man wore only loose fitting linen trousers. Suspended from a leather thong around his neck, and resting against his improbably muscled plastic torso, was a silver amulet in the shape of a five pointed star.

The scene was almost exactly as she'd imagined Maeve's Beltane celebrations and she grinned. Then she saw the knife.

A shiver sprinted down her spine as she looked at its curved blade. It reminded her of something. Something bad. She tried to dredge up the memory but all that surfaced was pain and paralyzing terror.

Stepping back, her eyes rose to read the shop's name painted in gold letters on a dark green background. *Morgan le Fey*. Arthur's half-sister. The witch.

Bloody hell! That's what was in Maeve's book. Witchcraft. Casting a circle.

Zoe almost ran down the hill and around the corner into Magdalen Street. How had she missed it for so long? The doll, the stone table (damn it, Maeve even called it an altar!) the leaves above the gate and in the jar in her room.

Crossing the road, she figured she finally understood Maeve's obsessive search for the doll. She wouldn't want it to get out that she dabbled in witchcraft. Imagine if that information found its way onto Trip Advisor. It would definitely be bad for business.

Zoe grinned briefly. She might post it herself. Once she was safely back in London.

She turned into a lane lined with parked cars. This certainly explained why she didn't like being around the altar. She remembered the black candles. That must be where Maeve did her spells. Maybe she'd picked up some vibe and that's why the table freaked her out.

Her footsteps slowed. Only she felt pure terror from it. And there was something seriously freaky about the doll. It felt almost evil, like dark magic.

Oh please! She shoved her hair back from her face. That was just too Harry Potter. This was the real world and in the real world magic didn't exist. If Maeve wanted to spend her time messing around with spells and incantations then that was her business.

At the brow of the hill was a kissing gate. She stepped through and stopped. This place was exactly like her picture. The ridge of the hill climbed gently towards the thorn and then rose up like the spine of a sleeping dragon. Beyond the thorn a well-worn path through nettles and brambles followed the curve of the hill.

Bypassing a duo of grazing sheep, she walked towards the tree. She knew its legend. Arriving on the Isle of Avalon, Joseph of Arimathea had plunged his staff into the soil. It had taken root and sprouted into a thorn tree.

The tree was badly mutilated, its branches cropped. The lady in the Tourist Information had told her it had been vandalised a number of times. The only hope of saving it had been to cut it back.

Multi-coloured ribbons tied to the railings surrounding the tree fluttered in the breeze. Zoe caught a white one. It had words written on it in black marker. Someone had written their prayer – in a language she couldn't read – and tied it here in the hope it would be answered. The tree seemed too small, too puny for the weight of the wishes and prayers it carried. Feeling she'd intruded, she let the ribbon go.

Zoe glanced at her watch – half an hour to sunset - and then at the sky. The clouds were fatter, crowding out more of the blue.

Rummaging in her bag, she pulled out a tattered silk scarf that she used to tie up her hair. She tore a strip off the end, found a space to tie the fabric to the iron railing and whispered, "Please let me see Finn this evening. I *so* need to talk to him. He's the only person who'd understand if I said..." Her voice dropped even lower, "Maeve's a witch or a Wiccan or whatever it is they call themselves." Letting the fabric go, she watched her prayer join the others.

She walked to a green painted bench. From here she had a perfect view of the paths from the town; the one she'd walked up from the gate and the other that rose steeply from the main road. Pulling out her sketchpad and pencils she tried to look busy. As if she wasn't only here to stalk the man she fancied.

The view across the town to the Tor was pretty enough. She sketched in the outline but her thoughts churned over what to say to Finn and her pencil wandered to draw his face in the corner of the page. She screwed it up, rammed it to the bottom of her bag and tried again.

She glanced at her watch. After eight already. If he didn't come soon he'd miss the sunset. The paths from the town were empty. She turned to look over her shoulder. There was no one on the hill. She swivelled the other way and her heart plummeted. Clouds quilted the sky totally obscuring the sun.

He wasn't coming.

Her shoulders slumped. The hope of seeing Finn had been like Prozac. Without it everything seemed a whole lot blacker.

She couldn't go back to Anam Cara. She'd stolen Maeve's bloody doll and been in her office. If she knew that she'd skin her alive. Zoe shuddered. She wasn't exaggerating. Maeve seemed capable of anything.

Real world, she reminded herself. Magic doesn't actually exist and people who do it are either sadly deluded or totally crazy. But that doesn't mean they're not scary. Maeve freaked her out as much as if she were Lord Voldemort himself.

And why the hell hadn't she figured this out earlier when she'd still had the chance to leave? Now it was too late. She had nowhere else to go. Her only option was to delay her return for as long as possible. But she couldn't do that here. The cloudy skies had hastened the night.

She trudged towards the gate. No matter what further damage it did to her overdraft she was getting out of Anam Cara tomorrow. Even if she had to beg her Mum for a loan.

Darkness congregated in the lane. A streetlight flickered half way down the hill. Hearing footsteps, Zoe glanced over her shoulder. A tall man strode purposefully. Suddenly aware that there was no one else around, she looked again. Caught a glimpse of dark clothes, short hair, a white face.

This was Glastonbury not Lewisham. She was probably totally safe. But she picked up her pace anyway. The footsteps sounded nearer. She risked another glance. He'd gained on her. Instincts honed from years of living in London kicked in. She pushed her legs to go faster, took a firm grip on the strap of her bag ready to swing it to defend herself.

"Hey Zoe, wait up!" the man shouted.

Chapter 12

Poised for immediate flight if it wasn't Finn, Zoe swung round. He strode towards her. She had just enough time to see that he didn't have any new injuries, and to realise they must still be in his future, when he was with her.

"Hi, how are you?" He seemed taller than she remembered. His chest, at her eye level, appeared broader and she suddenly felt tiny. Faced with the reality of his presence her pre-prepared witty banter flew out of her head and she answered his question reflexively.

"Are you okay? You look a bit...." Finn said, his eyes fixed on her face.

"I'm fine now I know it was you behind me and not some deranged stalker!" The words came out sharper than she'd intended. Heat crept into her cheeks.

"Jesus! I'm sorry. I never thought." Finn reached out, his fingers fleetingly brushing her sleeve. Zoe's heart bounced at his touch. His eyes were soft with concern. The dark circles beneath them had faded. A livid red slash marked his forehead where yesterday a plaster had been.

"Where did you come from anyway?" Zoe said. Had she left the Holy Thorn too soon?

"Along the road. I'm staying out that way in a little village called Sharpham." He gestured up the road and she saw that, like yesterday, he carried a small backpack.

"Oh!" His explanation was disconcertingly normal. And totally different to what she'd imagined from her drawing. But that's his future, she reminded herself. "I was at the Holy Thorn. Have you been there?" she said, falling into step with him.

"Yeah, years ago. I came with Padraig, my uncle. He was from Donegal, fiercely proud of his heritage and had a very low opinion of the English. But one Easter he came over and took me on a tour of sacred sites. Stonehenge, Avebury, those kind of places. We came to Glastonbury. Saw the Tor, the Holy Thorn."

Zoe smiled at the obvious affection in his voice. "That sounds great."

"I don't think I was as appreciative as he'd hoped. I was fourteen and a right pain in the arse."

"I find that hard to believe!" She laughed, sending a teasing glance his way.

Their feet slowed as they reached the junction. Finn tugged a black hat from his pocket. He put it on over his untidy hair, pulling it down until it rested on his eyebrows.

The main road turned at a right angle where the lane joined it. Cars hurried past, street lights turned the dark into a soft gloom.

Finn pointed straight ahead. "I'm going this way so I'll say goodbye then."

Zoe hesitated. If she walked with him she'd be back at Anam Cara much too soon but if she went into town she might never see him again. "I'll walk with you."

Finn frowned. Head down, he strode across the road. Zoe's stomach flipped as she followed him. She'd forgotten how confusing he was to be around. He'd seemed genuinely pleased to see her in the lane. Why had that changed?

When she caught up with him on the pavement, Finn said, "How's it going at Anam Cara?" He glanced over his shoulder as a car's headlights slid over them.

"Not great. I swear the place gets weirder every day."

"In what way?"

"How long have you got?" Zoe said, with a forced laugh.

"If it's that bad why don't you find somewhere else to stay?" Finn turned to look behind them as he spoke. Puzzled, Zoe copied him. She couldn't see anything to worry about. The pavement was empty. A few cars passed, their headlights briefly filling the road with light.

"Believe me, I'm trying." Zoe filled him in on her attempts to find a room elsewhere – making a joke about struggling artists to hide her embarrassment at her penniless state – ending with telling him she'd be at the hostel from Thursday.

She realised her lack of enthusiasm must have been obvious when Finn said, "The hostel's not that bad. I stayed there on Sunday night."

"But is your idea of *not that bad* the same as mine?" Zoe said, as they came to the zebra crossing. Finn's stride lengthened leaving her trailing behind. Reaching the pavement he stood with his back to the road.

He turned as she joined him and said, "I've stayed in some rough holes so I'm pretty easily pleased. If it's got hot running water and an inside toilet then I'm happy."

"I'm more of a fluffy towel and complimentary toiletries kind of girl!"

"I managed to scrounge a towel. That was about the limit to the luxuries." Finn grinned briefly. Zoe smiled with him. They passed a five bar gate leading to the mediaeval barn housing the Rural Life Museum. Mature trees crowded around it, their canopies casting shadows over the pavement.

"Actually, I'm surprised they let you in. They told me I absolutely had to arrive before midnight or I'd be sleeping on the street." Zoe flicked a teasing glance at him as she tossed her hair over her shoulder.

"The guy behind the desk did need...." Finn stopped abruptly, grabbing her wrist. There was nothing remotely flirtatious in his touch. His fingers were a tight band but she felt again the strange tingle on her skin. "How did you know I arrived after midnight?"

Zoe tried to shrug. "Didn't you mention it yesterday?"

"I don't think so." Finn's voice was steady but she could sense that his control was thin. Her gaze slid away. Had she made a mistake in trusting him? What did she actually know about him?

He tugged impatiently on her wrist. "Did Maeve tell you?" She didn't reply, didn't look at him and he said, "Please Zoe, this is important." Hearing the undertow of fear in his voice, she turned to look at him.

He dropped her wrist, made a gesture that seemed to say 'sorry'. In the twilight his eyes were unreadable. She couldn't walk away and leave him doubting her. She had to tell him what she knew. Only without revealing how she knew it.

"I saw you in the garden on Sunday night. After the tree exploded I looked out of the window and you were there." She saw shock register on Finn's face, instantly followed by the coldness she'd seen yesterday.

"How long have you known?"

"I didn't recognise you at first yesterday. I'd only seen you in the dark and for no more than a second. It was just that I had this feeling that I knew you but it only clicked when we were walking down the lane."

"When you stopped?" Shoulders hunched, Finn looked suddenly vulnerable.

"Yes," Zoe whispered. As Finn stared over her head, she studied his face, unable to decipher the emotions that flickered across it.

"I see now why you thought I was a stalker." Finn rubbed his hand over his face, his voice gruff.

"No! I didn't. I don't think you're a stalker... or a burglar or ...or anything like that." She gestured a little wildly. "Do you think I'd be here if I did?"

"But you know nothing about me. We only met yesterday."

Hearing him voice her doubts stung and Zoe spoke without thinking. “Because for some reason - I don’t why - I kind of trust you.” Realising how much she’d revealed, she looked down.

“You shouldn’t.” Finn shook his head, his voice bitter. “I’m risking your safety just by walking down this road with you. And if I ever thought more than two bloody seconds ahead, I’d have figured that out before I shouted.”

“I...I don’t understand.” But she was very afraid that she did. She’d not misread him earlier. He didn’t want her around.

“And that’s the best way.” Finn’s voice was unexpectedly soft. “Go back to London and forget you ever met me.”

Like she’d ever be able to do that. Then her chin rose. She looked up at him. If she wasn’t going to see him again there was one question she had to ask. “What were you doing in the garden on Sunday night?”

“I can’t tell you.”

“Why the hell not?”

“Because...” Finn scowled. Eyes fixed on his face, Zoe waited. Was that the only answer she was going to get? His mouth twisted. “You’d never believe me if I did.”

“But it’s to do with Maeve, right?” The breeze stirred the leaves above them, blowing Zoe’s hair around her face. She shivered and pulled her jacket tighter.

“Yes.”

“Then why can’t you tell me? I already know that there’s weird stuff going on at Anam Cara.”

“Zoe, let it go. You don’t need to know what’s happening.”

“Why not? I’m the one staying there, remember! I’m right in the middle of this and it’s awful and Tanya’s ill and I don’t know what to do about it.” Hearing her voice getting higher and squeakier, Zoe sucked in a breath. “She had healing with Maeve yesterday and she's been ill ever since. And Helena told me that Tanya's not the only one. Everyone gets ill after healing. And Maeve tried to tell me it was a *healing crisis*." Zoe's fingers sketched quotation marks in the air. "But that's crap. Tanya's really poorly. She looks awful. Really, really bad and she's throwing up all the time. And Maeve hasn't even bothered to see her. How crap is that? And I'm trying to take care of her but I don't know if I'm doing the right thing. And you're the only person I've met since I've been here who actually sees Maeve for the cold-hearted bitch that she is. Everyone else thinks she's fabulous. Even Tanya. Even…"

"Jesus, Zoe! Not so loud." Scanning the road, Finn stepped closer.

"Sorry." Zoe's hair fell across her face to hide her burning cheeks. "It's just that now I know Maeve's dabbling in witchcraft or a Wicca or..."

Finn grabbed her shoulder. "What?"

"Didn't you know? It's taken me a while to figure it out but I'm pretty sure..." Zoe's words were lost as Finn pulled her towards him. Her feet left the floor. Too stunned to think, her fingers fastened in his fleece and held on. He spun her away from the side of the road and into the deepest shadow. When her feet touched down, she sucked in a breath, her nose pressed against his chest. He smelled of fresh air and sunshine and something muskier that made her blood flutter.

"Shush," he whispered in her ear, his breath warm on her skin. "There's a car at the junction that might be Maeve."

"So?" Zoe muttered, trying to pull away.

Finn's arms tightened around her. "She mustn't see you with me. It's too risky."

She felt, rather than saw, him straighten as the car passed. His hand settled gently on her hair, holding her to his chest. She could hear his heart beating next to her ear. For one delicious second, she closed her eyes and allowed herself to lean into his safe, strong chest. His hand slid down her hair. Her scalp and her neck tingled and she clamped her mouth shut to stop from murmuring with pleasure.

Then he released her. "It's okay. She's gone."

They shuffled awkwardly apart. Zoe felt her cheeks flame scarlet. She hitched her bag onto her shoulder. "Was it Maeve? Did she see us?"

"It's her car. I saw the number plate. But she'd need x-ray vision to have seen you." Finn looked up and down the road as if he expected the car to reappear.

Fiddling with the button on her jacket, Zoe flipped her hair to hide her face. That hadn't been a cuddle or a hug. He'd done it because he thought she needed protecting.

"Sorry for manhandling you. You must have thought I'd lost my mind."

She raised her eyes to his. "What's going on? And don't trying fobbing me off again or say you can't tell me because it's not good enough. If things are so bad that Maeve can't see me with you then I think I have the right to know why!"

Blowing out a long breath, Finn rubbed the scarlet mark on his forehead. Then his eyes met hers. "Okay. But not here. There's a pub around the corner. Let's go there."

Zoe followed, not minding when his longer legs covered the ground more quickly. Her head was spinning. She needed time – like a week - to catch up.

The outside of the pub was badly in need of another coat of whitewash. A weak light shone on the sign, The Sun Inn, painted in blue and gold. Finn waited for her in the doorway. As she joined him, he opened the door and gestured for her to go first.

Half of the clientele turned to look at them and Zoe was very glad of Finn's solid presence behind her. This was not the kind of place she'd have come on her own. A row of drinkers stood by the bar. Others sat at tables watching football on the flat screen TV on the wall. In the back room a couple played pool and a bearded hippy read a newspaper with a pint of real ale in his hand and a scruffy dog at his feet.

Finn led the way over the grimy floral carpet. He pulled his hat off and dropped it on a round table in the corner farthest from the bar. "What can I get you?"

Zoe sank into a chair upholstered in worn red plush. "Red wine."

Finn walked across the room, pulling money from his pocket, looking like any other guy on the way to the bar. That he wasn't had become very obvious in the past half hour. Any other man would have laughed at her outburst, cracked a joke about her imagination running away with her. She shuffled the beermats around the table. She was about to get answers and suddenly she wasn't sure she wanted to hear them.

Finn set a large glass of wine on the table in front of her. She took a huge gulp, felt the warmth of the alcohol flow through her. After a moment of silence she said, "So?"

"So?" Finn raised his pint of Guinness. Chin up, eyes fixed on his, she waited. After licking the creamy froth from his lips, he leaned forward and in a low voice said, "Why do you think Maeve's a witch?"

Zoe winced a little when he said the 'W' word. "I only figured it out this evening. When I saw the shop in town, Morgan le Fey. Do you know it?"

"No. What's a shop got to do with it?"

"That's what made me finally realise what was going on. I can't believe I didn't figure it out sooner. It's just that I've never come across any," - Zoe hesitated then rushed on - "witches or wiccans or whatever they call themselves before."

Finn raised his eyebrows. "You're telling me a shop made you decide Maeve's a witch?"

"Kind of. It was more like the last piece in the jigsaw." Figuring she'd start with the least revealing part, she told him about Maeve's altar and the inexplicable fear she felt from it. He listened intently, interrupting occasionally to ask questions. Relieved to finally be able to talk about what she'd seen at Anam Cara, Zoe started to relax. When she explained about the leaves above the gate and in the jar in her room, Finn asked her to describe the ones she couldn't identify. Instead, she took out her sketchpad and drew them.

"Rowan," he said.

"Is that significant?"

"It's used as protection against evil or enchantment." Finn's mouth twisted. "Bay is to protect the house and holly strengthens the spell."

"How do you know all this?"

"Padraig was big on folklore. He taught me a lot." Finn's eyes were momentarily sad, then he grinned fleetingly. "Is that all? No offence but that doesn't sound much more than typical Glastonbury, New Age nonsense."

"No, that's not all! I saw a book in Maeve's office this morning."

"In Maeve's office?" Finn's voice rose. He glanced around the pub to see if anyone had overheard before leaning across the table, his voice not much above a whisper. "What the hell were you doing in there?"

"Looking for the telephone number for the doctor." When Finn's frown deepened, Zoe said, "Tanya needed to see a doctor but I couldn't find Helena to ask for the number. Maeve was still in her room or in bed or whatever she does in the morning and I couldn't find the telephone directory. I thought it might be in Maeve's office."

"And you went in there? That was an insanely risky thing to do. If she'd found you..." Finn shook his head.

"I know!" Zoe's hands flew out. "I knew when I did it that it was crazy but I was so angry with Maeve for the way she'd ignored Tanya and it wasn't locked so I just went for it."

"Jesus, Zoe!" Finn ran his fingers through his hair, making it even more tousled. "And you did this after you knew about people getting sick?"

Zoe nodded.

"You don't lack guts, I'll give you that," Finn said, a grudging admiration in his voice. Surprised, Zoe smiled at him. He didn't look away. The moment stretched and just when it became too intense he said, "Does Maeve know you were in her office?"

Zoe swallowed hard, taking a second to focus. Her thoughts had slid away to relive the moment when his arms had been around her. She shook her head. "I'm pretty sure she doesn't. But -" she bit down on her bottom lip "- that's only half of it."

Finn's eyebrows shot up. "Tell me you've not snuck into her bedroom as well?"

"I'm not that stupid!" Zoe spread her hands, palms up, on the table. "Well, maybe you'll think I am when I tell you about it. But I didn't mean to be. It was kind of one mistake that just snowballed."

"That sounds dangerous." Finn's mouth curved into a brief grin. "But first I want to hear about this book."

She explained about the black book falling from Maeve's desk and how she'd read a few words as she picked it up.

Finn leaned forward. "Can you remember them?"

"Something about a circle and a staff. Honestly, I should have figured it out then but I heard...."

"Can you remember the exact words? It's important."

"It was something about breaking the staff and

burning it in the centre of the circle," she said. "There was a diagram as well."

"Can you draw it?"

"I can try."

As she picked up her pencil Finn said, "Did you see the title of this book?"

"Yeah. It was *The Seventh Book*. I thought it sounded kind of creepy." Zoe's brow furrowed as she tried to remember what she'd seen.

"You're sure?"

"About the title? Absolutely," Zoe said, sketching in the last cross.

"Jesus! That's priceless." Finn barked out a laugh. "What a gift!"

She pushed the pad across the table. "What's so funny?"

He picked up his pint and saluted her. "Zoe, I owe you one for this."

"You do? Great!" Zoe took a sip of wine. "Then how about answering some of my questions?"

"Not until you've told me what else you've been up to." Finn's grin faded as he studied the sketch. "Can I keep this?"

"Be my guest."

He tore the sketch from the pad, folded it and zipped it into the pocket in his fleece. "Okay then, what's the other thing?"

Zoe took a deep breath. "You know the tree in Maeve's garden that was hit by lightning. Of course you do. You were there." Her eyes flickered to his face. "But what I don't understand is how you didn't get more injured when it exploded? I mean, the garden was shredded. It was like a bomb had gone off. But you seem to be more or less alright." Gesturing to his plastered fingers and the mark on his forehead, Zoe saw that his face had frozen.

For a long moment, Finn stared into this pint glass. "Zoe, there are some things I can't tell you, that it's better that you don't know. And this is one of them."

"Do you have *any* idea how annoying that is? Why won't you let me decide what I should and shouldn't know?"

"Because by then it would be too late and you'd already know."

Zoe crossed her arms. "Not necessarily. You could tell me just the headline and then I could decide if I wanted to know the rest."

"What if it's dangerous to know the headlines?" Finn leaned forward.

"Oh my God, Finn! Are you like MI5 or Special Branch or.... " Zoe threw her hands up. "Or is that something else you can't tell me for my own safety?"

"I swear I'm a conservationist." Finn smiled fleetingly. "Currently unemployed but that is what I do."

"Then what are you doing involved in something that you keep telling me is dangerous? It's not like it's some kind of environmental disaster."

Finn drank deeply from his Guinness, his eyes not leaving her face. "You were telling me about the tree?"

Biting her lip, she studied his face. This was not working out as she'd hoped. So far all she'd done was talk. But he didn't look like a man who was about to open up. "Okay, but I haven't forgotten about the answers you're not giving me." Eyes fixed on her wine glass, she gave him a carefully edited version of how she'd found the doll, with no mention of talking to the Green Man.

"Can you draw this doll?"

Zoe darted a glance at Finn's face. His eyes were narrowed, his nostrils flared. She blinked and dropped her gaze to the blank page in front of her. Why did he suddenly look so angry? Taking her time, she sketched the doll first with its bark wrapper, then without. She pushed the finished drawings towards him. There was silence as he studied them.

"How did you find it?" As his eyes flicked to hers and then away, Zoe caught a glimpse of terror in their depths. That shook her as nothing he'd said had done. She looked unseeingly away from him. If Finn was scared then what the hell was going on?

Finn repeated his question. Her fingers fiddled with her pencil as she answered. "Because of the lightning. I'd probably never have seen it otherwise. The bark wrapped round it was like camouflage against the trunk."

"I'd forgotten the thunder storm." He slumped back in his chair, brow furrowed. Zoe wanted to ask him to explain but some instinct warned her not to intrude. She looked away.

Twenty two players in brightly coloured kit ran across an emerald pitch on the flat screen. Pool balls rattled as they were racked. The drinkers at the bar erupted in laughter. Finn said her name once, then again. Turning her head, she was startled by the intensity in his eyes. "What happened to the doll after that?"

Zoe told him how she'd shoved the doll in her pocket when Helena returned. She skimmed over the part where she'd argued with Helena then faltered unsure how to explain what she'd done next that wouldn't make her sound certifiable. "I'd had a couple too many of these on Saturday night." She ran her finger around the rim of the glass. Finn's eyes were fixed on her face, watching her as if every word she spoke was critical. "And I had this ridiculous feeling about the bloody doll. I know it sounds stupid but it really freaked me out. It was like something from a horror film. And the more I looked at it all trussed up like that and scowling at me, the more I didn't like it. So I decided - I don't know why – to cut it out of the bark wrapped around it because I thought it'd make it less scary so..."

"What?" Finn grabbed the table, making the glasses wobble.

"Yeah, I told you, crazy idea." Zoe shrugged. "And it didn't even work. Stupid thing looked just as weird when I'd finished. I had to lock it in a drawer before I could even think about going to sleep."

"That was it? That was the only reason?" Finn stared at her. His grey eyes were dark with emotions that she was suddenly afraid to guess at.

"What can I say? I was drunk. And I *so* wish I'd never done it. The damned thing's caused me nothing but trouble. Because in the morning I found out that Maeve was looking for the doll and then I kind of panicked because I'd unravelled it and there was no way I could admit to Maeve that I'd taken it. So I got rid of it."

"Of all the...." He stared unblinkingly at the carpet.

Zoe could tell he was struggling with something. But she had absolutely no idea what. She doodled in the corner of her pad as her brain tried to make sense of his reactions.

Suddenly his gaze snapped back to her. "What time did you find the doll?"

"I'm not sure. Maybe around eleven."

"What time did the tree come down?"

"About half twelve, I think." Zoe frowned. Everything that happened at Anam Cara on Sunday evening seemed more significant now she viewed it through the prism of Finn's reactions.

"And you got rid of the doll in the morning?"

"I chucked it in the river. Near where we met." Zoe smiled briefly but Finn didn't respond.

"And the bark and the wool, what did you do with that?"

"I'd put them in the bin in my room and to be honest, I forgot about them in the morning. But after Maeve asked me about the doll yesterday afternoon and I had to lie to her about it – and that's not something I want to do again in a hurry - I went back to my room, grabbed them and dumped them in a bin in town."

"Had Maeve been in your room while you were out?"

Zoe hesitated. "Maybe. Someone had been in to put the jar of leaves and needles on the windowsill. But I thought it was Helena. She's the one who does all the work."

"Could she have seen the bark and the wool in the bin?"

"I suppose. If she was looking for them."

"Has Maeve asked you about the doll again? Said or done anything that shows she suspects you?"

"She asked me about it yesterday afternoon and after that I thought maybe she'd guessed. But I honestly think that was just my guilty conscience. No one's mentioned it since so I kind of stopped worrying about it."

"Don't underestimate her!"

"What do you mean?"

Finn leaned closer, his face only inches from hers. "I mean, that if Maeve has the slightest suspicion that you're involved in the doll going missing then you need to get out of there."

"I know. I've been trying. It's not that simple."

"I get that. But with what you know, what you've seen, it's too risky for you to be there."

"Don't you think you might be over-reacting? I'm definitely going to leave on Thursday. Isn't that enough?"

"If Maeve knew you'd taken the doll...." Finn's hands balled into fists. "You have no idea what she'd do to you."

"Then tell me!" Zoe threw her hands up. Finn slumped back in his chair, his eyes tight, his mouth a hard line. "If you want me to leave then you have to give me some damned good reason. Not more cryptic comments and warnings that I don't understand because" – Zoe's voice rose as she got more agitated – "they're just making me really scared."

Finn sat immobile for a long time. Then he ran his hand over his eyes and sighed. "What do you want to know?"

"Everything," Zoe said. "If I have to decide whether I stay there or not I want to know everything."

"I can't tell you everything." Finn raised his hand as she started to protest. "But I will tell you about Maeve. Enough for you to understand why I think you should leave."

"Okay, let's start with that."

Chapter 13

Finn waved away Zoe's offer to buy this round saying, "It's the least I can do." While she waited, Zoe doodled on the edge of her pad, creating a series of black, spiky shapes. Hearing him laugh, she glanced over. He was smiling, enjoying a joke with the barman. It seemed impossible that he'd just told her it wasn't safe for her to stay at Anam Cara.

She'd thought yesterday that he was confusing to be with, a man of light and shade. Now she was worried about the depth of the shade. There had to be a damned good reason why he was afraid of Maeve. And, despite what she'd said to him, she knew it wouldn't take much to convince her not to return to Anam Cara.

She glanced at her watch. Five past ten. How could she possibly find anywhere else to stay this late? Unless the pub did rooms or Finn....

Two packets of crisps dropped onto the table and, a lot more carefully, a red wine and a coke joined them. Easing his long legs into the chair opposite her, Finn gestured at the crisp packets. "Your choice."

"Thanks." Zoe picked up the cheese and onion. "I'm veggie so the smoky bacon's yours." She crunched down a mouthful of crisps and realised she was starving.

"I was veggie once." Finn tore open the crisps. "I was trying to impress a girl. Freya. She was on my MSc course. Smart, sophisticated, older than me. Way out of my league. Still have no idea how I persuaded her to go out with me. But then I was stuck with being veggie. The house was a meat free zone. I used to have to go out for sneaky burgers."

Fairly certain this was ancient history, Zoe laughed. "What happened?"

"We split up." Finn pushed up the sleeves on his grey t-shirt. "But not over my meat eating habits."

Zoe hesitated and then decided she had to go for it. If he was spoken for she needed to know. "So what about at the moment? You...seeing anyone?" she said, staring at the inside of her crisp packet.

"No."

"Oh!" Zoe's eyes flicked to his. Embarrassingly, she felt a blush steal across her cheeks.

"You?"

"No. I'm...I'm...single," Zoe said, unable to look away from his gaze. The eye contact held. The moment stretched to stillness. Zoe felt a barrier fall and she was falling with it, spiralling down into the grey haven of his eyes.

The pub door opened. A draft swirled in. Finn's head whipped round. Her pulse kicking up, Zoe mirrored him. A middle aged man with a bald head and a significant paunch was cheerfully greeted by the regulars at the bar.

With a grin, Finn shrugged. Zoe's eyes narrowed. He'd avoid talking about Maeve for the rest of the night if she let him. She took a gulp of wine and said, "So, Maeve? How'd you meet her?"

"Because my sister Catriona - Cat - stayed at Anam Cara last year." Finn folded his arms, resting them on the table between them.

"In October?"

"She first came in August. Not long after she'd split up with Andy, the latest in a long line of loser boyfriends. She came here to find herself." Finn's eyebrows rose. "Again."

"And Maeve promised to mend her broken heart?"

"Probably. I'm a bit thin on the details." Finn shuffled

the beer mats around the table as he spoke. “Cat wasn’t talking to me. I hadn’t been as sympathetic as I could have been about Andy.”

“Why? What did you say?”

“I think my exact words were ‘he’s an arse and you’re better off without him’.”

“Ouch!”

“Yeah.” Finn rubbed his forehead. “Not one of my better moments. Padraig, our uncle, had just died and I....”

Hearing sadness saturate his voice, Zoe reached towards him. For a second, her fingers hovered next to his arm. “Oh, I’m so sorry.”

“Thanks. It was really sudden. Heart attack. He was sixty three.” Finn looked away, his face tight. “I’d thought he’d be around for a lot longer yet.”

“You must have been close.”

“He was like another parent. It knocked me sideways.”

“Didn’t your sister understand? I mean, you’d both just lost your uncle. Couldn’t she cut you some slack?”

“I don’t know.” Finn’s lips twitched as if he were about to say more. After a pause, he added, “Cat’s eight years younger than me. She’s always treated me as the shoulder to cry on. And she wasn’t as close to Padraig...” He shook his head as if trying to dispel unwelcome thoughts.

“It must have been a tough time.”

“September was a total write off.” Finn’s eyes were fixed on the wall behind her head. “When I wasn’t working, I was in Donegal, organising the funeral, sorting out Padraig’s house. It took a while before I realised Cat hadn’t been in touch. In the end I figured she was waiting for an apology. I rang, left a message. She didn’t get back to me, not even a text. I tried again a week or so later. Still nothing. That wasn’t like Cat. She doesn’t hold grudges. I spoke to Mum. She told me Cat was in Glastonbury learning another kind of healing.”

"Karmic wave?"

Finn barked out a humourless laugh. "Of all the stupid bloody names! I thought it was just another of Cat's obsessions."

"Obsessions?"

"Cat gets infatuated with things. At the beginning it's the answer to all her prayers." His fingers tapped the edge of the table. "But when it stops being easy or someone upsets her she drops it and starts looking for the next thing. It's been Buddhism, yoga, life coaching and every kind of healing that you can think of.

"I thought this one would fizzle out like all the others. And, to be honest, it was a relief that I didn't have to listen to her going on about how it was changing her life. But then Mum let slip that Cat was taking unpaid leave from work to help out at Anam Cara."

"She was working for Maeve? I hope she treated her better than she does Helena."

Finn frowned. "I doubt it."

Zoe blinked at him. She was starting to feel a little blurry and gently slid her wine glass further away. She needed to stay focused. There were undercurrents to his words that it would be all too easy to miss. Picking up on an earlier thought, she said, "What does your sister do?"

"She worked at a spa in Leicestershire. Doing aromatherapy and reflexology. She enjoyed it and she was good at it. I couldn't understand why she'd miss work to make beds and mop floors for Maeve."

Hearing the past tense, Zoe felt a quiver of unease for Cat. "What did you do?"

"I waited 'til she was back in Melton Mowbray then I went to see her. Tried to talk to her." Finn hunched his shoulders, scowled into his empty glass. "It didn't go well."

When he didn't say any more, Zoe tried to fill in the gaps. "If your sister's anything like Helena then I can imagine. I tried to talk to her yesterday and it was a total waste of time. She acts as if Maeve is some kind of guru. It gets a bit freaky after a while. Like she can't think for herself anymore."

"In a weird way, that's good to know. I'd thought that because Cat's a bit fragile that Maeve used that to..." He glanced away, his jaw jutting. "It really pisses me off that she's still doing the same to other people."

"But how does she do it?"

"It's a form of mind control."

Zoe blinked. "Mind control! Seriously?"

"Yes, but I can't tell you how she does it."

"Come on, Finn!" Zoe's hands flew up. "You have to tell me that. She's doing it to my friends. Don't you think they have a right to know?"

Slumping back in his chair, he said, "I can't tell you because I don't know."

"Oh!" Zoe's hand rose to her mouth. "Sorry. It's just you said you'd tell me enough to decide if I'd go back and when you said..." She fanned her hands out. "Well, I thought you'd changed your mind." There was a moment of awkward silence.

He rested his folded arms on the table. "Give me time. I'm figuring this out as I go along." His voice was low, his eyes fixed on hers. "I've not told this to anyone. Not even Winston. Though he'll get the whole story when he gets here."

Zoe smiled tentatively, trying to hide the thrill she felt that he was confiding in her. She briefly wondered why he'd not talked about this in six months even to his family. But distracted by the intensity of his gaze, she asked the more obvious question. "Who's Winston?"

"He's a mate. He's coming down on Thursday. I'll ask him about mind control. He's got more experience of these things. I understand that's why Cat wouldn't listen..."

"Just one thing!" Zoe interrupted, her hand darting across the table. She miscalculated the distance and her fingertips brushed his forearm. The same tingling sensation, almost like pins and needles, ran across her fingers.

Finn's eyes met hers. In that second, she thought she saw a spark of desire in their grey depths. Then his eyebrows rose and he said, "What now?"

"If Maeve does this mind controlly thing -" Zoe twirled her index finger around her temple "- how come it doesn't work on me?"

"I don't know. But it doesn't work on me either."

Zoe thought for a moment. "I guess I already knew that. Because otherwise we wouldn't be having this conversation."

Finn's face froze. "No, we wouldn't. And I'd be missing a sister."

"What do you mean? What happened to Cat?"

"Five days after I'd seen her she disappeared."

"What?" Zoe didn't know what she'd been expecting but it wasn't this. Her earlier fear darkened. "Please tell me Cat comes out of this in one piece?"

"Barely." Finn's voice was grim. Zoe's eyes widened. She gestured for him to go on. "The first I knew was a phone call from Mum. That was Friday morning. The spa rang her after Cat didn't show up for work two days in a row and they couldn't get hold of her. Mum told me she was going to Melton Mowbray." His chin dropped to his chest. "I honestly thought she was over-reacting, that she'd get there to find Cat ill or in the middle of some meltdown and not answering the phone.

"But the flat was empty. Cat's car was gone. Mum called me. I told her to ring the police. I left as soon as I could but I was in Anglesey and it's a four-hour drive from there. When I arrived at Cat's the police were already there. Crawling over the place, going through all her things. Mum was in pieces. Father was on holiday in Florida. He got the first flight home. Arrived in time to make the television appeal. Thank God. I don't think I could have done it." He rubbed his hand over his eyes as if he were trying to erase the memories.

"Oh my God, Finn! I had no idea." Zoe knew her words were hopelessly inadequate but she felt too stunned to come up with anything else. Trying to remember if she'd seen anything about Cat's disappearance on television, she said, "This was October last year?"

"End of. Cat didn't go anywhere without telling someone. She wouldn't pop out to the shops without announcing it on Facebook." Finn's face was bleak as he relived the memory. "The police wanted a list of her friends. I told them about Maeve. The last two calls on her mobile were to Anam Cara. I thought that was suspicious. The police sent someone round to interview Maeve but" - Finn's face twisted – "she convinced them that she'd not seen Cat for over two weeks."

Zoe stared at him trying to take in what he'd said. "She did the mind control thing on the police?"

"Yes."

"That's..." Zoe swallowed hard. She didn't doubt him. She'd seen Maeve in action, knew how persuasive she could be. She'd just not imagined her using it on anyone other than her guests.

"Something of what Maeve told the police didn't ring true. But there was so much other stuff going on, what with the investigation and the media and my parents, I wasn't thinking straight. Then they found Cat's car in a shopping centre in Bristol. She didn't know anyone in Bristol."

"But you thought she might be in Glastonbury?"

"I thought it was worth a try. I had to do something. It was the waiting I couldn't take. And I...erm -" Finn's eyes slid away "- I couldn't shake the idea that Cat was at

Anam Cara."

There's more to that than you're telling me, Zoe thought but she let it go. She could see how hard it was for him to talk about it. "You came to look for her?"

"Yes. And got as far as the front gate. Maeve spun me the same tale as she'd told the police. But I didn't believe her. I kept asking questions. And she refused to let me in to see for myself."

"What did you do?"

"I waited until the middle of the night and then climbed the wall."

"Seriously?" Zoe stared at him. "Wasn't that a bit desperate? I mean, what if Cat hadn't been there?"

"By then I was sure she was."

"How?" As she asked the question, Finn folded his arms. "You're not going to tell me?" she said.

"Right. All you need to know is that I found her. She..." He swallowed hard, his mouth a thin line. "It was like a flashback to when she was anorexic as a teenager. I couldn't believe how much she'd changed. It was only nine days since I'd seen her. She was ill, really ill. Stick thin. She could barely stand, let alone walk."

"Oh my God! Poor Cat." There was silence for a moment. Zoe sipped her wine and tried to absorb what he'd said.

Suddenly Finn said, "What's wrong with Tanya?"

"She had healing with Maeve and afterwards she got really ill." Zoe's eyes widened. "Is that what happened to Cat?"

"Yes."

"But how? I don't get it."

"Maeve doesn't give energy to people. She takes it away."

Zoe's mouth fell open. "No?"

"It's perfect when you think about it. With the mind control she's got it all sewn up. If the patient feels ill after the so called healing she convinces them it's nothing to worry about, that it's all part of the process."

"That's what she did with Tanya. She told her it was a healing crisis."

Finn snorted. "It's a lot more than that."

"I can see that she's not a healer. It's the other part that's hard to handle, that she's *taking* energy from people."

"Think about it."

She remembered Tanya after her healing, looking totally drained; Penny at breakfast on Monday saying how bad she'd felt after Karmic Wave; Helena in the kitchen getting defensive when she'd asked about the others who'd been ill. She'd had doubts then, questioned the credentials of Maeve and Karmic Wave enough to Google them. Weren't Finn's words only a small leap beyond what she'd thought herself?

"O-kay," Zoe said slowly. "I mean if I hadn't seen what happened to Tanya then I'd think you were completely nuts."

Finn shrugged as if to say, 'fair enough'.

"But, as it is, I can kind of see that you might be right."

Finn leaned across the table. "You see why I don't think you should go back there?"

"God, yes!" she said and instantly regretted it. Finn had said he'd tell her enough to decide if she'd return to Anam Cara. She'd just admitted that she didn't want to but there were things she still wanted to know. As he opened his mouth she jumped in with another question. "How does she do it?"

"I'm not sure. My best guess is that it's the opposite of healing energy."

She frowned. "I don't understand."

"Have you heard of reiki? That's the most well-known form of energy healing."

"Sure. Anna swears by it."

“In reiki the healer takes energy that exists in the universe and gives it to the patient. I think Maeve does the opposite. She identifies an energy that she wants. I’m not sure how she does that. But through touching someone she can take that energy from them.”

Zoe hunched her shoulders. “And that’s what she did to Cat?”

“Yes. When I found her Maeve had been stripping energy from her for five days.” Finn’s eyes were fixed on his hands wrapped tightly around his glass. “Cat was so far under Maeve’s control it was like she’d been drugged. I had to get her out of there. And there was no time.

“I did the only thing I could. Picked her up and carried her. She was limp, like a bloody ragdoll. There was no way I could get her over the wall like that. The gate was the only option.” His jaw tensed, his voice was barely more than a whisper. “Maeve tried to stop us. But I got Cat out.”

Zoe sensed there was lot more than he’d revealed but she recognised the set of his face and knew he’d refuse to answer. She hesitated, then said, “I don’t understand why Maeve did it. I mean, that was like kidnapping. She could go to prison for that.”

“You’re forgetting that she can convince the police of anything she wants.”

“Is that why you didn’t ring them when you knew where Cat was?”

“I knew there was no point.”

Seeing the bleakness in his eyes, Zoe knew she’d have to push him. “Maeve must have wanted something really badly from Cat,” she said, her voice carefully neutral. “Even if she knew she could get round the police, Cat has a family and friends. They weren’t going to just let her disappear.”

Finn’s eyes flicked to her face, then away. “Let it go, Zoe.”

"I'm just trying to understand."

"Then stop."

"But why?"

"I said I'd tell you enough for you to decide whether you'd stay at Anam Cara. No more."

Zoe glared at him. He looked back impassively. After a few seconds she tilted her head and shrugged one shoulder. "Okay. Just tell me what happened to Cat. Is she alright now?"

"No. She's the same. Not better. Not worse. She barely eats. She hardly ever gets out of bed. She's got no energy, no interest in anything."

"Oh, poor Cat! And you think that's because of Maeve? What she did?"

"Yes."

"So when you got back from New Zealand you came to Glastonbury to confront her?"

Finn's eyebrows shot up but then he nodded curtly. "You could say that."

"It must have been one hell of a surprise when you turned up on Sunday night! What did Maeve say to you?"

Finn shook his head. Zoe folded her arms and waited. He didn't answer. "Okay, how about an easier one? Why is the doll so important to Maeve?"

"Do you need to know that to decide if you're going back to Anam Cara?"

"Definitely." Zoe kept her face straight and stared him in the eye.

"Liar." Finn grinned. "You decided ages ago."

Zoe opened her mouth to argue and then conceded with a half-smile. She glanced at her watch. Ten to eleven. "I can't go back there. Not after what you've told me. But how am I going to find anywhere else to stay at this time of night? And I have to go back sometime. All my stuff's there. And my portfolio. I have to have that. I've got a meeting with the publisher next week and everything I've done for King Arthur is in it."

Finn glanced at her and then away. "Why don't you have my bed?"

"I..."

"I won't be in it. I'll be out for most of the night."

Zoe realised she was staring at him and dragged her gaze away. It was so very tempting. And not only because then she wouldn't have to face Maeve. More time with Finn would be a bonus. But she had to be sure that he meant it. "That's really kind of you but I don't want you to feel like you have to."

"I don't." Finn looked at her steadily and for the first time since they'd arrived in the pub she felt reassured.

"Then okay. And thanks." Zoe smiled widely. "Though I feel bad about stealing your bed."

He shrugged. "There's a sofa bed. Don't worry about your things. You can get them tomorrow. In daylight. Sharpham's a couple of miles from here. I can't go back with you. There is a place I have to be, that I should have been a while ago. But I don't think it's a good idea for you to walk on your own."

"I can get a taxi."

Finn gestured as if to say 'why didn't I think of that' and headed to the bar to arrange it. While she waited Zoe finished her wine and slid her sketchpad into her bag.

Returning, he perched on the edge of the chair. "The taxi'll be here in ten minutes." From the pocket of his fleece, he pulled out a key with a plastic tag attached and held it out to her. "There's a row of three cottages. I'm in Kingfisher. It's the one at the far end."

Zoe smiled. "Thanks."

"You're welcome." Finn smiled back.

The moment lengthened until it pulsed with tension. Finn looked away first. He started balancing the beer mats like a house of cards. Watching him, Zoe wondered if he was regretting the offer of a bed.

As the silence between them reached the edge of awkward, Zoe said, "I really hope Tanya's okay. I won't feel so bad about breaking my promise to Dave if she's alright."

"Who's Dave?" Finn took the beer mat from under Zoe's glass and added it to his tower.

"It's a bit soon to call him Tanya's boyfriend as they only met on Sunday night and she passed out during their date last night. He lives here." Zoe dropped her voice to a whisper. "And he told me people talk about Maeve, about what goes on at Anam Cara."

"Is he a big bloke? Built like a brick shithouse?" Finn balanced another beer mat.

"Yes. How did you know?"

Finn's hands gently balanced another layer. "I've seen him around."

"Really? Where?"

He looked up, met Zoe's puzzled gaze. Shoving his chair away from the table, he said, "You ready to go?" The beer mat tower wobbled and collapsed. Grabbing his fleece Finn headed for the pub's back door.

Swinging her bag on to her shoulder she followed him. About to dismiss his words as yet another cryptic comment, she remembered the sense she'd had of being watched when she'd talked to Dave last night. Had that been Finn?

He held the door open and she stepped out into the poorly lit car park. The wind had picked up. It whipped Zoe's hair around her face and her hands rose automatically to control it. When she looked up, she saw that Finn had put his hat on. In his dark clothes he looked exactly like a character from a film about to embark on a clandestine mission. Only the blackened face was missing. "What *are* you going to do?"

Finn grinned. "I'll be on the Tor studying the habits of a nocturnal creature."

His reply was so unexpected that Zoe laughed. Then the pieces fell into place. The picture she'd drawn of him on the Tor at night, the sense she'd had of being watched. "It's Maeve, isn't it? You were watching Anam Cara last night and you're going back there now?"

"How the hell do you know that?" Finn's voice was an agitated whisper. He stepped closer, towering over her.

"I..." Zoe gulped, realising that once again she'd spoken without thinking and revealed more than she was supposed to know. "I just kind of guessed. I had that prickling on the back of the neck feeling yesterday evening when I was talking to Dave outside Anam Cara... And when you said nocturnal that made me think of Maeve. There's a creature of the night quality about her, don't you think? And maybe she is nocturnal. I know she doesn't usually get up for breakfast so maybe she's doing something at night..." Realising she was babbling, she trailed off.

Finn studied her face. Zoe smiled apologetically and tried not to look as crazy as she'd just sounded. "How do you do that?" he said eventually.

"Do what?"

"Read so much into what I say?" Finn frowned. "You've been doing it all evening. It's...it's weird."

Zoe forced a laugh that sounded a little unconvincing. "You've told me Maeve controls minds and steals energy from people. You're about to spend the rest of the night on the Tor watching her and you're saying I'm weird?"

Finn grinned wryly. "Good point."

A car with Tor Taxis painted in white on its door turned into the car park. Finn signalled to it. Relieved that he'd accepted her garbled explanation, Zoe tugged her jacket closer. Finn swung his pack onto his back.

"Why *are* you watching Anam Cara?" she said.

Finn pulled on a pair of black gloves. "Because it's not over."

The taxi stopped next to them. Zoe put her hand on his arm. “Be careful.”

Finn didn’t reply. His arm stretched out, he bent slightly towards her. *Was he going to kiss her?* Her fingers tightened around his forearm, she leaned in. His gaze slid to one side. He pulled the taxi’s door open.

Zoe’s face flamed bright red. She swung her hair to cover it, keeping her head down as she climbed into the back seat.

“Sleep well.” His voice was soft as the touch of a feather on her cheek. Surprised, Zoe stared up at him. She opened her mouth to respond, could think of nothing to say that didn’t sound utterly hollow.

He closed the door. As the taxi moved, she twisted to look back. Fear clutched at her stomach as she saw him stride out of the car park and turn up the road towards the Tor.

Chapter 14

Zoe sank back as the taxi swung around a corner. It sped out of Glastonbury and down a succession of straight roads lined with scrubby trees to stop at the end of a narrow lane that ran behind a farmhouse to a row of converted outbuildings. The taxi driver offered to wait while she went in saying, "It's a lonely spot at this time of night, love."

Zoe couldn't have agreed more. Grateful for the taxi's headlights, she crunched along a gravel path passing doors marked 'Bittern' and 'Kestrel'. At the end of the row was Kingfisher.

She fumbled getting the key into the lock, struggled to make it turn. When the lock clicked, she shoved the door open. Her hand patted along the wall until she found the light switch.

Calling it a cottage was seriously overselling it. It was a square room with an en-suite built into one corner. A double bed took up almost half the space with a pine wardrobe beside it. A galley kitchen filled the right wall. Grouped around the door were a sofa – the one Finn was going to sleep on, a mere two feet from the end of the bed – and a chair. A flat screen TV was screwed to the wall.

"Cosy," Zoe muttered, dropping her bag on the sofa. There was little evidence of Finn's occupation. An Ordnance Survey map covered the coffee table. Today's Guardian was abandoned on the floor by the sofa. She picked it up to see what he'd been reading. It opened at an article about global warming. She raised her eyebrows. If she was going to spend more time with him she was seriously going to have to swot up on environmental issues.

In the tiny kitchen she found an unwashed mug and plate waiting in the sink. She opened cupboards until she found a glass and filled it with water. Returning to the sofa she switched on the TV. For a few minutes she watched a chat show where the host joked smarmily with a Hollywood actress promoting a film to be released next week.

By then she'd be working at the cinema again. Her old life seemed a million miles away and she couldn't imagine going back. Not ready to deal with that, she pressed the remote, returning the screen to blank silence.

Picking up her bag, she walked to the door, checked it was locked and then retreated to the bathroom. A little later, she padded across the wooden floor in just her t-shirt and knickers, dumped her things at the side of the bed and climbed in.

A faint scent clung to the pillow reminding her of the moment when she'd been in his arms. For one blissful second she'd thought he was stroking her hair. Obviously she'd been wrong but there was no harm, curled up in his bed, in reliving it that way, in imagining that it had turned into a kiss.

Please let him be alright. It was all too easy to visualise him as she'd dreamt and drawn him. A lonely figure on the Tor surrounded by a wild sky. The wind rattled the windows. She pulled the duvet closer. Poor Finn, he wasn't even coming back to a nice warm bed.

She flicked the light back on and hopped out of bed. He'd given up his bed for her. The least she could do was make his.

Opening the wardrobe, she saw a couple of t-shirts and a pair of trousers all with the tags on, and on the top shelf, cotton trunks and socks in their packaging. Momentarily distracted by the image of Finn in only his underwear, it took her a moment to wonder why he had so few clothes and why they were all new.

She scanned the room again. Even for a holiday rental it was bare. In the bathroom there was only his razor and a toothbrush. No wash bag or toiletries. Where was his luggage? And the personal possessions people brought with them even for a few days away?

She peered again into the wardrobe. Behind a pair of mouldy looking boots was a zipped transparent bag with pillows, sheets and a blanket. She tugged them out and dumped them next to the sofa. As she tried to figure out how it folded flat, she wondered if she'd made a mistake in coming here. She swore as the mattress refused to lie flat, yanked hard until it capitulated.

What did she really know about him? He'd warned her about Maeve and made sure she didn't see them together. That had to count for something. Smoothing the fitted sheet and plumping the pillows, she figured that in the end, it came down to whom she trusted. As she'd said to Finn earlier, she trusted him. Flipping the duvet into place, she decided she'd ask him in the morning where all his things were.

Back in bed she stared at the ceiling. She'd been so naïve, such a stupid idiot, waiting on Wearyall Hill, hoping that Finn would turn up like some romantic hero and make everything alright. If she'd known what he'd tell her would she have gone? Because he'd opened her eyes to a reality that was far weirder than she'd ever imagined.

She'd been miles off worrying about Maeve dabbling in witchcraft. What was actually happening was far more terrifying. If she hadn't met Finn she'd have gone back to Anam Cara tonight. And, if he was right and Maeve had guessed that she'd taken the doll, then she'd have been in big trouble. Shivering, she pulled the covers closer and eventually slipped into a restless sleep.

***

A little before one in the morning, Maeve's suspicions crystallised. Clearly the girl would not be returning and, in that case, only one course of action remained. Throwing open her office door, she climbed the stairs. There had to be something in Zoe's room that would reveal who or what she was.

Unsure about what she hoped to find, Maeve searched manually this time. It was frustratingly slow to rifle through the girl's belongings but she quelled her irritation. Turning the rucksack upside down and shaking it, Maeve accepted that the words she'd spoken to the girl last night had been entirely futile.

She had, however, prepared for Zoe's continuing recalcitrance. Earlier this afternoon she'd instructed Helena to clean the hidden room. Time was running out. If there was no other option, she would not hesitate to use more direct measures to get answers. Last night she'd ascertained that Zoe had no discernible power. A few hours locked in the room, with food and water in very short supply, would undoubtedly make the girl more willing to co-operate.

She'd not contemplated that the girl wouldn't return. To Maeve, her entire evening wasted in waiting – except for her daily trip to the cash machine to augment the funds for her new life – it was an unmistakable admission of guilt. The girl had come to Anam Cara to release the Beltane sacrifice and, with that task completed, had left. The only puzzle was why she'd not departed on Sunday night. Why stay on, playing the innocent, and risking exposure at any time?

After opening the drawers in the bedside cabinet and finding nothing other than an elastic hair band and a packet of tissues, Maeve moved onto the wardrobe. There was some dirty washing at the bottom of it. Nose wrinkled, she rummaged through it. She checked behind the wardrobe and underneath it.

Then she bent to look under the bed. A dark square shape lay next to the wall. Maeve reached for it and as it slid into focus she recalled Zoe carrying it when she arrived. Unzipping the portfolio, Maeve removed its contents.

Perched on the edge of the bed, she flipped through the pictures. Most she gave only a cursory glance but four she looked at in more detail and put to one side. Then, for long moments, she studied each drawing, turning them to the light, focusing on each detail.

Brow furrowed, she returned to the picture of a familiar figure standing next to a tower silhouetted against a storm tossed sky.

Maeve walked to the window. The trees were hunched over by the wind. While she'd waited in her office, it'd turned into a wild night.

She looked at the Tor. Was he up there? Could it really be that easy? She glanced down at the drawing in her hand. If the girl had come here on a rescue mission then why draw these pictures? Why leave them here to be found?

Unless they were bait for a trap. Maeve turned and walked briskly across the room. That was a risk she was prepared to take.

Chapter 15

The window of Zoe's room returned to darkness. It had been a welcome distraction to watch Maeve move around the room illuminated like an actor on a distant stage. Finn had seen her viciously shake a rucksack, yank open drawers and pull something large and flat from beneath the bed.

She'd sat for several minutes with her back to the window. Then she'd looked up at the Tor and seconds later the light had gone out.

Finn relaxed a little. Maeve wouldn't be searching Zoe's room if she didn't suspect her. He'd made the right call in persuading her to leave. Which was a relief because he'd been doubting his motives. As well as being unhelpfully distracted by the thought of Zoe in his bed and what she was – or wasn't - wearing.

Now he was sure Maeve was onto Zoe, she was in the right place. And the reason he'd made the offer was irrelevant. His plan to stay away from her had been all wrong. He'd thought he was keeping her out of trouble. Instead she needed telling how much trouble she'd got herself into. His lips bent into a half smile. The information she'd given him was invaluable, especially about *The Seventh Book*. Just knowing that would give him and Winston an edge they very badly needed.

But then she'd got him to talk. Worse, she had this uncanny knack of seeing behind his words. Of course, she didn't always guess right. How could she? Yet somehow he'd still ended up telling her things he never spoke about.

It was beside the point that she'd taken it surprisingly

calmly. Opening up did not end well. Not with a secret the size of his. He knew that. He'd been there with Freya. It was pointless hoping it'd be different with Zoe.

No matter that he liked her. Or that he owed her, big time. That if she hadn't taken the doll on Sunday night he'd...

He swallowed hard, shoving that thought into a drawer at the back of his mind and slamming it shut.

Forcing his brain back to the task at hand, he raised his binoculars, caught the swing of the gate, a flash of blonde hair in the sudden glare of the security light. Maeve was on the move.

She didn't turn to the garage as he'd expected. Instead she set off on foot walking away from the town, quickly disappearing behind houses. Where was she going at this time of night? He focused on the few places which allowed him a view of the road. A minute later he saw her pass through one of those gaps.

The road skirted around the base of the Tor but he knew a path climbed from it to the lower slopes. She couldn't be heading that way, could she?

He moved out of the shelter of the tower, felt the wind buffet him as he searched for movement below. After fruitless minutes of scanning the slope he stepped back. There was no direct route to the summit from the road. She'd either have to turn and walk around the Tor to join the path up the ridge or head the opposite way to join the steps climbing up the steep side of the hill.

Hunching his shoulders, he zipped his fleece up to his chin and realised he was cold. The swirling energy of the Tor had been keeping him warm. Rubbing his arms, he extended his awareness to search for it. The ground beneath him felt lifeless. He couldn't go deeper with his shield in place. Quickly he weighed the risk. Deciding that if Maeve was out walking she couldn't be searching for him with spellwork, he released his shield.

There was a moment of sweet relief as if he'd eased off clothes that were too tight. Forcing himself to go deeper than he'd thought possible without his staff, he located awen deep within the hill, curled in on itself, like a snail in the protection of its shell.

For a moment he was confused and then, with an instinctive awareness, he understood. The energies of the Tor had retreated to protect themselves. They feared Maeve as he did. They knew she approached.

He stepped into the shelter of one of tower's buttresses, leaned against its solid, cold bulk. *How the hell had she found him?* He'd been shielded all evening and, even without that, she shouldn't have been able to locate him here. The energy of the Tor confused him and he was attuned to the earth. To Maeve, adept in spellwork, it should be a maelstrom of contradictory impulses, his energy hidden by those surrounding it.

He snapped his shield back into place. With awen gone he was exposed. And, whatever had brought Maeve up the Tor to look for him, he was not going back. No fucking way. He'd die first.

Abruptly, and irrationally, he thought of Zoe. Saw again her worried face as she'd told him to be careful. Wished he'd kissed her then.

Focus.

Slinging his pack on his back, he scanned the night. He had a clear view of the upper stretch of the path that ascended along the ridge. No one wanting to approach the top of the Tor unseen would take that route. If you wanted to surprise someone the steps that clambered up the steep side were a far better option. They were out of sight of the top for most of their ascent, coming out only a few feet from where he stood.

If she came up the steps he'd have very little time to react and he couldn't retreat down the path without being seen. If he saw her coming up the path, he could risk dodging down the steps if he kept low and moved fast.

His gloved hand whipped out, slamming against the wall. He was bloody well trapped until he knew which way she was coming. Was she confident enough to risk a frontal approach up the path or would she use stealth and come up the steps? If it were him, he'd take the steps. Scouting above their route, he listened intently, scanning the darkness for any sign of movement. Jumped like a girl when a barn owl hooted.

Moving back into the shadow of the tower he focused the binoculars on the point where the path became visible. Clouds skimmed across the sky, playing hide and seek with the waxing moon. He waited, his breath shallow, his heartbeat fast.

A denser black emerged from the night and resolved into a figure. A hundred metres away on the path, moving steadily towards him.

He stepped out of the shadows, bent low, ready to run for the steps. Glancing to his right, he froze. The darkness was fading. He recoiled into the shadow of the tower. Globes of light floated away from Maeve, one hovering over the path in front of her, the other drifting towards the steps.

They looked like Chinese lanterns but Finn knew they were hunting him. That Maeve could convert them to a weapon in a second. The steps were cut off to him now. Even at this distance, if she saw him move, she was strong enough to kill him. Without his staff he couldn't defend himself.

He looked behind him at the flat plateau encircled with darkness. The steep side of the Tor was slightly less precipitous than a cliff face. His only escape was down it.

He checked the position of the figure on the path. She moved quickly, head bowed against the wind. Wrenching the binoculars from around his neck, he stuffed them in his pack, stood with his back against the cold stone. The tower would hide him from Maeve's sight so long as he kept its walls between them. He peered around the edge of the empty doorway, checking he couldn't see her. It was clear. He had to go now before she got close enough to see through the arches and there was nowhere left to hide.

He sucked in a deep breath and sprinted for the darkness at the rear of the Tor. His feet pounded, sounding thunderous in his ears. He glanced over his shoulder. He couldn't see Maeve. But a globe floated closer, approaching the steps to his right, diluting the night into twilight.

He pushed his legs to go faster. Fixed his eyes on the comforting darkness. Too late he looked down, saw a low pedestal of stone in front of him. He swerved, banged his shin. Bit back the pain. Kept running.

Three more paces brought him to the edge. He didn't hesitate. Holding his breath, he grabbed a tussock of grass with one hand and launched his feet out into the night.

He landed heavily, the ground slamming painfully into the right side of his body, knocking the breath from him. Momentum took him further. He couldn't hold on as he slid downwards, his feet instinctively scrabbling for grip. He grasped a tussock, found a toe hold. Lay still, desperately sucking in air. When he'd stopped gasping, he rolled over onto his back. Looked up. Saw a dim formless glow, a lightening of the night. He swore under his breath. She was getting closer.

Slowly, trying to make no sound, he eased his feet down the hill. Slid a couple of feet. Froze when he saw a movement above him. He glanced up. Saw a light directly above his head. Beneath it the grass was illuminated as bright as day. He glanced left, thinking he'd move that way. Another globe hovered. Same to his right.

How many globes could the bloody woman control at once? He fought down the desire to pop them. Without his staff it would be suicide. A direct assault on Maeve's magic would confirm his presence and she'd hunt him like hounds after a fox. His only option was to creep away. Then, with luck, he'd live to fight another day.

Very carefully, he inched towards the safety of the darkness below. His feet landed on something solid. He lowered himself on to it. Realised he stood on one of the turf terraces that wound around the Tor. Crouching, he looked up.

The globes floated about three metres above him. Between them stood a dark figure, bent forward, looking down. Finn flattened himself against the side of the Tor. If Maeve saw him now he was a dead man.

He needed a distraction. His fingers scrabbled, found a pebble. Releasing his shield, he drew on awen. Without his staff it was puny but he felt a little less helpless. He welcomed the energy into his body; breathed with it, controlled it, shaped it. The pebble rose above his palm, and as he formed the thought, it flew in a high arc towards the steps, bouncing and rattling on the concrete as it fell. He glanced up in time to see Maeve spin away, her coat billowing around her. The globes followed.

Bent over Finn ran along the turf terrace heading away from the steps. Should he keep going, run round the Tor until he reached the gentler incline along the ridge? But then he'd be exposed, in easy sight of anyone on the top. Instead he crouched, gripped the edge of the terrace with both hands and walked his feet down the slope.

Gravity pulled his body down, his arms extending until he held on with only his fingertips. Bracing his feet, he let go. Slid a few feet further. One foot landed in a hole, kicked its way out. A moment later he realised he'd disturbed its occupant. He heard a scrabble of earth. A rabbit shot past him up the slope.

"Shit!" Finn breathed, covering his head with his hands. A second later, he felt the quiver in the earth as the light ball smacked into the turf. In his peripheral vision, he saw the rabbit tumble down the hill, falling over and over, its neck broken.

Seconds later the protective cover of darkness thinned to a dusky grey. He couldn't move. Could only imagine the lights floating down the slope, Maeve waiting on the edge poised to strike. He hardly breathed. The wind flattened his clothes to his body. He waited. Each breath felt like a minute.

The slope returned to darkness. The globes must be moving away. He didn't move. Didn't trust his legs. The wind moaned through the empty arches of the tower. Finn listened to it for long minutes, then with a deep breath inched further down. His feet hit another turf terrace.

He crouched low on it. The steps were ten, maybe twelve, feet below him. The gradient had lessened. He could scramble the rest of the way. He glanced up. The globes had disappeared. He took two steps down the slope and froze. A light emerged around the curve of the hill, shining on the steps beneath.

He spun and keeping low, sprinted around the curve of the hill. His foot slipped on the slope. He fell to his knees. One hand landed on a stone. It ripped through his glove, lanced into his palm. Glancing back, he saw another light emerge. Dropping to the ground, he rolled to face the side of the Tor, shaped his body to it. A second later, above the sound of the wind, he heard the sharp tap of heels on concrete.

He didn't move. Could only hope that his black clothes hid him. The feet moved down the steps. He counted them. Sixteen, seventeen. They came closer again. Twenty eight, twenty nine. Moving away. Thirty nine, forty, forty one. They faded after fifty five.

Finn waited. He lost track of how long he lay there. When he felt the energy of the Tor start to emerge, he cautiously rolled up to sitting. He took a deep breath. His ribs ached liked he'd been punched, his shin throbbed. Hearing rustling from the undergrowth he froze. A fox slunk out of the hedge and trotted away.

He felt sure Maeve had left the Tor but there were plenty of places near the road where she could lurk in wait for him. He limped around the Tor, heading away from the steps. Between the hill and the hedge lining the road was a gully where sheep slept protected from the storm. He walked along it until he reached a five bar gate, climbed that, skirted around a field and came to the road. Cautiously he looked left and right, listened. Then he sprinted across it, took the path over Chalice Hill.

He didn't slow his pace, didn't stop glancing behind him every few seconds. Passing through a gate the path entered a tunnel between a tangle of hawthorn trees and bramble bushes.

His feet faltered, then stopped. He pulled his hat off, scrubbed his hand over his eyes. How the hell had Maeve known he was there?

Chapter 16

A few hours later, Finn was woken by a light. He forced his eyes open, blinking against the brightness. "Zoe?"

"Sorry."

Propping himself up on his elbows, he looked at her over the back of the sofa. Hair hanging in front of her face, she crouched on the floor at the side of the bed, rummaging in her bag. Her legs were bare. Her t-shirt rode up her back, revealing a tight arse in purple knickers.

He closed his eyes for a second, wondered if he were dreaming. "What are you doing?"

"Sorry. I didn't mean to wake you. I just have to..." Her voice rose until it was almost squeaky.

He looked again. She sounded upset. She'd sunk to the floor, her back against the bed. Her hair, hanging like curtains, obscured her face. Definitely not a dream. He recognised the posture. He'd seen his sister curl up like that far too many times.

Flinging the bed clothes back, he got up. "What's wrong?" He sounded exhausted. There was a stain of daylight behind the curtains. He guessed it was around five o'clock. He'd had two hours sleep.

Zoe seemed oblivious to his approach. "What's going on?" he said, irritated now. He'd had a bad night. He didn't need ignoring as well. There was no response. "Zoe?" He crouched next to her, wincing when the dull pain in his ribs sharpened.

Her sketchpad balanced on her bent knees. Surprised, he tilted his head to look at her face. Her eyes were fixed on the paper in front of her, her brow furrowed with concentration. She gripped the pencil so tightly her knuckles were white. It moved swiftly, scoring the paper with rapid lines, shading between them. "Okay, you're drawing." He shoved his hand through his hair. "Why?"

Zoe didn't reply. It was as if he wasn't there. He briefly considered going back to bed. It didn't look like she'd notice. Then the fascination he'd felt on Monday when he'd seen her by the river resurfaced. He eased himself down to the floor and watched the picture take shape.

It was night. The sky clear, the moon close to full. A cloaked figure stood in the centre of a stone circle. The ring was small and incomplete, some of the stones almost swallowed by the ground. A fire burned in the centre of the circle. A hood hid the figure's face. One claw like hand was raised towards the sky.

Zoe's pencil moved on, revealing a person kneeling on the ground on the opposite side of the fire. The person became a man; wearing combats, walking boots, a fleece. His hands were behind his back. Finn bent his head to peer closer. A rope bound the man's hands. The pencil moved to the face, shaded untidy hair, outlined square lines of a chin.

"No!" Zoe gasped, her eyes widening.

"What is it? What's wrong?"

Her hands covered her face, her shoulders shook. Knees bent, she curled into a ball. The sketchpad slipped to the floor.

"Hey, it's alright." He gently touched her shoulder. For a moment, she didn't respond then suddenly she turned, folding in on him until her head rested on his chest. Instinctively his hand rose to her shoulder. Her hair cascaded over it, the colour of conkers, silky against his fingers. Her bare legs touched his, her skin warm.

Swallowing hard he focused his eyes on the wall and tried not to think. Her shoulders heaved as she cried and the scent of her hair – coconut and honey – wafted up to him. He swore silently and held his breath. He'd given into impulse and stroked her hair once already. He would not take advantage of a crying woman. No matter how badly he wanted to.

He looked for a distraction, saw the sketchpad on the floor and grabbed it with his free hand. Holding it above her head, he studied it. The finished picture had a touch of Gothic melodrama about it that didn't erase its sense of menace. Whether it was a man or woman behind the hood he couldn't tell, except that the hands were perhaps too small to be a man's. They looked like an old person's; the joints distorted, the skin too large for the bones beneath.

Why hadn't she drawn the man's face? The rest of the sketch was incredibly detailed. He could see logs crumbling in the fire, a talisman suspended from a thong around the man's neck, mud on his boot.

Abruptly she pulled away, wiping tears from her face with her fingers. "Sorry," she whispered.

"That's okay. You alright now?"

She looked at the floor. Following her gaze, Finn saw her pale, slim legs. He forced himself to look away. "I had a bad dream," she said, her voice so low he had to bend his head to catch her words. "Really bad. And then I had to draw it." She hesitated. "I know it sounds crazy. But if I draw the dream then it's like it can't hurt me anymore. If I don't draw it, it gets stuck in my head and I'm awake for the rest of the night."

Finn held the sketchpad out to her. "This is what you dreamt?"

Zoe flinched away from him. "I don't want to see it!"

"O-kay." Finn's voice was gentle, the one he used at work to sooth frightened creatures. "We won't look at it now."

"Sorry," Zoe repeated, pushing her hair away from her

face. "I know I sound crazy. But it's just that if I look at the picture the dream will get back in my head."

Ignoring the stabbing pain in his ribs Finn levered himself up from the floor. "Putting it over here," he said as he crossed to the coffee table. He dropped the sketchpad within easy reach of the sofa. He'd look at it again later.

When he turned, Zoe had moved to sit on the bed. She looked up, biting her lip uncertainly. "Sorry about that. I know I sound like a crazy woman." She folded her arms, across her chest. Her t-shirt pulled tight against her breasts. No bra.

Finn wrenched his eyes back to her face. "A little eccentric but not crazy," he said, trying to keep his voice light.

Her brown eyes were smudged with makeup, her hair was a mess. And still she looked hot. He wanted her, had wanted her all evening if he were being honest. She'd been giving out all the right signals in the pub. Would she knock him back if he made a move now? He sat next to her on the bed. Deliberately close.

"I'm *so* sorry that I woke you," Zoe said. "I wasn't thinking at all. I'd forgotten where I was and I just put the light on like I would at home..."

"Don't worry about it."

"Are you sure? I mean, you can't have been back for all that long. You'll have had no sleep at all." Zoe's worried eyes met his.

"I'll be fine," he lied, stifling a yawn. "Do you always draw your dreams?"

He was sat so close to her, their legs almost touching, that he felt her tense. "Only the bad ones," she said quietly.

He glanced at her. She was biting her bottom lip again. That wasn't very promising. He regrouped and tried a different tack. "You know, you had me worried for a minute when you were drawing. It was like you were in a trance or something." His voice was light, teasing. He nudged her shoulder gently with his.

"Was I? Sorry, I didn't realise. There's not usually anyone with me when it happens."

"Will you stop saying sorry? I don't mind that you woke me, okay. I don't even mind you crying on me." He pulled his t-shirt away from his chest, pointed to a darker patch. "Look, I'm drying out already."

Zoe smiled weakly. "Okay."

"That's better."

"I don't know why I cried." Zoe looked down, her hair falling forward. "I don't normally." She rubbed at the pile of the carpet with her toes. Her toenails were purple. Before he could shut it down his brain logged that they matched her knickers. Which was *not* a visual he needed now! He closed his eyes, sat entirely still and willed his body not to betray him.

Silence hovered between them for long seconds. When he'd got enough control, he reached out, gently swept her hair away from her face and let it fall over her shoulder. He bent to look at her face. "I told you I don't mind," he said, his voice a little huskier than normal. He cleared his throat, hoped she'd not noticed.

Zoe looked up at him. "I know. It's just that you invite me to stay and I repay you by waking you up in the middle of the night and crying all over you."

"But you made my bed for me. That counts for something."

"Seemed only fair after you'd given up this bed for me." She smiled, a wide genuine smile that lit up her eyes.

Now we're getting somewhere. He gestured towards the bed, raised his eyebrows. "And are you finding it comfortable?"

"Absolutely." She grinned. Then her face froze. She grabbed his hand, stared at the deep gash on his palm.

"What happened to your hand?"

Finn tugged it away. "I fell." He stared at the carpet, hoping she'd get the message that he didn't want to talk about it.

"And you banged your leg as well." Zoe gestured to the ugly red slash on his shin, crusted with dried black blood. "That must really hurt."

"It does."

"You poor thing," she said, her eyes full of concern.

"I'll live." He stood. The moment had gone. She'd reminded him why it shouldn't have been there in the first place. "Try and get some sleep," he said. Walking stiffly back to the sofa, he heard the swish of the duvet, the creak of the bed. He eased himself down, sank into the sofa's soft embrace. It was the only one he was going to get tonight.

The light went off. He heard Zoe turn over. He tried to shut out the awareness of her closeness, to forget she was only feet away. He lay entirely still, staring unseeingly at the ceiling. The bed creaked again and he fought down the urge to go to her.

Think of something else. Think of Maeve. That was guaranteed to cool desire.

"Finn?" Zoe whispered.

"Yes."

"Thanks."

He opened his mouth to ask what she was thanking him for. Then realising he didn't want to get into that, he said, "You're welcome."

He waited - his ribs aching, his leg throbbing evilly - until he heard her breathing slow. Then sitting, he glanced at the bed. She slept curled on her side, her hair spread over the pillow. He sighed. He'd massively overestimated his self-control when he'd offered her a bed for the night.

He put his hand on his aching ribs, rubbed his fingers along each one, testing they weren't broken. He'd ignored his injuries when he came in; been so exhausted he'd literally fallen into bed. Now he'd slept a little, the pain had become insistent. He should be rested enough to do something about it.

Deciding he'd no broken bones he placed his hands on his ribcage. Closing his eyes he drew on the energy around him, let it seep through his hands, visualised it breaking down the blood trapped in the tissue. Then he did the same with his leg, was pleased when he took his hands away to see that the wound had shrunk to a thin red line.

Bending easily now, he grabbed his pack from the floor and unzipped it. He took out a pen torch, held it over the drawing. Knowing it was a dream, he looked at it with new eyes. Padraig had taught him not to underestimate the power of dreams. The difficulty was knowing which ones had meaning and which were simply nightmares. That was hard enough with his own dreams. Figuring out someone else's was entirely new to him.

The drawing reminded him of pictures he'd seen from war zones. Captives forced to kneel before they were beaten or tortured. The same feeling of overt threat came from the hooded figure's stance. Whatever happened next he felt sure it wouldn't end well for the man.

Why was he faceless? Had Zoe dreamt him like that? He thought back, remembered her sketching in the chin, then saying 'no' and dropping her pencil as if she'd seen something she didn't want to draw. He frowned. It made no sense. But then none of her reactions to the dream or the drawing made any sense to him.

He dropped the pad back on the table and switched off his torch. He wasn't going to figure that out tonight. Maybe he'd have another go in the morning, ask her about the man. If she didn't freak out again when he showed her the picture.

He punched the pillow, turned onto his front, tried to

find sleep. His mind was too active, his brain replaying the events of the night. Trying to find a reason why Maeve had looked for him on the Tor. With zero success. He put that away to think about later. Moved on to what he had found out. Maeve was on to Zoe. And he wanted her a lot further from Anam Cara than the hostel. He didn't want to have to scale that bloody wall again to rescue her. Zoe should go back to London until it was over.

The hard part would be getting her to agree to it. In the morning he'd tell her he'd seen Maeve searching her room. Only he didn't think that'd be enough. Because, even after what he'd told her this evening, she had no idea of the danger she'd been in. And he couldn't explain without revealing everything, his own secret included. And he knew how that would end. Cue stunned silence and questions about his sanity.

That left him with an unsolvable dilemma. If he didn't tell her everything, she wouldn't leave Glastonbury. And if he did tell her, she'd think him insane, doubt every word he'd ever said and probably stay anyway.

Tomorrow he was going to Lyme to get his staff. It'd been stupid to have put it off this long, to think that keeping a low profile would work. Maeve wasn't going to give up that easily and he had to be able to protect himself.

Somehow he'd convince Zoe to wait until he got back from Lyme before she returned to Anam Cara to collect her things. He couldn't go with her but he could get Maeve out of the way to give Zoe time to pack and leave. After that, he had to say goodbye. He wouldn't risk her safety again as he had this evening. But he was going to ask if, when this was over, he could come up to London and take her out somewhere.

He'd just not mention that he had to live that long first. He exhaled heavily. After what had happened on the Tor he was entirely too clear about how likely that was.

Chapter 17

Heart pounding, her skin slick with sweat, Zoe woke. In her dream she'd been frantically searching Anam Cara desperate to find Finn. But in each room there was a hooded figure laughing triumphantly. Or a faceless man, on his knees with his hands bound behind his back, pleading for his life. Or cold, white hands reaching out to grab her. Waking was a moment of pure, sweet relief.

But it was short lived. As she recalled the events of the middle of the night, she rolled over, buried her face in the pillow and groaned. Couldn't she have had just one night off from the bloody dreams?

Slowly, she turned over and opened her eyes. Light percolated through the curtains. She could hear Finn's breathing. It seemed to saturate the room, reassuringly slow and even, as if he slept deeply.

She grabbed her clothes and tiptoed to the bathroom. Seeing herself in the mirror she could only hope that she'd not looked this bad in the middle of the night. She scrubbed the mascara smudges from around her eyes and brushed the knots from her hair. She craved a shower but wouldn't risk waking him.

Pulling her leggings on she thought longingly of the clean clothes in her rucksack at Anam Cara. The prospect of going back there, of facing Maeve, was pretty damned terrifying. Would Finn go with her? Now she wasn't staying there anymore, surely it didn't matter if Maeve saw them together. Tying her hair into a ponytail, she figured she'd ask when he woke up. After what he'd told her last night he couldn't honestly expect her to go back to Anam Cara on her own.

Opening the bathroom door, she tiptoed back to the bed. Finn had been really sweet last night, holding her as she cried, not complaining that she'd woken him. When he'd sat next to her, wearing only shorts and a t-shirt, his long, muscular legs had been so close to hers that their bare skin almost touched. He'd swept her hair back and she'd felt the spark return, thought he was going to kiss her. Then, in one of those sudden changes of mood that so confused her, he'd walked away.

She sighed. Maybe she'd imagined it. After all, who'd want to make a move on the total soggy mess she'd been last night. God knows what he thought when she flipped out about the drawing.

Automatically, she reached for her sketchpad but it wasn't there. Then she remembered Finn taking it from her. What had he done with it? She needed to see it, to know the worst before he woke. Scanning around the room, she crept towards the sofa bed. Spotting the pad on the coffee table, she snatched it up, saw the man's blank face and froze.

Immediately her mind filled in the blank face. It was Finn. He was the man kneeling on the ground, his hands tied behind his back. She gasped as the enormity of it filled her mind. Her hand clamped over her mouth as her stomach plunged.

Her eyes turned involuntarily to the sleeping figure on the sofa bed. He lay on his stomach, his arms flung out, his face turned towards her. The lines of tension he wore when awake had disappeared. He looked exhausted and rumpled and kind of adorable. She wanted to wrap her arms around him, keep him safe from the danger that lurked in this drawing.

But the danger was there. She'd tried so hard last night to avoid it. She'd thought if she didn't draw his face that it wouldn't be true. But the dream hadn't given up. It'd morphed into the nightmare that stalked her sleep.

She walked to the bed and sat down. Picking up her pencil, she took a deep breath and sketched in the lines she'd avoided drawing last night.

Unblinkingly she stared at the completed sketch. Finn's eyes were closed, his face serene. Why wasn't he fighting? It almost looked as if he accepted what was going to happen. She looked again at the hooded figure. Who was it? Screwing up her eyes, she tried to recall the dream. She had a faint memory of an echoing cry of triumph as the hooded figure raised its hand. It seemed strangely familiar but she couldn't place it.

If only Finn hadn't seen her draw this. Brow furrowed, she glanced over at him. There was no point wishing for that. He'd sat next to her, watched as the drawing took shape, wanted - when she'd stopped stupidly crying - to talk about the picture.

Sooner or later he'd ask her about last night. She couldn't tell him that she'd been so scared she stopped herself from drawing his face. That would seem crazy. But not as crazy as explaining she was only scared because she knew the dream would become reality.

She shook her head. She could imagine his reaction to that. He'd think she was delusional. Or insane. And she wouldn't blame him.

Right now, she felt like she really was losing her mind. Because this drawing was a whole different level of weird. A massive step beyond what she'd dreamt and drawn in Glastonbury. This was as bad as the dreams she'd had in October. The ones that had woken her night after night in the run-up to Halloween.

And what if those dreams were the same as these? If they were premonitions too? Suddenly there was a lump in her throat. She swallowed hard. She couldn't remember those dreams – they faded once she'd drawn them – but she was pretty damned sure they were even weirder than this one. So strange that only the fact that the sketches were good, even talented work – and a lot more original than anything she drew with her conscious mind – had stopped her from tearing them into a thousand tiny pieces. Instead, she'd shoved them to the back of the wardrobe.

Stop! She was just being ridiculous now. Those were nightmares. And she was going to have to lie to Finn and tell him that this was just a dream too. Okay, that would make the way she'd reacted last night seem a little mad but, at least, she wouldn't have to tell him the truth.

Her eyes slid back to the picture. A shiver brushed her spine. The hooded figure was going to hurt him. She knew it. This drawing was horribly, maybe even deadly, serious. It wasn't like the other sketches that only revealed his presence at a particular time and place. By drawing this she'd found out something about his future that really mattered. She couldn't keep that from him.

Did she really have to tell him now though? She thought for a moment, her teeth gnawing on her bottom lip. Couldn't she wait until she knew him better? Find a way to build up to it?

She glanced at the clock. Eight fifty three. How much sleep had he had? She hadn't heard him come in but he'd definitely been asleep when she put the light on. That had been just before five. What had he been up to in the hours after they left the pub? Had he been watching Anam Cara all that time?

She visualised him as she'd drawn him on Sunday night, standing in front of the tower on the Tor, binoculars in hand, his face grim. Her eyes returned to the drawing of the stone circle. What if this happened as soon as the one of the Tor had? She'd drawn that on Sunday night and on Monday - and again on Tuesday - he'd been on the Tor watching Anam Cara. She ran back through the days since she arrived at Anam Cara counting off the dreams. The picture at the Holy Thorn was the exception but would she bet Finn's safety on that? What if she could only see the future just before it happened?

Her drawing showed a three quarter moon hanging over the stone circle. That could be a clue as to when the dream would happen. It meant nothing to her. But it would to Finn. He was sure to understand the phases of the moon. She had to tell him when he woke up. She had absolutely no choice.

Her stomach plummeted as she pictured his reaction, the inevitable look of stunned disbelief. She couldn't face that. She liked him too much to watch his face change from shock to coldness to rejection.

There had to be an easier option, a way to tell him without having to see his face as she did it. Twisting her pencil between her fingers, her gaze dropped to her sketchpad still resting on her knee. She could probably explain everything better in a note anyway. And then he'd have time to think about it and decide if he wanted to see her again.

Her eyes closed for a second. She wouldn't hold her breath for that.

Tearing a blank page from her pad, she wondered if this was a coward's way out. Finn wasn't like other guys. He'd had to deal with some weird things of his own. Maybe she should be brave and risk telling him face to face?

Then she remembered how Mia, and years later, Anna had reacted when she'd told them about her dreams. How even they, the two people who knew her best, had dismissed her drawings as the product of an over-active, over-sensitive subconscious. That they'd been wrong - and her dreams had turned out to be premonitions - didn't make talking about them any easier. Quite the opposite, in fact.

She wrote 'Hi Finn' then she stopped, her mind as

blank as the page in front of her. Words weren't her strength. She could say so much more with pictures.

Finn's breathing stuttered. Tensing, she glanced at the sofa bed. The mattress creaked as he turned over. A few seconds later, his breath returned to its even tempo.

She bit her lip and started writing. Two drafts were screwed up and stuffed in her bag. The third – with some crossings out – was good enough.

She carefully folded the note around the drawing of the stone circle and wrote Finn's name on the front. Then she flipped the duvet back into place, put her shoes on and swung her bag onto her shoulder. She picked up the key to the cottage and crept over to the sofa. Quietly she put the note on the coffee table, the key on top of it. She looked at Finn for a long moment, trying to memorise his face.

"Please don't hate me or think I'm crazy," she whispered. "I'm trying to do the right thing here. If I didn't like you so much I wouldn't have told you."

At the door, she hesitated. With her hand already on the latch, she rested her forehead against the wood. Once she stepped outside she was on her own. In a world that was a lot more terrifying than the one she'd thought she lived in when she woke up yesterday.

She glanced back at Finn. Was she making a mistake? Should she stay? Give him the note and wait while he read it? Her mind ran through his possible reactions. None of them were good.

She pulled the handle down and stepped out into a bright sunny morning. Silently, she closed the door behind her.

Chapter 18

Hearing desultory chatter over the breakfast table, Maeve hesitated outside the kitchen door. Her hands rose to her face. She'd done her best with powder and foundation but the night's exertions had taken their toll. She'd drawn energy from Helena as the girl slept - enough to get her on her feet this morning - but she'd had precious little left for putting her face on.

Sliding her sunglasses on, she stepped into the room. Light streamed through the windows and even behind her glasses she winced. "Good morning," she said, taking the chair at the head of the table. She saw Penny stare before hastily looking away. Tony took one glance and dropped his knife. The clatter as it hit his plate stabbed into her brain. Only Helena appeared not to notice. She didn't look good either. Her face was pasty with dark circles beneath her eyes and her movements were even more clumsy than normal. Abandoning her own breakfast, she moved to hover by Maeve's elbow. "I'll have earl grey, grapefruit and wholemeal toast," Maeve told her.

As the girl returned to the kitchen, Maeve turned to her guests. "How are you this morning?" she said, trying to appear as normal as possible. Penny answered and, thereafter, Maeve interjected the occasional question, faking an interest in their paltry activities and the conversation flowed. Helena placed half a grapefruit in front of her. After a single mouthful, Maeve pushed it away. The sharpness that she usually enjoyed tasted like sulphuric acid on her tongue. Sipping her tea, she addressed herself to achieving her purpose.

It took far longer than she'd anticipated. Penny was willing but dithered when Tony expressed his concern for her health with surprising adamance. Maeve repeated again and again that his wife would benefit from the healing, staring at him as she tried to imprint the message in his brain but, disturbingly, it had little effect.

She felt a sharp moment of panic, a flowering of doubt. Was her strength so diminished that even someone as weak as Tony could resist her?

Then she saw the irritation on Penny's face and realised she could divide to conquer. With a few hints that Tony was being overbearing and possessive, she soon had the two of them bickering. Then it took only a few minutes before Penny asserted her independence and agreed to meet Maeve in the treatment room in half an hour.

Her task accomplished, Maeve stood and, with a quick word to Helena about her chores, left the room. Walking through the porch she heard Penny and Tony's raised voices and smiled.

She'd been a wife once. Many, many years ago when a wife was expected to obey her husband. She'd rarely obeyed hers. He was a stupid man. A wealthy acquaintance of her father's with just enough wit to flatter her naive seventeen year old self into believing she was in love. She could barely remember him now. Any affection she'd had for him had been eclipsed by Sebastian's birth, followed a year later by Tristan's. Her wonderful, golden boys who'd taught her what love really meant. Even after all these decades she carried the agony of their loss. Two gaping wounds that could never heal.

Opening the door into the garden wing she entered the treatment room. Thrusting thoughts of the past aside she went through the preparations for a healing. When she was ready, she stepped out into the small entrance hall. Opposite was the door to Helena's room with the main door on her left. On the wall to her right, hung a large picture showing the positions of the chakras. Pressing both hands against the picture, Maeve murmured, "Open". When she stepped back, the frame swung outwards revealing a low, narrow entrance. The smell of damp floated out to meet her as she ducked her head to enter.

The room was as black as a mine shaft, the only illumination coming from the daylight that slid through the half opened door. Maeve formed a light globe and released it. The space was barely four feet across, the ceiling sloping sharply down towards the back wall. The globe flickered like a guttering candle, yet another sign that her strength was low.

Helena had done as she'd asked. The room had been swept clean of its previous occupant's overhasty departure. A thin mattress lay next to the back wall with a folded blanket on top.

She'd been pre-emptive yesterday in considering confining Zoe in here. The girl's pictures had confirmed what she suspected. The girl had come to free her Beltane sacrifice. That gave her a lever. Whatever the relationship between the two of them, she knew he wouldn't stand by and let the woman who rescued him become the sacrifice in his place. His sense of responsibility made him weak. As he'd come for his sister, he'd come for Zoe. This time she'd be waiting for him.

She smiled. The globe glowed more brightly as if suffused by her excitement. She would make him suffer for all she'd endured since the tree exploded on Sunday night. She'd start by making him watch as she stole the girl's blood and drank it. Even the few silver sparks it contained would revive her and give her the strength she needed to complete the ritual.

The temptation to act immediately had to be quelled. In her extensive research she'd discovered that certain learned spellworkers believed *The Seventh Book* to be inaccurate on one key point. The ritual should be performed at first light on Beltane morn. That was less than forty eight hours away. A tracing spell would keep the girl in sight until she needed her.

It was an intricate spell that required preparation. However, as the girl had helpfully left her things behind, the vital ingredient was already at hand.

Chapter 19

Finn woke to the sun sliding through the curtains and absolute silence. It took him a second to figure out why that wasn't right. "Zoe?" No reply. Yawning hugely, he turned to look over the back of the sofa. The bed was made. Standing, he said again, "Zoe?" Was she in the bathroom? The light wasn't on. Three steps took him there. He knocked, said her name again, louder this time. Nothing. He threw the door open. The room was empty.

He turned and looked around. Her bag was gone, her clothes. Had she *left*? He glanced at the clock by the bed. Nine fifty three. It wasn't like he'd slept till lunchtime. Why had she gone?

He wandered back to the sofa, sat on the edge of the mattress. He'd promised his mum he'd be there for lunch. Much as he was looking forward to a home cooked meal he knew the price he'd have to pay. Neither his mum nor Cat believed in holding back and they had six months' worth of fear and anxiety pent up ready for his arrival.

His hand rubbed his chin. He needed a shave. There remained a dull ache in his ribs. His fingers probed the spot, making sure he'd patched himself up as best he could before he saw his mother. He didn't want to give her any more reasons to worry. He glanced at his leg. It looked like he'd injured it weeks ago. There wasn't much he could do about the latest gash on his palm. Zoe would be bound to notice if he didn't let it heal naturally.

Reaching for the clothes he'd thrown in the chair last night he saw a note on the coffee table. He snatched it up. Another page fluttered out, falling onto the mattress. He picked it up, opened it and froze.

The man's face had become his own. He blinked but the image held. It was him. He was the captive.

What the hell? Why hadn't she drawn this last night? He remembered Zoe dropping her pencil, her eyes wide with fear as she said 'no'.

Impatiently, he shook the note open.

Hi Finn,

I'm so sorry to run out on you like this but I don't know how to tell you what I need to say. The dream I had last night was about you. What I told you about my dreams was true. I do have to draw them to make them go away but I didn't finish this drawing. I realised it was you in the stone circle and I was so scared that I stopped. I think I hoped if I didn't draw it, it wouldn't be real.

But it is, or at least, it will be. You see (and this is the really freaky bit) I seem to be able to draw the future. I don't expect you'll believe me – I hardly believe it myself – but it happens. It used to be just family things, like dreaming about my sister with a baby before I knew she was pregnant, but since I came to Glastonbury it's got seriously weird. I've had one of these dreams every night and they've all been about you.

I didn't see you in the garden on Sunday night. I dreamt about you and drew you on Saturday night. I couldn't tell you. So I lied when you asked me, said I'd seen you out of the window. I'm only telling you now because I'm scared for you.

I'm sorry that I don't know who the hooded figure is. But if there's any possibility that this dream will happen then I have no choice but to tell you that you're in danger.

I know this sounds completely crazy. Thanks for the bed and for being so sweet last night.

Stay safe

Zoe

Finn's eyes flicked back to the drawing, his mouth

hanging open. It was a premonition. His heart began to race. It must be Maeve behind the hood. Who else would want to threaten him?

And it didn't look good. With his hands tied like that he was a dead man. And why did he look so bloody calm, almost like he was ready to die? He had to tell Winston. This was bad. Very, very bad.

He took two steps and froze. Zoe was a *seer.* He snorted. It was fucking unbelievable. Why hadn't she told him? Why had she thought *he* wouldn't understand? He shoved his fingers into his hair. After what he'd told her last night, shouldn't she have guessed that he'd accept this? Or, at least, given him a chance instead of running off?

Now he had to track her down, find out what else she'd seen. She said she'd dreamt about him every night since she came to Glastonbury. She'd arrived on Saturday. That meant there were another three drawings. He had to see them, find out how these dreams worked. Because he needed all the help he could get if he was going to get out of this stone circle alive.

He glanced at the clock again. If he left at half eleven he could still make it for lunch. He grabbed his clothes from the chair and headed for the bathroom. That gave him time to find Zoe, get her to show him these other pictures. If she had them with her. If they weren't at Anam Cara.

With his hand on the door, pieces fell into place. Zoe fretting about her portfolio, Maeve taking something large and flat from beneath the bed last night. Had Maeve seen these drawings? Did they reveal Zoe's gift? What if she'd left here to go back to Anam Cara to get her things?

His fist slammed against the door. "Fuck!" He'd not told her not to go. He'd been waiting until the morning to tell her about Maeve searching her room. Suddenly that seemed like eye-watering stupidity. Only he'd never imagined she'd just bloody leave.

He cast his mind back to what he'd seen last night. Maeve had sat on the bed for long minutes. If she'd seen the pictures – and it would be insanity to imagine she'd not - then, at the very least, she'd think Zoe had met him. Add that to what Maeve already suspected and Zoe could be in real trouble.

He needed to know what was in these pictures, what they revealed. Were they all as vividly prescient as this one? Because if Maeve had even the slightest idea that Zoe was a seer then she would crave her gift as ferociously as a vampire scenting blood.

Suddenly he was throwing on his clothes, stuffing his feet into his boots. He had to find her. He might be over-reacting. Maeve could be entirely too focused on finding him to be distracted. But after what she'd done to Cat – whose talent was far less extraordinary – and with Beltane only two days away, he wasn't taking any chances.

Snatching up his fleece, he riffled through the pockets searching for the scrap of paper with her number on. He swore when he remembered he still didn't have his mobile. Where the hell was he going to find a pay phone? He grabbed his keys, stuffed her note and the picture in his pocket and strode out the door.

Blinking in the sunlight, he pounded across the gravel to where he'd left the hire car. A grey-haired man, smoking on the picnic bench outside Kestrel Cottage, looked up as he passed and said, "Morning." Finn returned the greeting and then stopped. "Do you have a mobile I could borrow? It'll only take a minute and I'll pay for the call."

"Yeah, alright mate." The man took a phone from his pocket and offered it to Finn.

"Thanks." Turning away, he pulled out Zoe's number and keyed it in. His foot tapped as it rang. When she said, very tentatively, "Hello?" a huge swell of relief flooded through him that was immediately swamped by a wave of irritation.

"It's Finn." His voice was much sharper than he'd intended. "Where are you?"

"Oh, Finn! I'm so sorry. I don't know what to say. I..."

"Don't say anything. Just tell me where you are."

"The New Moon Cafe. On the High Street." She sounded confused and upset. He ignored that. He'd explain when he got there.

"I'll be there in ten minutes." He ended the call before she could argue. Giving the phone back to the man, he handed over a two pound coin. It was too much but he didn't have time to waste.

He spun the hire car out of its parking space and accelerated up the lane. Turning left he slammed his foot down hitting sixty in seconds. The arrow straight roads meant he only had to slow for the roundabouts on the A39. He ignored the thirty limit on Northload Street and floored it into the car park. Then he strode across the tarmac and down the narrow alley next to the church.

Just before he came out on the High Street he realised he'd forgotten to shield his presence. Pausing, he closed his eyes to focus his energy.

'Crap,' he muttered, realising he'd not asked Zoe where the cafe was. He scanned up and down - saw nothing that worried him - and figuring right looked more promising he headed down the incline.

The cafe was near the bottom, painted black with silver crescent moons around the name. He flung the door open. Her head whipped round as she heard the door open. She was chewing her bottom lip, her eyes pink rimmed as if she'd been crying.

She stood as he approached, her hands outstretched in apology. "Finn, I'm so sorry," she said. "I should have told you about the dream last night. I don't know why I didn't. And now you're mad at me..."

He didn't know what to say. The anger had evaporated the moment he saw her. He felt only relief. He needed her to know that. Putting his hand on her shoulder, he pulled her into an awkward one-armed hug.

Chapter 20

Stunned, Zoe stood there, her cheek resting against Finn's chest, her arms hanging limply by her sides. After she'd left the cottage she'd been convinced she'd never see him again. Then he'd rung, sounding furious and she'd been ready for anger. But this was….

Oh God! Her heart stuttered. *Was he doing this because Maeve was outside?*

Then his other hand was on her waist, pulling her closer as he folded around her and she knew instinctively that he meant it this time. Her arms moved, wrapping themselves around his broad chest to hug him back. She closed her eyes and the fear, tension and unshed tears melted away.

"Why didn't you tell me you're a seer?" he whispered against her ear.

"I'm a *what?*" Zoe pulled away to look up at his face.

His hands slid to her shoulders. "You're a seer. You see the future." He frowned. "Didn't you know?"

Zoe shrugged. "All I know is that I have these crazy dreams."

Finn dipped his head to look at her face. After a moment, she reluctantly met his eyes. His gaze was intense, his voice grave. "Don't ever say that. They're not crazy. They're a gift."

"Easy for you to say." Stepping back, she folded her arms.

"You'd be surprised. I understand more than you think."

"You do?"

"Yes." Finn scanned the room as he spoke. "Who else knows about your dreams?"

"Only my sister and my friend Anna. And they only know about the dreams of my family. I've not told them about the ones of you."

"And Maeve doesn't know?"

"No! Why would I have told her?"

"I thought not. But I had to check." Finn looked towards the front of the cafe. "What time is it?"

Slipping back into her seat, Zoe glanced at her watch. "Twenty to eleven."

"Bugger! We'll have to stay here but we have to move further back." He gestured to an empty table at the gloomy rear of the café.

"Okay but why?" Picking up her bag and jacket Zoe followed him.

"It's a bit more private." Pulling the chair out opposite he muttered, "It'll be fine so long as Maeve's still tucked up in bed."

"Oh no! You don't think.... I mean she wouldn't do anything here." Zoe gestured around her. "There's a room full of people."

"Which is the only reason we're still here." Finn plucked the menu from between the salt and pepper pots. He glanced at her. "Do me a favour, will you?"

"Sure," Zoe said and then bit her lip at her rashness. It didn't sound like a serious request but then you could never tell with Finn. What if he was about to ask her to do something she really didn't want to agree to? Like not seeing him again?

She'd cried when she left the cottage. Those tears had made her realise not only how far she'd fallen already but how scared she was. She didn't want her fear about what was happening at Anam Cara to drive her into leaving Glastonbury and yet, without Finn, the thought of remaining felt pretty damned terrifying. When the taxi dropped her in town, she decided to go to the hostel and ask them about cancellations. If there was a bed for tonight then she'd stay.

If not then she was heading for home. She wasn't quite sure how she felt when they told her there was a bed free in one of the dorms but she took it. When Finn rang she'd been trying to figure out if there was any way she could go to Anam Cara to get her things without seeing Maeve.

"Will you tell me when it's half eleven?" Finn asked, interrupting her thoughts. "I have to leave then. I'm going to Mum's for lunch."

"Where's that?"

"Lyme Regis."

"Isn't that, like, a really long way?"

Finn shook his head. "Only about an hour and a half."

"Oh," Zoe's hands rose to cover her slightly pink cheeks. "My geography is so crap."

"If I leave at half eleven I should make it. My sister has a thing about my timekeeping. She says *that's* crap. And as I've not seen her for....Well, let's just say it's more than my life's worth to be late."

"You're going to see Cat?"

"Yeah."

"You don't sound very thrilled about it."

He looked down, appearing to study the menu. "I don't know what I'm going to say to her."

"Why not?"

There was a long pause. At last, Finn muttered, "Because I let her down."

"No you didn't," Zoe said gently. "You got her out of Anam Cara. How is that letting her down?"

"But that's all I did." Finn dropped – with more force than necessary - the menu back between the salt and pepper pots.

She opened her mouth to ask what he meant but then seeing his jaw jutting stubbornly she closed it again.

Obviously there was more to it. She was trying to figure out her next question when Finn looked up, his face carefully blank, and realised that a pretty, blonde waitress stood next to their table.

"What can I get you?" The girl took a pen and pad from her apron, her attention focused entirely on Finn.

He gestured to Zoe. "What are you having?"

"I don't know. I haven't thought. I didn't feel like eating when I got here."

"Well, I'll have a full English."

To a non-meat eater it sounded surprisingly good. "Do you do a veggie version of that?" The waitress nodded, a little sullenly. "I'll have that then."

"And a coffee for me and a top up for Zoe," Finn said. She saw the waitress try, completely unsuccessfully, to catch his eye and bit back a smile. He looked very good this morning. The stubble and messy hair suited him. He looked rugged yet sexy as if he were about to climb a mountain or raft down a river.

And he was also – astonishingly after last night and this morning - with her.

Finn pulled the picture and her note from his pocket. Zoe's shoulders slumped a little. Why couldn't they just have breakfast and talk about normal things? The kind of conversation people had when they were getting to know each other, like where they grew up and what they did in their spare time. There was so much she wanted to know and there never seemed to be a right time to ask.

Finn gestured at the picture. "Are you alright if we talk about this now?"

"I'm *so* sorry about last night..."

Finn held a hand up. "Enough with the apologies, remember?"

She nodded slowly. "Okay."

He put the drawing on the table between them, smoothing the creases out with the side of his hand.

Frowning, he met her gaze. "I still find it hard to believe you dreamt this."

"You and me both," Zoe said, avoiding looking at the sketch. She hated the look on Finn's face. What could have happened to make him accept his captivity? Sitting opposite him now – conscious of the force field of confidence and determination that surrounded him - it was impossible to imagine him not fighting.

"What else can you tell me about this? Is there anything else - anything at all - you remember?"

"The only other thing was a voice. A kind of cry of triumph as it -" Zoe pointed to the hooded figure "- raised its hand."

"Did you recognise the voice?"

She shook her head. "It sounded a bit familiar but I can't place it. I'll keep trying. It might come back to me."

"Let me know if it does. It could be important."

She nodded. She didn't need reminding about why it was important. If she hadn't recognised that then they could have been having the kind of normal conversation she craved over breakfast at the cottage.

Finn hesitated and then pointed at the hooded figure. "I know the hands look like an old person's. But could you have got that wrong?

"I don't know. Once I've drawn the dream it fades, just like an ordinary dream. But if you think it's important then I'll try to remember."

"It is important. Because if it weren't for the hands I'd be one hundred per cent sure this is Maeve."

"No!" Zoe's hands flew up as if to push away his words.

Finn gave a tiny nod. "Yes."

"But why do you think it's her?"

"I can't think of anyone else who wants to kill me."

Zoe gulped, stared. "No," she repeated, willing him to be joking – a weird, sick kind of joke – but better than him being serious. “You don’t mean that.”

“Don’t look so worried.” Grinning confidently, Finn leaned across the table. “It’s not going to happen. Now I know what she’s got planned for me I’ll go in there prepared.”

“Oh my God! This is unbelievable. I never thought she wanted to -” her voice dropped to a whisper “- kill you.”

“Just because she wants to doesn’t mean it’s going to happen.”

“How can you be so calm about it?”

“It’s not a total surprise. I’ve known for...a while that Maeve would prefer me dead.” Finn took a deep breath. “But I’m not such an idiot as to think I don’t need all the help I can get, so if there’s anything else, if you know where this place is or when it’s going to happen...”

“I think it might be soon,” Zoe said quickly. Finn’s revelation about Maeve was making her head spin. At least talking about the moon gave her something practical to focus on. “Most of my other dreams, at least the ones that I’ve had since I’ve been in Glastonbury, have happened the day after I had the dream. So when I saw the moon” - she pointed at the picture - “I thought it might give us an idea of timing.”

Finn slapped his hand against his forehead. “Doh! Why didn’t I think of that?”

“I was trying to look it up when you arrived. I’d got as far as finding out it’s a waxing gibbous moon but as to when it’ll next happen…” She shrugged.

“From the look of this - ” Finn swivelled the paper towards him to get a better look “- I’d say it’s two or three nights before the next full moon. Can you find the date for that?”

Zoe picked up her mobile as the waitress appeared with a tray. Zoe’s latte spilled into the saucer as the girl plonked it down in front of her.

Stirring two sugars into his coffee, Finn said, “The

moon last night was only a couple of days shy of this. Which would make the full moon sometime in the middle of next week?"

Tapping her finger impatiently, Zoe waited for the webpage to load. When it finally did she scrolled down and said, "You're absolutely right. The full moon will be on the third of May."

"Making this..." Finn exhaled sharply. "I should have bloody known!"

"Known what?"

"Beltane."

"But you told me most of what happens at Beltane is harmless."

He pointed at the hooded figure. "That was before I knew you were staying with Maeve."

Zoe stared at him, her brain struggling to catch up. Then cold fingers of terror fastened around her stomach as his words made sense. She swallowed hard, trying to force down the sudden nausea and said, her voice a little shrill, "You don't mean it? We don't even know for sure that it's Maeve. And this could be any night." As she said it she realised it was ridiculous. She was trying to push away the fear, to avoid asking the really big question.

A ghost of a smile flitted over Finn's face. "Nice try but I'm sure. It's Maeve at Beltane." He stared out of the window behind her head. "Friday."

Sucking in a deep breath, she forced herself to ask the question that was making her stomach churn. "But why? Why does she want to kill you?"

Finn rubbed his hand over his face. "It's a long story."

In his eyes she saw, for a moment, the weight of all he was dealing with. "You don't have to tell me," she said hastily, surprising herself. Maybe Finn had been right last night and there were things it was better she didn't know.

"Thanks." He met her gaze, half smiled. "But you're in so deep you're going to have to know." The resignation in his voice surprised her. She watched him, waiting for him to say more. His eyes shifted to her phone, lying on the table between them. "Can I borrow your mobile? I need to ring Winston."

"Sure." Their hands touched as he took it and the same incredible tingle ran across her skin.

"Hi. It's Finn," he said. Zoe caught the echo of a deep voice. "Look, things are moving faster than I'd thought." She sipped her coffee and tried not to look like she was listening. She'd felt certain he was about to explain. Then, with another of his lightning changes of mood, the moment had gone.

"I've met someone who was staying at Anam Cara and she's..." There was laughter down the line and Finn broke off. He flashed a grin. "Yeah, she's right here. She's given me some really useful information. Maeve's using *The Seventh Book*.....Yeah, I know....Can you get your hands on a copy?" His eyebrows rose at something Winston said. He turned and walked out into the garden behind the cafe.

Through the open door, Zoe watched him pacing as he talked. What couldn't he say in front of her? He had so many secrets it was impossible to know which questions to ask first.

Returning, Finn handed the phone back. "Thanks. He's coming down later today."

"Oh, that's great." Zoe worked hard to put some enthusiasm in her voice. Of course, he would want his friend's help. Only the selfish part of her wasn't ready to share him yet. "What time'll he arrive?" she said, trying to figure out if she could hope to see him when he got back from Lyme Regis.

"It'll be late. He's in Glasgow. And even though he'll break every single speed limit on the way it'll still take about five hours." Finn put his hand on the drawing. "Do you mind if I keep this? I want to show it to him. He might see something in it that we've missed."

Zoe tensed, her eyes flicking to his face. She wanted to say no. She didn't like the idea of someone she'd never met knowing about her dreams. But if Winston could help keep Finn safe then she had no choice. "O-kay," she said slowly. "If you think it'll help."

"I'm sure it will." Finn leant back in his seat. "You know, it could be a huge help to us that you're a seer."

Zoe's shoulders hunched. "I wish you'd stop calling me that."

"Why? It's what you are."

"But I don't want to be."

"Sometimes we don't get to choose. We just are and we have to learn to live with it." Finn smiled ruefully. "Or at least that's what Padraig told me when I said exactly the same thing."

"But I don't want to learn to live with it. I want it to stop!" Zoe knew she sounded petulant but she couldn't help herself. "And why are you being so damned understanding about it anyway?"

"I have an idea what you're going through."

"How?" Zoe's hands flew up. "How can you possibly?"

"Like I said, I understand more than you'd think," Finn said. She opened her mouth to protest but he cut her off. "You said you have these dreams about your family. Have you had them all your life?"

"No. Or at least." Zoe looked away, sighed. She really wasn't comfortable talking about this. She felt exposed enough already. She opened her mouth to fob him off then her glance fell on the drawing of the stone circle and her concerns seemed insignificant. Folding her hands around her coffee cup, she stared into it. "The dreams started just before my Dad left. He and Mum were rowing all the time. I started having dreams of him on his own in a strange house. It was an awful place, almost derelict, paint peeling off the walls, that kind of thing. There were always huge abstract canvases in the background. Dad was sometimes painting but mostly drinking -" she paused, bit her lip "- or crying. I had the dreams night after night and after I'd had one I couldn't get back to sleep. I was exhausted. One night I was awake and I just started doodling on some paper. Next thing I knew it was morning. When I woke up I saw that I'd drawn the dream."

"How old were you?"

"Fourteen."

"Tough." Finn nodded. "I was twenty five when my parents finally called it a day. That was bad enough. When the dust settled and Mum was alright in her new place in Lyme I went travelling. Started in Chile and worked my way up to Alaska. Met Winston on that trip."

"I wish I'd had that kind of escape. Although I probably wouldn't have gone to Alaska." Zoe flipped her hair over her shoulder. "With hindsight I can see that my Dad had some kind of nervous breakdown. He was a secondary school teacher and he just couldn't take it anymore. He moved to a cottage in the Scottish borders, miles from anywhere. It was nearly two years before he'd let me visit. When I got there I had a really strong sense of déjà vu. Of course, I told myself I was imagining it." She stared at her hands as she remembered the confusion of her younger self. "I see now I'd dreamt about it, the house, his work, the whole thing." She paused, took a breath. "He's actually quite successful now. He had an exhibition in London in January. But he wouldn't even come down for it."

"You don't see much of him?"

"I go to visit once a year or so. Just for a few days. I always feel like he's relieved when I leave."

"Parents - who'd have 'em?" Finn's grin was rueful, yet understanding.

Comfortable silence spread between them. Finn broke it with another question. "How do your dreams work? Do you draw everything that happens or are the drawings the edited highlights?"

"It's kind of hard to explain." Zoe fiddled with the teaspoon on the side of her coffee cup. "Mostly it's just flashes of an image. But they're so vivid, like a clip from a film, repeated over and over until it wakes me up. Then I draw what's stayed in my mind. And when I've drawn it, it's gone."

"Have you tried to remember any more? To go back to the original images from the dream?"

"No, I've always just been pleased when they fade from my mind." She pointed to the sketch. "Some of them, like this, are terrifying enough when they're on paper."

"How long have you known you're a see...I mean, dreaming the future?"

"Since Sunday morning."

"Bloody hell! No wonder you're not over the 'it can't be happening to me' phase."

As he spoke the waitress slapped two plates down on the table. "Is there anything else I can get you?" she said, leaning towards Finn.

"Not for me," he said, giving her the briefest glance.

"I'm fine," Zoe said.

The plate was warm, the fried eggs and mushrooms still sizzling from the pan. But she wasn't hungry anymore. Reluctantly, she picked up her cutlery and scooped up a forkful of baked beans.

"What happened to make you work it out?" Discussing matters of life and death clearly didn't impact on Finn's appetite, she realised, seeing him wolf down his breakfast.

"You." Zoe waved her fork at him. "On Saturday night I dreamt about you in the garden. Then in the middle of

Sunday night, I got woken up by the tree exploding followed by the scream from Maeve's room."

"What?" Finn said, his mouth full.

"There was this really loud, high pitched scream. It sounded like she was in agony. In the morning she tried to convince us she'd seen a mouse but that was bullshit."

Finn grinned. "Don't hold back there."

"I won't. Not now you've told me what she's been up to." She gestured to her phone. "I've been trying to contact Tanya on Facebook. I don't have her mobile number and I just want to know she's alright."

"Don't tell her where you are!"

"I wasn't going to. I'm not a complete idiot." Zoe scowled at her plate, channelling her irritation into stabbing mushrooms. Chewing them, she kept her head down avoiding his gaze.

"Sorry. That was out of order," he said after a moment. Zoe raised her eyes to look at him. His smile was apologetic. "I'm honestly only trying to keep you safe."

"You know," she said, "It's hard to stay mad at you when you put it like that."

"And, what's more -" Finn's smile transformed into a grin, "- it's the truth."

Zoe looked down to hide a smile of pure delight. "When I think how Tanya trusted Maeve and how she abused that it makes me so bloody angry I could punch her."

"Hold that thought. She's done something else you won't like."

"What?"

"She searched your room last night."

Zoe's cutlery clattered onto her plate. "What? Why?"

Finn raised his eyebrows. "Do you really have to ask?"

"Then she knows about the doll and that I went in her office?"

Finn shook his head. "Suspects. I don't think she

knows for certain."

"But that's bad enough. How am I going to get my things? I can't go back there. Not knowing that!"

"I've got a plan. But it means waiting until later today. When I get back from Lyme."

"But what about my things? If she thinks I'm not coming back she might get rid of them." She snatched up her phone. "I should ring. Tell her I'll be there later to collect them."

Finn grabbed her hand. "You can't ring!" Zoe felt the tingle that always came when he touched her. She ignored it. She stared at his fingers, not saying anything, until he released her.

Finn held his hands up. "Sorry. I'm being an arse."

"I need my portfolio. Everything I've drawn for King Arthur is in it." Zoe's hands wove back and forwards as she spoke. "Everything else I can live without if I really have to. But I have to get my work back."

"We will get it. But it has to be later. I don't think she's going to get rid of it. She seemed to find what's in it far too interesting."

"What do you mean?"

"Maeve went through your portfolio last night."

"Oh my God! Then she's seen the pictures. The pictures from my dreams. They were in there." Zoe swallowed hard and put one hand on her stomach. The nausea had returned. "She knows that I've met you and that you're still in Glastonbury."

"Okay. Hold up," Finn said. "You need to tell me about these other drawings."

"They're all of you. In different places. In the garden after the tree exploded, I drew that on Saturday night. And later that night I drew you walking down the road into Glastonbury. Then on Sunday I dreamt about you on the Tor at night. And..."

"You drew me on the Tor?" Finn interrupted sharply.

"Yes."

His fist slammed onto the table. The plates and coffee cups rattled. "Fucking bitch!"

Heads turned towards them. Zoe leaned over the table, said urgently, "What is it? What's wrong?"

There was a moment of silence. His face was coldly furious. He sucked in a deep breath. When he spoke his voice had a hard edge of bitterness. "That explains how she knew where to find me last night."

Zoe gasped. "Oh no!"

"Yes." Finn hissed out the word. "After she'd looked at your pictures she headed up the Tor. I saw her coming and I... left."

"God, Finn!" Zoe's hands swept out. "I should have told you last night. I knew you were going up the Tor and I never thought about the drawing. If I'd not left it there..."

"Who persuaded you not to go back?" Finn eyes were intent on hers. "That was me. And I'm sure it was the right call."

"But if I'd just taken the dream drawings with me..." Zoe reached towards him, her hands hovering an inch away from his forearm. "I knew I shouldn't leave them lying around. I just never thought she'd search my room."

"Don't beat yourself up about it. You're new to this. We all make mistakes at the beginning."

"What do you mean? New to what?"

"I'll tell you later. Now eat." Finn gestured at her half full plate.

Zoe put her cutlery down. "I've lost my appetite."

"You can't let her get to you," Finn said. Zoe gave him a look that said *get real.* "And if you don't eat," he added. "I'll feel bad about telling you what happened last night."

Zoe sighed, picked up her fork and pointedly stabbed a mushroom. "Happy now?"

His answering grin was fleeting. Silence settled while

Zoe ate. Finn stared out of the cafe window. Then suddenly he said, “Do you think Maeve could tell from your drawings that you’re a seer?”

Zoe blinked. “I don’t think so. Maybe if she’d seen that one.” She pointed at the drawing on the table. “But the others I could have drawn after I’d seen you in those places. I suppose with so many pictures of you she might think I know you better than I did. Or at least, better than I did before we met last night.”

“You mean she’ll think from the pictures that we’re working together.”

She shrugged. “I suppose so.” Her thoughts had been running more along the line of Maeve believing that she and Finn were an item.

Finn tapped the drawing with his finger. “Do you think it’s significant that all the dreams you’ve had in Glastonbury have included me?”

Zoe focused her entire attention on cutting up her fried bread. “I don’t know.” She actually had a very good idea but she sure as hell wasn’t going to explain.

“And why’s this one the only picture with someone else in it?”

Zoe gestured as if to say *who knows*. Finn sat silently while she ate the last few bites. Laying her knife and fork on her empty plate, she glanced at her watch. “Just so you know it’s nearly twenty past.”

“Okay, thanks.” Finn looked around for the waitress and asked for the bill. Then he shoved his plate aside and leaned forward. “I want you to do something for me.”

Zoe’s heart sank at his tone. “That sounds serious.”

“I want you to go back to London. Just for the next few days until Beltane is over.”

“No way!” Zoe said, instantly forgetting that only a couple of hours ago she’d been thinking of leaving. However much she liked him she wasn’t going to let him change her plans. “I’ve got a meeting with the publishers next Wednesday. That's only a week today. And I'm still nowhere near ready. Camelot and Lancelot and Guinevere aren't finished. And the whole final battle is a complete blank." Her voice rose. "I've done what you asked and I left Anam Cara and now I'm in the lousy hostel for the rest of the week. But that's as far as I'm going."

Finn rubbed his hand over his eyes. "I thought you were going to say that."

"Then why did you ask?"

"Because it'd be safer for you not to be in Glastonbury for the next few days. We know Maeve suspects you of taking the doll and -" Finn hesitated "- let's face it, the reason you took it is so damned unlikely…"

"Thanks," Zoe said dryly.

Finn ignored the interruption. "…that she's bound to think you had a better reason, one that's more of a threat to her."

"That's total guesswork."

Finn raised an eyebrow. "Not completely."

"Then you're going to have to explain this because you've still not told me why the doll's so important to Maeve or why you think it's not safe for me to be here."

"There's no time to tell you now."

"So will you tell me later?"

"Yes- " Finn raised his hand "- if you'll promise me one thing?"

Zoe's eyes narrowed. "What?"

"Will you get out of Glastonbury for today? I'd ask you to come with me but I've not been home in six months and Cat's still pretty fragile." A flicker of pain passed over his face when he mentioned his sister. "You're welcome to come for the ride if you want. Lyme's a nice place, kind of arty. I think you'd like it."

"You honestly think I'm not safe here on my own?"

"If you stay away from Anam Cara you'll probably be

fine."

"Only probably?"

"Yes."

Fiddling with her teaspoon, Zoe hesitated. The thought of a few hours in the car with him was very tempting. But she had a sense that this time with his family was important and she didn't want to intrude, even as a passenger on the journey. And she had work to do. If she was ever going to be ready for the meeting with the publishers she couldn't afford any more distractions. "What if I went to Wells?" she said. "I was thinking of going there tomorrow anyway. The cathedral is supposed to amazing. Perfect Camelot material."

Finn took her hand. The tingle ran up her skin to her elbow. "I'd be happier if you were further away but alright. Just be careful and stay in public places. If anything happens that you're not sure about, anything at all, then ring me. I'll give you Mum's number as well, okay?"

"Okay," she repeated faintly, his worry for her safety inflaming her fears.

Finn picked up her phone with his free hand and held it out to her.

He dictated his number followed by his mother's and waited until she'd keyed them in. "I'll text you when I'm leaving Lyme."

The waitress slapped a saucer with the bill on the table. Zoe reached in her bag for her purse. She opened it and winced. She'd got ten pounds and some shrapnel. Would that be enough? She took the note out and put it on the saucer.

"I'm getting this," Finn said.

"No. You don't have to do that."

"Zoe, you've changed your plans for today because I asked you to. It's the least I can do." Pushing his chair back, he headed to the counter. She picked up her tenner and tucked it back into her purse. At least now she could afford lunch.

She heard the waitress laugh, turned to see her blatantly flirting with Finn, flipping her hair over her shoulders as she smiled up at him. Zoe's shoulders tensed. She fought back the desire to go over there and turned to stare out of the window.

Two women in their thirties in flowing skirts and scarves wandered past chatting animatedly. A couple with a baby in a buggy and a bickering toddler were followed by a middle-aged woman with hennaed hair. Zoe felt a sudden stab of envy. She didn't know what these people were doing in Glastonbury in the middle of the day but she guessed they weren't talking about people wanting to kill them in two days' time.

She glanced at Finn. He stood by the counter pocketing his change. He saw her looking and grinned. She smiled back before looking quickly away. *How did he do it?* He'd unfolded to her a world in which a woman who pretended to be a healer had kidnapped his sister, stole energy, controlled minds, wanted him dead and would threaten her if she went back to Anam Cara. So why did she feel so very safe with him?

Chapter 21

"Hey Cat! How you doing?" Finn said, opening the door to the conservatory. His sister lay on the rattan sofa, and despite the heat of the midday sun pouring through the windows, she wore a heavy, hooded jumper. A cream rug covered her legs.

He'd been prepared by his mother's words on the phone, and again when he arrived, but there was still a sliver of shock at how thin and ill she looked. Not quite as bad, he thought, as when he'd seen her last. A little more colour in her cheeks, a little more flesh on her bones but the hollowness in her blue eyes remained.

A tall, polished wood staff leaned against the arm of the sofa. The compulsion to reach for it was almost overwhelming. He knew exactly how it would feel in his hand, the sense of completeness that would flow through his veins as the staff connected his heartbeat to the pulse of the earth. Shoving his hands in his pockets, he stepped back. He wanted his Mum and Cat to believe he'd come to see them.

"Oh, Finn! You're here. You're really here." Pushing fine, blonde hair out of her eyes, Cat held a skeletal hand out to him. Then just as he'd feared, she began to cry.

Scanning the room for a box of tissues, Finn squeezed her hand and keeping his voice light said, "Come on, Cat. Anyone would think you weren't pleased to see me."

Spotting a box of tissues on the coffee table, he hooked it up with one finger and dropped it on his sister's lap. Stepping away he brushed his hand against his staff. The surge of energy, after so long without it, was like coming home. Tears sprang to his eyes. He bit down on his reaction, turned his face away.

"I'm sorry. I can't help it," Cat whispered. "It's been such a long time and I've had nothing to do but worry about you. There were times when I thought I'd never see you again."

"You can't get rid of me that easily." He looked out at the garden sloping steeply behind the house, glanced up as a black-headed gull screeched overhead.

Cat blew her nose. "What happened to you? Where have you been?"

"Glastonbury."

"I know that!" Frowning, Cat folded her arms. "But have you've been at Anam Cara all the time? Since the night you came to find me?"

Finn leaned his head against the window. "I was there until Sunday night."

"How did you get away?"

"I'm not entirely sure." He hesitated, searching for the right words. "I had help."

"Who from?"

Finn shook his head. He had no intention of mentioning Zoe. He knew Cat would seize on any mention of a girl and bug him with endless questions. "Not anyone you know."

"But it was someone with magic?"

Finn raised his eyebrows. "You could say that."

"Wow! That's amazing. You were really lucky. You could have been – well, you know..."

"Yes." His voice was grim. He knew exactly what he could have been.

"That night, the night you came to get me – what happened? Why couldn't you get away?" Cat leaned over the back of the sofa. When he didn't speak, didn't turn his head, Cat said, "I waited in the car like you said. The gate slammed and I started the engine thinking you'd be right behind me. But you didn't come. I kept watching the clock, thinking just another minute and you'd come."

Finn's shoulders sagged.

"Then the gate flew open," Cat continued, the words pouring out faster. "For a split second I thought it was you. But it was Maeve. She ran towards the car and I was so terrified I slammed my foot on the accelerator. I didn't think. I still don't know how I managed to drive – I felt so weak that night that I honestly didn't think I could - but I had to get away. And I didn't think of you and I didn't stay for you. And because of that she..." Cat's face crumpled as she mopped tears from her cheeks.

Finn scrubbed a hand over his face, blew out a long breath. This was what he'd been dreading. When the worst of the tears were over he pulled a chair next to the sofa. "You only did what I told you to do. I knew the risks." He glanced through the glass ceiling and swallowed hard.

He'd massively underestimated the risks. And Maeve. But he'd do everything possible to keep that knowledge from his sister.

Cat's hands, clutching crumpled tissues, dropped from her tear stained face. "You did? You knew before you came to find me that she's a spellworker?"

Finn's eyes narrowed, his jaw tensed. "Of course I did." Shoving the chair back, he moved to the window. "But after you'd gone I... Well, things didn't go entirely according to plan."

And that was the understatement of the century. He picked up a carved wooden apple from the window sill. Turning it over and over in his hands, he sensed the faintest memory of sap, the wood's remembered connection to the earth. Like a nicotine patch on a quitting smoker, it slightly calmed the twitch in his fingers, the insistent desire to hold his staff. "I got you away from Maeve and that's what matters."

“I’m so very, very sorry.” Cat spoke so quietly he barely caught the words. “You’ve been gone for very nearly six months. God knows what she’s done to you, what you’ve been through – I know you probably won’t tell me – and it’s all my fault. If I hadn’t gone to Anam Cara, if I hadn’t believed in Maeve and trusted her, then none of this would have happened.”

“You’re forgetting that Maeve controls minds.”

“But I should have realised,” Cat said. “When I think back, I can see that there were things that didn’t add up and I ignored them. If I hadn’t done that then you wouldn’t have had to come for me and none of this would have happened.”

Her eyes, brimming with tears, were fixed on him. He wouldn’t - couldn’t - talk about what he’d suffered, wouldn’t add to the guilt she already carried. “Stop it. It doesn’t help,” he said softly.

Cat’s fingers dipped into the neck of her jumper and pulled out a silver chain with a pendant on it. Recognising the stone as a black agate - supposedly a protection from psychic attack – Finn’s mouth tightened but he said nothing. If it helped his sister sleep at night, he wouldn’t be the one to tell her that against Maeve the crystal was as much use as a chocolate fireguard.

“You know, it’s a good job you’d given me your mobile. If it hadn’t had GPS I don’t know how Mum would have found me,” Cat said, picking up the story of that night. “I drove as far as I could. Then the adrenaline must have worn off and, all of a sudden, I was exhausted. I pulled over and rang Mum. I thought she’d be at home but, of course, she was in Melton. It turned out I was somewhere near Frome. She came to get me but it took hours and I was really frightened that somehow Maeve would track me down. Then Mum brought me back here. And -” Cat shrugged sadly “- I’ve been here ever since.”

Finn took a deep breath. He had to ask, however much

he didn't want to hear the answer. "But you feel better than when you left Anam Cara, right?"

"I suppose so. I was in such a bad way there that almost anything would be an improvement. It's just that I've got no energy. I can't walk any distance. I get tired when I stand up. I even get tired watching TV or reading a book. I've tried everything, all the therapies I can think of. You won't believe this but I've even been to the hospital. The doctors can't find anything wrong with me either."

Finn's eyebrows shot up. She must be deeply worried about her health if she was willing to put her faith in the medical profession.

Knowing she'd want to tell him in detail about her hospital visits – and the inadequacies of doctors compared to alternative therapists - he said quickly, "What did you tell Father about when you disappeared?"

"I said I went to Anam Cara because of the split with Andy - which is true. And I got ill when I was there and was too poorly to ring anyone - which is also true, just not the whole truth." Cat frowned. "Somehow, I'm not quite sure how, he's got the idea I had flu. For a long time he thought I was suffering from post-viral fatigue. Now he's decided it's depression." There was a pause. Cat shredded a tissue between restless fingers. "It's not, is it? It's because of what happened at Anam Cara? That's why I can't get better."

"Don't say *can't,*" Finn snapped. He'd lost six months of his life because he'd rescued her. He was damned if he'd let her give up on getting well.

"Call it what you like," Cat said wearily. "It amounts to the same thing. I'm still here and I'm still ill."

Finn perched on the edge of the chair next to her. He waited until she looked at him and said slowly, "You will get better." He would do everything he could to make it happen. But he needed Cat to believe it. Just in case he didn't make it.

"Oh God, don't you start." Pushing her hair from her face, she glared at him. "I've had enough from Mum and Father. I thought you'd understand."

"I do understand. But you have to fight it. You can't let Maeve win."

"What do you think I've been doing for the past six months? It's just I can't get away from it. Every time I go to sleep, I dream of her and that room and..." Cat's mouth twisted, her eyes filling with tears.

Finn plucked a tissue from the box, said, "Here."

"If only I could tell people what happened I'm sure that'd help. Father's sending me to a therapist. But how can she help me when I can't tell her what really happened?"

Finn returned to lean against the window. This was exactly what he'd been dreading. Cat didn't pull any punches. Whatever she felt she would tell him.

Maggie, his mother, had – so far, at least - spared him. He knew the reproaches and blame were there. They'd hung in the air between them, unspoken, when she'd released him after hugging him on the doorstep. Not that he'd defend himself when she did find the words. For six months she'd not known if he was alive or dead. She'd got one child back, only to lose the other.

Staring at the reflections in the glass, his thoughts returned to Zoe. Amazing that she'd only known she could see the future since Sunday. He understood now why she'd left the note this morning. He remembered the turbulence of trying to accept his own powers. It had taken months in Donegal with Padraig before he'd even started to come to terms with it.

There must be somewhere decent in Wells they could get a drink when he picked her up. A beer might help him find the words to explain. Because it was time. She'd told him her secret. Least he could do was reciprocate.

Obviously not with the whole truth. She didn't need to know what had happened that night at Anam Cara. But enough of Maeve's thirst for power for her to realise the potential danger. She'd seen enough, already guessed enough that what he told her would, he hoped, be just the final pieces in the jigsaw. He knew she could be stubborn – she'd shown that earlier when she'd wanted to take the bus to Wells - but that was only because she didn't understand the risks. Once she did she'd agree to go back to London.

"Where's my mobile?" he said suddenly. It must be nearly two hours since he'd left her in the car park in Wells. She could have been trying to get hold of him. And, as he knew, a lot could happen in two hours.

"I thought you'd want it so I brought it down with me." Cat slid her hand into the pocket on the front of her jumper and held it out to him. "I've kept it charged and switched on just in case you tried to ring."

Tapping in the code to unlock it, he said, "Has it rung today?"

"No. Why? You expecting a call?"

Scanning his many unread text messages, Finn said, "I wondered if Winston had rung." About to add that his friend was coming down later, he stopped himself. That was information best kept from Cat and Maggie. The less they knew about his plans for the next few days the better.

"You know Winston came here?" Cat said. "When he was in Glastonbury looking for you."

Imagining the state Cat had been in at that time, Finn's first thought was Winston deserved a bloody medal. Instead, he said, "He told me he'd been to Glastonbury but not that he'd come here. That was good of him."

"I told him everything I could remember, in case any of it helped with -" Cat gestured forlornly "- you know, finding you."

"Thanks," Finn said inadequately, slipping his mobile

into his pocket. The weight of worry Maggie and Cat had suffered pressed down on him. Trying to push it away, he asked a question guaranteed to fire a different set of emotions, "Where does Father think I've been?"

"Mum and I told him you got a great job working in Brazil on a rainforest conservation project."

"And he believed you?"

"Of course. Why wouldn't he?"

"Do you know how hard it is to get jobs like that? What the competition's like? And I have no expertise in rainforest habitats."

"Don't get all technical about it." Cat waved her hand airily. "Mum and I thought you should be somewhere that's really hard to get to and has hardly any telephones so he wouldn't be surprised if we didn't hear from you for months."

Finn turned back to the window. "Or at all."

"Don't say that. Mum and I always knew you'd be alright, that you'd get away from...her."

Picking up the wooden apple again, Finn resisted the temptation to remind her of her earlier words. Tossing the fruit from hand to hand he said, "You can say her name, you know? She's not Voldemort."

"Don't joke about it!"

Avoiding her eyes, he increased the arc of the apple's flight. "Where's Father?"

"Spain."

"Golf?"

"What else?" Cat hesitated, her eyes on her brother's face. After a moment, she said quickly, "Actually he's coming back today. He's taking me to the therapist tomorrow because Mum's got to work."

"Thank Christ I came today then."

"He's been really worried about me." Cat's fingers closed around her pendant and she pulled it back and forth on its chain. "He's been here a lot and he's been really supportive, taking me to the doctors and the hospital."

"Bet Mum's thrilled about that."

"Don't be mean, Finn."

"What's made you his cheerleader?"

"I'm not. But he's surprised me, that's all. And I think, maybe, what happened in the autumn might have made him realise what's important."

Finn raised his eyebrows but didn't push it. He hadn't come here to fall out with her. "So how's Mum been taking him coming round all the time?"

"She'd never say it but I know she hates it. She goes into a frenzy of cleaning before he comes, is icily polite while he's here and then goes for a long walk on the beach when he leaves."

He nodded, unsurprised. The clatter of plates came from the kitchen. Lunch must be nearly ready.

He gestured to his staff. "I'm going to need to take that with me."

"I know. That's why you've come."

"It's not the *only* reason I've come. I wanted to see you and Mum."

"Yeah, right," Cat said, twisting round to reach the staff.

"Have you had it with you all the time?" When he'd pressed it into her hand at Anam Cara he'd thought it was only for a minute or two. He shook his head. He'd been a bloody cretin.

"It makes me feel better," she replied. Finn smiled. He knew exactly what she meant.

Instead of holding it out to him, Cat folded her arms around it, her eyes suddenly wide with fear. "You need it because you're going back there, aren't you?"

He opened his mouth to deny it. The lines of tension etched on his sister's face, her red-rimmed eyes made him stop. If he didn't tell Maggie and Cat what was coming then he protected them from worry over the next few days but was that the right thing to do? Should he leave them totally unprepared if the worst did happen?

He couldn't lie to himself. Despite the confidence he'd shown with Zoe earlier, there was a chance, a not insignificant chance, that he wouldn't come back. That whatever he and Winston planned, with the foreknowledge Zoe could give, wouldn't be enough to stop Maeve killing him. If that happened he didn't want his family to keep hoping he'd make another miraculous return.

Sinking into the chair next to Cat he took her hand. "Yes. I'm going back. I have to finish this. Winston's coming down later to help."

Cat let the staff tip forward until it was within his reach. "You will be careful, won't you? Really careful. I couldn't bear it if I lost you again."

Finn's fingers closed around the wood. Pulling it from his sister's hand, he slammed it to the floor and the precious connection flowed through the staff, along his arm and into his heart. He felt the pounding of the sea against the shore a mile and a half distant, the tender roots of springtime burrowing through the soil, groundwater squeezing through fractures in the rock beneath his feet. Muted because it flowed to him through concrete and tile but present and identifiable and connected to him again.

Cat's voice intruded. "I'm serious, Finn! Promise you'll be careful?"

"Alright, sis. I'll be careful." Finn's tone was mocking. With his staff in his hand and the connection returned he felt euphoric, lightheaded.

Suddenly, he wanted to see his sister smile, to wipe the worry from her pallid face. Even if it was only for a minute. He still held the wooden apple. With the energy flowing through his staff, it was child's play. Grinning, he channelled a trickle of awen, enough to make the apple spin in mid-air.

Cat folded her arms. "And now you're just showing off!"

"So?"

"So I'm not impressed by your party tricks."

He knew that and it'd always pissed him off. She was one of the few people he could do them for. "Humour me, will you? It's been a long time."

With a flick of his wrist he sent the apple spiralling through the air to whirl above his sister's head. He tapped his staff on the floor and the apple broke into two pieces, white blossom cascading out of it, petals falling like confetti over her. With a quick laugh of pure pleasure, he caught the two halves, closed his hand around them and fused them back to a whole.

Then he looked at Cat. Tears were streaming down her face, sobs shaking her body.

"It wasn't that bad!" he said.

"It...it was beautiful." With shaking fingers she plucked petals from her clothes.

"Then why are you crying?"

"Because that's it, isn't it? The reason Maeve wouldn't let you go." When Finn didn't reply she added, "It's because of your magic?" Taking his silence for agreement, Cat leant forward, her hand clutching at his sleeve. "Then don't go back. Forget what I said earlier about -" Cat screwed her face up and spat the word out "- Maeve being the reason I've not got better. I was just feeling sorry for myself."

"Like that makes a change," Finn muttered. He knew it was harsh, knew exactly how she'd react. He didn't care, wanted only to stop her words, to halt the emotions they were triggering.

Cat drew away as if she'd been scalded. "I was going to say, if you're going back to Anam Cara for me then don't. But -" she folded her arms "- forget it."

Finn rested his forehead against his staff as his hands

ran reflexively up and down it. Eventually the sofa creaked as Cat turned to him. “I’m scared for you,” she whispered.

Rubbing his hand over his face, he fought the desire to make light of her worry. “It’s going to be different this time. I’ve got this -” he picked up his staff “- and I’m not on my own. Winston’ll be there and there’s a seer in Glastonbury who’s giving me some invaluable help.” He leaned forward, entirely focused now on making his sister understand. “I have to do this. Maeve’s still taking energy from people. I know most of them won’t suffer any permanent damage. But what about the next person who arrives there with a gift or who, like you, carries magic in their blood? Would you have them go through what you did?”

“No. Of course not.” Tears pooled in Cat’s eyes as she stared at her brother. “But that doesn’t make it your job to stop her.”

“Who else is going to do it? The Order’s gone.” Finn spun away to stare out at the garden. “It’s too late anyway. Even if I drop it, Maeve won’t.”

“Oh my God! Are you sure?”

Zoe’s drawing of the stone circle flashed uneasily into his mind. “One hundred per cent certain,” he said.

***

In Wells cathedral, Zoe frowned at her drawing of Lancelot and Guinevere snatching a clandestine moment together. The stone staircase that climbed from the aisle to the Chapter House made the perfect backdrop for the legendary lovers. Guinevere looked unattainably lovely in an exquisite dress. Lancelot exuded confident physicality in his chain mail, sword at his hip, helmet in his hand.

It was his face she had a problem with. She’d just

finished sketching it for the third time and he still looked exactly like Finn. Thinking some swear words she couldn't say in the house of God, she picked up her rubber and erased Lancelot's head.

Closing her eyes she took her mind back to Sunday afternoon, sitting in the sunlight in Glastonbury Abbey. The drawing she'd done that day came to mind. She saw Lancelot in bright armour, the effortless way he held his sword and his remarkable resemblance to Finn.

She shook her head. She must be remembering it wrong. Taking out a different softer pencil she tried again. This time she didn't bother finishing. The deep set eyes, the stubborn chin and the unruly hair showed she'd made the same mistake again. *Oh for f... heaven's sake!* She didn't normally have a problem remembering work she'd done before. Was she so infatuated that his was the only face she could draw?

Pushing tendrils of hair away from her face, she had to admit she'd thought of him a lot in the hours since they'd parted. Especially the moment after they'd left the cafe when - during what had almost become an argument about whether she should accept his offer of a lift to Wells - he'd said, "Why is it so hard to understand that I need to know you're safe?" She'd stared at him, wondering if he really cared as much as his words suggested. Then he'd grabbed her hand and headed towards the car park and she followed, stunned into temporary silence. She'd not even put up much of a fight when he asked her to stay in Wells until he could pick her up.

She hoped he'd be back soon. And not only because she wanted to see him. She needed her portfolio. She shook her head trying to chase away the fear sparked by the thought of going back to Anam Cara.

She had no choice. She'd made good progress today – inspired by the gothic architecture of the cathedral, Camelot was finally taking shape – but she couldn't manage without the work she'd already done.

Deciding she'd finish this sketch when she had the picture of Lancelot in front of her, she slid it into her pad and stood up. Stepping carefully on the worn, shallow steps she walked up the staircase she'd just drawn.

Chapter 22

Late afternoon shadows crept across the grass in front of Wells cathedral. Zoe sat on a bench with her back to the waist high wall surrounding the cathedral close. A little sleepy from her disturbed night's sleep, she ate grapes and Facebook messaged Tanya while she waited for Finn. He'd texted over an hour ago saying he was about to leave Lyme Regis.

It'd been half past four when the flurry of preparations for evensong distracted her long enough to realise she was starving. She'd wandered back into the sunshine, bought a sandwich, coffee and some fruit and eaten them in the garden at the back of the cathedral. Then she'd walked around its exterior, drawing flying buttresses and beautiful gothic arches until tiredness had caught up with her.

Her phone beeped again. Picking it up, she saw another message from Tanya. Zoe had started by apologising for not going back yesterday but Tanya had told her not to worry. She was a little better today, the throwing up had stopped but she still felt weak as a baby. Feeling like the least she could do was provide a distraction, Zoe had given Tanya a heavily edited account of meeting Finn. Tanya's latest message said, "*You lucky lady! Tell me everything. What does he look like?*"

Actually you've seen him, Zoe thought. He's the man you saw in the garden on Sunday night. The one Maeve convinced you wasn't there. Obviously she couldn't tell Tanya that so she settled for the typical girly reply of "*Gorgeous!*" She felt vaguely unsettled after she'd sent it.

She'd made it seem so straightforward to Tanya whereas actually there were so many complications, so many things he hadn't told her, that she'd absolutely no idea where to start with unravelling them.

Her phone beeped and she snatched it up. It was Finn wanting to know where she was. She'd expected that she'd meet him in the car park where he'd dropped her this morning and they'd go straight back to Glastonbury. This text opened up a whole other set of possibilities. Rapidly, she texted back. Then she felt breathlessly, giddily excited. She pulled her hair out of its ponytail and brushed it, applied a smear of lip-gloss.

Her phone flashed with another message from Tanya. "*When you seeing him again?*" it said. "*Now! I'll fill you in later*," Zoe sent back.

Trying not to look as if she had nothing to do but wait for him, Zoe kept her phone in her hands, scrolling through Facebook to catch up with what her other friends were doing, but unable to stop herself glancing up every time she heard footsteps. Reading her friends' posts made the unsettled feeling return. Their lives continued as normal – jokes, nights out, bad days at work – whereas her life had spiralled into something completely unexpected. What comments would she get back if she posted, 'Met a really great guy. Strange thing is I dreamt about him before I met him. Turns out I'm psychic! But that's not the weirdest. Now the woman who owns the B&B where I stayed wants to kill him!' They'd think she was joking. Five days ago she'd have thought the same.

A hand touched her shoulder. She jumped sky high as a voice she knew said in her ear, "Hey Zoe!"

"Where the hell did you come from?" she said, swivelling in her seat. Finn vaulted effortlessly over the wall, carrying a tall polished wood stick.

"That way." Finn pointed in the direction of the mediaeval gateway guarding the entrance to the cathedral close. He looked different in a blue shirt that brought out the colour in his eyes, smart indigo jeans and polished shoes. He'd shaved and his hair was almost tidy. Abruptly she remembered that she was wearing rather crumpled clothes she'd put on yesterday morning.

Zoe's hand covered her pounding heart. "You scared me."

"Sorry," Finn said, with a grin that was anything but apologetic and Zoe found her heart racing for an entirely different reason. "Why don't you let me buy you a drink to make up for it?"

"I thought we were going to Anam Cara to get my things," Zoe said as she stood.

"We will. Let's have a drink to get our courage up first."

"Alright, if you insist. The only problem is..." She fanned her hands out.

"What?"

"It's going to take a lot more than one to make me brave enough to face Maeve!"

Finn laughed. They walked across the square of grass in front of the cathedral, leaving the close through the gothic arch of another gatehouse. "What's that?" Zoe pointed to the stick in Finn's hand.

"It's my staff. My sister had it."

Zoe frowned. "What's it for?"

"I'll tell you when we get there." Finn pointed to a large half-timbered hotel across the market square. Zoe glanced up at him again. It wasn't just the clothes that were different. There was something more indefinable. A kind of confidence that made him seem – which was obviously totally impossible – even taller.

Finn opened the hotel's door and gestured for Zoe to lead the way into a low ceilinged bar. Other customers were talking quietly in suits and shirts relaxing after a day at work. "Red wine?" he said and she nodded. Returning with half of Guinness and a glass of red, Finn pointed at a few tables in a courtyard outside that caught the last rays of the sun.

"Good idea."

She followed him out. Only a few of the tables were occupied, a couple were having an intense conversation near the door and a lone smoker cradled a pint glass. Finn chose an empty table at the far end of the row. He pulled the chair out for her, held it while she sat. He's being very attentive, she thought, as he took the seat opposite and carefully propped the tall stick against the arm of his chair.

Almost as if this was a date. It can't be, she told herself sternly, trying to catch the hope that had taken flight. But it soared away, gleefully reminding her that he'd asked her for a drink, that he looked dressed for a date.

She stared down into her wine glass, fighting back a huge delighted grin. Finn took a gulp of Guinness before asking about her day. She found that she didn't have much to say as she couldn't tell him about her problems with Lancelot's face and she didn't want to admit she'd been in contact with Tanya. She quickly changed the subject and asked about his Mum and Cat. She could tell from the hesitations and way he shoved his fingers through his hair when he spoke of his sister that the visit had been as difficult as he'd expected. The highlight had clearly been lunch which he described with the relish of a starving man.

"Sounds like a real feast. Your Mum must be thrilled that you're home from New Zealand," Zoe said.

Finn tensed, his grey eyes suddenly cold. "You could say that."

Zoe frowned. *What now?* Why had her seemingly innocuous comment made him close up again? She considered pushing it, asking him directly why her words made him uncomfortable but she didn't. Just in case this was actually a date she'd keep it light, stay away from the difficult stuff for once.

"You're lucky," she said with a bright smile. "My Mum's a lousy cook. Fortunately her new man, Max, is really good and she no longer lives on Marks & Spencer's ready meals. I honestly grew up thinking St Michael was the patron saint of cooking."

Finn laughed, a warm, deep sound that sent shivers deep inside her. He took a sip of Guinness and then launched into a convoluted tale about him and Winston on a camping trip in Western Scotland that involved a Swiss army knife, two trout and an awful lot of whisky. And suddenly, effortlessly, they were having the kind of 'getting to know you' conversation that she'd been craving.

Before she knew it their glasses were empty. Finn asked if she wanted another one. "Dutch courage," he said and the spell was broken.

She shook her head. "I'd love to but I don't think I should. If I've got to face Maeve then I need a clear head."

"Right." Finn sounded distracted. His hand strayed to the wooden stick propped against the arm of his chair. He looked at her for a long moment, his eyes studying her face. "Before we go there's something I said I'd tell you."

Remembering what they'd talked about this morning Zoe nodded. "Why the doll's so important to Maeve?"

"Yes, that's part of it. But there's more to it than that."

She took a deep breath. This was finally it. The moment she'd been pushing for when he'd reveal the meaning behind all those cryptic comments. "I'm listening."

Finn leaned forward, his eyes on hers. "What I'm going to tell you will challenge some things you think you know but it will answer your questions. But you're going to have to keep an open mind. Okay?"

She thought she saw something that looked

surprisingly like apprehension in his grey eyes. "I'll try," she said slowly.

"When you said on Tuesday night that you thought Maeve was a witch you were nearer the mark than you realised."

"But I thought you said..." Zoe interrupted.

"I didn't say she wasn't," Finn reminded her. "She's actually much more powerful than a witch. She's a spellworker."

"A *what*?"

"It's a form of sorcery."

Zoe couldn't hold back a quick, humourless laugh. "Sorcery! Seriously?"

"I know it's hard to believe, that's why I asked you to keep an open mind."

"O-kay."

"When you took the doll from the tree and cut its bindings you broke a spell. A spell that was vitally important to Maeve."

Zoe shook her head as if to dismiss his words. "I don't get it. Why are you telling me this?"

"I want you to know what Maeve can do and why you're in danger."

"Is this about me leaving Glastonbury?"

"Partly, yes. I know you've got your work, but I thought about it on the drive back from Lyme, and you could go somewhere else connected with King Arthur. Like Tintagel or Caerleon."

Zoe looked down into her empty glass. "What you're really saying -" she said, trying hard to keep the hurt from her voice "- is that you don't want me in Glastonbury?"

"Yes, for your own safety." Finn leaned across the table. "We know from your drawing that things are going to get ugly and I don't want you caught up in that."

Her eyes flicked to his. He kept going on about her safety. So far the only reason he'd given for her not being safe was because Maeve was some kind of witch. But that would mean he believed that Maeve could hurt her with magic and spells.

"But witchcraft doesn't actually work," Zoe said. "I mean, I know that there's plenty of people in Glastonbury who believe in it and if you say the doll's important then I can see why me taking it would piss Maeve off. But not enough to want to hurt me."

"How do you know witchcraft doesn't work?"

"Because it doesn't. Everyone knows that."

"Do they?"

"Yes!" Zoe's hands flew up in her frustration. "I know people believed in witches and magic in the past but that was because they had no other way to explain the things that didn't make sense. But that was hundreds of years ago. We have science to explain those things now."

Finn shook his head. "So much for an open mind."

His words touched a nerve. She *was* open-minded but she wasn't a bloody fool. "I didn't know you were going to try to convince me to believe in witchcraft and magic. What's next?" Her voice rose. "You going to tell me that dragons exist?"

Finn looked away, his hand moving again to his staff. He drew in a long, deep breath. When he turned back, his face was tight with tension. "You see the future. That's a form of magic."

"It doesn't feel like magic," Zoe muttered. "Not to me."

Finn leaned closer. "But you believe in it or you wouldn't have told me about it."

"Only because I have no choice! Because I saw it with my own eyes and I couldn't deny it."

Abruptly Finn shoved his chair back. "Right." He walked across the courtyard to where a rose tree climbed a trellis against a white painted wall. Returning he said, "Hold out your hand."

"Why?"

Finn raised an eyebrow. "Just for once can you do what I ask without arguing?"

Zoe reluctantly extended her hand. On to her palm fell a small red brown twig with a leaf unfurling from it.

Back in his seat, Finn said, "What's your favourite colour?"

Unsure where he was going with this, Zoe frowned. "Purple. Why?"

"You'll see." Finn's hand enfolded hers. The familiar tingle came with his touch and then suddenly it intensified, became a pulsing warmth that soaked through her skin to the bone beneath. Startled, she looked at him. His eyes were closed, his other hand wrapped around his staff.

"What's happening?" she said, trying to pull her hand away.

Finn's grip tightened. "Shush. Hold still."

The sensation faded to the usual tingle she felt when Finn touched her. With a flourish, he lifted his hand from hers. On her palm lay a rose bud, its petals a rich aubergine. For a long moment, Zoe stared at it, her eyes wide with confusion.

"How did you do that?" she said, her voice cracking.

Finn grinned. "Magic."

"It was a trick? You had this up your sleeve or something?"

"It's not sleight of hand. This is the real thing. I channelled the energy from the earth through my staff to make the twig blossom. Then I gave it a bit of help with the colour. Do you like it?"

"It's beautiful. But I don't... I don't understand." Zoe's breath caught in her throat. She waved a hand in front of her face and swallowed hard. "I felt like a tingle on my skin that got warm, really warm, and then there was this." She picked up the rose bud between her thumb and index finger holding it at arm's length as if it were toxic.

"The tingle you felt was from the energy I channelled."

Zoe blinked at him. It felt like he was speaking an entirely different language. "What energy?"

"The earth's energy."

"You can channel the energy of the earth?"

"Yes."

"And that's what the staff's for?"

"It strengthens the connection. Without it, the energy I can access is limited. Although it's enough for small things, like stopping your drawings from falling in the river."

Zoe stared at him, eyes wide. "But I saw you catch them..."

Finn grinned. "Only because I'd stopped them first."

Completely lost now, Zoe shook her head. "I don't get it."

Finn rubbed his hand over his face. "What don't you get?"

"How any of this is possible!"

Finn was quiet for a moment, his eyes thoughtful before he said, "You've heard of the ancient druids?"

Still confused, Zoe nodded. His words conjured up images from the books she'd read about King Arthur. Pictures of men with long beards cutting mistletoe with a sickle. What had that got to do with Finn's impossible claims of magical powers?

"The power that I have is inherited from the ancient druids. There's not that many people still have it and it usually runs in families, mostly down the male line. Padraig had it. I inherited it from him. And Winston. He's got it."

"So you're telling me you're a *druid*?" Zoe spat out the last word.

"Yes." Finn smiled widely. "But I don't want you to confuse me with the people you see in white robes at Stonehenge at the solstice. They're revivalists and the term 'druid' is now associated with their form of nature worship."

"Oh my God!" Zoe dropped her head into her hands. She sucked in a deep breath. Then she looked up and said firmly, "Okay, joke's over now Finn. Tell me how you really put the rose in my hand."

Finn shook his head. "I'm not joking."

She stared at him. She recognised the signs; the tightness around his eyes, the jut of his jaw. So either he was far more of a practical joker than she'd realised or he was telling his own, totally screwed up, entirely warped version of the truth.

Desperately trying to think she let her hair fall forward around her face and closed her eyes. This couldn't be happening! After she'd almost begged him to tell her what was going on at Anam Cara this was what she got? A tale of witches and druids?

When she looked up, Finn's eyes met hers. She saw sadness in them as if he feared what she'd say next.

"You really believe this, don't you?" she said softly.

Finn leaned towards her. "I'm not insane if that's what you're thinking. And I'm not making any of this up. Maeve is a spellworker. She wants the magic in me, the connection I have to the earth. That's why she wants to kill me."

Zoe raised both her hands, palms towards him, trying to push his words away. "This is too much." Standing, she slung her bag on her shoulder.

Finn grabbed her hand. "Zoe, look at me." When she didn't he pushed on, his words rapid. "I know this is hard to accept. I know what I'm asking of you. But just think, will you? You've seen what Maeve can do. You've seen what she's done to Tanya. And remember how much the doll freaked you out? That's because you felt the power in it. You even picked up on what Maeve uses her altar for." His hand smacked down on the table, making the glasses quake. "Damn it, Zoe! I swear I'm telling you the truth."

Beneath the frustration, she heard a thread of desperation that made her drop her gaze to meet his. Slowly, emphasising each word, Finn said, "This is happening. In Glastonbury. And *you're* part of it."

She looked into his grey eyes. She knew he was serious, that he believed it. But just because he believed it didn't mean it was real. "Let go of me, Finn. I...I need..." She shook her head. "I don't know what I need.... except I have to be to be away from -" her hand swept in an arc that took in the rosebud, the wooden staff and Finn "- all of this weird crap!"

Finn dropped her hand, slumped back in his chair. She caught the hurt in his eyes before the familiar, bleak mask slid over his features. She turned and walked away.

Chapter 23

Maeve had always hated needlework. Forced to do it as a child, she'd spent endless hours turning out samplers, tablecloths and handkerchiefs. These days she only sewed to make poppets and hardly any of the skills she'd been forced to learn were used in roughly tacking the seams together.

Leaving a hole in the side of the little doll, Maeve turned it so the seams were inside and took down four canisters from the shelves above her table. She stuffed the poppet with sage and elfwort to increase psychic awareness, holy thistle to help find what is lost and tarragon to rejuvenate her purpose.

Then she opened her grimoire and took out the envelope. Carefully she removed the hair bobble and laid it on the table. Using tweezers Maeve eased the hairs away from the elastic, careful not to break them. She held the bobble up to the light to check she'd got them all and then, still using the tweezers, inserted the hairs into the centre of the poppet's body. A few stitches sewed up the hole in the doll's side. Maeve snipped off the lavender thread and picked up a black pen. Deliberately she drew large eyes, a pert nose and long flowing hair. The girl had a ready smile but she couldn't bring herself to reproduce that. Instead she drew a thin grimace of a mouth.

No one but her would recognise it as a likeness of Zoe. But then no one else needed to.

***

Zoe shoved the hotel's front door open and stepped out into the market square. Glancing over her shoulder, she was relieved to see that Finn hadn't followed her. Turning left, she quickly walked away. She checked her watch. It was just before seven. She needed a bus back to Glastonbury. She would go to Anam Cara to get her things and then she was going home. Hopefully tonight. She'd have to check what time the last National Express coach left Bristol. But if not tonight then definitely first thing in the morning.

Her feet sped up, she shoved her hair away from her face. She'd had enough. She wanted her old life back. She wanted a world in which no one believed in spells or magic or druids or seers. They'd been having such a great time. For once they'd been relaxed and having fun together and then he'd ruined it, telling her all of that crap about spellworkers and sorcery as if it answered all of her questions, as if he were letting her in on a big secret.

What kind of naive, trusting imbecile did he think she was? She bit down on her bottom lip as tears flooded her eyes. Why did she keep picking the liars and the crazies? She'd believed everything he'd told her about Maeve kidnapping his sister and controlling minds and stealing energy. Was any of it true? Did his sister actually stay at Anam Cara? Did he really go to get her in October? Could she believe anything that he'd told her?

She didn't know anymore. That was why she had to go home. Her world made sense at home. Maybe when she got back she'd be able to figure it all out, understand why she'd believed him and fallen for him. A tear slid down her cheek. She brushed it away, swallowed, sniffed. She wouldn't cry. Not here in the street. She wouldn't let him do that to her. She'd only known him since Monday. Only two days. When she got home, she'd see it for what it was. Just a holiday romance. Her stupid overactive imagination being captured by a handsome stranger.

But what about the dreams? Another tear fell. She chewed her lip to keep the others back. She'd thought the dreams meant there was something special between them, that he might be the one. Why else would she have dreamt about him before she met him? And what about last night, the dream of him in the stone circle? What did that mean?

She had absolutely no bloody idea.

Pushing her hair back, she stopped and looked around. Across the road from where she stood was a church with a tall tower. She glanced back, saw a green painted signpost and retraced her steps. One of the hands pointed the way to the bus station and she turned.

She soon found that 'bus station' was a rather grand title for a few shelters in a corner of a car park. Checking the timetable, she found she had a fifteen minute wait until the next bus to Glastonbury. There were a couple of teenage girls sitting in the bus shelter. They were gossiping animatedly about friends and boys and, after an initial disparaging glance, ignored her entirely.

Watching them, Zoe knew what she needed. She dug out her mobile and pulled up Anna's number. Please let her answer, she prayed as she listened to the phone ringing. Then her friend's voice burst down the line, "Zoe! How are you? How's Glastonbury?"

Zoe swallowed hard trying to shift the lump that had suddenly formed in her throat. "I'm okay," she managed to say.

"How's King Arthur?"

"Good. I've made some real progress. I'm actually starting to think I'll be ready for the meeting next week."

"That's fantastic! I knew Glastonbury would inspire you. And Maeve? Isn't she great? I told you she was just what you needed."

Zoe screwed her eyes up, took a deep breath. "Not exactly."

There was a moment's silence before Anna said,

"Why? What's wrong?"

"I met someone. Finn. I had a dream, one of the strange ones, about him on Saturday night. Of course, I didn't know it was him then. I just drew this really good looking guy. And then, when I met him on Monday I didn't recognise him straight away. I was drawing down by the river and he stopped my drawings blowing into the water."

With the memory came Finn's explanation. Her drawings caught on the wind, tumbling over, heading into the river. Then they stopped as if they'd hit an invisible wall. It'd seemed like a miracle. But Finn said he'd done it. With magic...

She forced the thought away and kept talking. "He told me all this stuff about Maeve. Crazy stuff and I believed him. I don't know why now. It was just that she wasn't anything like you'd said and I couldn't understand why everyone else loved her like you do but I couldn't get on with her. And she kept trying to force me to have healing and join in with the meditation and then I found this scary little doll on the Green Man's tree..."

"The *what* tree?" Anna interrupted.

"The Green Man. In the garden at Anam Cara." There was silence and Zoe added, "It was on the big oak tree near the wall. You couldn't miss it. It looked like a real face with hair and everything."

"I don't remember," Anna said. "You know you should have tried the meditation. I'm sure you'd have got something out of it. Maeve's got a real gift for making the sessions special. She knows just the right thing to make you relax and feel safe. It's almost like she's reading your soul."

God, it was just like talking to Helena! This was exactly the reason she hadn't rung her friend back sooner. "Well, anyway I met Finn again on Tuesday evening. I had another dream about him at the Holy Thorn and I went there hoping to see him. I actually bumped into him on the road and we...” She broke off wondering how to explain. She could hardly say, ‘he picked me up and swung me into the shadows so that Maeve wouldn’t see us together.’ Instead, she continued, knowing it sounded lame, “We went to the pub and then I stayed at his last night.”

“Really! Wow! So how was he?” Anna asked, with a smile in her voice.

“We didn’t. He... he slept on the sofa.” Zoe took a deep breath. “But then I had another dream and this one really upset me. He held me while I cried and I thought...”

“Oh Zo! That sounds serious,” Anna said gently. “What happened?”

“This morning, because he’d actually seen it, I told him about my dreams and he was really cool about it. And then he went off to see his family and he met me in Wells about an hour ago and told me all of this crazy stuff about -” Zoe broke off, she couldn’t tell her friend that Finn thought Maeve was a sorceress “- how he’s a druid and he can do magic by using the power of the earth.”

“You know that’s what I love about Glastonbury!” Anna said. “People just come out with things that no one would ever say in London.”

“No, it’s more than that. He *really* believes it. This evening he had this staff with him. It’s like a wooden stick that’s nearly as tall as I am and he says he can channel the power of the earth through it. And he put a leaf from a rose bush in my hand and something happened and when he took his hand away there was a rose bud.”

“Neat.”

“But it’s got to be some kind of trick, right? You can’t *actually* do that using the power of the earth!”

“Let’s not skip over the important point here. He gave you a rose.”

“So?”

"So he likes you!"

Zoe sighed. It didn't seem to matter anymore. There was a pause and then Anna said, "So do you like him?"

Zoe closed her eyes. "I did."

"Oh, Zo!" her friend said softly. "Whatever this Finn's done, you've got to remember he's not Gareth." When she didn't respond, Anna added, "All I'm saying is it wouldn't be surprising if you found it hard to trust again."

"It's not that!" Zoe said, her voice a bit too loud. Sometimes she found it just a little irritating that Anna - having met the love of her life and soon-to-be husband in fresher's week – thought she was so well qualified to give advice on relationships. "It's not me," she added, more quietly.

"Then what is it? So he's into druidry, it's not that big a deal."

"But he really believes in it. In magic and sorcery and I don't know what else..."

"Earth magic? That's part of what druids believe. That's why they go to Stonehenge at the solstice."

"He said he wasn't like them," Zoe muttered.

"What?"

"Nothing," Zoe said a little louder. She knew her friend was trying to help but she was just making her feel more isolated. Without telling her about Maeve how could she explain how frightened she'd been and that Finn had made her feel safe?

"How did you leave it with him?"

"I didn't."

"Do you want to see him again? Because maybe you just need to take it slow, find out more about what he believes. You said you told him about your dreams and he was cool with it. That's got to be a good thing."

"I don't know," Zoe murmured, tears choking her throat. "Right now I just want to come home."

There was an audible sigh before Anna said, "Why

don't you sleep on it, sweetie? See how you feel in the morning?"

Zoe brushed a tear from her cheek. She felt utterly exhausted, all those disturbed nights catching up on her. "I'll probably have to. I'm waiting for the bus back to Glastonbury now. Then I have to get my things." Her stomach clenched at the thought of going back to Anam Cara. "And I don't know if there'll be a bus to Bristol in time to catch the last coach."

"It's great that King Arthur's going well and it'd be a shame to rush home just because of this guy. I know Glastonbury can be a bit overwhelming but don't give up on it. You might feel completely differently in the morning."

Too tired to argue, Zoe changed the subject, asking Anna about her wedding plans. As they chatted the bus for Bridgewater pulled in. The teenage girls got on and with their departure the bus station seemed very empty.

When Zoe rang off, she saw she'd got a text from Finn. *"I'm on my way to Anam Cara to get your things. I'll drop them off at the hostel"*

She felt a brief flash of anger that he'd assumed she couldn't do it herself. It was immediately extinguished by relief. He was actually doing her a huge favour. Regardless of the fact that she no longer knew if anything he'd told her was true, she still didn't want to face Maeve.

Then she shook her head. If she'd needed any more proof that he believed everything he'd told her then here it was. He obviously thought he had to do this to protect her from whatever Maeve - the supposedly evil sorceress - had planned for her.

But that was insane. Okay, Maeve dabbled in witchcraft. That was the only way to explain the doll on the tree, the stone table, the leaves above the gate. But that was all. There were plenty of people in Glastonbury who did stuff like that.

But what about the Green Man? How did he disappear from the tree after the storm? And everyone getting ill after they had healing with Maeve? How did she explain that? Or the weird way Maeve had of getting people to agree with her?

She paced restlessly around the bus shelter. There wasn't any sensible explanation. She checked her watch. The bus should have arrived by now. Not that she was in a rush anymore. She was stuck until Finn dropped her stuff at the hostel.

And as the hope of going home disappeared, she knew why she'd craved it so desperately. What if again tonight she dreamt something that showed his life was in danger? How the hell would she cope with that? She couldn't have a freak out like last night in a dormitory with twenty strangers.

But it was more than that. It was Finn. How he'd reacted when she'd told him. That he'd understood. For the first time she'd found someone who accepted her dreams, who actually thought them valuable and important. She'd believed for so long that something was wrong with her brain. For a few wonderful hours Finn had made her feel that there wasn't.

Chapter 24

His feet pounded on the steps, his legs flexing and straightening as he powered upwards. His mind focused solely on movement, he tried to leave his thoughts in the shadows at the base of the Tor.

Breathing heavily, he reached the summit. He looked around, remembering last night. His hand tightened around his staff. His defence. Now he had it things were different. Tonight, he wanted to get Maeve out of Anam Cara - for long enough for Winston to pick up Zoe's things - and he was prepared to do whatever it took to draw attention to his presence here.

Propping his staff against the tower, he took the binoculars from his rucksack and surveyed Anam Cara and its garden. A light shone through the open curtains in the room next to Zoe's but he couldn't see any movement within. There were lights in the ground floor but the rooms he now knew to be Maeve's were in darkness.

His foot tapped out a rapid beat, his fingers drummed against the binoculars. He took them from his eyes and paced across the concrete surrounding the tower. Behind the town, the last rays of the sun sent fingers of orange light across the sky. The Mendip and Quantock hills had been absorbed by the night. Dusk stole the light from the Levels. Above his head, a three quarter moon shone. A reminder of Zoe's picture, a portent of his future.

Zoe. He didn't want to think about Zoe.

Instead he thought about Maeve, about what it would take to provoke her to leave. Of course, it was risky to offer himself as bait. He could live with that. It was better than what Maeve had planned for him.

Walking back to his vantage point, he looked again at Anam Cara. Nothing had changed. He swept the binoculars away and focused on the lights of the town on his right. She was down there, maybe at the hostel. Probably cursing him, doubting every word he'd said to her. He should have bloody known that she wouldn't believe the truth when she heard it.

He'd held it together until the door had shut behind her. Only then had his head dropped into his hands. When anger swiftly followed, his fist crashed onto the table. Her wine glass fell, smashing on the paving stones beneath. He'd sworn loudly and comprehensively. The couple at the nearest table stared at him, eyebrows raised. Standing, he picked up his staff. He intended to leave the rose – like him it had failed to make her understand – but at the last moment, he'd stuck it in his pocket and headed for the exit at the rear of the courtyard. Minutes later it hit him that she might head back to Anam Cara and he sent her a text. There'd been no reply. He hadn't expected one.

From below, he heard a powerful engine snarl. Striding across the flat top of the Tor, he looked over the steep side – close to where he'd thrown himself over the edge last night - focusing the binoculars on the road below. The single light of a motorbike flashed behind the hedges, the engine throttled back and stopped. Got to be Winston.

Ten minutes later, his friend appeared at the top of the steps. "Bugger me!" Winston puffed, leaning heavily on his staff, his Scottish accent smoothing the edges from the words.

"You want to cut down on the deep fried Mars bars." Finn stuck out his hand and hauled his friend up the last steps.

Winston's hair was as black as his leathers. He wore it in a ponytail, tied up with a leather thong. In his late thirties, half a head shorter than Finn, he was thinner with a wiry strength. His face was angular with slightly swarthy skin, dark brown eyes and a wicked grin.

Punching Finn on the shoulder, Winston said, "Too many hours behind the desk, that's what the problem is. Just wait, I'll be fit as a fiddle when I'm back in the field." An archaeologist at Glasgow University, specialising in the Neolithic period, Winston had directed digs all over Scotland.

"Yeah, right! All you do is stand there and tell the hot girl students what to do."

"That's how they learn." Winston grinned. "And in the interests of academic balance I should point out that they're not all girls. We have male students too."

"Surprised you've noticed!"

"Less of the cheek, McCloud! Five hours I've spent on the bike riding to your rescue. You said there'd be beer and curry when I got here and then you drag me up Glastonbury bloody Tor."

"Change of plan," Finn said. "There's beer in the fridge back at the cottage. But right now I need your help to get Zoe's things out of Anam Cara."

"Zoe's the seer?"

"Right."

"Why can't she pick up her own gear?"

"Because Zoe took the poppet from the tree and having no clue what she'd done she lied to Maeve about it..."

"Brave," Winston interjected.

"Yeah, she is that. Though she had no idea who she was dealing with..." Breaking off, Finn stared away into the night, his jaw tight.

"What happened to the poppet? Did Zoe give it to you? It could tell us how Maeve was strong enough to hold the spell for so long. Because even for a spellworker it was a powerful piece of magic."

Finn shook his head. "Zoe threw the poppet in the river. I got her to draw it for me though. I'll show it you when we get back to the cottage."

"That's a shame. It would have told me a lot more if I could have examined it. But I suppose it's better than nothing," Winston said. "Zoe can answer any questions I've got when I've seen the drawing."

Finn scowled. To give himself time to think, he reached his hand out and directed energy to his staff. It leapt the few feet from where it leaned against the wall of the tower and slapped into his palm. As his hand closed around it, he knew he wasn't ready to admit that Zoe wouldn't answer any questions. That she probably would never speak to him again.

"There's more to this, isn't there?" Winston frowned. "Some other reason Zoe can't go back to Anam Cara?"

Finn took a deep breath. If he got the explanations over with he could stop talking about her. "Last night Maeve found Zoe's portfolio and in it were the drawings from Zoe's dreams. The ones of me. At the very least, Maeve suspects we're involved. At the worst, she's guessed Zoe's a seer."

Winston whistled. "And the witch'd want that! Though not as much as she wants you. Although I suppose she might decide the seer's the easier target. She could take her and then come back for you."

Hearing Winston put his worst fears into words, Finn's hand tightened around his staff until his knuckles went white. It took a huge effort to keep his voice calm as he said, "And that's why Zoe's not going back to Anam Cara."

"Aye, I get that." Winston nodded. Then he added casually, "Just so I know, are you?"

"What?"

Winston raised an eyebrow. "Involved?" he said, making the word heavy with innuendo.

"No!"

Winston shrugged. "Only asking."

"Well, don't."

Winston stared at his friend's face. Then he hefted his staff and said briskly, "Alright! What's the plan?"

"I need to get Maeve out of Anam Cara long enough for you to get in, pick up Zoe's things – I'll show you which is her room – and get out. I'm going to have to be the bait. I'm the one Maeve wants."

"And before we do this you've checked Maeve's at home?"

"I've been watching the house. I've not seen her leave."

"We need more than that. You got the number?"

"We can't ring her!"

"I don't see why not. I'll do it. She might recognise your voice." Winston held his hand out. "You got the number?"

Convinced it was a bad idea, Finn scrolled slowly through the previously called numbers on his phone until he found it. He'd called it half a dozen times in October. He pressed the screen and handed the mobile to his friend.

"It's a good job I'm here," Winston said, putting the phone to his ear. "You're a bloody amateur."

"Taking out two vamps does not make you an expert," Finn said.

"Two vamps *and* a demon. You missed that one. Excellent fight. I..." Winston broke off and his voice deepened until he sounded like a young Sean Connery. "Good evening. May I speak to Maeve?"

Finn rolled his eyes. Winston had used his voice to reduce many women to putty but he was damned sure he was wasting it on Maeve.

There was a pause and then Winston said, "Oh, right. And who might I have the pleasure of talking to?"

Finn thought he heard a giggle down the line.

Definitely not Maeve then.

"No, thanks," Winston said. "That's kind of you but I need to speak to her myself. Do you know what time she'll be back?" He nodded. "Thanks a lot, Helena. Nice to talk to you. I'll ring again later."

Winston handed the phone back. "Time to go."

"She's not there," Finn said, feeling like a total idiot. What the hell had Maeve been up to while he'd wasted his time watching a house she wasn't even in? Winston was right. He was a bloody amateur.

"Apparently Maeve's out doing whatever spellworkers do in Glastonbury on a Wednesday night. Her Aussie friend didn't know what time she'd be back so we'd better get a move on."

"I'm going." Finn slung his rucksack on his back and shoved the binoculars at Winston. "You'll keep watch."

"Did the witch eat your brain?" Winston said. "I'm going in. She's never met me."

"But Cat said you came to..." Finn trailed off. He had to find words to thank Winston for coming to Glastonbury to look for him but it wouldn't be easy and this definitely wasn't the time.

"I did. But I never got past the gate. From the outside there was no sign of you."

Finn hesitated. It was the sensible option to let Winston go in. Only it didn't feel right. He'd got Zoe into this. He didn't like relying on Winston to get out her of it.

"Of course, if you want to play the hero for Zoe," Winston added, a grin spreading over his face.

"Leave it!" Finn said. He should explain that Zoe had walked away - if he didn't Winston would keep this up all night - but he couldn't find the words.

"Is that a no?"

In the hope of shutting Winston up so they could get on with this, Finn said, "If you want to go in there then by my guest."

"Excellent!"

"Okay. Let's move." Finn started towards the steps.

"Just one thing," Winston said. "If I'm going to risk my life to pick up this girl's luggage I'd like to know why I'm doing it."

Finn glared. "I told you."

"No, you told me what Maeve thinks. Not why getting Zoe's bags is so bloody important that you'd go back to that place and risk another face-off with the witch."

Finn's gaze dropped. "I ...I got Zoe into this. Or at least, she was in it before I met her but I dragged her in deeper."

"I see." Winston nodded. "Sounds like she's not the only one who's in deep."

It took Finn a second to catch his friend's meaning. Then his eyes narrowed. "Fuck off!"

"If you insist." Winston shrugged, took a step back. "But I've only just got here."

Finn shook his head. "Remind me why I asked you to come?"

"For my wit and wisdom. And because you wanted to let your mate in on the action!"

Finn's answering grin was brief. Zoe's drawing of the stone circle was bright in his mind. He could die on Friday, knowing that made it difficult to match Winston's enthusiasm. Instead, he focused on the job at hand. "Okay. We're going to take my car round to Anam Cara in case we need to make a quick exit." He'd left the hire car in Lyme and returned in his elderly, rather battered 4 x 4. Built like a tank with a diesel engine that did 0-60 in about five minutes he knew it wasn't designed to be a getaway vehicle but he felt safe in it.

"The bike'd be quicker," Winston said.

"Yes but you're the one going in. And if Maeve comes back and starts throwing light globes the car'll give better protection. Trust me. You don't want to be on the receiving end of one of those." Finn started down the steps as he spoke. "Anyway, we'll have Zoe's stuff to carry when you come out."

"I hope she packed light," Winston said, following him.

"As well as her bag, there's a portfolio. That's the most important thing. The drawings, the ones of me, are in there."

"I've never met a seer who drew her visions. That should make interpretation a whole lot easier. Seers normally talk in such generalisations that it's impossible to figure out what they're telling you. But having your Zoe around's going to be a huge help. Give us a real advantage."

Finn swung round, pointed the tip of his staff at his friend. "No way! We're keeping her out of this. It's too dangerous."

For a split second, Winston looked startled. Then he dropped one hand on Finn's shoulder and pushed past him. "Don't you think that should be up to her? I know you're out of practice with women so I'm going to give you some advice. They really hate it when you make decisions for them."

Scowling at his friend's back, Finn opened his mouth to tell him where to get off. Then he shut it again. What was the point? She'd already made her decision. She didn't believe him. That was the end of it.

He started running down the steps. "Come on!" he shouted as he barged past Winston. "I've seen arthritic grannies move faster than you!"

He heard a muttered curse, followed by the heavy thud of Winston's footsteps. Finn grinned fleetingly and upped the pace.

***

The hill fort was an ancient place, believed by some to be the site of Camelot. In daylight it held its mysteries close. In the night, it was an enigmatic rise in the landscape, a place that few dared visit.

A light globe illuminated the steep hedge lined path. Over her shoulder Maeve carried a black velvet bag. The lights of the village disappeared as she climbed. Darkness beckoned to her.

Coming to a gate, she passed through it and then turned. She needed to be sure she would be undisturbed. She raised her hand, said the words to create a shield that blocked the way.

The path opened out into a wide oval expanse, once a settlement of the ancient Britons. Its defences were grassy banks, encircling the hill. They kept enemies out and shielded the interior from prying eyes. That's why Maeve came. When she needed the additional power from casting out of doors, she could be certain she'd be alone here.

At the centre Maeve stopped. From her bag she took out her robe, put it on. Then moving a little to the north she paced out her circle. Salt marked the circumference. Candles were placed at north, south, east and west. Picking up her athame she pointed it at each candle in turn and they flamed into light. She placed the kindling she'd brought with her in the centre of the circle. Next to it she laid the poppet and her grimoire.

She cast the circle and called the fire into being. As the flames took hold, she opened the grimoire. Reading the words by the light of the globe above her head, she murmured the words to start the ritual, "Ishtar, Cerridwen, Innana, Shakti, Yoruba, Danu, Kali and Aine. I call on you to protect, empower and inspire my magic."

Then, telling the goddesses what she wanted to do, she held her hand in the smoke of the fire and sliced the athame across her palm. Blood surged. She closed her hand around the body of the poppet.

As her blood merged with the poppet she felt the goddess's power within her and knew the spell worked.

Chapter 25

Alone at a table in the courtyard of the hostel, Zoe stared into the bottom of her glass. The wine had done its job. Her thoughts had stopped frenetically spinning and the world had lost its focus.

A nightlight glowed in a jam jar on the table in front of her. Cheers from the bar – where football fans from a bewildering variety of nations were watching a game on the big screen - swirled out and joined with the chatter and laughter of the other hostellers. The noise didn't touch her. She was isolated in a bubble of her own silence.

Her phone flashed and beeped. She picked it up. A text from Finn. *"Your bags are at the front desk. No problems with picking them up. If you decide you want to talk then ring me. If not, then good luck. Finn."*

She closed her eyes, dropped her head into her hand. She'd hurt him. She could feel it in the words, the curt 'good luck' which meant 'goodbye'. The prospect of never seeing him again was suddenly terrifyingly real. He wouldn't contact her again. If she didn't ring him then that was it. Over.

Swallowing hard, Zoe took a deep breath and slugged down the last of her wine. She stood and then wobbled, had to grab the table to steady herself. She saw people looking, felt a blush rise to her cheeks and swung her hair to cover her face. Slowly, not hurrying in case she tripped over her feet, she walked towards the main entrance. Her bags were in the custody of the totally disinterested man behind the desk and she was soon heading for the dorm, rucksack slung on her back, portfolio tucked under her arm.

It was all she'd dreaded from a hostel, a large room, packed with metal bunk beds. Some of the bunks were already made up with sheets and blankets. One or two had people lying on them, reading or, headphones in, listening to music. Spotting an unoccupied bed, Zoe dropped her rucksack and portfolio on the floor and claimed the bottom bunk.

She pulled her portfolio towards her and slid open the zip. Quickly, she flipped through the contents checking if all her King Arthur sketches were there. Nothing seemed to be missing although they were in a different order. The drawings of Finn that she'd tucked away at the back were now on top. Did that mean Maeve really had gone through her portfolio last night?

Remembering how troublesome Lancelot's face had been, she flipped through the drawings again, thinking, at least, this was a problem she could solve. She tugged out the drawing she'd done on Sunday and rested it on her knees. Then she blinked, frowned. Lancelot looked like Finn. Admittedly he wore armour and his hair was a lot tidier but the resemblance was unmistakable. Which was as weird as hell because she'd drawn this twenty-four hours before she met him.

Forget it for now, she told herself. Look at it again tomorrow. As she slipped Lancelot back into the portfolio the picture of the Green Man fell forward. She shoved her hair out of her eyes and picked it up. She remembered now. He'd been her inspiration for Lancelot.

Then she gasped. The Green Man looked like Finn too. But he was suffering. His mouth clamped into a thin line, holding back pain or grief, the empty eyes haunted. She frowned, blinked and blinked again. The picture remained the same. The Green Man looked exactly like Finn. How was that possible? Why the hell would Maeve have a carving of Finn on her tree?

She shook her head to try to clear it. Feeling a little dizzy, she closed her eyes. It made no sense. Like so many things that had happened today it made absolutely no bloody sense. And she'd had more than she could take of this insanity. She wanted to lie down, close her eyes and sleep dreamlessly until morning when she could go home.

She shoved the portfolio under the bed and yanked open her rucksack. Something fell out. She bent to pick it up. "Oh," she whispered. She twirled the rose between her finger and thumb. It really was beautiful. The purple petals were softer than velvet, the scent as opulent as the colour.

How had he done it? How could he create something so gorgeous from just a twig and a leaf? He couldn't have known what colour she'd choose. Did he have roses in all the colours of the rainbow in his pockets ready to pull out?

She laid the rose on her palm, remembered the tingle and the heat she'd felt as his hand covered hers. Then, when he'd moved his hand away, the rose had been there. As simple and as utterly inexplicable as that.

***

On his knees, hands bound behind him, Finn watched from the centre of the stone circle as the hooded figure brandished the broken stick at the sky and screamed a torrent of meaningless words. With the movement the hood fell backwards and revealed a face. It was the face of a crone and that face was laughing.

The high triumphant laugh followed Zoe as she struggled through layers of sleep. She woke, skin drenched in sweat, heart thumping. Automatically she reached for the bedside light but her fingers found only air. Then she remembered where she was.

Except for a thin line of light around the blinds at the windows, darkness smothered the dorm. Rubbing her eyes, Zoe sat and reached down to pick up her sketchpad and pencil. Her fingers closed around the rose – resting on top of her pad - and she grabbed it too.

Not completely awake she walked, one hand extended to make sure she didn't bump into anything, towards the door. The corridor was unlit but from an un-curtained window came a thin grey light. Walking towards the window, she found herself in a kitchen. Switching on the light, she pulled a chair from the table and sat down.

For a long moment she simply twirled the rose between her fingers, brushing it against her cheek, inhaling its perfume. Then she reluctantly put it on the table, bent her knees, rested her sketchpad on them and closed her eyes. Immediately the dream sprang back to life and without thinking she started to draw.

When she finished she dropped the pad on the table, rested her head on her knees and curled up. She could feel tears, a hard ball trapped above her diaphragm. But she felt too scared to cry. The crone was back. She didn't need to look at the sketch to know that she'd drawn her again. She'd stalked her dreams for night after night in the autumn. Why the hell had she come back now?

Eventually she prised her head off her knees. She picked up the rose again, pulled her sketchpad towards her.

The crone wore the hooded robe. She held two broken sticks over the fire at the centre of the circle. Finn had got it wrong. It wasn't Maeve. She brushed a finger over his familiar face. The furrow between his eyes, the tension in his jaw made it look like he was concentrating hard on something. She frowned, peered closer. He held something in one of his hands. It looked like a thin bladed knife. Was he trying to escape?

He had to see this. Whatever she felt about him,

however confused she was, she couldn't keep this from him. Maybe she could meet him, for just long enough to explain about the drawing, before she caught the first bus out of here.

Only home didn't seem like a safe haven anymore. Because she'd drawn the crone before. In the autumn she'd had a string of bad dreams in the run up to Halloween. The drawings had so terrified her that she'd hidden them in the back of the wardrobe hoping she'd never have to look at them again. Only now she would have to because, somehow, it was all connected. And that made no sense at all. How could the nightmare figure from October be the person behind the hood?

Suddenly all she wanted was to see Finn, to tell him about the crone. She looked at her watch. Quarter past five. His text had said 'ring me' but she was fairly sure he hadn't meant at this time in the morning.

And if she did ring, what would she say? There was still all of the head-spinning stuff that he'd told her about druids and spellworkers and magic.

Could Anna be right? Had she over-reacted last night? She brushed her fingers over the rose's soft petals. Maybe. She'd felt the same stunned disbelief as when she'd found Gareth had lied to her. Had that made her reject Finn's words without thinking?

Did what he'd said about the earth and energy make some kind of sense? Lots of people believed in an innate energy in the earth and that there were places – Glastonbury, Stonehenge, Avebury – where it spilled over. That was why people flocked to these special – some would say sacred – sites. Would it really be such a huge leap to believe that Finn could somehow use that energy? Especially when she held something he'd created with it?

But what about Maeve? What about all he said about her? Could any of that possibly be true? She closed her eyes, thought of Tanya and Helena, the altar, the doll, the Green Man's face disappearing after the storm.

Abruptly the memory became crystal clear. Standing in the garden by the shattered wreck of the Green Man's tree and seeing that his face – the face that looked exactly like Finn - was missing. She'd felt it then. Something was going on at Anam Cara. Something that didn't - no matter how hard she wanted it to - make any kind of logical sense.

Which meant it had to be something else. Something outside of the world she knew and believed in.

Finn's words from yesterday, when she stood up to leave, leapt into her mind. She remembered his hand on her arm, the way his grey eyes had pleaded with her to understand, how he'd asked her to embrace the truth of what she'd seen and felt. But she hadn't. She'd walked away.

Shoving her chair away from the table, she almost ran back to the dorm and grabbed her bag. In the kitchen, she closed the door, dug her phone out and pulled up Finn's number. Her finger hovered over the screen. Was this the right thing to do or was she being completely crazy?

She looked at the rose and her finger hit the screen. Once she'd done it she knew it was a bad idea. About to cancel the call, she heard it ringing. Taking a deep breath, not sure if she wanted him to answer or not, she put the phone next to her ear and counted the rings. Finn answered on the sixth, his voice thick with sleep.

"Hi, it's... Zoe. I'm so sorry to wake you. I seem to be making a habit of it." She laughed unconvincingly. "It's just that I've had another dream."

"What?"

"It's about you. You're in the stone circle and the hooded figure, it's not Maeve." Zoe's voice rose. "It's this woman with a crone's face."

"It's *not* Maeve. You're sure?" Finn's voice

sharpened.

"Yes, I'm sure. But I've seen this crone woman before. I dreamt about her again and again in October. Do you think that's important?"

"Yes." She heard him yawn and then he said, "Are you okay? Because you don't sound okay."

"No." The word came out high and squeaky. Zoe screwed her eyes up, bit her lip to try to hold it together.

"What's wrong?"

"She really scares me. The crone woman. The dreams I had in October, I don't remember them but I know they were terrifying and if she's the person in the stone circle then that's bad, Finn. I just know that's bad."

"She's not going to hurt you."

"No, she's going to hurt you!"

There was a long silence then Finn said, "I thought you didn't care about that."

"Oh, God! Please don't say that. I just got confused..." Zoe gestured wildly. "Everything you told me… it was too much but when I had this dream I realised that I was wrong and I...I want to see you."

"Now?"

"I know it's ridiculous because it's not even light," she said. "But yes."

"Are you at the hostel?"

"Yes."

"I'll be there in ten minutes." The line went dead and Zoe stared at her phone. A grin spread across her face. Then she looked down, saw her pyjamas and dashed to the dorm to get dressed.

A little over ten minutes later, Zoe stepped out of the front door of the hostel wearing jeans, trainers and a purple hoody. Her portfolio was tucked under her arm. Silence cradled the town as the light changed, slipping from night to day.

Both the High Street and Magdalene Street were

deserted. No sign of Finn in his little red car. Restlessly she walked towards the market cross. After she'd paced twice around it, she made herself sit on the stone base. At the sound of an engine, her head whipped round. A big, blue off-road vehicle approached.

It slowed and then pulled up by the kerb. There was a man driving it. He looked like Finn. Then she was on her feet because it was Finn. He got out of the car and walked towards her. His hair was rumpled from sleep, his clothes looked like he'd fallen into them. She walked towards him and then her feet were running.

Suddenly he was there, his arms around her, pulling her towards him, holding her tight. Her hands slid around his back, grabbing handfuls of fleece to tug him closer. He cradled her head and stroked her hair, whispering her name. Her face was pressed against his safe, strong chest. She closed her eyes and basked in the moment.

Then he moved. She looked up, ready to step back but his eyes were on hers with a look that held. A slow smile spread across his face sending shivers of anticipation through her. Then his lips met hers. Gently at first, moving tantalisingly slowly then, as she opened her mouth, his hands pulled her closer as his lips became more urgent, more passionate.

And then there was another feeling, an entirely different sensation to anything she'd ever felt. It started where he touched her, spread from his lips, his hands until every inch of her skin tingled. As the kiss deepened, the tingling became more intense. Confused, she pulled away, looked up at him, frowning.

"What's wrong?" he said, his hand stroking her cheek.

"I felt the strangest thing."

Finn's face froze. Abruptly he let her go, stepped back. "I thought you wanted..."

"Of course, I did! I do! I've been waiting for you to kiss me for days." She stepped after him, grabbed his hand and returned it to her waist. "But there was this tingling feeling. It was just kind of strange."

Finn pulled her close again. "Are we talking good strange?"

"Definitely good." Zoe stood on her tip toes and brushed his lips with hers. "I've felt it before when we touched but then when we kissed it was all over."

Finn raised his eyebrows. "Really? *All* over?"

"Yes." Zoe giggled. This time the kiss started deeper, one hand locked in her hair, tilting her face to meet his. His other sliding down her back to pull their bodies closer. The tingle rose faster, seemed part of her body's urgent response, the desire that raced through her. When his lips moved to trail down her neck she found enough breath to say, "Definitely all over." The look he gave her made her heart beat faster and then his lips were on hers again and she forgot to think at all.

Passing footsteps made them pull apart. "If we keep this up someone's going to tell us to get a room," Finn whispered against her ear. "I've got one but unfortunately Winston's in it."

Winston. She'd forgotten all about him arriving last night. And if he was at Finn's then they definitely weren't about to finish – in his lovely, big double bed – what they'd just started.

"All I've got is a bed in a dorm so I vote for your place," Zoe said, reluctantly removing her arms from around his neck. "Except I guess Winston's not going to like being woken up this early."

"He'll get over it. He's dying to meet you. He's never met a seer who can draw her visions."

"Oh no! What have you told him?" Zoe's hands rose in agitation. "I'm *so* not a seer. My dreams don't even make sense."

"Shush." Finn brushed a finger over her cheek. "It doesn't matter. We'll figure out who this crone is." He gestured to her portfolio lying at the bottom of the Market Cross. “Is that coming with us?”

“Yes. I thought you’d want to see the drawings of all the dreams I’ve had since I came to Anam Cara.”

“We do.” Finn stepped away to pick up her portfolio and the tingling sensation disappeared, making her feel abruptly bereft. Opening the passenger car door, he slung her portfolio onto the back seat.

Zoe stared at the car seat, the bottom of which was at the same level as her chest. “Could this *be* any higher?” She put her foot on the ledge and grasped the seat to climb in.

“You need a hand?” Finn said. Before she could reply, his hand was on her bum boosting her up. Zoe lurched into the seat and had to grab the steering wheel to steady herself.

Face bright red, she turned to him. “I think you enjoyed that a bit too much!”

Finn simply grinned, slammed the door and walked around to the driver’s side. When he got in next to her Zoe said, “You were driving a little red car yesterday.”

“Hire car,” Finn said, starting the engine. “This one’s mine. Brought it back from Lyme yesterday.”

Zoe looked down. Her feet barely touched the floor, making her feel uncomfortably like a child. “This one’s built for giants.”

Finn laughed, the rich, wonderful sound that sent shivers through her. “You’ll get used to it. And I’m always happy to give you a helping hand.” He winked.

Half way up the High Street they turned down a narrow side road. “Thanks for bringing my things last night. I really didn’t want to go back to Anam Cara...” She broke off as a thought hit her and she blinked at her own stupidity. Had she really been so obsessed with her own problems that she’d not realised how dangerous it was for him? “But you shouldn’t have gone! What if

Maeve had seen you?"

"She was out. Winston went in, charmed Helena and came out with your stuff. All I did was sit in the car and keep watch."

"That was lucky," Zoe said quietly. Her reaction made her realise that she must have accepted that Maeve wanted to harm Finn. Glancing out of the passenger window, she added, "I'll thank Winston when I see him. I'm sorry I didn't text you last night to say thanks. I should have done only I....I had a bit much to drink."

"You're not the only one. Winston and I were up half the night. I was filling him in on all that's happened and we got through a lot of beer."

At the roundabout with the A39, Finn went straight across, heading down a lane that knifed across the flat fields of the Levels. Zoe was silent for a few moments watching low, bent trees and small fields flash past. There was something else she had to say and it would be easier when she didn't have to look at him. "I'm sorry I freaked out yesterday," she said, her voice low.

Finn glanced quickly at her before his eyes returned to the road. "That's okay. I told you too much at once. I should have realised that you'd need time to figure it out."

Zoe laughed a little hollowly. "Yeah, like a decade! But we don't have that kind of time. I figured that out after I had this dream. And then I remembered what you said yesterday and I realised -" as she strove to explain it, she understood what had really driven her to ring him "- that I've been scared ever since I found out that Maeve was looking for the damned doll. I know I don't understand much of what's going on but I do know that the only time I've felt safe is when I've been with you."

"That's good to know." Finn hand's reached over to rest on hers.

Moments later he moved his hand to change gear, turning into the narrow lane that led to the cottage.

Stopping the car in the parking space, he said, "You need a hand getting down from there?"

"I'll manage," Zoe said. She felt particularly ungraceful as she slithered out of the seat, clinging to the door frame. Luckily, Finn was busy getting her portfolio and his staff from the back seat so he didn't see her ungainly exit.

Meeting her at the front of the car, he wrapped his arm around her shoulder. Zoe peeked up at him. "Is Winston really going to be okay about us waking him up? I feel bad. It's only just after six."

"Let's get this straight. It's alright to wake me up at 5.20am. And at about the same time yesterday. But you feel bad about waking Winston?"

"Well, I've never met him."

"True. Just so I know, do you make a habit of this? Is being woken up at five something I need to get used to?"

A warm glow started around Zoe's heart and spread outwards. *He was planning on getting used to her.* "I promise I don't make a habit of it," she said, happiness bubbling inside of her.

"Good." Finn stopped, looked down and then they were kissing. Another long, hungry kiss that left them both breathless.

Holding her close Finn said, his voice low and husky, "You know, I could just kick Winston out."

Zoe laughed. "Maybe later he can go do something that'll keep him busy for a couple of hours."

Finn's eyebrows rose. "A couple of hours, heh?"

Zoe nodded. "At least!"

"Okay, let's get on with it." Finn strode towards the cottage. "Sooner we get this figured out, sooner we get the place to ourselves."

Finn's hand held hers and, laughing, Zoe found herself almost running to keep up. Reaching the cottage door, Finn hammered on it with his staff before he unlocked it.

"You decent, Grant?" he called, shoving the door open. "Because we've got company."

A deep Scottish voice said, "What the hell?" Finn stepped inside and Zoe, knowing how small it was, hung back to give Winston time to wake up. She glanced around her. Back the way they'd come, the sunrise turned the sky a pale orange and in the distance the Tor and its tower were silhouetted against the changing light.

Finn opened the curtains and the window before beckoning her inside. "Winston's in no fit state to meet a lady so he's scarpered into the bathroom. Come on, I'll put the kettle on. Do you want coffee?"

"Please," Zoe said. The tiny cottage had transformed since yesterday. Then it had seemed almost empty, an impersonal rented space. Now stuff covered every available surface. A collection of old books was piled on the coffee table, a laptop rested in the bottom of the armchair with papers layered on top of it. Panniers and a sports bag cluttered the floor. The kitchen surfaces were crowded with plates, take away cartons and empty beer bottles. There was also an unmistakable smell of curry.

Finn piled plates in the sink before filling the kettle. That suddenly seemed deeply incongruous. Weren't electric kettles a bit conventional for a druid? "Can't you boil water with the power of the earth?" she said, walking over to lean against the kitchen counters.

He studied her face, his eyes wary. "Is that a joke?"

Zoe met his gaze steadily. "I really want to know. I think, maybe, I'm starting to get that you're a druid. The rose helped." She smiled, a little ruefully. "It was a smart move to give it to me again. Because I finally realised that I'd felt the energy or the power that you used to make it. I don't understand how you channel energy from the earth but I'm starting to see that you can."

Finn took a single step towards her. Wrapping his arms around her waist, he pulled her close. His cheek rested on the top of her head. “Thank you,” he whispered.

Chapter 26

They were standing like that, not another word spoken, when the bathroom door opened. "Oh, hello!" Winston said, sounding like someone from a 'Carry on' film, and they sprang apart. Her cheeks burning, Zoe swung her hair to cover them. But then Finn was making introductions. "Zoe, this is Winston Grant."

Winston grasped her hand and, to her surprise, kissed her on the cheek. "Much as I could have done without the wakeup call, it's good to meet you. I've heard a lot about you."

"Good to meet you too," Zoe murmured, wondering what exactly Finn had said. Winston wasn't anything like she'd expected. In dark grey t-shirt and tight jeans with shoulder length black hair flowing around his face, he was very good looking in an edgy kind of way.

"And McCloud," Winston said, pointing at Finn as he walked backwards towards the bed. "Less smooching and more coffee making!"

Finn made a rude hand gesture at his friend before taking three mugs and a jar of instant coffee from a cupboard. "To answer your question," he said quietly to Zoe, "I *can* use the earth's energy to boil water but it takes a lot longer than a kettle."

"Oh," Zoe said, realising his answer didn't surprise her. "I guess that's kind of handy if there's a power cut."

Finn laughed and Zoe joined in. She saw Winston glance over at them. I'm changing their dynamic, she thought. It's a boys club and I've just barged in.

When the coffee was made she took a mug over to

Winston. He thanked her and she said, “I’m really sorry about waking you up so early. It’s just that I had another dream and I think it’s important.”

“Is it of Finn in the stone circle again?” Winston sat on the edge of the bed putting on his boots.

Zoe swallowed. It was hard to get used to the fact that someone she’d only just met knew about – and, even more amazingly, accepted - her dreams. “Yes.”

“Then you were right to call whatever the time.” Winston’s voice dropped. “And I’m glad you’re here because now he’ll stop fretting about you.”

“Fretting?” she whispered.

“Aye.” Winston winked. “Though he’d kill me for telling you.”

“Oh,” Zoe said, inadequately.

Winston took a swig of coffee. “It’s a good job he met you. Maeve can produce some seriously powerful magic and we’re in danger of being totally bloody outclassed. Even the two of us together. If your dreams can tell us what to expect then he’s in with a chance.”

“But it’s not Maeve,” Zoe said. “That’s why I thought this dream was important, why I had to tell Finn about it straight away. The hooded figure is this woman with a crone’s face.”

“I’m not sure that changes as much as you think. This woman – whoever she is – is almost undoubtedly a spellworker and she’s got it in for Finn. He’s never used magic as a weapon in his life. Goes against everything he believes in. I’m a wee bit more -” Winston gave a small shrug “- pragmatic about these things. There’s some bad shit out there and someone’s got to deal with it.”

Eyes widening, Zoe spun to look at Finn. Oblivious to her concern, he sat on the sofa flicking through a large black book as he drank his coffee. “Oh my God, I didn’t know....” Zoe trailed off. She felt *so* out of her depth here. The idea that magic could be used as a weapon was another thing that had just leapt out of the pages of a book. But the fear in Winston's words was unmistakable.

She hurried over and sat next to Finn. Unable to stop herself, she reached out and brushed his arm, needing to feel the reassurance that always came when they touched. Finn briefly glanced at her, a half smile warming his eyes. His fingers captured hers. He brought their clasped hands to rest on the sofa cushions and Zoe realised that the tingle had gone.

Puzzled, she glanced at him, squeezed his fingers but nothing changed. She was about to tell him but stopped when Winston moved the laptop onto the floor and sank into the chair opposite.

"You know, Zoe, I've met a few people who claimed to be able to see the future," Winston said. "Mainly they were a bit delusional but Finn says you're the real deal."

Zoe blinked. "Does he?"

"And from what I've seen of your picture of the stone circle, I'd say that he's not wrong." Winston leaned forward, his dark eyes watching her face intently. "So what else have you got for us, Zoe the seer?"

With a flutter of anxiety, Zoe unzipped her portfolio and took out a drawing. "This is the dream I've just had." She handed it to Finn. He studied it for a long moment and she saw his face harden with tension.

"Whoever this crone is she's not just got it in for me. She wants my staff as well." He passed the drawing to Winston.

Zoe gasped. Of course! Why hadn't she realised that the broken stick the crone held over the fire was his staff? His hand reached out to reclaim hers and she gently squeezed it, hoping to convey through that single touch all of her care and concern for him.

"That's not good." Winston picked up the thick black book that Finn had been looking at earlier and opened it at a page marked with a scrap of paper. "Aye, it's part of the ritual. It says the staff has to be broken in the presence of its owner."

"She has to have me and the staff in the circle to make this work?"

"That's what the book says. The ritual requires you and the staff at sunset at Beltane," Winston said.

"Alright," Finn said. "But how's she going to make me do it? Why would I give up my staff knowing it's going to be destroyed?"

"By the look of this -" Winston gestured to Finn's image in the drawing "- you're in no position to argue."

"True." Finn grimaced. "Do you think..." He broke off, looked down at Zoe and added quickly, "Never mind."

For a moment there was silence with both men seeming lost in their own thoughts before Winston said, gesturing to both of her drawings of the stone circle, "I know which of these you drew first, Zoe. But is that the order they're going to happen in?"

She shook her head. "I don't know. I'm sorry. I don't remember anything about my dreams after I draw them."

"But you remember dreaming of the crone?" Finn said.

"Yes. Back in October last year," Zoe said.

Winston's eyebrows rose. "When in October?"

"At the end."

"Around Samhain?" Winston said.

"He means Halloween," Finn explained.

"Then yes. I dreamt of this woman actually on Halloween because I remember thinking how bloody appropriate it was," Zoe said.

A look passed between Finn and Winston. "Why? What is it?" she said, glancing between the two of them.

"Maybe nothing." Finn smiled briefly but his eyes stayed tense. "Was that the night of Halloween?"

Zoe thought for a moment. "No, I was working at the

cinema on Halloween and it was a late one with a horror movie double bill and I remember thinking if anything's going to give me nightmares it's this. But then I didn't have any more of the really freaky dreams until I came to Glastonbury."

There was a pause. The guys exchanged another glance before Winston said, "You had other dreams about the crone around the same time?"

Zoe nodded. "I had a series of them. Night after night running up to Halloween."

Winston tapped his fingers on the drawing. "Did you draw those dreams as well?"

"Yes, of course."

"And did you keep them?" Winston said.

"Yes. I have a rule about throwing things out. It's stupid really but I started it when I was a student and couldn't tell good work from bad. So I keep everything unless it's obviously rubbish. These drawings were freaky as hell but technically pretty good. I shoved them to the back of the wardrobe and forgot about them until I drew the crone again this morning."

"It's lucky that you kept them. We're going to need to see them," Winston said. "They could be important."

Zoe looked between the two of them, read the identical tension on their faces. "There's something you're not telling me," she said quietly.

A significant look passed between the men before Winston nodded very slightly. "We think the crone could be Maeve," Finn said. "It'd be one hell of a coincidence if there were two women who want to kill me at Beltane."

"But the crone doesn't look anything like Maeve," Zoe said. "She's nowhere near that old." Unbidden the memory of Maeve's face, looking tired and almost elderly over breakfast and then startlingly rejuvenated only hours later popped into her mind. "Oh!"

"What?" Finn said.

"This might sound a bit crazy but could Maeve be using wi-" Zoe broke off. She knew it was silly but somehow she couldn't bring herself to say the word. Not in connection to Maeve "- erm, spells to change the way she looks?"

"It's okay to say it, you know." Finn leaned in, his voice deep and low as he whispered in her ear, "Witchcraft."

"It's alright for you." Zoe nudged him in the ribs. "You're a druid. Witchcraft and magic are part of your world but it's all new to me."

Finn grinned. "You see, you can say it."

"And I was asking a serious question before I was so rudely interrupted," Zoe said.

"You're wasting your time asking him serious questions," Winston said. "But I'll give you an answer. It's possible. Maeve could do that. Why do you ask?"

Zoe explained about the change in Maeve's appearance on Monday. Finn nodded. "That sounds like magic."

"I don't get it," Winston said. "No spellworker has unlimited power. Why would she use it to give herself a facelift?"

"Vanity?" Zoe said. "That's usually why women worry about their appearance."

Winston pointed at the hooded figure in the drawing. "Or because she looks like a circus freak if she doesn't?"

Zoe's eyes opened wide. "You're not really suggesting that without magic she'd look like that?"

"I don't know." Winston pushed his hair away from his face. "Maybe. At the moment all we've got to go on is your drawings. That's why it's important that we see these other dreams, the ones you had back in October. The more information we have the better prepared Finn'll be for what's going to happen in this stone circle."

Unable to argue with that, Zoe turned to Finn. "How

soon do you need to see these other drawings?"

Finn's fingers tightened on hers. "Soon."

Zoe sighed. "I was afraid you were going to say that." She glanced up at him, saw caution in his eyes, tension in his jaw. He thinks I'm going to argue, she guessed. But she couldn't. If the drawings from October would somehow help to keep him safe then she had to go home to get them. She knew without asking that Finn wouldn't agree to her coming back.

"Looks like you're getting your way after all," she said slowly. "I'm going home."

Finn studied her face for a long moment. "Whether it's Maeve or not in the stone circle I need to know you're safe."

"I know. I get that." Zoe looked down for a moment to summon up the courage for what she wanted to say. Flipping her hair away from her face, she peeked up at him. "But it's *too soon*." Fearing she'd said too much, she held her breath.

Finn didn't meet her gaze. "It's only for a few days. Until this is over."

That wasn't the answer she'd been hoping for. She wanted to know that he felt the same. She stared at her hands, wishing she could take her words back.

"Can I see the other pictures from your dreams?" Winston said.

"But Finn's not seen them," she said. They were all of him. It didn't seem right to show them to his friend first.

Winston's eyebrows rose. "Tell me when you're ready to share." Crossing to the small kitchen area, he muttered, "I need more coffee for this."

Zoe took three drawings from her portfolio and handed them to Finn, keeping back the one of him at the Holy Thorn. As forty-eight hours had passed since she'd drawn it she was starting to think that picture was nothing more than wish fulfilment.

Sipping her coffee, she nervously watched Finn's reactions. He studied the one of him on the Tor for a moment and then muttered, "I can see why Maeve knew where to find me."

He dropped that onto the coffee table and looked at the sketch of him walking through the rain on Saturday night. He put that down without comment, turned to the drawing of the garden after the Green Man's tree exploded. "I look fucking terrified."

"That's why I knew you weren't a burglar or an axe murderer." She hesitated before adding, "I still don't know why you were at Anam Cara on Sunday night."

Sitting close to him she felt his body tense, watched as his head turned away. "Because of Cat."

"But Cat was at Anam Cara in October. I know she's still really ill and you've been away in New Zealand but why were you there in the middle of Sunday night?"

There was a long moment of silence before Finn said quietly, "Let it go, Zoe."

She stared at his familiar features. What more was he keeping from her? Was it something to do with him being a druid, something that – after the way she'd reacted last night – he didn't think she'd understand?

Finn picked up her other two dream drawings, studied them again before slowly shaking his head. "It's one hell of a talent you've got, Zoe Rose. You have no idea how good you are."

Feeling a burst of pride at his words, she smiled shyly at him. She'd felt burdened by her dreams for so long that it felt amazing to know he valued them. Their gaze locked and Zoe forgot about dreams and doubts as she lost herself in Finn's eyes. The moment shattered when Winston plonked two cups of coffee on the table in front of them and picked up Zoe's drawings.

"They're remarkable," he said, after studying them intently. "There are records of seers having visions of this clarity but I've not heard of anyone in modern times with a talent like this. And because you're an artist it's all down on the page. Every single detail!" He picked up the latest drawing and glanced at Finn. "You're going to need a knife."

Finn nodded. "Looks like it."

"And you'll need to practice cutting the ropes," Winston said. "Make sure you don't slit your wrist in the process."

"I think I can cut a bloody rope," Finn said.

"With your hands tied behind your back?" Winston said. "If you drop the knife then you're..."

Finn's jaw tightened. Glaring at his friend, he interrupted, "I know."

Zoe looked between the two men. Recognising the tension in Finn's face, she knew he didn't want to talk about this. Picking up the two drawings of the stone circle, she decided to change the subject. "There's something I don't get."

"What?" Finn said.

"It's this leather thong around your neck." She pointed to it in each of the drawings. "I've never seen you wear anything like this. Is it some kind of talisman?"

"Let me see?" Finn said. Zoe handed the drawings to him. Winston moved to stand beside his friend.

"Beats me," Finn said. "It's not anything I own."

"It's a wee bit girly." Winston grinned. He leaned down to study the drawing more closely. "It looks like a piece of wood on the thong. Could be some form of protection but it's not anything I recognise."

Zoe looked up at him. "Do you think it's important?"

"Could be. But we need to know what it is first." Winston shrugged. "Add it to the list of things to find out before tomorrow."

Finn groaned. "Great."

"Time to fire up the laptop." Winston picked it up off

the floor.

"Have you got an internet connection?" Zoe said. When Winston nodded, she added, "Can you do me a favour and look up the times of coaches from Bristol to London?"

Before Winston could respond, Finn said, "I'm taking you home."

Winston instantly and vehemently opposed that idea, saying it would waste time they needed to prepare for Beltane. Zoe's immediate reaction was to tell Winston to butt out. The prospect of a few hours alone with Finn was unbelievably precious but then she remembered what Winston had told her. It'd take six, maybe even seven hours for him to make the round trip. Six or seven hours when Finn wouldn't be learning the skills he needed to keep himself alive.

Aware of Winston's gaze, Zoe turned to Finn and told him as gently as she could that she thought his friend was right. "I came on the coach and the bus. I'll be fine going back that way."

"Not the bus," Finn said. "At the very least, I'm taking you to Bristol and seeing you safely on to the coach to London."

Zoe couldn't argue with that. An hour or so together on the drive to Bristol wasn't much. It certainly wouldn't make up for the time she'd hoped they'd have today but, right now, she'd grab with both hands anything that delayed the moment when they had to say goodbye. From behind his laptop Winston shrugged as if to say 'whatever'.

"Right, that's settled then." Finn stood. "I'm starving. Who wants breakfast?"

He headed over to the kitchen area. Throwing open the fridge door he said, "I can offer you bacon and eggs. Or for the veggie, eggs and eggs."

Zoe laughed. "I'll have eggs then."

"Have a look at this, will you?" Winston gestured at his laptop. Moving to stand behind him, she saw a photograph of a stone circle on the screen.

"Is this the circle from your dream?"

"I don't think so." Zoe picked up her drawings and held them next to the screen. "The perspective's different so it's tricky to compare but I think the fallen stones aren't in the same places."

"Bugger. That was my best guess," Winston said. "I'll keep looking."

A few steps took her to the kitchen area. "Is there anything I can do?"

"That depends on how you want your eggs." Finn tossed a frying pan onto the cooker. "I can do fried or boiled. If you want anything else you're going to have to cook them yourself."

Zoe leaned against the kitchen counter. "I could eat a fried egg sandwich."

"Then the only thing I want you to do is stay and talk to me."

She smiled. "I can do that." Except her mind was full of the dark and deadly worries that Winston's words had created. Did Finn really not know how to use magic to hurt people? Was that something you had to learn? And why had Winston said it went against everything Finn believed in? She decided to start with an easy question and work up. "When did you know you were a druid?"

"When Padraig told me when I was fifteen," Finn said, dropping rashers of bacon onto the grill pan.

"He had to tell you? You didn't, like, just know?"

"I knew some strange stuff was happening around me. Electrical equipment had an unhealthy habit of bursting into flames when I got frustrated. I don't know how many calculators I got through. My parents stopped replacing my computers. Then, one day, I was having a row with Father and everything breakable in the room shattered.

That was the final straw for my parents. Father wanted to send me to a boarding school for troubled teenagers. Instead Mum packed me off to Padraig in Donegal. I thought it was some kind of punishment. Turns out she suspected what was happening and had sent me to the only man who could help me."

"Because Padraig was a druid too?"

"Yes. The first few weeks were hell for both of us. I was one angry kid. He had this habit -" Finn smiled affectionately "- of pulling objects out of the air. I thought it was some kind of stupid trick and I felt far too old to be taken in by kid's stuff like that. But when a tent appeared on the kitchen table halfway through dinner and he told me I was going on a camping trip I realised there was something else going on.

"He took me to a woodland about thirty miles from his house. There's not a whole lot of trees in Donegal. These were in a valley with a stream running down the middle. He left me with the tent and enough food for a week. Told me to learn about the earth, the water, the trees and what connected them. I thought he was raving. But when I started to feel the earth pulsing beneath me when I lay down at night I thought I was the one losing my mind. When Padraig came to collect me he asked me if I'd felt anything. It took me a while to come clean. When I did he smiled and said, 'All these weeks I've been thinking you were nothing more than a spoilt eejit. Turns out your mother was right, boy. It is in your blood. You're a druid'."

"Wow!" Zoe said. The word seemed massively inadequate but she couldn't think what else to say.

"That was the start." Finn broke eggs into the sizzling frying pan. "I went back every chance I could after that. The following year, when I was sixteen, I spent another week in the wood to choose my staff. That's a rite of passage every druid goes through."

"What happens?"

Finn shook his head. "Sorry. Can't tell you."

"Why not?"

"Because it's a secret druidic ritual passed down from the ancient Celts."

"Oh!" Zoe leaned against the kitchen counter and pouted with disappointment. The move had the effect she'd hoped for. Finn wrapped his arms around her waist and leaned towards her. The kiss was slow and lingering. "Nice try but I'm still not going to tell you," he said.

"You're no fun!" Zoe laughed, pushing out her bottom lip.

"I promise I'm *lots* of fun," Finn whispered against her ear, in a low voice that sent goose bumps across her skin.

Zoe giggled. "Ooh! I like the sound of that." *Just come back so I can find out.*

Stepping out of his arms, she sucked in a deep breath to dispel the panic. Why did Finn have to take on the crone anyway? She understood why he couldn't go to the police but wasn't there someone in his world he could turn to? Some kind of magical law enforcement that handled problems like this?

A few minutes later when they were sitting around the coffee table with plates balanced on their knees, Zoe said, "I know this might sound like a really stupid question but why do you have to deal with Maeve? Isn't there someone you can call on whose job it is to deal with druids and spellworkers who break the rules?"

Winston grinned. "You mean like a Ministry of Magic?"

"Exactly." Zoe nodded, surprised he understood. She'd thought Harry Potter was maybe a bit low-brow for Winston.

Winston shook his head. "No. Not anymore."

"There used to be," Finn said. "They were called The Order. A council of five druids and spellworkers elected to uphold our laws. If they were still around they'd have dealt with Maeve."

"So where are they?" Zoe said.

"They're dead," Finn said. "They all died on the winter solstice six years ago."

"Oh, how awful? What happened? Was it an accident or..." Zoe's eyes widened, her hand rose to her mouth. "No! Are you saying it was magic?"

"Yes," Finn said. "They all died in different ways. Two were apparently natural causes. Bryn Williams had a heart attack, Eve Penbury a brain haemorrhage. Nina Stewart drowned. Harry Field crashed his car into a tree on a road he drove every day. And Tamara Blythe, the newest and youngest member of the Order, just disappeared."

Surprised by the regret in Finn's voice, Zoe said, "You knew them?"

"I met all of them but it was only Harry that I knew well. He and Padraig went way back."

"And as we have no idea who did it or how it was done there's been a serious of lack of volunteers to form a new Order," Winston said.

"But why would anyone do that? Why kill all those people?" Zoe said.

"I have no idea. Even after all this time no one does although there's no shortage of theories," Finn said. "But that's the reason there's no one for us to go to. Why we have to deal with this ourselves."

"But you've never done anything like this," Zoe said. "Isn't there someone, anyone you can ask for help?"

"I did. He's right here." Finn glared at Winston. "And that was information he wasn't supposed to share."

"Too late, mate. Get over it." The Scot shrugged.

"So *you've* done this before?" Zoe said to Winston.

There was a moment of hesitation before he said, "Sure."

"And you can teach Finn how to defend himself?"

"Absolutely."

Zoe looked between the two of them. Winston winked at her, slumped in his chair as if he didn't have a care in the world. Finn leant forward, knees apart, hands resting on his legs. They looked confident. So why did she feel like they were suddenly conspirators? "There's something you're not telling me," she said slowly.

There was a moment of uncomfortable silence. Winston shrugged as if to say 'your problem, mate'. Finn nodded pointedly in the direction of the kitchen. Taking the hint, Winston picked up the empty plates. "I'll be over there doing the washing up."

"Winston knows what he's doing," Finn said. "He's faced evil and come out alive. He's going to keep me safe."

"But he said you'd never used magic to hurt anyone before, that it goes against everything you believe in." Zoe spoke low and urgently. "How long will it take you to learn? Is that what you don't want to tell me? That there's not enough time?"

He ran his fingers through his hair. "We've got time. Don't worry about that. When sunset comes tomorrow I'll be ready."

"Couldn't you just do it the easy way and shoot her before she gets to the stone circle?" Zoe said.

"Wouldn't that solve our problems!" Finn laughed briefly and mirthlessly. "But no, it won't work. Any half decent spellworker can generate an energy field that keeps them safe from bullets. The only way to stop them is to destroy that field."

"So how do you do that?"

"With magic."

Zoe thought for a moment and then said, "But once you destroy their energy field couldn't you shoot her then?"

Finn's eyebrows rose. "I didn't think you'd be a fan of firearms."

"I'm not normally but right now I'm keen on anything that keeps you safe."

"I can't fault that logic." Finn's smile was tight and weary. "But it won't work. If she were concentrating she could stop the bullets or worse send them back the way they'd come. The only sure way to defeat a spellworker is with magic."

There were lines of stress around his mouth, his eyes. She reached out and took his hand. "I know you probably don't want to hear this but I'm...*scared* for you."

"I know. That's why I should never have dragged you into this. If I'd walked away after we first met then you wouldn't be going through this now."

"Oh, don't start that again! If I hadn't met you on Tuesday night I'd have gone back to Anam Cara and who knows what would have happened."

"I can have a bloody good guess." Finn shoved his hand through his hair. "You're right though, it was too late. Your pictures make that clear. Even before we met you were in this. Right in the middle, dreaming and drawing and changing everything."

Zoe searched his eyes. Saw the fear she felt reflected back together with a softness that made her breath catch. "But I didn't have a clue what I was doing," she whispered.

Finn swept a strand of hair away from her face, his fingers lingering on her cheek. "Doesn't matter."

Chapter 27

Maeve woke to a persistent knocking. Opening her eyes, she said wearily, “Who is it?”

Helena’s voice came faintly through the door. “I’m sorry to bother you but it’s Penny. She’s ill. Tony’s really worried and he’s insisting on seeing you.”

Maeve cursed under her breath. She’d been desperate enough yesterday to ignore the potential complications of a concerned spouse. She’d intended to be careful, to limit the amount of energy she’d taken during the healing. Apparently she hadn’t been careful enough. “Tell him I’ll be down shortly,” Maeve said, climbing out of bed. “And come back in ten minutes. I’ll have an infusion ready for Penny.”

Walking to the window, she jerked the curtains open and sunlight flooded the room. She averted her gaze from the damage to her garden and stared out at the wide sweep of the Levels. By this time tomorrow she’d be far from here, ready to embark on her new life and these petty troubles would be forgotten.

Returning to the table she filled the kettle from a bottle of local spring water and switched it on. She stared for a moment at the canisters on the shelves. The infusion must revive Penny enough for her to leave. She needed uninterrupted space to prepare for the Beltane ritual.

Taking down three canisters - angelica to renew energy, borage to speed recovery and ginger to remove pain – she spooned the appropriate amounts into a mug. After pouring in boiling water, she reluctantly placed her hand over it to infuse the contents with a little of her own energy, just sufficient to have the desired effect. Then she left it to cool.

She walked over to the mirror, gazed critically at the wizened wreck of her face. She'd been doing this spell for decades. From tomorrow she wouldn't need it anymore. She'd be strong enough to permanently turn back the years, to restore the looks she'd lost to grief.

Placing the mug of infusion on a tray, she put it outside the door. Then she poured spring water into a silver bowl and cast a circle. Above the centre of the circle she suspended from a hook in the ceiling the poppet she'd made yesterday.

Speaking the words to invoke the goddesses, Maeve lifted the silver bowl and passed her athame three times over it deosil. Then she spoke the words of the spell, "Once, twice, three times by this blade by the mighty winds and the boundless sky, thrice do I charge this water to show me where she be."

Slowly, careful to avoid ripples, she raised the bowl until she saw the little doll reflected in the water. An image shivered into being behind the poppet's reflection. It wavered and clarified until it showed streets and stone buildings. Maeve smiled briefly. She recognised this place. The girl was in Bristol.

***

Finn bent to put her rucksack and portfolio on the floor and Zoe couldn't help but appreciate how fit he was. In both senses of the word! He'd carried her luggage during their dash through the streets of Bristol and was barely out of breath whereas she felt unattractively sweaty and red in the face. Not a good look when she was about to say goodbye to him not knowing when - or if - she'd see him again.

Finn slid his arms around her waist, pulled her into a

tight hug. “Well, we made it,” he said. It’d taken longer than they’d anticipated to navigate Bristol’s one way system and they’d had to run from the car park. Only to find when they arrived at the coach station that the National Express to London was ten minutes late.

With her head resting on his broad chest, Zoe felt the familiar tingling sensation creep across her skin. For a moment she simply enjoyed it. Then she tilted her head back to look up at him. “You’re doing it again.”

“Doing what?”

“Making my skin tingle when you touch me.”

Finn’s eyebrows rose. He touched his lips to hers. “Like when we kissed this morning?”

The sensation intensified and she giggled. “Exactly like that. But the weird thing is it’s doesn’t happen all the time. It went away when we were in the cottage.”

Finn grinned. “Are you sure you’re not imagining this?”

“Absolutely not!” Zoe punched him playfully. “It wasn’t there in the cottage or the car.”

Finn regarded her silently for a moment, his grey eyes thoughtful. Then saying, “Let me try something,” he took a step back.

“O-kay,” Zoe said, wondering where he was going with this.

“Has it gone?”

“Yes.”

Finn moved back and wrapped his arms around her again. “What about now?”

Relaxing into his embrace, she shook her head. “Still nothing.”

There was silence for a moment before he said, “And now?”

Because she was waiting for it she felt the tingle start where his body touched hers and then ease outwards across her skin. “It’s back.”

"Thought so." Finn smiled a little smugly. "You're feeling the energy from my shield."

"Your *what*?"

"Shield." His voice dropped. "You know I told you about spellworkers creating energy fields. This is similar but on a much smaller scale. I direct a pulse of energy over my skin and it keeps me hidden from other people with magic. I don't need it at the cottage or in the car because I've put other forms of protection around them."

"So without it Maeve could use magic to find you?"

"Yes."

"Oh my God! I had no idea... I mean I didn't realise you could use magic to do that." The increasingly familiar feeling of being totally out of her depth returned. While at the same time she felt a stab of panic at the danger he faced.

"I had no idea you'd be able to feel it," Finn said. "I'll have to ask Winston if that's normal. Last time I was in a relationship there wasn't any need for shields."

Zoe's eyes flicked up to his. "Relationship?" she said softly.

"I know it's not been very conventional so far but I thought... That is, if that's what you want?"

Zoe's face lit up. "Absolutely! Yes! That's what I want."

"You're prepared to date a druid?"

"If you're prepared to date a woman with crazy dreams!"

"You're a seer. And I'll risk it." Gently he traced a finger along her cheekbone. Zoe closed her eyes, savouring his touch and the amazing sensation creeping through her skin. "Do you mind it?" he said, his finger trailing down her neck. "The tingling?"

She shook her head. "Actually -" she glanced at the rows of waiting passengers and stood on tiptoe to whisper in his ear "- it's kind of exciting. If you know what I mean?"

Finn's eyebrows shot up. "How exciting?"

Zoe's gaze darted to the waiting passengers. "I'm not telling you here!"

"Later then? I'll ring you."

Blinking, Zoe nodded. He was being so damned normal. *W*ell, not exactly normal because their newly confirmed relationship didn't have a normal. But he was acting as if things were normal around them. As if he weren't in this life and death situation. As if they were guaranteed to see each again very soon.

She swallowed trying to force back the surge of emotions. She wanted to cling to him, beg him to be careful, tell him - in case she never got another chance – how much she cared. Only she knew instinctively that was the last thing Finn wanted. He was the one in danger. All she had to do was go home and wait. If Finn needed normal then she'd give him that. She could fall apart when the coach pulled out. Forcing a smile, she said, "Don't let Winston work you too hard!"

"I can handle him." Finn grinned confidently. "He's probably sent you a dozen emails with possible matches for your stone circle by now."

"He really doesn't get it that I don't remember my dreams after I've drawn them, does he?"

"He's relying on you. He's convinced you're our secret weapon."

"Oh, don't!" Zoe said, bowing her head.

He put his finger under her chin and tipped her face up. "We need your dreams. Without them we'd be completely blind."

"I know and I'll ring you," Zoe said, repeating the promise she'd made earlier in the car. "Only I'll try not to wake you in the middle of the night next time."

"That's probably for the best. I need my sleep tonight. I'm not going to get much tomorrow."

And there it was again. Impossible to get away from. Tomorrow night. When he might die.

Dread crept into her heart and Zoe wrapped her arms tighter around him. Instantly he responded, pulling her closer until her body pressed against his. Gently, his hand stroked her hair. "What you doing Saturday night?"

Zoe shook her head. She really couldn't think that far ahead. "I don't know. Nothing, I don't think."

"I was hoping you'd say that. Would you like to go out? I'll come up to London. We'll go somewhere fancy with tablecloths and wine lists."

"But, it's Beltane and we don't..."

Finn cut her off. "No buts. Do you want to go out with me or not?"

"Yes, of course I do."

"Then it's a date."

Zoe hastily blinked back tears. Not trusting her voice she looked up at him and nodded. Then standing on tiptoes she fastened her fingers in his hair and pulled his head down. After one delicious moment of anticipation Finn's lips met hers. The kiss was deep, passionate, loaded with emotion. Then they clung to each other, eyes closed, locked in the moment.

Suitcase wheels rattled, feet shuffled forwards as people around them started to move. For another second she clung to Finn, willing herself to hold it together, not to turn into a total teary mess.

Taking a deep breath she pulled away. The gate had opened. People were boarding. Finn picked up her luggage. Without meeting his eyes, she swung her rucksack on to her shoulder, took her portfolio.

Pulling her ticket from her pocket she said hurriedly, "Don't wait. I'll be okay from here. You don't need to stay and wave me off."

Finn nodded. "Alright. I'd better get back. See what Winston's up to."

She scanned his face, trying to commit it to memory. "I'll see you Saturday," she said softly.

Finn's hand slipped beneath her hair, cradled her face. "Saturday," he murmured. "I'll be there."

Turning, he strode down the concourse. When he reached the glass doors onto the street, he looked back, raised his hand. Biting her lip to hold back tears, she did the same.

Chapter 28

"I assure you I've done everything I can to ease Penny's healing crisis," Maeve said to Tony for what felt like the fiftieth time. The words were, of course, a lie. She could put back the energy she'd taken but she had no intention of doing so. She had the most important ritual of her life to perform tonight and her need was far greater than Penny's.

It was more disquieting that Tony's concern for his wife could override his subjugation to Maeve's control. No matter how slowly she spoke or how long she held his gaze her words were not having their usual effect.

"How could you let this happen?" Tony said in a vehement whisper, pointing at his wife tossing listlessly on the bed. "This isn't like any healing crisis I've ever seen. Look at her! She's in pain."

"She just needs a few hours sleep," Maeve said. "Give the infusion time to do its work and she'll fine."

"She'd better be!" He moved towards the bed and took his wife's hand. "Do you want me to stay while you sleep?" he said.

Deciding this was an opportune moment to make an exit, Maeve stepped hastily out onto the landing. Helena hovered there. "How's Tanya today?" Maeve said.

"She's doing much better," Helena said. "I've taken her some tea and toast."

"Wait here." Maeve rapped sharply on Tanya's door. Hearing a quiet 'come in', she swung it open. The room stank of sweat and sickness. Tanya sat up in bed, a pallid, greasy haired mess in crumpled pyjamas.

Maeve strode over to the window and threw it open. "Let's get some fresh air in here. It'll do you the world of good." Turning back to the bed, she smiled down at Tanya. "Helena tells me you're much better today. You can go home."

"I'm not sure I feel well enough. It's a long drive and I still feel really weak."

"Tanya." Maeve looked her in the eye and spoke slowly, emphasising each word. "You are well enough. You will go home today."

"Okay, Maeve. If you're sure."

Maeve smiled fleetingly. "Good girl. Start packing and I'll send Helena to give you a hand."

"Yes, alright. Thank you." Tanya dragged back the bedclothes and slowly stood. She took a tentative step forward, wobbled and put her hand on the wall. She glanced uncertainly at Maeve.

"Well done," she said absently, stepping around her guest.

Closing the bedroom door Maeve beckoned to Helena. "Help Tanya to pack. Make sure she leaves as soon as possible and don't listen to any excuses."

"No worries," Helena said. "I'll get her going."

Her breakfast tray waited in the office. Sipping earl grey tea, Maeve opened *The Seventh Book* at the marked page. Slowly she read and reread the steps necessary for the ritual until she felt certain she'd memorised it.

A little before noon she returned to her room and repeated the spell to ascertain Zoe's location. This time the image wavered, briefly coalesced into a straight road with many lanes filled with cars and lorries before breaking into shimmers of colour.

Maeve put the bowl down and perched on the edge of the table. Where was the blasted girl going? The spell could only reveal her current location. A little less than two hours had passed since she'd been in Bristol. She could be on any motorway within a hundred miles of that city heading in any direction. But if she waited until the girl arrived then it could be too late to go after her.

There had to be some way to find out the girl's destination, someone who knew where she might run to. Tapping her foot impatiently Maeve ran over in her mind what she knew about Zoe. She'd given a London address when she booked but it was unlikely that the girl would go home. If, indeed, that was her home. The thought of London triggered a memory of the girl's arrival and abruptly she had a solution.

Throwing open the door she called her employee's name. A few seconds later she heard the heavy tread of Helena's feet on the stairs. Before the girl reached her, Maeve said, "Find me a telephone number for Anne. Or was it Anna? I can't remember her surname. She stayed here a couple of times last year." About to turn away she remembered the girl's pictures. They'd been useful before. Possibly they'd provide some clue as to where she was going. "And bring me the portfolio Zoe left behind."

Helena's willing smile faded. "I can't. I'm sorry. It's not here."

"What do you mean it's not here?"

"Zoe's portfolio isn't here. A guy came to collect it and her rucksack yesterday evening."

Maeve stared at her employee. Then she held the door open. "Inside!" Shoulders hunched Helena walked past her. Firmly shutting the door, Maeve pointed to a straight backed wooden chair. "Sit."

"I'm sorry. You were out and the guy who came said he knew Zoe and she'd asked him to pick her things up and I thought..."

"Quiet!"

"Sorry," Helena mumbled, staring at the floor.

Maeve walked over to the mirror and, staring unseeingly at her reflection, struggled to control her fury.

That he would return to collect Zoe's luggage spoke of a confidence she hadn't believed him capable of. He must have known she'd gone out or he'd never have dared return. Zoe's picture of him standing on the Tor flashed into her mind. He must have been watching the house, waiting for his chance. But even then there'd been a risk. She could have returned at any moment. It didn't make sense. Unless there was something in Zoe's luggage – something that she'd missed – for which he'd take that chance.

"What time did he come?" Maeve said, without turning round.

"I guess it was about nine. I was watching TV and then the intercom on the gate buzzed and I thought maybe it was you, that you'd forgotten your keys or something. But it was the Scottish guy who'd rung earlier and he said he'd come to pick up Zoe's things."

Maeve spun to look at her employee. "Scottish?"

"Yeah, he'd got this lovely accent. Kind of like Ewan McGregor."

"What did he look like?"

"He was a good looking guy with dark hair in a ponytail."

Maeve was silent for a long moment. He had an accomplice. She'd not anticipated that. For a second she felt a stirring of something uncomfortably close to apprehension. Then she remembered who she was dealing with. Whether there was just the Scot or a dozen other druids prepared to fight beside him, it wouldn't matter if she had Zoe.

Helena broke the silence with a further stream of apologies. Maeve ignored them. After displaying such incompetence there could be only one further use for the girl.

With effort she modulated her voice and smiled. "You're leaving me after today and I want to give you something before you go. Find me that telephone number and then go to the treatment room. Relax and I'll be there in a little while to give you some healing."

"Oh, thank you, Maeve. That's really kind. I'll get that number for you right away," Helena said, edging out of the door.

Maeve took two suitcase from the top of the wardrobe and began to pack. From under the bed she pulled out the black leather bag that held her savings and zipped it closed. She must be ready to leave the moment she obtained the information she needed.

In her office she found numbers for two Annes and an Anna waiting on her desk. The first was delighted to hear from Maeve but didn't know anyone called Zoe. The second went straight to voice mail and impatiently she left a message. The final call was productive. A few plausible lies were told. The girl was very receptive and promised to call back when she had more information.

Leaving the house through the French windows, Maeve lit the four candles on the altar and took a moment to invoke the power of the goddesses. What she was about to do would ideally take place here but, with Penny and Tony still in the house, that was impossible.

She entered the garden wing and opened the door to the treatment room. Helena lay on her back on the therapy couch. She sat up awkwardly when Maeve walked in. "Relax, dear. This is your time," Maeve said, her voice low and soothing. Quietly she moved around the room, drawing the curtains, lighting incense, starting the nauseating New Age music, placing a blanket over Helena's plump body.

"Now I want you to imagine you're filled with light," Maeve said, placing her hands on Helena's heart and throat chakras. Immediately the girl's aura sprang into focus, a dirty brown layer of insecurity overlaying it. She swept that away. Beneath was the muddied red of repressed anger, orange for addiction and a surprising streak of turquoise indicating a talent for healing.

Maeve closed her eyes and allowed the energy from the aura to flow into her. Calm stole over her and she pulled more deeply, sucking the last drops from the body beneath her hands. Helena started to writhe. Her breathing laboured, she begged Maeve to stop.

Moving her other hand to the girl's throat, Maeve pressed down on the trachea, choking off words and breath. The girl clawed at her grip but she exerted more pressure. Very soon the struggles ceased.

As she usually did at the end of a healing Maeve washed her hands and silenced the music with a flick of a switch. Mechanically she began to fold the blanket but then stopped herself and pulled it over Helena's bulging eyes.

Disposing of the corpse was the most tiresome part of killing. She didn't have time to dig a grave. She could leave the body here. She'd be living a new life by the time it was found. But the police would undoubtedly be called and that could lead to complications.

As she blew out the incense a thought occurred. At midnight it would be Beltane. The festival of fire. Nothing cleansed and destroyed like fire.

Chapter 29

Grateful to be at home after hours of travelling, Zoe closed the front door. The final leg of the journey by tube had been over-crowded, unfriendly and a little grimy. A lot like the way London seemed after Glastonbury.

Dumping her bags at the bottom of the stairs, she headed through the lounge to the kitchen. While she waited for the kettle to boil she made a couple of slices of toast. It was a very long time since breakfast and she was starving. The memory of Finn cooking eggs made her smile briefly before the fear returned, settling over her like a suffocating blanket.

Desperate to do something, however little, to help she'd spent the coach journey hunched over the screen of her mobile searching for photographs of stone circles. As they'd reached the M25 she'd found a picture of the Nine Maidens in Devon, which looked almost exactly like her drawing and she'd emailed the link to Finn.

Abandoning her rucksack and portfolio where she'd dropped them, she picked up her bag and carried her tea up the two flights of stairs to her room. As she opened the door, her mobile rang. Hoping it was Finn she snatched it from her bag. Then she saw Anna's name.

Her friend had texted earlier. Zoe's response had said only that she was fine and on her way home. Anna had replied immediately wanting to know how she'd left things with Finn. Realising that would only lead to more questions Zoe had ignored it.

Dropping the phone on the bed, Zoe let the call go to voice mail. If only she'd not told Anna about Finn last night. Now her friend would have far too many damned questions. Questions that she couldn't possibly answer without telling Anna that her beloved Maeve was actually a crazy, homicidal witch.

Zoe turned to look at the wardrobe. Behind those very ordinary fake wood doors were the pictures of the crone. Pictures that so terrified her in October that she hoped she'd never have to look at them again. Only for you Finn, she thought, tugging the doors open.

The bottom of the wardrobe was, as usual, a total mess. She dropped to her knees and rummaged through piles of shoes and old clothes until her fingers closed on the square edges of a sketchpad. Pulling it out, she sat back on her heels, took a deep breath and opened it.

The first few pages were filled with sketches she'd done for a commission last year. Quickly, she flipped past them until she found the first of the drawings from October. A picture of a pale, thin girl crouched in the corner of a dark, windowless room sobbing. Not recognising the girl, Zoe only looked at it for a moment before she turned the page.

She gasped. In this drawing, the crone stood over the lifeless form of the same girl. She held a knife with a thin curved blade that dripped with blood. There was a bone deep gash in the girl's forearm. Blood flowed from it into a shallow bowl. As she looked more closely Zoe's stomach lurched. The girl lay across a circular stone table. A table that looked exactly like Maeve's altar.

"Oh my God!" Zoe breathed. Finn was right. Maeve was the crone.

Terror flooding through her, she swallowed hard. This changed everything. It had to. Finn couldn't go to the stone circle. Not once he knew Maeve would be waiting for him.

She reached for her phone, had Finn's number on the screen before she remembered there were two pictures she hadn't looked at. Reluctantly, she turned the page.

And there he was. In the garden at Anam Cara, his back against a tree, the crone pressing that same evil looking knife to his throat.

"No!" Zoe's hand rose to her mouth. She looked closer, saw the terror in his eyes. Then she shook her head. This couldn't have happened. He would have told her if Maeve had caught him, wouldn't he?

There was one drawing left. With shaking fingers, she turned the page.

Finn's body was pinned against the tree. Thin branches wound around his upper arms, roots curled around his calves. His torso sank into the trunk, fingers of bark snaking out to cover his thighs. His mouth was open in a silent scream as the tree devoured him. Maeve, dressed in a long dark robe, stood watching, her crone's face laughing.

Zoe shivered. Nausea swum up from her belly. She flicked back through the pictures. She desperately wanted them not to be real. For these drawings to be nothing more than nightmares. But Finn was in them. And she'd dreamt of him, these impossible, screwed up dreams, six months before she met him.

Again she reached for her phone. She had to talk to him, to hear his voice. She pressed the screen to dial his number, silently praying that he'd answer. When it clicked through to voice mail she could have cried. "It's me, Zoe," she said, her voice tight. "I've found the drawings, the ones I did in October. And you were right. It is Maeve. She's the crone. But I… -" her voice rose and she bit hard on her bottom lip to stop the tears, "- you see, you're in the drawings too. And I don't understand what they mean. Because in the picture she's caught you and she's threatening you. And then there's this tree and it's like it's trying to eat you and the bark's creeping over you and…"

Her voice cracked as a memory broke through. "Oh! I…I…" She closed her eyes for a moment, stunned by what she'd remembered. "Just ring me back when you get this, will you?"

Then scrabbling to her feet, she ran for the door and flung herself down the stairs. In the hall, she dropped to her knees and yanked open her portfolio. Frantically she scrabbled through the sheets of paper looking for two drawings.

She laid them on the hall carpet. The Green Man and Lancelot. And they both wore Finn's face.

Yesterday, in a red wine soaked haze she'd been able to ignore this. Now she couldn't. Not after she'd seen the picture of the tree.

It wasn't that Finn looked like the Green Man. Finn *was* the Green Man.

Zoe sat back on her heels and fought back the desire to laugh hysterically. Because suddenly so many things made sense. He'd not arrived at Anam Cara during the thunderstorm. He'd been there, trapped in the tree. Somehow he'd got out during the storm. Maybe the lightning strike had freed him. Could that be why he'd been barely injured by the explosion? Because he'd been at the centre of it?

And that explained how the Green Man had disappeared the morning after the storm. It wasn't a Green Man. It was Finn, held by Maeve's magic, trapped in the tree.

Every single one of his evasions abruptly fell into sharp focus. With tear-filled eyes she stared at the picture of his bark covered face. "Why didn't you tell me?" she whispered. "Why the hell didn't you tell me what she'd done to you?"

A tear fell on to the page and she brushed it away. "I talked to you. That first day when I thought I'd made a hideous mistake coming to Anam Cara I asked for your help and then on Sunday night when I was drunk I -" she suddenly laughed, her voice high with an edge of hysteria "- I felt like you could really hear me."

Her hand rose to cover her mouth as the tears came and she gave into them, her body shaking as the confusion and fear of the past few days flowed out of her.

When she finally dried her tears on her sleeve her anger had dissolved and she knew that she loved him. She wouldn't feel this sickening, overwhelming, almost paralysing terror if she didn't. Because now she understood what Maeve was capable of. Finn had been telling her the absolute truth. Maeve planned to kill him in the stone circle tomorrow night.

Slowly she prised herself off the floor and walked upstairs. She picked up the sketchpad, tore the pictures out and laid them on her desk. Then with shaking fingers she took four photos with the camera on her phone and emailed them to Finn.

Chapter 30

In a wood to the west of Glastonbury, Finn lined up six empty Guinness cans on the top of a fallen log and walked across the clearing to where his friend stood. Above Winston's outstretched hand hovered a bubble of bright light. "The globe makes the energy easier to control when you're learning," he said in the dry tones of a lecturer. "But the down side is that your enemy can see it coming."

Remembering Maeve's light globes on the Tor on Tuesday night, Finn nodded.

"When you're able to control the globe and you can use it accurately then the next step is to unpeel it and use the energy without its wrapper. But that's harder to work with. The globe's like throwing an egg. It's got a shape, you can predict how it'll move. The pure energy's more like throwing egg yolks."

"Messy," Finn muttered.

Winston didn't crack a smile. "And, more importantly, likely to go anywhere. Including all over you. There are druids who've tried this without being properly prepared and ended up hospitalised with first degree burns."

"Great! If Maeve doesn't kill me, my own magic could." This was one of the reasons Finn had never wanted to learn offensive magic. Back when he'd been sixteen and delighted with his powers, he'd reached out an invisible hand and pushed a kid who'd been bullying Cat from his bike. Bragging to Padraig about it later had resulted in a lecture about magic not being a weapon. Of course, he'd rebelled against that. But when he'd won his staff and learned about the interconnectedness of the world and the energy in it, he'd understood what Padraig had meant. Since then it was only in a few hairy situations when travelling that he'd even been tempted.

"You're probably not going to get that far in the time we've got," Winston said. "We'll start with small globes. They're easiest to handle but they've not got much power in them." Winston raised his hand and the bubble of light flew through the air and hit the first of the Guinness cans.

"Nice."

"Your turn."

Finn drew awen through his staff. An orb of light flickered above his palm. "Focus the energy," Winston said. Concentrating, Finn frowned. The light in the globe started to glow steadily. "Good." Winston pointed at the row of cans. "Try for the middle one."

Finn pulled his hand back as if he were throwing a ball and released the globe. It spun erratically before hitting a tree trunk six feet from his target and releasing only a shower of sparks.

"You're not keeping the awen focused after you've released the globe," Winston said. "That's why your aim's crap and the globe faded on impact."

Finn sighed, stripped off his fleece and dropped it at the bottom of a tree on the edge of the clearing. He knew Winston was trying to help but if Maeve broke his staff all of this was irrelevant. "Without my staff I'll be lucky to light a candle. I sure as hell won't be able to generate a light globe."

"I might have a wee bit of an idea about that," Winston said, his hand rising to his throat. "There was a druid I met in India. Irish guy, bit of a loner. He'd been to some places I'd never even heard of and he showed me how he got his staff over the border without any difficult questions."

"How is that going to help?" Finn said impatiently.

Winston shrugged. "It's a long shot. I need a bit more

time to see if I can make it work."

"Alright but even if I've got my staff I need bigger guns than light globes."

"How the hell are you going to control the big guns if you can't throw one of these?" Winston formed a light globe as he spoke.

"Maeve uses three of them at a time. I've seen her do it. I need something else or I'm dead."

"When you stop being crap at this, we'll move on to something bigger."

Finn scowled. "If this is how you speak to your students I'm surprised none of them have shoved you in a trench."

Winston grinned. "A cute Aussie tried last season. I didn't put up much of a fight."

Finn created another globe. "I don't want to hear about you exploiting your students for sexual favours."

"None of them have ever complained. And you're in no position to talk. I've had to put up with you and Zoe. That display this morning was sickening."

"Leave her out of this!" Finn bounced the globe above his palm, sending it higher and higher into the air. "I'm armed and dangerous." He released the ball of light as he spoke. He aimed for the middle of the five remaining cans. The globe struck the centre of the log and burst into flames.

"Definitely dangerous," Winston muttered. He pointed his staff at the flames. They flickered and died. "Again. And try not to incinerate anything this time."

The lesson continued. A little over an hour later, Finn could hit the cans on five out of six attempts and Winston decided to increase the size and power of the globe. As he replaced the six seriously dented cans on the log he explained the damage a bigger globe could do. Finn nodded, already shaping a larger orb in his hands.

Across the clearing, in the pocket of his fleece, his

mobile rang. And then, a little later, it beeped as an email arrived.

***

When the doorbell rang Zoe was tempted to ignore it. When it buzzed again insistently she put down her pencil and headed downstairs expecting that her housemate, Jake had forgotten his keys again. But when she opened it Anna stood on the doorstep holding a bottle of wine.

"Are you okay?" her friend said. "Why didn't you answer your phone? I've been worried."

"I'm fine," Zoe said quickly. "Honestly. You didn't need to come round."

Anna gave her a quick hug. "But I thought you needed cheering up. You sounded so upset on the phone last night."

"That's sweet of you. But really I'm fine." Zoe led the way through to the lounge.

"Then why have you come home?"

"I..." Zoe shrugged helplessly. "It's kind of a long story. I'll get some glasses." She reached for the bottle.

Anna held it away from her. "No, I'll do it. You look shattered."

"I am." Zoe sank into the sofa. "I was up ridiculously early."

"Because of this guy?" Anna called from the kitchen.

"You could say that." Zoe heard the familiar clink of bottle against glass and frowned. Wine really wouldn't help her keep her story straight. She would have to tell Anna that she'd sorted things out with Finn. But then how could she explain coming home early? Anna knew her too well to be satisfied with half-truths and evasions.

What was keeping her? Zoe tilted her head back to look through the door. "Everything alright?"

"Fine." A moment later, Anna walked through the

door holding two large glasses of red wine.

"How come you're not at work?" Zoe said.

"I left early. They owed me some flexi-time."

"You didn't have to do that." Zoe frowned. She'd been upset on the phone last night but not suicidal. Wasn't it a bit of an over-reaction for Anna to leave work early and trek across London to see her?

"Don't worry about it. I'm here now." Anna ran her fingers through her dark curly hair, not meeting Zoe's gaze. "Cheers!"

Zoe lifted her wine glass and took a sip. The red wine had a slightly unpleasant tang. "This taste alright to you?"

"Sure." Anna swirled it round her glass appreciatively. "It was nearly ten quid a bottle so it should be okay."

Zoe took another sip and again the sour taste hovered on her tongue.

"So what happened with Finn? Did you talk to him again before you left?" Anna said.

Zoe gulped down a mouthful of wine to give herself time to decide what to say. "Actually yes. And we kind of worked it out."

"You did!" Anna leaned forward. "What happened?"

"Well, I met him this morning and we talked and I remembered what you'd said and -" Zoe tapped her finger on her glass trying to decide what to say next, "- and we decided to give it a go."

"So where is he now?"

"In Glastonbury."

"Then why did you come home?"

Zoe glanced away. "A friend of his had come to stay so we couldn't spend much time together and I'd done everything I wanted to in Glastonbury and I thought I'd make more progress at home." Her eyes slid back to meet her friends. "He's coming here on Saturday though and he's taking me out."

"He is?" Anna looked confused. "So you're together now?"

"Yeah." Zoe couldn't repress a huge grin. When Anna didn't respond, her smile faded. Last night her friend had been encouraging her to give it a go with Finn. Why was she being so cool now?

"Why didn't you tell me?"

"Sorry." Zoe felt suddenly guilty. Anna had been genuinely concerned about her and, lost in worry about Finn, she'd pushed her away. "I should have rung you back. It was just that…." Again words failed her because there was so much she couldn't explain.

Luckily, Anna didn't seem to notice. "Last night you were really upset about him being a druid," she said. "What made you change your mind?"

Zoe stared into her wine glass. She couldn't answer that question honestly. So she grinned and said, "I just remembered how fit he is!"

***

When only one Guinness can remained intact, the others having been reduced to shards of aluminium, Finn decided he'd earned a break. Winston handed him a bottle of water and he gulped down half of it. Then, rolling his shoulders to shift the tension, he headed across the clearing, propped his staff against a tree trunk and took out his phone. There was a missed call from Zoe. He dialled his voice mail and, as soon as he heard her speak, he knew she was upset. His frown deepened as he listened. When the message ended he said, "Shit!"

"What is it?" Winston said.

"Zoe. She's got the pictures from October and she says one of them is of a tree eating me." Finn touched the icon to access his emails.

Winston's eyebrows shot up. "Have you told her?"

"No."

Winston blew out a long breath. "Good luck with that then, mate."

Finn clicked on the first attachment to the email. There were long slow seconds as the file downloaded and then the screen filled with a picture of a pale, thin girl curled up in the corner of a dark room.

Instantly the memory returned. The moment when he'd opened the hidden door and found his sister, terror in every line of her face, cowering in the farthest corner of the room. Finn swallowed hard. "Winston, you need to see this." He held the phone out.

"This is Anam Cara?"

"Where I found her."

"Fuck! Poor Cat." Winston handed the phone back. "What else?"

Finn gestured as if to say 'who knows' and opened the next photo. It was Cat again. When he saw the crone holding the bloody knife, the wound on his sister's arm, an explosive anger surged through him. He swung round, wanting to hit out, to hurt something. "The fucking bitch! I'm going to fucking kill her!" Reaching out his hand, his staff flew into it. He slammed it against the earth, felt the connection to awen pulse through him.

"Hey!" Winston's hand gripped Finn's arm.

Finn narrowed his eyes, yanked away. Then he took a deep breath, walked a few paces, came back. "Look." He held his mobile out to Winston.

The Scot was silent for a long moment. Then he said, "Actually *we're* going to fucking kill her!"

Fleetingly, Finn smiled. He slapped Winston on the shoulder and a look passed between them. "Go on. Look at the next one," Finn said.

Winston studied the screen for a long moment before he said, "Well, we can be sure about one thing. Maeve is the crone. In this she's in the garden at Anam Cara threatening you with that knife."

Finn nodded. He didn't need to see the picture. He remembered all too clearly. "That's when I knew I was in real trouble. She wrapped a force field around me and flung me half way across the garden. I landed against the tree. She didn't need the bloody knife. I couldn't move a muscle."

"That's powerful magic. Even for a spellworker."

"Tell me about it," Finn murmured. Then he took a deep breath and added, "Come on. Let's get it over with."

Winston pressed the screen and then he grimaced. "Jesus, Finn! That's brutal."

"Yeah, it was."

"Do you want to see it?"

Finn shook his head. He needed no reminders. The agony and terror already haunted him.

He was silent for a long moment then he said, "Give me the phone." When Winston handed it to him the screen was blank and he was grateful for that.

"You going to ring her?"

"Yeah."

"Right. I'll -" Winston pointed across the clearing, "-be over there."

Finn put the phone to his ear, listened to it ring. He had no idea how he would explain. He just knew that for Zoe he was going to try.

***

"We haven't decided where we're going yet. Somewhere nice," Zoe said. Or at least that's what she tried to say but she had problems with her words. They kept coming out slurred. She looked at her wine. She hadn't even finished the glass. "Just how strong is this?"

"I'm not sure. Nothing out of the ordinary. Are you alright?"

"I feel like I've drunk -" it took two attempts to get that word out "- the whole bottle."

"Probably it's because you're tired. Why don't you put your feet up? Close your eyes for a few minutes. I don't mind."

"No, I'll be fine." Zoe scrubbed her hand over her forehead. She suddenly felt really hot. "Would you mind getting me some water?"

"Sure." Anna went through to the kitchen. She came back with a glass and gave it to Zoe. She slugged the water back and held the cool glass against her burning cheek.

"Better?" Anna said.

Zoe shook her head. She rested it against the sofa cushions and closed her eyes for a moment.

"That's right. You take it easy." Anna's voice seemed far away. Dimly aware of her friend moving about, it was too much effort to open her eyes. A moment later Zoe heard Anna say, "Yes, it's working. Exactly as you said. What do you want me to do now?"

Zoe blinked repeatedly trying to bring the room back into focus. She turned her head to see Anna on the phone, pacing restlessly up and down the hall. "You were right," her friend said. "She and Finn are together." There was a pause and then she added, "Okay. I'll stay with her until you get here."

Zoe eyelids slid closed and she gave up the fight for a moment. The next thing she knew Anna was sat next to her, stroking her hair. "What's going on?" Zoe tried to ask but the words were hardly distinguishable.

"You're going to be fine. Just rest," Anna said softly. Hovering on the edge of the darkness, Zoe knew she shouldn't be feeling like this. Her lids flickered helplessly as she tried again to push through the blackness.

Then her phone rang. *Finn.* She tried to grab her mobile but it fell through her numb fingers and slipped to the floor. Head swimming, she bent to pick it up. Anna snatched it away.

"Give me the phone," Zoe said shrilly, the words slurred.

"Sorry, sweetie." Anna pressed the screen and the ringing stopped. "It's your new boyfriend and I've been told not to let him speak to you."

"No!" Zoe exclaimed, the single word surprisingly clear.

With a monumental effort she tried to grab the phone from Anna's hand. "Oh, no you don't," her friend said, easily moving it out of her grasp. Unbalanced by the movement, Zoe collapsed face down across her friend's lap. "Why you doing this?" she mumbled.

Again Anna stroked her hair. "Stop fighting it, sweetie. You need to rest for a while. That's all."

No, she needed to tell Finn. Holding that thought she tried to struggle upright but Anna's hands were firm on her shoulders. Long seconds later unconsciousness claimed her.

***

"Well?" Winston said.

Finn shrugged, trying not to look worried. "No answer." He couldn't help feeling a bit relieved that he'd got a temporary reprieve, a little longer to figure out how to explain. But beneath that he was pretty sure he'd never get the chance, that he'd never hear from her again. And he couldn't blame her. What woman could handle that her new man had spent six months trapped in a tree? Winston was probably right and he should have told her but he'd honestly thought she'd never need to know. Or at least, not yet. Not until they knew each other a whole lot better.

He pushed his fingers through his hair. There was nothing else he could do. She'd either ring back or she wouldn't. He slipped his mobile into the pocket of his jeans. If she did ring he wouldn't miss it this time.

"We're going to try breaking force fields," Winston said. "We know Maeve likes to use them. If you can shatter it then it'll recoil on her. When that happens it's like an enormous elastic band snapping. The recoil physically hurts but only for a second or two. You'll have to be ready to follow through."

"With the killer blow."

"Exactly."

"Come on then," Finn said, hefting his staff from hand to hand. "Make a force field."

Winston grinned. "Like you're going to break it!" He closed his eyes to concentrate and, at that second, Finn pushed outwards with the palm of his hand, directed the awen and let it go. Winston staggered backwards as if he'd been punched in the stomach and fell flat on his arse. Finn burst out laughing.

Winston stood up, brushed away the leaves that clung to his clothes. "At least you're aim's improving." He bent to pick up his staff and, as he straightened, the air around his body solidified into a transparent bubble. "Come on then, if you think you can take me!"

"No problem," Finn said with a lot more confidence than he felt.

***

Zoe heard a buzzing noise. Someone moved her head. She murmured restlessly, her eyes flickering half open. "It's alright," Anna's voice soothed. Zoe's cheek came to rest on something soft and her lids closed again.

As if from very far away she heard the front door open and her friend quietly say, "Come in. She's through here."

Who's here? But even that thought was hard to catch hold off. She was sinking back towards unconsciousness when a cool hand touched her forehead.

A familiar voice said, "You've done well, my dear. How long has she been out?"

No, it can't be! This must be a dream.

"About half an hour."

"Good. Then the drug should last at least another hour." The word 'drug' penetrated the haze enough for Zoe to force her eyelids open for a second. She saw legs. A short flowery skirt; that was Anna. And grey trousers.

"What was it that I gave her?" Anna said.

"A tincture of valerian, skullcap and poppy."

"But she will be alright? I mean, it won't hurt her, will it?"

"Don't worry, my dear." The words were spoken slowly and with emphasis. "No harm will come to her."

Chapter 31

"I think Zoe's right." Winston held two sheets of paper next to the screen of his laptop and looked between them. "The stone circle's the Nine Maidens."

"On Dartmoor?" Finn picked another slice of pizza out of the box on the coffee table and bit into it.

They'd stayed in the wood long after darkness fell. Practising again and again the skills he would need tomorrow night. He was shattered, his muscles ached and yet he felt strangely wired. It'd been good to handle some serious energy. He'd felt the return of the bone-deep connection to awen. He would need that if he was going to make it through tomorrow night alive.

"Aye. And the Saint Michael line goes straight through the middle of the circle," Winston said, dropping Zoe's drawings onto the pile of papers and maps cluttering the table.

Finn's eyebrows rose. "You're serious?"

"Would I joke about the most important ley line in England?" Grinning, Winston leaned over and grabbed the last piece of pizza.

"You'd joke about anything!" Finn laughed. Then Winston's words hit home. "But this could be bloody brilliant. Think of the energy I can take from the ley line." As he spoke his gaze fell on Zoe's drawings and he saw Maeve brandishing his broken staff over the fire. "Course that's only going to work if I've got my staff. If this drawing of Zoe's is right and Maeve breaks it then not even the St Michael line is going to save me."

"Aye, I know." Winston's voice was unexpectedly soft. "I'm still working on that."

Finn glanced at his friend. "I don't want to pressure you but we're on a schedule here."

"It's not as easy as I first thought."

Finn stared at the carpet. He didn't want Winston to know how much his words earlier had sparked a hope. If his friend couldn't make whatever it was work then he was well and truly screwed. He picked up the Ordnance Survey map of Dartmoor and said, "I'll head over to the Nine Stones first thing in the morning. I want to dowse it, find out exactly where the energy goes."

Winston nodded. "Alright. I think I'll stay here. See if I can figure this out. I'll come down later on the bike."

"How far is it?"

"Couple of hours max. Even in your heap of junk."

Finn ignored that. He was used to Winston insulting his car. "You think Maeve knows about the St Michael Line? Is that why she chose this place?"

"Spellworkers aren't generally interested in ley lines. However I suppose it's possible that she…" Winston reached for *The Seventh Book.*

Finn completed his sentence. "Plans to use the ley line after she's taken my connection to the earth."

"Aye, that's possible. But if that happens you'll be dead." Winston opened the thick black book.

"Thanks for reminding me," Finn muttered.

"I thought so." Winston tapped his finger on the page. "The ritual doesn't require a ley line."

"Then why'd she chose this place?"

"Could be one of two reasons. There was a burial chamber in the centre of this circle. It's long since been robbed out but perhaps the chamber's enough for what she needs."

"Bones of the ancestors," Finn said.

"And the circle's beneath Belstone Tor and about a

mile from Belstone village. Some people believe Belstone Tor's named for the god Bel."

"The Celtic God of fire? That'd be appropriate seeing as it's Beltane tomorrow."

"Exactly and that ties in with the Saint Michael line. The Celts' major celebration of Beltane was at Avebury but there would have been fires all the way along the line to welcome the sun on the morning of the first of May."

"Stop! It's way too late for a lecture on the history of ley lines." He picked up his phone and, for the fifteenth time since they'd got back to the cottage, checked the time. Seventeen minutes past eleven and Zoe still hadn't rung him back. He was running out of reasons why she hadn't called. Unless, of course, she didn't ever want to speak to him again.

Was it worth another call? Just in case she'd missed his message. Maybe that would shake the nagging sense he'd had all evening that something wasn't right. Only if he rang her again in front of Winston he'd never hear the last of it.

Standing, he rolled his shoulders and said, "I'm going for a quick walk before bed. Stretch out these aching muscles."

"Right. I'm going to make some calls. See if anyone knows how I can get hold of the Irish guy I was telling you about."

Finn grabbed his fleece and stepped out into the night. The breeze whipped at his jacket as he put it on. Striding down the gravel path away from the cottages, he crossed the car park and headed down the lane. Under the shadow of a large sycamore, he pulled out his mobile. He hesitated for a moment before pressing the screen to dial her number. As he listened to it ring, he remembered this morning at the bus station. Saying goodbye had been harder than he'd anticipated. He'd only known her four days. Logically it was ridiculous to miss her. Yet somehow it felt like he did.

The ringing stopped and, expecting the call to go to voice mail, he scowled. Then after a long pause a voice said, “Yes?”

It didn’t sound like her. “Zoe?” he said uncertainly.

“Zoe’s sleeping. But I thought you might call.” The voice was dreadfully, shockingly familiar.

“What have you done to her?”

“I gave her something to help her sleep. If you do exactly what I say then no harm will come to her.”

“You bloody bitch! How the hell did you find her?”

“It was remarkably simple,” Maeve said. “Zoe’s friend Anna was most helpful. Zoe may be capable of resisting me but Anna has always been charmingly responsive.”

Rage boiled through Finn’s veins and for a long moment he didn’t trust himself to speak. Then he drew a ragged breath and, his voice vibrating with anger, said, “What do you want, Maeve?”

“You, of course. It was foolish to think you could escape. All you’ve done is make the end worse for yourself.”

“I doubt that!”

Maeve laughed harshly. “You will suffer. I’ll see to that. You owe me, Finn McCloud.”

“For what? You trapped me in a bloody tree for six months.”

“Out of interest, how did you escape?” Maeve’s voice softened. “I know the girl had something to do with it.”

“She had *nothing* to do with it!” Finn snapped, picturing Maeve taking her anger out on Zoe. He swallowed hard and added, “It was the lightning.”

“You’re lying. I know the girl has some power. I can see silver sparks in her aura as she sleeps.”

“You stay away from her!”

“Or you’ll do what? Come barging into my garden

again and try to take her back?"

"I got Cat out!"

"Indeed. But you were the greater prize. My Beltane sacrifice."

"Then let's end this. Where and when?"

"Oh, I'm not going to make it that easy for you. When it's time, I'll let you know."

Finn blew out a long breath as he tried to hold on to his anger. "You'll tell me now."

"I'll tell you when I'm ready. But know this, if you don't come I'll take the girl as consolation. Those silver sparks of hers will keep me going long enough to track you down."

"Oh I'll be there! And if you've done *anything* to hurt her I swear I'll kill you!"

"Don't make threats you can't keep, Finn McCloud. It makes you sound weak."

The line went dead.

Swearing loudly and profusely Finn kicked at the unresponsive tree trunk. Then sucking in a deep breath he sprinted back to the cottage.

Chapter 32

In a service station outside Salisbury Maeve dropped the phone onto the passenger seat and smiled. The druid's call was a gift from the goddesses. A sign that her plan couldn't fail.

She'd intended to ring the druid sooner. She'd wanted to pile on the emotional pressure, to play on his wonderfully predictable sense of responsibility. Unfortunately Zoe's mobile phone had proved as uncooperative as its owner. The damned thing needed some kind of code before you could use it and unlocking spells only resulted in the battery shooting out. Maeve had been ready to throw it out the window when unexpectedly it'd rung.

She looked over her shoulder at the girl sleeping across the back seats. The blanket had slipped, revealing the gag that obscured half of the girl's face. She'd given her another dose of the tincture before they left London. It should ensure that she slept for another couple of hours. Maeve twitched the blanket back into place. It hid the bonds at wrist and ankle. There were spells that would have done the same job but using physical restraints would help to preserve her energy.

She sipped the remains of her cup of earl grey tea – served in one of those paper cups that ruined the taste - and consulted the map. Not wanting her backseat passenger to be seen she'd decided to avoid the motorways. The route was slower but she was in no hurry. They had half the night to get there.

She needed him at the stone circle an hour before the

sun rose at 5.30. If she called again at around 2.30am that would give him sufficient time to get there and no time at all to prepare anything that could disrupt her plans.

She'd get the girl to make that call. An obvious tactic but it would serve a useful double purpose. It would, in case he doubted, convince him that she had Zoe. And any sign of distress in the girl would turn the screw tighter and deeper.

A little later, Maeve tossed her empty cup out of the car window and took another look at her passenger. Reassured that she still slept deeply, she started the engine and re-joined the A303 heading west.

***

At first there were only dreams. Dreams that were too vivid, the colours psychedelically bright. Finn screaming as bark crept over his skin. The doll resting in the palm of her hand as lightning flashed overhead. Maeve wearing her crone's face, laughing and laughing. Finn in the centre of a stone circle plunging his staff into the earth. A dragon opening its mouth to roar. A line of light racing towards him through St Michael's Mount, a wooded hill fort, the shell of a church on top of a hill, Glastonbury Tor, Avebury, a ruined abbey. All of these places somehow connected by the light that surged across the country to converge on Finn.

Something filled her mouth, making it difficult to breathe. Pain in her arms, her wrists, her shoulders. A dull ache in her left temple. Dryness in her throat. Eyelids that were heavier than lead.

The drone of an engine. A sensation of movement. She was lying down, her legs uncomfortably bent. Something covered her head. Slowly she prised her eyes open. Saw nothing but blackness. Her hands flexed against their bonds and her fingers touched fabric. Straining painfully against the roughness binding her wrists, she grasped a handful of the material and it slid off her face. Blinking, she saw the interior of a car, dimly lit by the dashboard. Visible around the headrest was Maeve's blonde hair.

With that memory flooded back. The strange taste to the wine. Feeling dizzy. Finn ringing. Anna snatching the phone away. Maeve at her house.

Tears prickled behind her eyes. How had it come to this? Anna had drugged her and betrayed her. They'd been best friends for years. Why would she help Maeve?

And now she was being driven through the night to a stone circle somewhere on Dartmoor.

Then another thought hit her and a wave of terror like nothing she'd never experienced before washed over her. Because Finn had said that if Maeve knew she was a seer she'd kill her to steal that gift. She screwed her eyes tight shut, dry sobs choking her throat. For a terrible moment, she struggled to catch her breath around the bulky gag and involuntarily tried to move her arms. The searing pain at her wrists shocked her into stillness.

Carefully, she inhaled through her nose trying not to move at all. For a few moments she concentrated only on her breathing. Imperceptibly, the panic faded and she began to think. The dream was important. The images had been even brighter, more persistent than usual. She had to remember it. It made no sense to her but to Finn it could be vital.

If she ever got the chance to tell him.

Pushing away that thought, Zoe closed her eyes and did something she'd never attempted before. She tried to hold onto the images from her dream.

She had no idea how much time passed. Her concentration was so intense that the movements of the car ceased to register until it bounced heavily and came to a halt. A sharp click was followed by a whirring as a seatbelt was released. Then Maeve spoke, "Zoe, dear. I know you're awake."

Oh for God's sake! Did the woman have eyes in the back of her head? She briefly considered ignoring her and pretending to sleep then she remembered that Maeve wasn't just the patronising owner of Anam Cara who she found so bloody annoying. She was a spellworker and if she could trap Finn in a tree for rescuing his sister then who knew what she'd do if Zoe defied her. She opened her eyes and looked up.

Maeve leaned around the driver's seat. "I want you to do a little something for me."

Feeling she had no other choice, Zoe nodded. "Good," Maeve said. She got out of the car and opened the door next to Zoe's head. Swiftly, Maeve untied the gag. Zoe gulped in air, her throat painfully dry.

"Sit up," Maeve said. "And I'll get you some water."

Zoe dropped her feet to the floor. That was the easy bit. Sitting was much harder. Her bonds cutting into her skin, she pushed down with her shoulder, flexed her elbow and levered herself upright. Maeve thrust a bottle against her lips and she drank, water spilling down her chin and soaking into her hoody.

"What do you want?" Zoe muttered.

"Right now, I want you to talk to your boyfriend and tell him where to meet us." Maeve slipped into the seat beside her. "What's the code for this blasted phone of yours?"

Zoe hesitated. She didn't want to do anything that would help Maeve get Finn to the stone circle. Then something sharp pressed against her neck. She tried to squirm away from it but it bit deeper.

"And don't think about lying to me!"

A warm trickle of blood slipped down her skin. "It's 3486," Zoe said. Maeve keyed in the numbers and then pressed the screen a number of times. She frowned, deep lines creasing her forehead. With the spellworker distracted Zoe took the opportunity to look around, hoping from some clue as to where they were.

The clock on the dashboard said 02:15. She'd been out for hours. The drug had left a thudding headache behind it. Through the windscreen she could dimly make out that they were parked on the verge of a narrow road lined with tall hedges.

She was turning her head to see what was behind them when Maeve pressed the phone against her ear. She heard it ringing. Bit her lip wondering how the hell she would explain that she'd been kidnapped.

"Maeve." Finn's tone was coldly formal.

"No, it's Zoe." She was momentarily so overwhelmed by hearing his voice that she didn't take in what he'd said. Then it hit home. He'd expected Maeve to call from her phone which must mean he'd already spoken to the spellworker.

"Thank Christ! Are you alright?" His relief burst down the line.

"Kind of." She bit her lip to keep back tears. It was much harder to keep it together when he sounded so close.

"Has she hurt you?"

"No." Aware of Maeve's proximity, Zoe hesitated but then the words poured out. "I'm so sorry. Anna came round with a bottle of wine and she put some kind of drug in it and I was really out of it and then when you rang she wouldn't let me talk to you. I think I must have passed out after that. I know Maeve turned up because she's here now and….and I'm scared."

There was a sharp intake of breath.

"This is not your fault," Finn said. "I should have…"

"Enough!" Maeve snapped, whisking the phone away. "The girl's fine. She'll come to no harm if you do exactly what I tell you."

Zoe leaned closer but she couldn't hear his response. Maeve laughed scathingly. "As I've already said, you're in no position to threaten, Finn McCloud. Meet me at the Nine Maidens stone circle an hour before sunrise. It's on Dartmoor, a mile from the village of Belstone."

Zoe's eyes widened when she heard the name. She'd been right. Maybe knowing that had given Finn some time to prepare. Could he be at the stone circle already? A tiny bubble of hope formed inside of her.

Without waiting for Finn to reply, Maeve rang off and tossed the phone onto the front passenger seat. Then she turned to Zoe. "You'll see him again soon. Of course, he's going to die shortly after so perhaps that's not much comfort."

"Or maybe he'll kill you. Have you thought about that?"

Maeve laughed scornfully. "You really do believe in the boy. How touching!"

Zoe glared at her, determined not to be intimidated. But when the spellworker picked up the gag and pulled it tight between her bony hands, she couldn't keep it together any longer. Cringing away she said, "Please no. Not that again."

Maeve stared at her, her watery blue eyes disturbingly close. "I suppose no one but me will hear you scream. But if you do, I won't hesitate to use this."

Zoe nodded frantically. "I'll be quiet."

"And stay down." Grabbing her shoulder, Maeve pushed her flat. The blanket flopped over her. She heard a car door open and shut, the sound repeated as Maeve returned to the driver's seat.

The engine started up. As they started to move, Zoe closed her eyes and blew out a long breath. Maeve didn't plan to kill her. She wanted to use her as bait. And maybe Finn would defeat Maeve. Okay, he hadn't seemed very confident about that when she left, but he was a druid. He had the power of the earth on his side and, even if he hadn't used magic as a weapon before, surely that was enough?

For a microsecond the bubble of hope grew. But then behind her eyelids she saw her drawing of the crone holding Finn's broken staff over the fire. Without that how could he fight? Or summon the line of light she'd seen in her dream?

And if Maeve did kill him. She swallowed hard. What would happen? She was bait now but once the trap had been sprung she'd be a witness to murder. A witness that Maeve couldn't control or influence. There was no way the spellworker would let her walk away.

A chill crept through her veins and she shuddered. Finn wouldn't only be fighting for his own life at the Nine Maidens. He would be fighting for hers as well.

Chapter 33

Zoe's world had shrunk to the uneven ground beneath her feet and the agony at her wrists. Head down against the bitter wind, trying to ignore Maeve and the eerie balls of light that hovered around her, she kept on putting one foot in front of the other.

For a brief, insane moment when they'd left the path from the village and Dartmoor had spread around them in bleak, desolate darkness she'd thought about making a run for it. Her hands remained tied behind her back which would make it difficult but the night offered protection. Or so she'd thought until, with a couple of muttered words, the spellworker had produced three balls of light. As if she'd read Zoe's thoughts, Maeve had explained that they were weapons as well. And in case Zoe planned anything stupid, she'd offered to demonstrate their power. Zoe shook her head and started walking in the direction Maeve pointed.

She'd fallen once, tripping on a root. Unable to put her hands out to save herself, she landed flat on her face in the mud and heather. Maeve hauled her up. That was when her wrists had gone from painful to agonising and blood had begun dripping down her hands.

There'd been a brief moment of hope when she saw a square building emerge from the dark. She'd thought it was a house. Planned to scream as they walked past. But when they got closer she'd realised it was a deserted barn, the roof half fallen in. The disappointment was so sharp she had to bite back sobs. After that she'd kept her eyes on her feet and trudged on.

Maeve pointed. "We're nearly there."

One of the light balls floated ahead to illuminate the ring of stones. For a second Zoe felt relief that the nightmare walk was over. That vanished when she realised this was the place where she and Finn might die.

Maeve strode into the centre of the circle, dropped her black velvet bag and looked around her. It was smaller than Zoe had expected from her drawings. The tallest of the stones barely came up to Maeve's chest. One far larger stone had fallen and lay outside the circle.

She walked around the perimeter and slowly, careful not to jolt her wrists, sat on the fallen stone. The cold seeped through her clothes and she shivered uncontrollably. In jeans and a hoodie she wasn't dressed for a night time walk on Dartmoor. Her jeans were ripped at the knee where she'd fallen and her trainers were caked in mud. She thought enviously of the layers of fleece that Finn always wore. Wherever he was she felt certain he wasn't shivering.

Scanning the dark moorland, she searched for some sign of him. Had he been to the Nine Maidens already? Could he be close by? Watching and preparing for the confrontation to come? She thought he might be. She didn't feel as alone as she had on the trek across the moor. But - she thought, shivering again - that could be just wishful thinking.

A cry from Maeve made her turn. What she saw was chillingly familiar. Wearing a long black robe the spellworker stood in the centre of the circle, a fire flickering by her feet. "Come here!" Maeve said.

Groaning inwardly, Zoe eased herself to standing. She half expected to feel something as she stepped into the circle - some sense of the energy that Finn had talked about - but there was nothing.

"Stand here." Maeve pointed to a spot next to the fire. Welcoming the warmth, Zoe did as instructed. Then she saw the curved knife glinting in the firelight and took three quick steps back.

"I hope you're not going to be difficult about this," Maeve said, moving towards her.

"About what?"

"I need a little of your blood for the ritual."

"Like hell you do!" Backing away, Zoe crashed painfully against one of the upright stones. Eyes fixed on Maeve, she tried to slide round it but suddenly she couldn't move. It was as if the air around her had solidified, holding her in place, pinned against the stone. Instinctively she struggled but only her head moved, the rest of her body was immobile. She opened her mouth to scream.

Maeve's cold hand smacked over it. Her face came closer; the watery eyes alight with excitement. "My dear girl," Maeve said, holding the knife in one hand, a silver cup in the other. "We can do this the easy way or the hard way and I definitely recommend the easy way."

The spellworker grabbed Zoe's shoulder and spun her round. Too scared now to fight back, Zoe's cheek landed against the rough surface of the stone. The invisible barrier tightened around her body.

Zoe screwed up her eyes and clenched her teeth together. The ropes on her wrists tightened agonizingly. There was a second of exquisite relief when the bonds fell away.

Maeve caught her right arm in a cold grasp and shoved the sleeve up. The point of the knife felt icy against the soft skin inside Zoe's elbow. The blade pierced. She gasped as a searing pain shot up her arm. Instinctively she tried to pull away. The force that held her intensified.

"Don't struggle!" Maeve said. "You're only making it worse."

"Like you care," Zoe muttered.

"You never give up, do you? I should have spotted that

the first day we met when you persisted in your tiresome interest in my Green Man. But you're right. I don't care. You're a means to an end. That's all."

Zoe didn't waste what breath she had on answering. There was silence until Maeve said, "There! That should be enough."

Abruptly the force that had held Zoe disappeared. She slumped to the ground, holding her right arm to her chest. Maeve raised the chalice and drank deeply. Unable to believe what she saw, Zoe stared. Her stomach churned and, feeling sick, she clamped her hand over her mouth.

"Thank you for this." Maeve raised the chalice to her. "Your blood will give me the strength I need to kill your boyfriend."

"You bitch!"

Maeve laughed. "Time to give up, dear. He's not going to save you." She walked around the inside of the circle, sprinkling the remaining contents of the silver cup on the ground.

Warm blood trickled down Zoe's arm. She groped in her jeans pocket and found a not terribly clean tissue. She pressed it hard against the wound. When it quickly turned bright red she felt the edge of rising panic. The gash needed bandaging and fast. Maeve obviously wasn't going to help. She could think of only one option.

Keeping an eye on Maeve, she slid her arms out of her hoodie and pulled it over her head. She grimaced when she saw her wrists. Layers of skin had been flayed away and the lacerations were encrusted with dried blood. She stripped off her t-shirt, gasping when the freezing wind hit her bare skin. Shivering uncontrollably, she rolled the t-shirt into a thick strip and wrapped it twice round her arm. With the help of her teeth she tied it as tight as she could. Fingers numb with cold, she pulled her hoodie on. The bulky bandage wouldn't fit down the sleeve. Instead, she cradled her wounded arm against her body.

Her head dropped back against the stone. Trying to slow her erratic breathing, she heard Maeve intoning words that made no sense. The older woman moved steadily closer. The thought of being sprinkled with her own blood forced her to move. She stumbled across the circle heading for the rock she'd sat on before.

The fire burnt enthusiastically now, its heat impossible to resist. For a precious moment it warmed her. Then Maeve was crossing towards her and Zoe moved away. She heard Maeve say, her voice commanding, "By the will of the goddesses, this circle I seal."

There was a shiver in the air around her and immediately the wind dropped. Reaching the gap between two stones, Zoe went to step through it and bounced back. Putting out her hand, she touched something invisible but solid. She moved further round, reached out and found the same barrier.

She swung to face Maeve. "What is this? What did you do?"

"It's a force field. It seals the circle. Makes it my sacred space. No one gets in or out without my permission."

"And that's what you needed my blood for? To trap me?"

Maeve smiled coldly. "Only temporarily, my dear. I have no more desire to prolong this than you do. When your boyfriend comes you can go."

"Then you can let her go, Maeve!" Finn's voice came, loud and confident, from the darkness outside the circle.

"Thank God!" Zoe breathed, spinning to look for him.

One of Maeve's light balls shot towards the place where his voice had come from. Its glow revealed him striding towards the stones, wearing a waterproof jacket over a thick fleece. As he got closer, she saw that the staff he carried was different to the one he'd had yesterday. It was taller and thinner with a fork at the top of it.

"You're early," Maeve said.

"That depends on when you expect the sunrise. I'm reliably informed that the sun will come over the horizon in exactly one hour." Finn pointed across the moor at, what Zoe guessed must be, east.

"Then you're wrong," Maeve said.

"If you prefer to trust the Met Office to the wisdom of a druid then you obviously don't understand the power you're so desperate to possess," Finn said.

"And will possess. Do not doubt that, Finn McCloud."

"I'm not as easy to kill as you seem to think. You couldn't do it last time and -" Finn raised his staff "- I'm armed this time."

"Not for long. If you want the girl back you'll break your staff."

"Not bloody likely!"

Zoe's eyes were fixed on Finn. She heard his shouted warning and turned. Maeve's knife was flying straight at her. Automatically she ducked but, like a heat seeking missile, the knife swerved towards her. For a second, Zoe thought she was about to die. Then the blade stopped millimetres from her neck.

"Don't hurt her!" Finn yelled. "It's me you want."

"Then break your staff. Until then I'm happy slicing bits off her. Perhaps her screams will change your mind." Maeve's hand flexed and the knife turned, its point digging into Zoe's skin.

Eyes screwed tight, Zoe stood rigid, too terrified to even breathe.

"Okay! I'll do it!" Finn shouted. "But let her go first."

Zoe's eyes flew open and she gasped, "No Finn! You can't..."

Finn didn't glance at her. "Release the knife and let her out the circle. Then I'll break my staff."

"Do you think I was born yesterday, Finn McCloud? I'm not letting the girl go while you're still armed."

"And I'm not breaking my staff until I know she's safe."

"Could you? The knife? Please?" Zoe said, breathlessly. Maeve curled a finger and the knife retreated slightly. With her eyes fixed on it, Zoe added, "Will you both stop talking about me as if I'm not here?"

"Be quiet! This is between me and the druid," Maeve said, without looking at her.

"Oh, for fuck's sake!" Finn said. "You brought her here. Let her speak."

Zoe's eyes slid between the two of them. It was a stand-off, each of them glaring at the other. She said quickly, "What if Maeve let me out of the circle but kept the knife on me until Finn breaks his staff? Wouldn't that work? It seems to me that'd give you both what you want."

"No," Finn said. "It's too risky. She could wait until I'd broken my staff and then kill you anyway."

"You're right, I could," Maeve said. "But it's you I want, Finn McCloud. If you do what I tell you, the girl's safe."

Across the barrier created by the force field, Finn's eyes met Zoe's. "I'm not happy about this."

"I know but it's okay." Zoe swallowed hard and tried to sound braver than she felt. "I can do it."

Maeve strode over to her. Grabbing the knife, she pressed the flat of the blade against Zoe's skin. "Those were brave words," the spellworker whispered, forcing Zoe to walk forwards. "But if you make one wrong move this knife will pierce your jugular and you'll bleed to death in minutes. Not even your druid will be able to save you."

At the perimeter of the circle, Maeve said, "Goddesses, by my leave, let this girl pass." The spellworker released her grasp. Instantly the knife returned to hover at Zoe's throat.

With her eyes fixed on it, Zoe took the next tentative step. There was a weird sensation, like sliding through jelly, and then she was free. Finn stood five paces away. She wanted to run to him but she didn't dare move any further.

"Alright, Maeve. I'm breaking it now." He raised his knee, laid the staff over it. There was a loud crack as it broke. Holding up the two pieces, Finn winked. For a second, Zoe was astounded then it made sense. That staff wasn't his.

"Throw the pieces into the circle," Maeve said. He tossed them in a wide arc. They ricocheted off the furthest stones and dropped to the ground. "Now step in yourself."

"Not until I've spoken to Zoe."

"That was not part of our deal!"

"You said you wouldn't hurt her if I did what you asked. I've followed your instructions exactly but you took blood from her anyway. That was out of order."

Maeve hesitated. "Count it as your last request, Finn McCloud. One minute. And the knife stays on her."

Finn didn't waste time replying. Striding towards Zoe, he stripped off his coat. Taking great care not to touch the knife, he slid it round her shoulders. "You're frozen. Let me see your arm."

"You saw that?" Zoe pulled up her hoodie to reveal the makeshift bandage.

"Yes. We were here about an hour before you." Finn gently untied the blood soaked t-shirt and cupped her elbow with his hands.

"We? Winston's here?" Zoe whispered.

Finn nodded.

She felt a tingling warmth spreading out from her elbow. "What are you doing?"

"Healing you."

"Don't waste your energy," Zoe said. "The bleeding's stopped. I'll be fine."

"But I need to know you're fine," Finn said, with a fleeting smile. When he took his hands away, she saw that the wide gash had become a thin pink line. His hands slid down to her wrist and she felt the same warmth there. "I should never have insisted on you going home. If you'd stayed with me this would never have happened."

"Don't go there." With the tiniest movement, Zoe shook her head. "You're here. That's what matters."

Finn's hand moved to her other wrist. His voice dropped. "If I… don't… you know, make it, Winston will take care of you. Get you away from here."

"About that. There's something I need to tell you, something that might help. Is she listening? I daren't look."

Finn shook his head. "No. She's at the other side of the circle picking up my staff."

"But that wasn't…?"

"Shush!" Finn laid a finger on her mouth. "That's just the beginning." His hand rose to the talisman at his throat. Zoe's eyes widened when she saw that it was exactly like the one she'd drawn. His finger rested on the small piece of wood and he raised his eyebrows. For a second, Zoe was lost then the shape of the talisman registered.

"Is that what I think it is?" she said.

Finn nodded.

"Thank God!" Without thinking, Zoe reached for him, flinching as the knife pricked her skin. "Owww!"

"Are you alright?"

"Yes, I just forgot for a second. Come closer. I don't want Maeve to hear this."

Wary of unintentionally jolting her, Finn stepped in until their bodies were only a centimetre apart. "I want to hold you," he whispered in the ear that didn't have the knife hovering next to it. "But one wrong move and the athame could…"

"I know," Zoe breathed, staring into his eyes. As she

looked, they became soft. Suddenly she felt as if the ground were shifting beneath her feet.

"What is it, sweetheart?" Finn's finger brushed a smear of mud from her cheek.

"I had a dream on the way here. I saw you plunge your staff into the centre of this circle and a dragon roared and then there was a line of light linking all these places. Some of them I didn't recognise but there was St Michael's Mount and Glastonbury and…"

"Oh, that's bloody brilliant!"

"What is?"

Finn grinned. "You'll see."

"Time's up, Finn McCloud!" Maeve called.

"I'm just saying goodbye," Finn said.

"Spare me the bleeding hearts. If you're not in here in thirty seconds then I'll kill the girl. One twist of my knife and she's dead."

Simultaneously with her words, Zoe yelped as the knife pricked her skin.

"Stop it!" Finn shouted. His hand reached towards the hilt but he pulled it back. "I can't," he whispered to Zoe. "If I touch it she'll know I've still got my connection to awen."

"I'm counting," Maeve said before adding the words that would allow Finn to enter the circle.

"Don't say goodbye," Zoe whispered. "I can't bear it."

Finn took her hand in both of his. "You don't have to. I'm coming back. The next time I see you take your top off I'm going to be this close. That's a nice bra you're wearing."

Zoe didn't know whether to laugh or cry. "That is *so* not the way I pictured you first seeing it."

"Jesus! I want to kiss you but I daren't risk it. The knife's too close to your vein."

Zoe's eyes were huge with unshed tears. "This is *so* unfair!"

“I know.” Finn’s voice deepened. “I’ll make it up to you.” He lifted her hand to his lips and, eyes fixed on hers, tenderly kissed the palm. “As soon as the knife moves, head for the hill behind you. Winston’s there.”

Without a glance back, he stepped through the force field into the circle.

Chapter 34

When the pressure lifted and he was free of the spell that bound the circle, Finn stopped. Pushing his fingers through his hair, he peered around him. He'd left pebbles earlier, dotted along the ley line to mark its course. He scanned the tufty grass inside the circle, spotted the ones he'd left to indicate where it entered and exited the circle. He couldn't see the pebbles near the centre and realised those must be on the other side of the fire. He'd just had time to dowse the course of the ley line before they'd seen Maeve's light globes crossing the moor.

In the centre of the circle, the spellworker raised her hand and neatly caught her knife. At least she'd kept her word and let Zoe walk away. If he died then he'd go knowing he'd saved his sister and Zoe. That was something. But he'd hoped to do so much more.

"Come here!" Maeve pointed to a spot between her and the fire. When Finn didn't move immediately she added, "Or do I have to come and get you?"

Finn shook his head. That was the last thing he wanted. The success of the plan depended entirely on his proximity to the ley line.

He started to walk towards the centre of the circle, moving in an arc away from Maeve. As he got closer to the fire, he saw the pebbles on the opposite side of it.

He glanced at the spellworker. Her cold, glassy eyes met his and he hastily glanced away. She started to move towards him. Finn ignored her. Kept walking. He had to get to the other side of the fire. He saw Maeve raise the hand that held the knife. Hoping to distract her, he said the first thing that came into his head, “Why are you doing this?”

“Doing what?”

“Trying to take my connection to the earth.”

Maeve stopped, looked away. “You wouldn’t understand.”

“Why not?”

“Because you’re a druid.”

“So?”

“You were born with power!” She spun towards him, spitting the words out. “How can you understand what it’s like to have nothing? To have to steal energy from other people just to stay alive?”

“That’s why you’re doing this? You wish you’d been born a druid?”

“No! Druids are fools. Bound by antiquated rules and ridiculous ideals. But your connection to the earth will free me from spells and rituals, from begging the will of the goddesses.”

Finn kept his eyes on the nearest pebble. Only two more steps. “And what will you do when you’ve got that?”

“Live,” Maeve said quietly, as if she spoke to herself. “Without the disguises.”

“Just out of interest, how many people have you killed along the way?” His foot nudged the pebble. “Before me, I mean?” The ley line’s energy was beneath him, pulsing through the soles of his boots.

The spellworker shrugged. “I forget. It’s been a long time. Their faces fade.”

There was a long moment of silence. Finn walked along the ley line towards the fire. Two paces away from it he stopped.

Heart pounding, he took a deep breath. He had to do this. It was part of the plan. He just hoped he was a good enough actor to pull it off.

He held his hands out towards her. "Okay, let's get on with this."

Maeve eyes narrowed suspiciously. "If this is some sort of trick, Finn McCloud?"

Finn produced what he hoped was a derisive laugh. "I've broken my staff and I'm trapped in your force field. What kind of tricks do you think I've got left?"

Maeve frowned, her eyes watchful. He would have to push it. "And death's got to be better than listening to you whingeing about how crap your life's been!"

In two steps she stood in front of him. Her hand swung out, slapped him across the face. Finn bit back the swear words, tensed for another blow.

"Turn round," Maeve said, grabbing his shoulder.

Careful to keep his feet in the same position, Finn complied. His hands were wrenched backwards. He felt her cold grasp on his wrists, the rope against his skin.

Instinctively he struggled. It was one thing knowing he would be bound. Something entirely different to experience it. As the rope tightened, a cold sweat crawled down his back, clung to his palms. He felt the panic return, the memories rushing in, dragging him back to the terror of the tree.

Maeve pressed on his shoulder. "Kneel."

As he went down, he glanced at the sky. Behind the moon the darkness thinned. Sunrise was coming. And with it - if he didn't keep it together - his death.

***

Frowning, Maeve bent to place the four black candles around the fire. The druid's calmness was unsettling. It was almost as if he'd given up, that he'd welcome death. That was unacceptable. She wanted him to suffer.

She pushed back the wide sleeve of her robe and checked her watch. Half an hour until sunrise. She had time.

Picking up the chalice, she looked inside. “Your girlfriend left some blood behind. Won’t that be useful.”

“You said you’d let her go.”

“Don’t tell me you believed that.” Maeve took the poppet of the girl from her pocket. Slowly, she wiped it round the inside of the chalice. “I can’t let her live. Not after what she’s seen. And with this -” she held the blood smeared doll up for him to see “- I can find her wherever she goes.”

“You bloody bitch!” The colour drained from the druid’s face. He struggled against his bonds. “You’ve got me. That’s what you wanted. Let her go!”

Laughing, Maeve dropped that chalice to the ground and picked up the one she’d purified for the ritual. “Is that why you gave yourself up? Because you thought you’d save your girlfriend?” When he didn’t reply, she continued, “You’re always trying to save people, Finn McCloud. Your sister, now this girl.” She leaned in, laid the flat blade of her athame next to Finn’s cheek. “Poor Catriona didn’t look too well when I last saw her. Does Lyme Regis not agree with her?”

The druid’s head jerked back. She waited until she saw his nostrils flare, his mouth open ready to curse and then slashed his cheek. His eyes, wide with rage and hate, met hers.

Holding the chalice to catch the blood, Maeve smiled. “I let your sister live in case I needed her for the ritual. When you were trapped in the tree I couldn’t have taken your blood to cast the spell. But your sister’s would have worked as well.”

“Fuck you!”

She laughed. “See what you’ve achieved by escaping, Finn McCloud?” She peered into the cup. It held sufficient blood for the ritual but she kept it there a few seconds longer. “Now your girlfriend will die too.”

He muttered words she didn't catch. She turned. "What did you say?"

He glared at her through narrowed eyes.

"Still trying to defy me?" She picked up his broken staff, swung it back and struck him hard in the stomach.

He doubled over, gasping for breath. "Not so full of smart answers now, are you?" She saw the effort it took for him to straighten, for his eyes to meet hers again. Maeve raised an eyebrow. "Say goodbye to your precious staff."

Lips tight shut, he looked away, his cut cheek turned towards her. The temptation was irresistible. She touched the end of the staff to his face, stroked it along the skin waiting for a reaction. When the muscles in his neck and jaw tensed, she raised the staff and brought it down hard on his cheekbone. Heard a satisfying crunch.

His head dropped to his chest. She shoved the tip of the staff under his chin and levered it up. "You will watch it burn!"

She poked one half of the staff into the fire, waited for it to catch. The wood flamed brightly. When it had charred she pulled it out and placed it on a crystal dish.

She waved the dish in front of the druid's face. "What's it like seeing your power turning to ash?"

"You know nothing -" he croaked "- about druid power."

She bent until her face was level with his. "But I will," she breathed. He flinched as if he expected another blow. Maeve smiled. Finally, he was getting the right idea.

She checked her watch. Fifteen minutes to sunrise. It was time.

***

Finn's cheek was agony. He sucked in a deep breath, winced when it released a shooting pain in his stomach.

"Ishtar, Cerridwen, Innana, Shakti, Yoruba, Danu, Kali and Aine," Maeve said loudly. She pointed her athame at each of the candles in turn and a flame leapt into being. "I call on you to protect, empower and inspire my magic."

This was it. He'd read *The Seventh Book*, knew the ritual would need all of Maeve's attention. He had to stop the spell before she drank from the chalice. Once she'd done that his blood would strengthen her and she'd be harder to kill.

Flexing his hands, he leaned backwards. His fingers touched the top of his boots. He strained against the rope but couldn't reach inside the right one. He shuffled that boot to the side, dropped his shoulder and tried again. Sweat crawled down his back. The bonds at his wrists gnawed at his skin but his fingers closed around the hilt of the knife. He glanced at Maeve.

"Hear me now all powerful goddesses, thy servant offers blood from her own veins as a tribute to your power and knowledge." On the final word, Maeve sliced her hand. Drops of blood fell into the fire. It flamed more brightly.

Carefully, Finn started to rotate the knife. His hands were clammy, his fingers thick and clumsy. If he dropped it now he was a dead man. Feeling the blade against his wrists, he exhaled. He manoeuvred the point under the rope. Eyes fixed on Maeve, he began to cut.

"I, your servant who pledges her loyalty, make this offering of the druid's blood." The spellworker raised the chalice above her head. "Goddesses, hear me! I, thy servant, call to you!"

The flames leapt upwards. Maeve stepped back. The chalice hovered, as if suspended by an invisible thread, within the fire.

Finn felt the knife slice through the rope. Maeve turned towards him. He froze. She picked up the crystal dish, stepped back to the fire. He released a breath, swallowed hard. Tightened his grip on the knife and tried again.

"By breaking his staff the druid has revoked his connection to the earth." Maeve raised the crystal dish to the sky. "I offer the druid's staff to the goddesses." She threw one half of the staff into the fire.

The flames changed colour. Became green, yellow, red, brown, the colours of the earth. "The power of the druid's staff I intermingle with the druid's blood." She dropped a handful of the blackened wood into the chalice.

As he pushed the blade back and forth through the rope the tip of the blade snagged. Finn's fingers slipped on the handle. The knife fell.

Maeve raised her hands towards the lightening sky. "Goddesses, at the raising of the Beltane sun join thy powers and give strength to thy servant who is in need this hour."

He bent his head. He sucked in a deep breath. Said a prayer of his own. Through his knees, he drew on awen from the ley line. Tensing every muscle in his upper body, he strained against the bonds. Sweat dripped into his eyes. There was a snapping, an unravelling and his hands were free.

Maeve lifted the chalice from the flames. "Goddesses, may the lifeblood of the druid flow through my veins, may the energy of his staff strengthen my heart." Eyes closed, she started to drink.

Finn yanked the talisman from his neck. He reached down and slammed it against the earth. Instantly, his staff shot up to its full height. He scrambled up, drew on the energy of the ley line and focused it. The chalice flew from Maeve's hands. Blood spilling out it hurtled to the ground.

The spellworker shrieked, "No!"

"I told you that you knew nothing about druid power."

Suddenly the air tightened around him. He couldn't move.

Maeve walked towards him, her hand raised palm out. The force field pushed him backwards. His feet scrabbled to stay on the ley line. He tried to fight back, to push his staff to the ground but the invisible power that held him was too strong. It dragged him across the circle and then, with a flick of Maeve's hand, flung him at the largest of the standing stones.

He crashed against it. Heard a crack. Felt instant agony inside his shoulder. His head swam. His vision blurred.

Then the memories broke through. Full moon over the garden at Anam Cara. The force field pinning him against the tree. Maeve's knife at his throat. Her high pitched laugh. Blinding panic as the tree's roots curled around his ankles. Fighting the branches knotting at his wrists. His strength waning as the tree sucked him in. The absolute certainty that he was about to die. Screaming in terror as bark covered his face.

Wrapping his arms around his staff, he cowered against the stone. *This was it. This time Maeve would kill him.*

The tip of his staff touched the stone. A tingle of awen seeped through the staff into his hands. Instinctively he drew on it, sensed it unravelling from deep within the stone. The earth magic of the St Michael line channelled through the circle of stones. It flowed through his hands into muscle, nerve, bone. He breathed with it, felt his heart rate slow, the memories dissipate.

He focused his mind on the invisible bonds that held him. Pushed the ley line's energy out. He had a sense of the force field flexing like an elastic band. He pushed harder and it snapped.

Striding towards him Maeve stopped as if she'd been struck.

Leaping up, Finn threw himself into the space between

this stone and the next. His body collided with the force field sealing the circle. He braced against it, pressed his hand against one stone, his staff against the other. Drawing the energy of the stones into him, he pushed out.

He heard Maeve cry, "I summon the God of Fire. Let this circle be his."

Flames swept around the stones. As the heat hit him, Finn flung himself away.

Maeve laughed. "You can't escape, Finn McCloud."

He darted around the inside of the circle. The crystal plate flew towards him. He doubled over, kept running. It smashed into a stone and shattered. Shards of glass sliced across his forehead, his scalp.

Spotting the pebbles marking the position of the ley line, Finn reached out with his staff and plunged it into the ground. He gasped at the strength of awen surging through him. Zoe had said something about a dragon roaring. This felt like a dragon. An angry dragon trapped in the earth for thousands of years. When it felt like he could hold no more, that awen would burn him up, he thrust the energy towards the force field.

The flames dropped. He felt the barrier stretch and he pushed harder.

In his peripheral vision he saw something flying towards him. He ducked. The knife swerved, heading for his face. His free hand rose instinctively to ward it off. The knife kept coming. Slid agonisingly through skin and muscle.

He stared at his palm for a long second. The tip of Maeve's knife in the flesh between his index finger and his thumb. The handle on the other side. Bright red blood.

He heard a roaring. *The dragon.* He had to let lose the dragon. He raised his staff, pointed the tip at Maeve. Released the surge of St Michael's energy that filled him.

The spellworker flew backwards, crashed against an upright stone, tumbled to the earth. He blinked at the static body. Raised his staff to fight again. The body didn't move.

The wind swirled around him. The force field was gone.

He stumbled over to where Maeve lay. There was blood on the stone, blood staining her blonde hair. He pushed her shoulder. Her head rolled over. The face that looked back at him was the face of the crone. The watery, blue eyes were lifeless.

There was burning in his hand. Scorching up his arm, consuming everything. He grasped the hilt of the knife and pulled. Blood spurted. His head swam. He dropped his staff. His legs buckled. He fell.

Chapter 35

Watching from the hill, Zoe saw him fall. "Finn!" she cried. The wind carried the sound away.

Next to her, Winston said, "Shit!"

Zoe grabbed his arm. "Is he alright?"

"How do I know?" Winston swung his rucksack on to his back. "I'm going down there."

Zoe started forward.

"No!" His hand shot out. "I promised Finn I'd keep you safe. Stay here until I find out if Maeve's dead."

"Oh!" She looked away, swallowed hard. "Okay."

As Winston sprinted down the hill the sun crept over the horizon, bathing the clouds in orange light. The moorland emerged from darkness, a huge expanse of bleak heather dotted with outcrops of rock. She shivered and huddled deeper into Finn's coat.

The past half an hour had been almost unbearable. Even though Winston had told her the plan it had still been torture to watch. When the fire died and Finn stood upright in the centre of the circle she felt like cheering. But then he'd fallen.

If he hadn't made it. If he was... She wrapped her arms around herself. She didn't want to even think that word.

Winston ran across the circle, dropped to his knees beside Finn, bent over him. Eyes wide, Zoe prayed to a God she didn't think she believed in. Winston took a bottle from his rucksack, poured the contents over Finn's head. Zoe's tired eyes tried to focus on his face. Had he…? Then his hand rose to his face and Zoe's knees suddenly became weak.

Winston hauled Finn towards the nearest upright stone, helped him to sit up. Then, staff raised, he walked across the circle, crouched next to the unmoving black shape. He was still for a long time before he walked across the circle and picked something up. Returning to Maeve he raised his hand. Sunlight glinted on the thing he held. As if the world had suddenly slowed down, Zoe realised it was a knife. Winston's arm moved, plunging the blade into the body.

She screwed her eyes up, her hands rising to cover her face. Whatever Maeve had done she hadn't wanted to see that. When she looked again, Winston stood next to Finn.

Her hands flew out. What was going on? She bounced up and down on the spot. Then Winston waved his arms as if semaphoring and she broke into a run. Dodging rocks and leaping over tufts of heather she sprinted down the hillside.

Gasping for breath, with a stitch in her side, she dashed into the circle and then stopped. He wasn't alright. Blood was smeared across his face, dripping from his wet hair. His cheek was all mashed up. Winston was bandaging his hand with a strip of black cloth.

"It's okay," Winston said, mistaking her hesitation. He nodded at the pile of crumped black robes. "She's…"

Eyes fixed on Finn's face, Zoe didn't take in his words. She walked over, dropped to her knees beside him. "Oh my God! What happened?"

"She fought dirty." Finn managed a weak grin. His uninjured hand took hers. "But I made it. I told you I wouldn't die."

Zoe bit her lip but the tears came anyway. "Hey!" Finn's fingers tightened on hers. "I thought you'd be pleased to see me."

"This is pleased." She smiled, brushing the tears away with her fingers. "When you fell I thought…"

"I passed out." He glanced up at his friend. "Winston

brought me round by pouring a pint of cold water over my head."

"It worked," Winston said. Looking at Zoe, he added, "He needs a doctor. Will you take him to the hospital?"

"Course. But can't you heal him?"

Winston shook his head. "I'm pretty sure he's got fractures. He says his ribs hurt. His collar bone could have broken when he hit the stone and who knows what damage has been done to his hand." He gestured helplessly. "If I heal him the bones could set wrong. He needs x-rays."

Zoe stared. "That bad?"

Winston nodded.

She glanced at Finn. His head rested against the stone. His face was grey, his eyes closed. "You're not coming with us?" she asked Winston.

"I'll help you get him to the car and then I'm coming back. I've got to… clean up here."

Zoe nodded, grateful to Winston for what he hadn't said. She couldn't think about Maeve. She had to keep it together for Finn. She stroked his unhurt cheek, saw his eyes flicker open. She forced a smile. "Okay, Finn. You and I have a hot date at the hospital."

***

The nurse behind the reception desk in Oakhampton Minor Injuries Unit listened disinterestedly as Zoe listed Finn's injuries. She handed over a clipboard. "Get your boyfriend to fill in this form and bring it back."

Zoe walked over to the row of plastic chairs where Finn waited. As she sat down next to him he said, "Did she say how long?"

She shook her head. "Paperwork first. Then if you're lucky you might see a doctor." His injured hand rested awkwardly against his chest. With his good one he reached for the clipboard.

"Why don't I fill this in?" she said.

His nod was such a small movement she barely caught it. "Thanks."

She picked up the pen, scanned the form. It wanted all the usual information; address, date of birth, details of his GP, any existing health conditions. "There's so much I don't know about you," she said.

"Does it matter?"

Her eyes rose to his face. "No. Not after tonight."

***

In a different waiting room outside the x-ray department Zoe tried not to fall asleep. On the opposite wall was a large TV with the sound turned off. Too tired to read the subtitles, her eyes were continually drawn to the changing pictures.

There was a shot of Glastonbury Tor, followed by a burnt out house. Zoe blinked, focused. A reporter stood in front of Anam Cara's blue gate. "The police are investigating the fire at the property and are keen to speak to the owner," the subtitles read.

She leaned forward. "We believe that a body was found in the property but this has yet to be confirmed," the reporter continued. Behind her a man in white plastic coveralls ducked under the line of police tape. "However, it's clear that the police are treating this as a crime scene."

As the reporter handed back to the newscaster, she fumbled in the pocket of Finn's coat and pulled out his phone. The BBC website had no more information. Frantically she tried other sites but found only rumours and speculation. Sagging back in the chair, she cursed the fact that her own phone was still in Maeve's car. She needed to ring Tanya. She didn't have Helena's number but maybe Tanya would.

When Finn emerged from behind the thick double doors a few minutes later he looked even paler and more exhausted. Thinking she'd tell him later, she tried to smile as she walked towards him but something in her face must have alerted him. "You okay?" he said.

"It's Anam Cara. There's been a fire. And they've found -" her hand rose to her mouth "- they've found a body."

Finn frowned. "She said she couldn't remember."

"What?"

His eyes met hers. "It doesn't matter."

***

Hours later, Zoe unlocked the door to the cottage and stood back to allow Finn to pass. His tightly bandaged hand rested in a sling. His fractured collar bone had been strapped up. The wound on his cheek had been taped and he'd been told to put ice on his cheekbone to help the break heal. There was a bald patch on his scalp where the doctor had shaved his hair to stitch the gash. The only good news had been that his ribs were only bruised.

Zoe put the bag of drugs on the coffee table. Without thinking she picked up two dirty mugs and an empty pizza box and took them over to the kitchen. When she turned, Finn sat on the bed. Wincing he bent over and slowly untied his boots. She bit back the offer to help. He'd already made it clear that he wanted to do as much as possible for himself.

Laying down he let out a long breath. She filled a glass of water, took a packet of painkillers from the bag. As she put them on the bedside cabinet, his uninjured hand fastened around hers and pulled her down to sit on the bed.

"Stay," he said.

"Of course. I'm going to make up the sofa bed."

"No. Here. With me."

"Are you sure? The doctor said you need to sleep. I don't want to disturb you."

"Fuck the doctor."

She shook her head. "Thanks but he's not my type. I'd rather have you."

"Good. Hold that thought." He pulled her towards him and kissed her very gently.

Chapter 36

Walking up the spine of Wearyall Hill in the last of the evening sun, Zoe could see that Finn was tiring. His breathing was laboured, his face pale. Even with his druid's ability to heal it had seemed overambitious to walk into Glastonbury this evening. But when she reminded him of the doctor's instruction to rest and suggested that they drive, Finn said he needed to be outside. She guessed that was a druid thing too.

Reaching the brow of the hill, the Somerset Levels spread out like a green patchwork quilt below them. "Wow! You can see for miles from here!" She spotted a bench, gestured to it. "Let's sit down, shall we?"

Finn ran his good hand over his face, puffed out a long breath and nodded. Further down the slope was the Holy Thorn. Two women stood around it. One wore flowers in her hair. From a very different kind of Beltane, Zoe thought.

In the distance, behind the thorn tree, rose the Tor. Beneath that was the burnt out shell of Anam Cara. "I just want to know if it's Helena they've found," she said. Earlier she'd contacted Tanya through Facebook. She didn't think the body would be Penny's or Tony's. They would have left together.

"I know, sweetheart." Finn squeezed her hand.

"How long's it going to take before they identify her?"

"It could be a while. They'll probably need her dental records from Australia."

Zoe nodded, bit her lip. "If it is her then it's so bloody unfair. Helena adored Maeve. She'd have done anything for her. I just don't understand why she'd kill her."

"When I was trying to keep her talking I asked how many people she'd killed. She said she couldn't remember."

"Oh my God!" Zoe's eyes widened. "So there could be more bodies?"

Finn nodded. "If not at Anam Cara then somewhere else."

Zoe's eyes were suddenly full of tears. She sucked in a deep breath, pushed her hair away from her face.

"To say she was evil doesn't really cover it," Finn said. "But that's the only word I've got."

"You're right. It doesn't cover it," Zoe said, her voice high and tight.

"How you doing with all of this?"

Zoe looked down at the pink and tender skin on her wrists. "Fine."

He shook his head. "I didn't mean that." He touched her temple. "I meant in here."

She glanced at him. The concern in his eyes made tears threaten again. She looked down at the grass by her feet, twisting her hands together. "I haven't really thought about it. It's all a bit too much and I've been so worried about you and..."

Finn tugged her hand. "Look at me." When her eyes met his, he said, "In the past twenty four hours you've been drugged and kidnapped, bound, threatened and seen a woman die."

The tears were really close now. Zoe's gaze dropped. "Thanks for reminding me!"

"I'm just saying that if you weren't upset there'd be something wrong with you."

She half laughed, half sobbed. As her hand rose to her mouth, Finn raised his arm and she curled into his shoulder. He didn't speak, simply held her while she cried. When she finally pulled away, she said, "I must look terrible."

Finn's smile was warm. "Not terrible. Just soggy."

They sat in silence, staring out across the flat landscape. Zoe tugged on the hem of the t-shirt sticking out from under her hoodie. It was Finn's and far too big for her. "There's something I need to ask."

"That doesn't sound good."

"I…" Her eyes flicked up to meet his and then away. "It's about the tree." She hesitated, hoping she didn't have to say anymore. When he remained silent, she said, "Why didn't you tell me you were the Green Man?"

"Oh! That." His hand slid from her shoulder.

"Yes, that." Zoe risked a glance at him. She'd expected to see tension in his jaw, tightening around his eyes, the signs that indicated this was something he wouldn't tell her. Instead he looked simply exhausted.

"I honestly thought you'd never need to know." He leaned forward, his eyes fixed on his uninjured hand.

"And if I hadn't dreamt about it would you have told me?"

"I don't know. Maybe, sometime." He suddenly sat back, looked her in the eye. "Try to see it from my side. I meet this gorgeous girl who I really like. The last thing I want to do is tell her I've spent six months imprisoned in a tree."

"So you let me think you'd been in New Zealand?" Zoe's hands flew out. "Doing something really boring with soil!"

"I did work on a soil erosion project in New Zealand. Only it was two years ago."

Zoe folded her arms. "I don't care about the soil thingy. I care that you didn't tell me about Maeve and the tree."

"I'm getting that." He twisted awkwardly to look at her. "I let you go on thinking I'd been in New Zealand because it was easier than telling you what really happened." Seeing her about to interrupt he added, "I didn't want to talk about it. Not to you. Not to anybody."

"You told Winston."

"Because I had to. He'd come to Glastonbury to look for me in October and he had to know what Maeve is - was capable of. But I haven't told anyone else."

"Not even your sister?"

"No, she'd been through enough."

The drawings of the pale, thin girl came into her mind and Zoe nodded. "Yeah, I can see that. But there's still something I don't understand."

Finn raised an eyebrow. "Just the one thing?"

"Stop it! I'm serious." Zoe's grin softened her words. "I don't understand how Maeve trapped you. I mean I know you'd not used magic to fight before but you still had all your druid power. Wasn't that enough to fight her off?"

Finn frowned. "It might have been if I hadn't been such a bloody idiot."

"What do you mean?"

"I didn't realise what she was. I thought she was just some New Age freak messing with forces she didn't understand. I never dreamt she had any real power." He shoved his good hand through his hair. "When I saw the light go on in the house, I knew I had to get Cat out. I didn't know what kind of hold Maeve had over her and I wasn't going to risk her talking her into going back into that cell. Cat was so weak she could barely stand. I drew awen into my staff and gave it to her."

"Oh!" Zoe's hand rose to her mouth.

"Exactly." Finn met her wide-eyed gaze. "The staff gave Cat enough strength to get to the car and then, when Maeve came after her, to drive away. But I'd got nothing left to fight with and when I realised what she could do..." He trailed off.

Zoe nodded. She knew what happened next. She'd

seen the pictures.

"I never imagined that you'd dreamt about it. When I got your call…"

"I was pretty freaked out."

"Then when I couldn't get hold of you I thought…" He ran his hand over his face. "I thought I'd never see you again."

Zoe slipped her hand into his. "No."

"I wouldn't have blamed you if you'd bailed. It's a lot to deal with. Druids, spellworkers, magic. A whole world you didn't know existed a week ago."

"Yeah, I know." She hesitated, looked down at their clasped hands. "But I can see now that this seer thing is a kind of magic. Not like what you and Winston can do but..." Her free hand arced upwards as she tried to find a way to explain. "But I'd have been a lot more scared at the stone circle if I hadn't had the dreams and known you were coming. So I guess the dreams can be a good thing."

"More than that. If it weren't for you, it'd be my grave Winston's digging." When Zoe opened her mouth to protest, he said, "No, I'm serious. Without your drawings I'd have been completely screwed. I'd have turned up at the last minute, desperate to get you out of there. There's no way she'd have released you until I broke my staff and then I'd have had nothing. I'd be dead and she'd be coming after you and Cat."

Zoe stared at him. "You'd really have broken your staff to get Maeve to let me go?"

Finn gave a small shrug. "Yes. It was my fault you were there."

"Even knowing you had no chance against her?"

He nodded.

"Wow, Finn!" Zoe said. "That's…I don't know what to say…"

"Don't say anything yet. There's something I want to ask."

"Okay."

He leaned forward. "Have you ever been to Donegal?"

She blinked. "No. Why?"

"Because Padraig left his house to me and Cat. It needs a lot of work doing on it before we can sell it and I'm thinking of heading over there. I want you to come with me."

"I'd love to!" Zoe beamed. "But I can't really have another holiday just yet though so it'll have to be…"

"No," Finn interrupted. "I'm not talking about a holiday. I want you to come with me. Live with me."

"Seriously?"

"Yes. You might think this is much too soon seeing as we've only known each other for five days. But after the five days we've just lived through I don't think that matters. I know you, Zoe Rose. Okay, I don't know where you went to school or what you like for breakfast but I know the important things and when I was in the stone circle you were the reason I kept fighting."

"Oh!" To give herself time to think, she replied to the easier bit. "I can't believe it's only been five days. Before I met you feels like another life." She fiddled with the cuffs of her hoodie for a long moment before she met his eyes. "But what you're asking, that's big."

"Too big?"

Zoe shook her head. "I'm not sure. I…." She stared at the neat square fields stretching away from the hill, watched the tiny cars travelling the straight roads. She thought about what she'd be going back to. Anna - the only person who could possibly understand what she'd been through - had betrayed her. Her other friends would think her crazy if she told them a fraction of what she'd experienced. Her art classes were finished until September. She'd give up the job at the cinema in a heartbeat and if the publishers liked her preliminary work then she could complete the commission anywhere. So why was she hesitating? She turned to look at him. "I want to be with you. I really do."

"Then say you'll come," he said, staring at her with an intensity that made her heart beat faster.

"I…I…There was a guy. Gareth. He, well, it doesn't really matter but we split up about a year ago."

Finn's gaze dropped. "I see."

"No!" Realising she'd given him the wrong idea, Zoe laid her hand gently against the side of his face. When his eyes met hers, she said, "It's not that I'm not over him. I'm totally over him. But he hurt me pretty badly." She hesitated, trying to find the right words. "I think maybe I'm just a bit scared."

"I ask you to live with me and you're scared?" Finn said. "You were brave as a tiger when Maeve was threatening you."

"But she was only going to hurt me physically. You could break my heart."

Finn was silent for long, painful seconds. Zoe was about to try to make a joke of it when he said, "I can't promise you that I won't. But if it helps, I'm in love with you."

"Oh!" Zoe's hand rose to her lips. "You didn't say that before."

"I don't go around rescuing people I don't care about."

"I know. I just needed to hear it." Her eyes were full of tears again but this time she didn't mind. "I'm in love with you too."

"So? Will you come to Donegal?"

"I've got to go back to London for the meeting with the publishers on Wednesday. But after that, yes, I'll come."

Finn pulled her to him with his good arm and hugged her tightly. It was pretty awkward with his sling and bandaged hand in the way but the peace that she felt when he held her was just the same.

As they moved apart, he said, "Come on. I'm starving. Let's go get something to eat." He pulled her up and slung his good arm around her shoulders.

Walking down the grassy slope, she said, "You know when you were in the tree, was it like you were asleep?"

"I suppose. I remember it swallowing me. Wish I could forget that part. But after that I don't remember anything until you broke the spell and I started to wake up."

Zoe stopped, stared at him. "I did what?"

"You don't know?"

She shook her head. "Know what?"

"By cutting the bark from around the doll you broke the spell that bound the tree. If you hadn't done that I couldn't have escaped."

Zoe's eyes widened. "But I didn't have a clue what I was doing!"

"Doesn't matter." Finn's eyes were solemn. "I owe you, Zoe Rose. You've saved my life twice."

"So if I hadn't got drunk and gone to talk to the Green Man you could still have been trapped in the tree?"

"Well, by now Maeve would have performed the ritual and I'd be dead but yes."

She blinked, trying to take in what he'd told her. It did make a kind of sense. He'd told her that Maeve used the doll in a spell. She'd just not connected that to Finn's captivity in the tree.

Then Finn said, "You *talked* to the Green Man?"

A blush stole over her cheeks. She glanced away, shrugged. "I was lonely. I didn't like Maeve. I had to talk to someone."

"But it could have been a tree spirit or a demon."

"Would that have been bad?"

"A demon definitely. Tree spirits are mostly harmless."

Zoe's hands flew up. "Well, I didn't know about any

of that then. I just had a good feeling about you."

"You did?" He wrapped his arm tighter around her shoulders and she stepped closer to him. "And whatever you said is safe because I don't remember."

Zoe threw a flirty glance at him. "The Green Man was much nicer than you. He didn't answer back!"

His hand fastened in her hair, tilting her head backwards. "He couldn't do this though." The kiss was deep and passionate, promising much for when they were alone.

When she stepped back, Zoe saw Finn wince. "Sorry. Did I hurt you?"

"Worth it." His fingers traced the line of her jaw and along her neck. "Wish I wasn't so banged up. What I want to do to you..."

"Yeah, I know. You will. We will. Druids heal fast, remember?"

He laughed, took her hand. As they drew level with the Holy Thorn, Zoe pulled away, "Just a minute. There's something I need to do."

She walked around the tree, searching for the offering she'd left on Tuesday evening. The scrap torn from her scarf fluttered with the other ribbons. Catching it she thought back to what she'd asked for that evening. Nothing had turned out as she'd expected but Finn was in her life and for that she was thankful.

Running the fabric through her fingers, her voice barely audible even to herself, she said, "When I was here on Tuesday I asked to see him again and I did and I want to say thank you for that. And if you had anything to do with keeping him alive then I'm really, really grateful." She unclosed her fingers and the ragged strip of fabric joined the other ribbons surrounding the tree.

Looking up she was surprised to see Finn on the other side of the Holy Thorn. His uninjured hand rested in his pocket, his eyes were fixed on the distant Tor. Feeling it would be wrong to disturb him, she walked a few paces down the hill. When she turned back, her eyes widened.

His good hand gripped the iron railing surrounding the tree. His head was bowed as if he were praying. Behind him the red ball of the sun hung in the sky. It was exactly as she'd drawn him on Monday night.

She turned away. When she'd drawn this she'd felt as if she were intruding. That sense was even stronger now. She'd come here to find him too soon. The injuries that had confused her on Tuesday made perfect sense now. And if this dream had happened then she couldn't deny it anymore. She really could see the future.

Her hand slipped into the pocket of her jeans. She pulled out a scrap of paper. Waking in the middle of the afternoon, she'd struggled to remember where she was. With the dream burning through her brain she'd stumbled over to the coffee table, found a piece of paper and a blue ballpoint. The sketch was rough but the picture was clear enough.

In a large church, sunlight streamed through a jagged hole in a modern stained glass window. The light created a pattern on the floor and in the centre of it lay a man dressed in a kilt. Blood spread from a wound on his head and pooled around his body.

Zoe swallowed hard. She couldn't see the man's face, didn't know where this place was. But she knew she'd become what she'd feared. The woman who saw terrible things before they happened. She had no idea how she would live with that.

Hearing Finn's footsteps she shoved the picture back into her pocket. He'd been through enough for one day. She'd show him tomorrow. Or, maybe, the day after.

"You ready to go?" he said.

She smiled. "Sure."

He took her hand. "I believe I promised that for our first proper date we'd go somewhere fancy."

Zoe grinned. “Actually, you said somewhere fancy with tablecloths and wine lists.”

“I’m not sure Glastonbury’s got anywhere that fancy but let’s go and see.” Hand in hand they walked down the hill into the town.

Acknowledgements

Setting out to write your first novel is a bit like a journey into another world. When I started writing I had no idea if I'd make it to the end and if I did what this book would look like. It's been a long process, three years to write the book, another two years for it to find its way out into the world and, in that time, an awful lot has happened to me and the people around me. I'm absolutely certain that I've bored my friends and family to distraction by talking about Finn, Zoe and Maeve as if they were real people and banging on about Glastonbury and magic when I should have been doing something more useful. Thank you for putting up with me and for resisting the temptation to say (even if you were thinking it) that I could more usefully spend my evenings improving my crocheting skills!

First of all I have to thank my amazing alpha-readers, Jane Stockdale, Amanda Kershaw, Jean Scaife and (until nephew came along) Maynard Case. Your enthusiasm for the story and demands for more chapters are what kept me going and each of you has been absolutely crucial in getting this story finished.

Then there's my lovely beta-readers, Jo Bartlett, Julie Heslington, Annette Valentine, Cynthia Else, Dave Pearce and Vicky Weston. You gave me the confidence to believe that the book was okay really and that it didn't need a told re-write from start to finish. Dave, I hope you'll forgive that the moon still doesn't work entirely correctly over Glastonbury in late April. I'm calling it a local phenomenon created by the unique energy of the place and not a plot hole caused by my lack of understanding of all things astronomical.

I owe a huge debt to the New Writers Scheme run by the Romantic Novelists Association. Getting in the scheme helped me to take my writing seriously and it's because of the NWS that I met the fabulous Write Romantics. I will never know the name of the NWS Reader who reviewed 'Beltane' but your feedback and comments helped so much. Thank you for explaining the concept of 'deep third' to me and for your enthusiasm for the story.

I also want to thank Chris Bartrum and the wonderful Bartrumbury crowd. I was so nervous when I read the first chapter to you in December 2012. It's been such a boost to know that you want to hear more and the silence in which you've listened to each instalment has been the greatest compliment possible. If any of you are impatient to find out what happens and buy the book I hope you'll forgive the inclusion of the prologue. I know it gives quite a lot away and that many of you have been enjoying the slow reveal.

There's been an awful lot of ups and downs on the road to publication and I've had my fair share of wobbles and moments when I was completely ready to give up. For the past two and a half years the road has been a lot less lonely as I've had the amazing Write Romantics to cheer me up and keep me going. Ladies, you are the absolute best and I'm so grateful to have you in my life. Extra special thanks must go to Jo for being cheerleader extraordinaire and to Julie and Sharon for long afternoons of tea and cake in Beverley putting the writing world to rights.

During the writing of his novel I visited Glastonbury many times and after staying in a few places (none of which were anything like Anam Cara, I hasten to add!) I found the haven that is the Arimathean Retreat. It has become my spiritual home from home and, although the book has been finished for quite some time, I still feel a need to return at least once a year. A massive thank you to Karen and Lisehanne for making me so welcome and helping me through some of the darkest times.

I also want to thank the people in Glastonbury who have shared their experiences and talked to me so openly about their religion and their passion. I apologise for any mistakes that I've made and ask you to remember that this is a work of fiction. And, ladies, I promise that there's some amazing life-affirming spellworkers in the next book.

Finally, I want to thank my Mum and Dad for pretty much everything. We're not a very demonstrative family and I know that if I say too much I'll embarrass them. They always encouraged me to read and never complained about yet another visit to the library. They've supported me in so many practical ways during the writing of Beltane and helped me get back on my feet during the worst of times. You're the best and I really hope you're up for another trip to Orkney so I can finish the research for the next *Spellworker Chronicles* book.

Also by Alys West

The Dirigible King's Daughter

When Harriet Hardy moved to Whitby, the Yorkshire town newly famous from Mr Stoker's sensational novel, she thought she'd left her past and her father's disgrace behind her. But then an amorous Alderman and a mysterious Viscount turn her life upside down and she's never been more thankful that she doesn't leave home without her pistol.

But when defending her honour lands her with an attempted murder charge, Harriet's only option is to turn to the mysterious Viscount for help. Fortunately, he turns out to be not so mysterious after all and, fortified by copious amounts of tea, she sets forth to clear her name.

As the court case looms Harriet fears she'll forever be tarnished by her father's scandalous reputation. Can she avoid conviction and find a happy ending? Or will she always be trapped by her past as the daughter of the notorious Dirigible King?

If you like Georgette Heyer or Gail Carriger then you'll love this sparkling romance with a steampunk twist.

About the author:

Alys West writes contemporary fantasy and steampunk. She started writing when she couldn't find enough books to read that had all of the elements that she loved; fantasy, romance and suspense, although her love of *Buffy the Vampire Slayer* may have had something to do with it too. Writing steampunk was a natural development from her obsession with tea. It also gave her a great excuse to spend her time looking at Victorian fashions and call it research.

Alys is doing a MA in Creative Writing at York St John University and also teaches a creative writing workshop for Converge, an arts project for people with mental health issues.

When she's not writing you can find her at folk gigs, doing yoga and attempting to crochet. You can find out more about Alys on her blog www.alyswest.com, follow her on Twitter at @alyswestyork or find her on Facebook at Alys West Writer. It makes her week if she hears from someone who's enjoyed one of her books so please do get in touch if you've got the time.

Also from Fabrian Books

This Other Eden

by Sharon Booth

Eden wants to keep her job, and, as that means spending the summer caring for three young children in the wilds of the Yorkshire Dales, she has no choice but to go along with it. Her consolation prize is that their father is unexpectedly gorgeous. Sadly for Eden, she's not quite herself any longer…

Honey wants to spend the summer with her married politician lover. The only problem is, there are quite a few people determined to put obstacles in her path. But what Honey wants, Honey usually gets…

Cain wants a knighthood and is willing to sacrifice almost anything for it. If his daughter is putting that goal in jeopardy, it's time to get tough…

Lavinia wants to keep her marriage intact, and if that means turning a blind eye to her husband's philandering, she'll do it. But that doesn't mean she can't have someone else spying for her…

Eliot wants to care for his children, and to be left in peace to heal. When he gets an unexpected guest, he wonders if it's time to start living again. But is this sheep farmer having the wool pulled over his eyes?

Cake baking, jam making, gymkhana games and sheep showing. Blackmail, deception, spying and cheating. Laughter, forgiveness, redemption and falling in love. A lot can happen during one summer in Skimmerdale…

Made in the USA
Las Vegas, NV
24 April 2021

21956004R00215